Born in India, Clifton Aubrey Lath moved to England in 1963. He went to school in Harrow and joined a band in the seventies as a drummer and vocalist. During this time, he also began writing songs and short stories. *The Lonesome Clown* song was born from this creative period. In 1990, he got married and had three children. Later in 2002, he achieved a Guinness World Record for singing non-stop for 24 hours. Clifton then produced some music videos for his songs and uploaded them to YouTube. He currently runs a family business with his wife and children, finding time to write whenever possible.

I dedicate this book to my wife Kirti and my family, Maya, Kewal and Raul, also my grandson Raben.

Clifton Aubrey Lath

THE LONESOME CLOWN

AUSTIN MACAULEY PUBLISHERS

LONDON * CAMBRIDGE * NEW YORK * SHARJAH

A CIP catalogue record for this title is available from the British Library.

ISBN 9781035870288 (Paperback)
ISBN 9781035870295 (Hardback)
ISBN 9781035870301 (ePub e-book)

www.austinmacauley.com

First Published 2024
Austin Macauley Publishers Ltd®
1 Canada Square
Canary Wharf
London
E14 5AA

Introduction

This story is about a young man trying to decide on his life choices, a life on the road filled with excitement or a life married to his college sweetheart. A life with security which is driven by his parents' business which one day will be his. Set in the Midwest town of Green River Wyoming, in the late nineties, a place steeped in western folklore and history.

Historic landmarks forged by the early settlers who trailed a path during the 1830s via Missouri from the east coast to Oregon on to the Pacific West coast. Pioneers who dug out of the barren rocks and soil to carve a path for the Union Pacific railroad, a journey of over 2000 miles and six months travelling through harsh landscapes and extreme heat. As a result, towns sprouted up along the way, which would go on to become major cities, all thanks to the wagon trains of the past. The native American plains Indians who populated the land over ten thousand years ago and started building villages along the Missouri river. Offered fierce resistance over many years but was subdued eventually, mainly by the United States Cavalry. The outlaws who wanted an easy way to make a living by taking everything by force, some were decent, others were not.

And so western legends were born on both sides of the law, legends like Jesse James, William Bonny, Butch Cassidy, Wyatt Earp, Doc Holliday and Wild Bill Hickok, to name but a few.

Towns created along the way, Salt Lake City, Carson City, Cheyanne, Reno and Rock Springs, plus many, many more. Put a pin anywhere on the mid-western map and you will find historical affliction.

Green River, a tributary to the great Colorado River, runs through the town of Green River, clear waters run along its winding path, a life source for the town and country.

An ever-expanding town with a rich colony of multinational people, the Rogers moved here in the 1960s from Dakota. They decided to set their roots and opened a stove showroom in the town, Jim Rogers, Debbie Rogers and their son Jake.

This story is based on him and the path that he is going to take to decide his future, this is his story…

Chapter One

The sun was high in the sky as the roof of the Houston Astrodome stadium rolled back its roof to let the daylight into the arena. The stadium was built in 1963 and could seat 70,000 people, the world's first multi-purpose domed sports stadium.

The date is 1974, the rodeo was in full flow as a lonely tired figure made his way to his dressing room, the sound of the crowds was at a crescendo slowly fading as he delved further into the corridors of the stadium heading to a place of quiet.

The sound of a creaky door opening into a darkened room, footsteps leading into a dressing room, a dressing table with a bulb-laden mirror is in front of the rodeo clown. He was in his late forties and suffering from an almighty headache brought on by heavy drinking from the night before. He sat down on a stool in front of the wooden dressing table and stared into the mirror; how did his life get this bad? He thinks to himself as he tries to form some sort of enthusiasm.

He was in one of the many dressing rooms at the rodeo arena, a legend among rodeo clowns, but on a downward spiral. He had a weathered old leather suitcase about fifteen inches by fifteen inches and opened the lid, inside is his clown make up and fedora hat along with a half bottle of Jack Daniels. He took out the bottle and opened it, took a gulp of whiskey and breathed out after swallowing, he looked again at the mirror. He doesn't smile, just started taking his makeup out and proceeded to apply his trademark face.

All clowns have a dedicated design which they protect vigilantly! To you and me, it's just another face. He then took out a photo of his wife, who left him a long time ago, she could not take any more of his travelling all over the country. His constant drinking brought on by the pressures that he was put under because of his work, he still loved her and stared at her picture and has a tear in his eye.

He had a family, a father and mother, and a wife who he left him to pursue his dream. His wife still living, left him for another man because he was never there for her. He left home to pursue a dream, one that made him famous, but at what cost!

The rodeo clown has a reputation and is tolerated by the people who employ him, but for how much longer, only time will tell. His stage name is Bandy, real name Leslie Goldhawk, and he blamed himself for the breakup of his marriage, hence the incessant drinking and ruination of his body.

There is a large crowd in the stadium, waiting for this legend to entertain them. The stadium is packed and he is still taking a trip down memory lane, thinking about his father taking him to see the carnival and his first ever rodeo show, when he was only seven years old. He had a wry smile on his face as he remembered the excitement he felt at the mighty horses galloping past him, that smile soon disappeared as he continued with his makeup.

That is where his love affair began with the rodeo and has been burned deep within him ever since, like a drug that needed to be fed into his veins intravenously.

Earlier that day, he visited the North Dakota Cowboy Hall of Fame, which covers the history of the travelling shows made famous by Buffalo Bill Cody. He was a buffalo hunter turned showman and travelled around the world with his famous show, a living legend from the west.

Today is the fourth of July, in rodeo terms "Cowboy Christmas" and for the cowboys who take part with more determination to do better. Six seconds, the magic number for them, that's how long they must stay on the bull to qualify, it can seem like six minutes to some. Bandy has finished his makeup and finally put on his fedora hat that has been well worn, but it's his favourite and he always wore it for every show. It's probably his lucky charm. He got up from his chair and took one more sip from his glass and toasted his wife's picture and then walked towards the dressing room door and opened it.

The auditorium noise got louder and the music blasts through the speakers all around the arena, he was ready to make his entrance.

He got the all clear from the steward and got introduced by the host sitting high in the stands in his control booth, 'Ladies and gentlemen boys and girls, please make welcome the man of the hour, Bandy, the Rodeo Clown!'

The music plays Mareeba's Rodeo song by Slim Dusty, an Australian country singer who made it big in America. A song about the rodeo and it's loud, as it's elevated above the crowd noise, the crowd went crazy as he entered the ring. Bandy took off his hat as he entered the ring of hard, sandy ground beneath his feet, he is smiling and looking around the arena waving his hat, he had done this many times before.

He made his way around the ring and towards the main gates where the rest of the rodeo clowns are waiting to take their positions. Bandy is the head clown and they wait for his orders, but because of his drinking habits and his injuries, he just gave the orders and made an appearance for the crowd.

Chuck Connors, a rodeo clown in his fifties, who has known Bandy for over ten years, has worked closely with him and has seen the master at his best, now looked after him and kept him out of harm's way.

He is careful not to make Bandy look bad in front of the crowd because they have paid good money to see him, just enough to keep him safe and everyone else.

Halfway through the show and Bandy is showing tiredness. He is getting slower and Chuck has noticed this and is showing concern.

'Hey! Bandy, why don't you take a break, I'll take it from here,' said Chuck.

Bandy looked at him with hazy eyes, his head pounding still, he approached Chuck. Pointing at the crowd, he turned to Chuck, 'You see that, they have come to see me,' he pointed a finger toward himself, 'And I won't let them down,' he has decided to make one final appearance in front of the bull. A swan song of sorts, maybe he is tired of life!

'I'm just saying to have five minutes, you look worn out.' Chuck handed him a bottle of water and a couple of paracetamols. 'Here, take these please.'

Bandy took the bottle of water and throws it behind Chuck, he looked at him angrily. 'Let me do my job.'

And is waiting for the next bull to enter the ring, Chuck walked away and shakes his head in disbelief, he can only wait and be ready for the inevitable to happen. The bull is released and the cowboy rode out, there are two other mounted riders on standby, ready to rescue the cowboy when he is dismounted by the bull.

The rodeo clown's job was to distract the bull while the riders pick up the cowboy, experience is essential for this role and athleticism is a key requirement.

Within four seconds, the cowboy is thrown off the bull and the riders speed to his recovery, the rodeo clowns spring into action, Bandy is slow to react and is the last clown out. The other clowns run past the bull trying to get his attention away from the cowboy who was sitting on his back, it seemed to work as the two riders safely grab hold of the cowboy and take him back safely to the gates.

Bandy is trying his best to attract the bull. Chuck shouted out from behind the gates, 'Bandy, we got this.'

But he can't hear him with all the noise of the crowd behind him. The bull stopped and looked around and noticed Bandy and then put his head down and charged towards him, Chuck was shouting as loud as he can and was signalling to the other clowns to distract the bull. But within seconds, Bandy was thrown high into the air, caught by the bull's shortened horns and landed near the gates. His almost lifeless body lies on the ground and is speedily recovered by the attendants who drag him to safety behind the gates.

By now, the other clowns have got the attention of the bull and successfully lead it through the gates and shut the gate behind it, they quickly run over to Bandy who is in a bad way. The medics are quick to respond as well and are soon tending to him, there is some blood around his checked shirt and it looked like it's coming from his side.

'Bandy, are you OK, buddy!'

Chuck looked concerned the crowd are silenced, then sighs ring out around the arena, sounds like a muffled wind as the medics place Bandy onto a stretcher. It is a dangerous job being a rodeo clown, but it's a well-known fact and that's why they get paid so well.

As the medics carry Bandy away on a stretcher, the crowd all give him a standing ovation as Bandy was taken away by the paramedics, they applaud out of respect as he is taken away through the tunnel, and into an awaiting ambulance, his career is now over. The career span of most rodeo riders is not long, because of the dangers they face daily with their craft. Time to reflect and decide what to do next, the injury is not life threatening but it will stop him from being a rodeo clown, Bandy is approaching his fifties. A new chapter awaited this outcome and he will have to dig deep to move on.

He will have to look at other ways of earning a living and still be involved within the rodeo business, Bandy still knew enough people to help him. This would be the time to call in a few favours and see who his real friends were.

In the hospital, Bandy woke up in a private room paid for by the sponsors of the rodeo, even though he went down the drink route, they still look after him. He was in pain from his injuries and very lucky to be alive. The doctor came in to see him as the nurse leaves the room after giving Bandy some pain killers.

'Good morning, Mr Bandy! I am Dr Ramos, I checked you over when they brought you in, you have three broken ribs and your chest plate was damaged. You are a very lucky man; your aorta was ruptured but not life threatening.'

'What does that mean exactly, doc?'

'Well, if your aorta was damaged, then we wouldn't be having this conversation, so you were very lucky indeed.'

'How long do I have to be here, doctor?'

'Oh, you should be ready to leave in a couple of days, I'm just waiting for your X-rays to come back and then after some rest, you are free to go.'

Bandy thanked the doctor and thanked god for being alive, he now had some serious thinking and plan his future.

Chapter Two

Fifteen years later, and after graduating from Western Community College in Green River, Jake Rogers who was born in Green River, with a suntanned complexion and dark hair, aged 19. With his girlfriend Corrine Smith, tall slim with auburn hair also of this town and in her late teens, picked up their caps that were thrown up earlier into the air and landed on the grass, as a time-honoured college tradition. It is May and the quaking Aspen trees that surround the college grounds are flowering and the catkins from the trees, surrounded by tufts of cotton are taken from the trees by the wind and flown away to land and sprout new trees in years to come.

One of America's best loved trees for their greenish white cream coloured bark and their unmistakable colour in the fall give it a stunning appearance. Also, in the wooded hills the fallen leaves of the Aspen at fall are an essential food for deer and beavers, nature's ecological larder. Wyoming is a beautiful land, abundant with trees and shrubs, rivers and lakes and awe-inspiring mountains that covered the landscape.

Nathan Jones, Rick Wallace and Tammy Norris have all graduated together, best friends since first grade, they are all smiling and congratulating each other.

'Well, what are your plans for the future?' Jake asked his friends.

'Well, I'm gonna take some time to decide on my future. My folks want me to go to the military academy, but I don't think that's my thing,' said Rick.

'I'm not going to waste my time on university, I think that I will get a job and stay local,' said Nathan, who was of red Indian blood. Nathan was of Cheyenne blood, his ancestors go back two hundred years, to the historical epic march in 1879. Led by the two chiefs Little Wolf and Dull Knife, who left the reservation in the south and marched with 972 people and were given permission to hunt, but there was nothing to hunt. The Federal Government promoted bison hunting to allow settlers to build ranches and raise cattle without any competition from the bison.

The Cheyenne had enough and decided to escape and make their way north back to their Wyoming homeland. A seven hundred mile walk in poor conditions with the United States Army in constant pursuit. They eventually surrendered and were housed at Fort Robinson but were told they had to go back south. They escaped again and eventually settled in south eastern Montana, near the Black Hills.

Some of the Cheyenne fought with Crazy Horse and Sitting Bull at Little BigHorn, the site of General Custer's last stand.

Just then, Jim Rogers and his wife Debbie came over to the gang, Rogers had a black jacket with grey trousers and Debbie wore a light blue pleated dress.

'Congratulations you guys, you all look so good in your tunics, can you group together so I can get a photo of you,' said Jim.

The weather was good, clear skies and warm, it was the beginning of spring and there was happiness all around, and this would be captured and caught on camera, kept for eternity. They moved together and posed for Jim to take a photo; these things will always bring back memories for them in years to come. Jake and Corrine stayed while the others went to see their parents, George Smith, Corrine's father, came over to say hello.

'Hi, I'm Corrine's dad, how are you doing?'

He held out his hand to shake hands with Jim and did the same with Debbie, 'It's nice to meet you, George, I've heard a lot about you, we finally meet,' said Debbie.

'Yes, so nice to put a face to the voice,' said Jim.

George was in his fifties; he was five foot eight and quite lean but well built. He worked at the arena and was in charge of security, George was happy in his work. George lost his wife a few years ago to cancer, and was a single dad, and was proud of his daughter, he agreed to go back to the Rogers' home for further celebrations.

'So shall I see you around two in the afternoon?' said George.

'That should be fine,' replied Debbie.

George and Corrine left the Rogers and headed off home to get ready for the visit later that day.

'Seems like a nice man,' said Debbie.

'Yes, he is easy to get on with,' replied Jim. They also left the college with Jake and made their way home which was only ten minutes away.

Chapter Three

Jim and Debbie Rogers owned a stove business in the town and had a public showroom; they specialised in wood-burning stoves. Jim was in his sixties and Debbie in her fifties, Jake worked there as well, he would look after the warehouse and sort out all the deliveries.

Business was good and it gave the family a good lifestyle.

Jake had dreams of one day going to California, he dreamed of seeing the Pacific Ocean, he had seen all the travel programmes and it looked good to him. He and Corrine would plan to go there for their holidays but for now, he would carry on working with his mother and father and see where that took him. Corrine and Jake were going out with each other and have been together since preschool, so they know each other pretty well.

Corrine had a job at the local beauty salon, she worked for Dalores Gonzalez a Mexican divorcee in her fifties, who employed half a dozen staff. Corrine had been working there for over one year now and Dalores treated her like her own daughter. Especially after Corrine lost her mother two years ago and really missed her, Dalores was friends with Corrine's mother.

Jake and Corrine hung out with their friends at the Red Feather bar on the corner of N 2nd E street, once a week in the evenings; where they would meet for food and drinks and discuss future plans and things to do.

During the weekend, they would hang out at the Verizon Coffee House, on River View Drive, Jake and Corrine knew the owner, Peppe Gonzalez, not related to Dolores. There wasn't much to do in Green River, the town came alive when concerts and shows came to town, especially the rodeo.

The Rogers family lived in Ironwood Street near the Green River; in fact, they could see the river from their back garden fence. Their garden was tree lined towards the back of the lawn, green ash and elm trees lined the path to the river. Jake and his dad would go fishing there regularly. Debbie would leave food out for the wild deer that she had made friends with over the time that they lived there.

Green River ran through the town snaking its way through Ashley National Forest and through Utah winding its way through Colorado onwards to join the mighty Colorado River and into the Grand Canyon.

Wyoming consisted of rugged mountains, wooded hills, high elevation deserts and they boasted eight national forests. Nine million acres of wilderness adorned the state, with its semi-arid climate.

Corrine's father worked as a security guard at the Sweetwater Events Complex, it hosted everything from Rock Concerts to rodeo shows. He had been working there for eleven years. Little did he know this place would be the catalyst for Jake's venture into the rodeo circuit and the future that he had not planned for.

They arrived at the Rogers house and George Smith and Corrine pulled up on the drive and parked the car. Jim was already at the door waiting for them. George stepped out of the car, a Lincoln continental, a very comfortable car and had a very good air conditioning unit built in. The reason that American cars were mostly large in size is because they needed to be comfortable for the long journeys, this was a vast country with a vast road network.

The weather was warm with a breeze and it was a dry heat.

Jim was at the opened door, welcoming George; he had on a red tee shirt and blue jeans.

'Welcome to our humble abode,' said Jim.

George shook his hand and entered the house with Corrine, Jake was behind the two of them and had his hand on Corrine's shoulder. Their home was a single storey three-bedroom house which Jim extended by adding a roof extension, giving them another bedroom and bathroom, this was Jake's room and it gave him a great view of the Green River.

Debbie was getting the food ready for a BBQ; she had steaks on a platter all seasoned and ready to cook. 'You alright with burgers and chicken, George?'

He turned around to look at Debbie. 'You don't have to go to all that trouble,' said George.

'No trouble at all,' said Debbie.

'But let me help you' he replied as he went over to her.

'Well, you can give me a hand setting up the BBQ,' said Jim.

George followed Jim out to the back garden, their garden was mostly patioed with some green lawn in the middle, there was a small swimming pool and a summer house mainly used for storage.

A brick-built BBQ which Jim made himself was near the summerhouse and while he was getting it ready, he asked George if he could get the charcoal from the summerhouse and together, they could get it lit and ready for the food. Jake took Corrine up to his room and put away his college things, Corrine walked to the rear window and looked out at the river.

'I never get tired of looking at this view, it's so calming,' she was looking out at the river view at the end of the garden.

The leaves were beginning to form on the branches of the green ash and the elm with its Y shape and when in full bloom, it had a beautiful umbrella canopy. Jake walked over to her. 'Yeah, it's great,' he gave her a hug and they kissed, this is not the first time that she had been in his room.

'Jake, dear, the BBQ is on and it will take half an hour OK!' said Debbie.

'OK Mum, we'll be down.'

They eventually made their way down and outside to the garden, Jake picked up a bag of potato chips from the counter on the way.

Not a cloud was to be seen in the big light blue Wyoming sky 'The big sky country' as it was known. They were all now in the garden, it was not a blazing hot day, but warm enough. Jim had a fridge in the summerhouse where he kept the beer and wine along with soft drinks.

'Jake, can you do the honours with the drinks please.'

Jake got up from his wicker chair, and as he walked towards the room, he said, 'Sure Dad, what would you like to drink, Mr Smith?' asked Jake, he looked at Jake.

'I'll have a beer, thanks Jake,' said George.

As he sat down in the wicker chair by the pool, Jake went into the white summer house through the half glass panelled doors and went to the fridge. He took out a bottle of white wine for his mother and father and a couple of cans of Coors beer, and Corrine drank coke. When everyone had their drinks in their hands, Jim made a toast.

'Here's a toast to our kids, congratulations! You are now starting life as an adult proper, good luck to both of you.' He raised his wine glass and everyone followed suit.

The burgers were now ready and Jim put them onto a plate and the chicken wings were already on the table, Debbie had potato salad that she made yesterday and a green salad was rustled up pretty quickly.

They all sat down and tucked into the food, George started talking about his place of work, and a particular event that was held there a few years back.

'You know, at the Wolves Stadium,' he recalled. 'There was a rodeo a little while ago, and I remember this one in particular, because of the bull. This bull was the meanest animal that I had ever seen, eyes as black as coal, I swear he had the devil in his eyes. Anyway, there was this cowboy who went up against him, and he had a reputation for being mean to the bulls that he rode. But this bull, I think his name was El Toro! He was having none of that and within a couple of seconds, unmounted his rider and then proceeded to charge straight at him. I have never seen fear in a man's eyes, he froze!'

'What happened?' asked Jake, who was intrigued at George's story, 'What happened to him?'

'Well, the bull ran into him and lifted him up in the air, that boy was lucky, he survived but never rode again.'

Jake's face was full of excitement while the story was being told, 'What happened to the bull?' asked Jake who was at the edge of his seat.

'Nothing, he just got a better rep as a mean animal, just a famous bull now and still going strong in the circuit today, so I've been told.'

This story got Jake thinking, he was deep in thought and Corrine asked him what he was thinking about. 'Oh, I was just wondering how a bull like that was made to join the rodeo circuit.' He was actually thinking about facing that bull, what it would be like! But he didn't want to tell Corrine that.

After lunch, they sat in the garden under cover in the shade, even though it wasn't hot the sun could be troublesome, Jim had sat everyone down and they were all fed and relaxed, life was good at that moment. Jake got up to go to the summerhouse to get more drinks, Debbie got up and followed him. Once inside, the summerhouse Jake went to the fridge and opened the door.

'You guys seem to be cool, how are you getting on with George?' asked Debbie.

'Just fine, he's OK! You and Corrine have been going together for quite some time now, any plans for the future?'

'I don't know Mum, I haven't really given it much thought, maybe it's time to move our relationship forward?'

'Thanks Mum, I will talk to her tomorrow.'

'No rush, Jake, but just make sure it's for the right reasons.'

And they left with drinks in their hands for all. Corrine was smiling as she saw Jake heading towards her, 'It's about time, we thought that you got lost for a minute,' said George, they laughed and took their drinks from Jake.

Just then Jake said that he was going to go in for a swim, he was getting a little warm and needed to cool off.

'Corrine, you want to take a dip!' He looked at her and smile then winked at her.

'Are you sure you want to go in, it's not that hot.' But she got up to go with Jake to put on her swimwear, they held hands as they left the others.

'Don't worry, the pool is heated,' said Jim.

Corrine kept some of her clothes at Jake's place, as they used the pool quite a lot in the past. They both went inside the house to get their swimming costumes.

'How about you George, do you fancy a dip? I can lend you some trunks if you want,' said Jim.

'No, I'm a summer swimmer, the weather has to be just right, in the eighties or more.'

'I just would like to relax, too much good food, and good company.' He pointed to his stomach, Debbie was of the same opinion and they just were happy to relax and watch the kids enjoy themselves.

Jake got into his room and Corrine followed, as she walked in, he grabbed her and brought her towards him and gave her a big kiss on the lips. He put his hands on her breasts and squeezed them.

'What was that for?' asked Corrine, who pushed him back a little.

'I just could not resist,' he said. 'We have time.' He had a wide smile on his face. 'Jake! Control yourself! Not here, as tempting as it may be.'

He looked at her and then got their swimwear, Corrine went into the bathroom to change while Jake changed in the room. She came out of the bathroom in her swimwear, a two-piece bikini.

'You see, you should not have worn that, you know the effect that has on me,' remarked Jake.

He looked her up and down, 'We had better go downstairs before we get carried away.'

Before long, they had both come back outside, Jake had on a pair of jeans shorts and Corrine wore a light blue bikini, Jake jumped in first causing a splash,

Corrine eased herself in gracefully. The water was warm as she submerged just exposing her head above water, the sun beating down on it made it seem warmer than it was, but it was still refreshing. The pool was not too deep, eight feet at the deepest end, the teal colour tiles that were around the bottom of the pool gave it a cool feel. It certainly cooled them down and just watching the two of them in the pool made the others want to go in. The afternoon went well and everyone was happy at that moment.

Chapter Four

The next day was a work free day being a Sunday, there was no work today as the shop was closed. Jim would sometimes go in to work to catch up on paperwork, and if Debbie was up to it, she would go in with him.

But she was in a relaxing mood that day, they would come around now and then, Jim was going into work, he was only going to be there for a couple of hours. When you run your own business, dedication is an important part of the business, that's what makes a successful business. Jim also had to arrange a surprise for Jake and had to make a call to organise that. He left the house and got into his car, put the key in the ignition and eased his car out of the drive, a journey he made daily. I suppose if we stop and look at what we do every single day, we would think to ourselves, why? But with no immediate answer, we carry on regardless with our normal lives, always looking forward to something.

A trend was starting in America, people from the cities were buying land in wide open spaces to build their own homes and try to live a self-sufficient lifestyle. This would probably be a thing for the future, where people would get fed up with the rat race and try to find solitude in the wilderness.

Jim parked his car outside his shop and turned the engine off, he unlocked the car door and got out of the car, he looked at the shop and walked toward the door. The street was quiet and the road empty of cars, it was still early and the sun was beginning to shine uninterrupted by any clouds. It was a sublime day, a 'glad to be alive day.'

This was still their heat season. It was busier in the colder months as people would light their wood burners to keep their houses warm and save on the heating bills. With wood a plentiful source, the running cost of the stove made it a cheap form of heating.

Jim opened the door and walked into the shop. There was mail on the floor just behind the door. He closed the door and collected the mail from the floor. He quickly looked through the letters, but most of them were bills. So, they were put to one side on the table next to the door. He got to his desk and sat down; he didn't turn the light on in the shop as it was bright enough because of the large windows at the shop front. He looked over some papers and picked out a couple of quotes that he was in the middle of preparing yesterday. As it was quiet, he thought that he would finish the quotes and get them sent by post. There was a new mailing system being introduced. It was called an email! Technology! Advancement for the future, or a means to an end, it could be sent by computers all over the internet. Some people call it electronic mail, the first email was sent in 1971 by a computer engineer, Ray Tomlinson to himself. Technology has come so far in such a short time, but is it a good thing!

A couple of hours later the phone rang and Jim picked it up, it was Debbie, she missed him at breakfast.

'Hi, dear, are you OK?'

'Yes, I'm fine.'

'You left so early; did you have breakfast?'

'I had some toast and coffee, I just wanted to finish some paperwork in my office.'

'Well, don't overdo it, we need to go shopping later so don't be too long.'

'OK dear, I should be about an hour.'

Jim put the phone down and continued with his paperwork, he was reminded of how important his business was, it was the lifeblood of his family. Without it, they would be relying on other places to work, and putting your fate in their hands. Living would be out of their hands, this made him more determined to succeed, and that came with hard work. That's why he chased every quote and made sure the bank balance was always healthy, for security and longevity of his business. He replied to most of the quotes and was quite pleased that he came into work, and also quietly confident of converting the quotes to orders.

The phone rang again, it was Debbie, 'Jim! Are you finishing work?'

He looked at his watch, 'Sorry babe, I didn't realise it was so late, give me five minutes and I will pick you up, OK!'

'OK, see you soon.' Jim put his paperwork away and turned off his computer and just made a final check that everything was off before leaving the shop.

A few minutes later, he picked up Debbie and they went to the Green River Department store on N 1st E Street, 'The barbers will be open, Jim, you better get your haircut while it's not so busy.'

'Do I need a haircut? It doesn't look too bad.'

'Just get it cut, we are here now!' Jim gave in and walked into the department store and he went into the barbers which was just by the entrance inside the store. A small barber's with three adjustable chairs for customers having their hair cut. Debbie was going to walk around and do some shopping. She headed to the clothes department leaving Jim to get his haircut. She would catch up with him later and they would have to get some groceries and drinks on the way home.

Chapter Five

Later that day, Jake got up around 11am and decided that he was going to take Corrine out and talk to her about their future together, his mother's talk was still on his mind.

He got dressed and called her on his mobile phone. 'Hi Corrine, are you awake?'

'Yes, of course! We don't all have the luxury of lying in, you know; what's on your mind?'

He thought for a minute, did his mother speak to her as well, his face was a little puzzled. 'Er, nothing, just thought that we can go down to the coffee house and have some breakfast.'

'Yeah, that sounds good, give me half an hour and I'll be ready, but it will be more like lunch by then.'

Jake would pick her up in his Mum's car, as he didn't have his own wheels yet, he could use his motorbike, but it would not be comfortable for Corrine.

A little later, Jim and Debbie came back home with a smile on their faces, Jake was a little surprised to see him back so soon.

'What happened! Dad, you're back early.'

'Yes, I know, give me a hand with the shopping, will you,' Jake went out to the car with his father to help with the groceries and then he took them inside. Then Debbie came over to Jake and helped him put away the shopping, Jim signalled to her and she took hold of Jake's hand.

'Son, we have a surprise for you.'

Debbie was in on the surprise and knew what was about to happen, she said to Jake to step outside the house. He wasn't sure what they were talking about but went with them anyway. They all went outside and waited in the drive, Jake looked at them wondering what the surprise could be.

'Well, I'm here, what's the surprise?'

Just then entering the road he could see a vehicle pulling up into their drive, it was a Chevrolet Silverado 1500 truck in garage white finish, it was brand new and it was heading for the Rogers' household, it pulled up outside their house and the driver got out. It was a friend of George's who owned a car sales forecourt, he gave Jim a really good deal on this car, and he approached Jake.

'Jake Rogers?' He asked.

Jake was stunned, and speechless, he put his hand on his head and said, 'Yeah, that's me!'

The driver handed him a set of keys and a folder with the car paperwork inside. 'This is for you.' Jake took the keys and looked at his mum and dad.

'Really! You did this for me, wow, thanks, can we afford this?' asked Jake, as he went to the car to look it over.

'This is for all your hard work at college and help at the shop, you've earned it, son,' said Jim. 'And anyway, I got a good deal on this.'

Jake looked inside the car, it had black leather seats and had the customary three seats at the front. It was a beast with a black grille and bumper at the front and black wing mirrors, it was what he dreamed of and here it was in front of him.

'Well, take it for a ride, you were going to meet Corrine, weren't you, show her the car,' said Debbie.

'Have you been listening to my calls, Mum?'

'Just a mother's instinct,' she winked at him as Jake got into the car and put the key in the ignition, still in disbelief.

'Don't worry, you're insured, I arranged that earlier,' said Jim. 'Thanks Dad, I just can't believe this is happening!'

Jake was in such a good place, his smile would not leave his face for a long time, not today! He turned the key and it started first time and purred.

'Take care, son, so you are all set for the road, we'll see you later,' said Jim.

'OK Dad, thanks again, I was going to pick up Corrine, boy, will she be surprised. Wow! I still can't believe it, see you later.'

He gently pulled away then built up speed as he pulled out of his road and onward to meet Corrine, he was in a happy place. Jake would surprise her, he couldn't wait to see the look on her face, when she saw the car. He was soon at Corrine's house, a similar house to Jake's but a little smaller in size, with a green lawn and brick paved drive. He called her on the phone.

'Hey, Corrine, I'm outside, are you ready?'

'I'll be out in a minute,' said Corrine. 'But why are you not at the door?'

Jake parked outside her drive in front of her dad's company van. She thought for a moment, 'Why did he not come into the house?'

When Corrine came out, she just stood there with her mouth open.

'Hi babe, it's me and my new car, do you like it?'

'Are you kidding, is it really yours?'

'Yup! Mum and Dad got this for me, what do you think?'

'What's not to like, can we go for a drive?'

'Sure thing, we'll take it for a spin and then get some breakfast,' said Jake.

Jake got out of the car and went to the passenger side door and opened it for her, she got in and he closed the door like a gentleman would do. They drove off onto the highway and drove to the edge of town and then a little further, the car was a dream to drive.

They finally arrived at Cafe Rio, it was a Mexican restaurant and Corrine's mother was half Mexican and used to bring her there from time to time. Corrine missed her food, she used to cook Mexican food three times a week at home. Corrine learned a few recipes and would experiment on her father, but it never tasted like her mother's cooking.

Jake parked the car outside in the car park and they went inside and waited to be seated. They were shown to a corner table near the large glass window, and were seated, the waitress gave them a menu. There weren't many people in the restaurant but it was early and the lunchtime rush was a couple of hours away. Jake ordered breakfast for both of them. He ordered Huevos Rancheros eggs in salsa, eggs Mexican style and some chorizo. While the waitress went away to order the food, Jake put his hand across the table and held her hand.

'Corrine, I brought you here because I wanted to spend some time with you alone.'

He looked around the room, 'Well, nearly alone, anyway, we have been seeing each other for quite a while now, and I thought it was time we saw a bit more of each other.'

'What are you saying Jake?'

He looked into her eyes; she had a smile on her face.

'You already know, don't you?' asked Jake.

'No! I don't know, what are you talking about?' said Corrine.

'OK, look, I think that I want to spend more time with you, like, every day! What I'm trying to say is, will you marry me?'

She was quiet for a moment then suddenly everyone in the restaurant cheered, and Jake felt a little embarrassed, he didn't realise his voice was so loud. Corrine looked around at the people and then looked at Jake and put both her hands on his hand.

'You know that you are supposed to get down on one knee to do this properly, don't you!'

As he was about to speak, Corrine spoke first, 'Yes, I'll marry you.'

The waitress heard as she was bringing their food to their table.

'Wow, that's fantastic, congratulations.' The rest of the people in the restaurant cheered and clapped for them.

It wasn't the most romantic proposal in the world, but it was sincere and as a way of congratulating them, the owner let them have breakfast on the house. After breakfast, while they were leaving the restaurant Jake thanked the owner and the waitress, and they got another round of applause from the customers.

Jake and Corrine waved and thanked them as they left the restaurant and back to his car, hand in hand. They both had smiles on their faces.

Chapter Six

Jake was going back to his house to break the good news to his parents and later go to Corrine's place and speak to her dad. Sitting inside the new car was like sitting in a cool box, the air conditioning came on instantly when he turned on the engine, it was that good. They soon reached home and Jake stood and looked at his car, the smile he had all morning was still with him. They quickly went into the house.

'Mum, Dad! Are you in?' asked Jake.

'Well, where else would we be, we are in the back, son,' said Jim.

They made their way to the garden hand in hand and his mother and father were sitting on the wicker chairs. Jake and Corrine stood in front of them. Debbie already knew what was coming.

'Well, we did it! We are getting married,' said Jake.

'Oh, that's wonderful dear,' said Debbie.

'Yes, brilliant news!' said Jim.

They got up from their chairs and hugged Corrine in turn, and Jim went over to Jake.

'I'm proud of you, son, we kinda knew this was going to happen, you know.'

He put his hand on Jake's shoulders, to show affection. 'Have you told your father yet, Corrine?' asked Jim.

'We were going there next, we had to tell you guys first,' replied Jake.

'Well, I'm pleased for both of you, there's a long road ahead, and we will be there to help in any way,' said Jim.

'You guys better go over to George's now and we will organise a celebration dinner tonight, on us,' said Debbie.

'OK Mum, we will talk later, make the reservation for five people,' said Jake as he and Corrine left and went outside and got back into the car and drove off.

The sun was still in its glory as it shone relentlessly down on Green River, this was the best spell of weather the town had seen for a long time. Winter was very harsh and seemed to last forever.

Jake and Corrine were at her house and they were going to tell her dad the good news, as like a lot of the folks in Green River, when the weather was good, they spent more time outdoors. George was in the backyard doing some gardening, he liked to upkeep the rose bed that his wife started and didn't like to see it die. She also had a vegetable section because she grew most of the ingredients that she used in her cooking. Corrine saw her dad on his knees taking out the weeds. Corrine went round the back of the house through the side entrance because he would be working in the garden.

'Hi Dad.'

He turned around and saw the two of them enter the yard.

'Hey you guys, how are you, Jake?' He said as he got up slowly, he had trouble with his back especially if he was working at ground level.

'I'm fine, Mr Smith.'

'What are you kids up to! You look happy,' he went over to the table and got a bottle of water to drink.

'Dad, we have some news to tell you!'

'OK! What news?' said George.

'Dad, Jake would like to talk to you,' Jake then spoke.

'Yes, Mr Smith.'

'Please, Jake, call me George.'

'Er, sure, OK, you know that Corrine and I have been seeing each other for quite a while now, well, I would like to take care of her and would like to very much to marry her, sir.'

George looked stone faced at Jake, intentionally, Jake was unsure what George was going to say and Jake looked uneasy. He had never seen him like this before, a cold sweat trickled down his face, partly to do with the heat and partly due to fear! But then he never had to ask for his daughter's hand in marriage before.

'So, you want to marry my daughter, and where are you thinking of staying? Have you got plans?'

'Er, yes, sort of! Well, we thought that we would stay with my mum and dad for a little. Until we got a place or our own that is.'

'Oh, you did, did you!'

Then he could not keep his straight face any longer and burst out with laughter, he put his right hand on Jake's shoulders.

'I am so happy for both of you, I know that you will look after Corrine.'

Jake was relieved, and he saw the funny side and smiled. He wiped the sweat off his face and relaxed a little.

'Let's have a drink to celebrate,' said George.

As he went to the fridge in the kitchen and took out two bottles of Schlitz beer and poured a glass of white wine for Corrine.

'Here you are you two, here's to the future, and as long as I am around, I will be there for you,' they raised their bottles and glass and toasted to the future, George was very happy that his daughter was getting married to Jake, he thought highly of him.

'Oh Dad, Jake's parents are organising dinner at a restaurant tonight, are you OK with that?' George walked over to the both of them.

'I didn't have plans for tonight, so that's fine, I look forward to it, just let me know what time.'

'Oh, I almost forgot, Jake's got a new car, do you want to have a look, it's outside!'

'Sure, let's take a look,' and they walked to the side gate in the garden and onto the drive where Jake had parked his car.

'Wow, that's some car, Jake.'

'Mum and Dad got it for me, for graduating, it's a step up from my bike.'

'Well, at least you will both be comfortable driving around in that, I am happy for you Jake.'

'And I almost forgot, Corrine, I was going to give this present to you later, but since you are here now, just wait here, I'll be right back.'

George went back into the house and a few minutes later came back out with an envelope, Corrine thought it was money, 'You don't need to give me anything Dad, he spoke to both of them.'

'I have been wanting to do this for a long time, ever since your mother passed away.' He gave the envelope to Corrine. She opened it and inside was a document which was five pages stapled together, she took it out and saw the header. Corrine's eyes lit up. 'Dad! This is the deed to the house, what's going on? Why?'

'Well dear, I am not getting any younger and the house is gonna be yours eventually when I die.'

'Don't say that, Dad, you're not going to die anytime soon.'

'Look, Corrine, I want you to have this, it's yours anyway, this just makes it legal, I'll still be living here, but I want you to know that all this will belong to you.'

'I don't know what to say.'

'There is nothing to say, now let's look forward to dinner tonight.' She had a tear in her eye and Jake cuddled her, and thanked her father for what he had done, he was shocked at the speed in which everything was happening.

Their future was set and some pressure was taken off the couple, which made the wedding a lot easier to arrange now. Jake told Corrine that he would see her at the restaurant later and kissed her goodbye.

'See you later, Mr Smith.'

'Jake, call me George, please, we're almost family.'

'OK, George, but it feels weird, see you later.'

Jake got into his car and drove off, trying to digest what had just happened and also earlier in the day. He certainly won't forget today for lots of good reasons.

Chapter Seven

Debbie had booked a table at Don Pedros Mexican restaurant on Wilkes Drive, which was walking distance from their house. The food was homely and the atmosphere was Mexican themed. They had eaten there a few times and knew the owner quite well.

Antonio Garcia moved to Green River from Denver Colorado ten years ago and liked the town, because it was peaceful and he liked the people as well.

He ran the restaurant with his wife and daughter, his daughter went to the same school as Jake, so they knew each other. The restaurant had basic wooden tables and chairs, likened to the cabanas in Mexico. He wanted to bring the old style of design to his restaurant, and was happy with the result.

Later that evening while the Rogers were getting ready, Jake was still excited about the proposal and the gift of the car. He thought of how lucky he was, most people don't have the luxury of parents who planned for the future like he did.

He considered himself very lucky, so he decided to tell his friends Nathan and Rick about the proposal, so he rang them. They were surprised at first but were happy for him, Corrine had already spoken to Tammy, her best friend.

Tonight, would not only be a celebration but also time to think about the wedding and make plans for dates and who they were going to invite.

Jim Rogers had a brother who lived in El Paso Texas, and he and his wife had two children, he has a sister, Jill who was married and had three children. She lived in Dakota, Jim's mother and father passed away a few years ago. So that's the only familial connection he has, they used to live in Montana and had a small ranch, Jim and Debbie used to live with them before they made the move to Green River.

They sold the ranch and his parents went to live with Jill, his mother gave Jim a large deposit from the sale to put down on the house they were buying in Green River. And some money went towards the business that they started.

The business was their only means of earning money now as they used most of their savings. Jim could not work for anybody; he liked to call the shots and have control and make his own future, and it was working quite well at the moment. The Rogers made sure they put some money away for a rainy day!

'Jake! Are you ready?' called Debbie.

After a few seconds he answered, he was still on the phone to Rick. 'I'll be down in a minute,' he said.

And said goodbye to Rick who he was speaking to about the dinner, he called Corrine to let her know that they would meet her and her dad at the restaurant at 07.30pm, he came downstairs dressed in a white shirt and blue jeans with a black belt and fawn jacket, casual yet smart.

Debbie and Jim were already dressed and ready to go, she had on a one-piece navy-blue dress and matching shoes while Jim had on a black suit and red tie.

'Take the tie off, dear,' said Debbie, it's not that sort of place!

He always listened to her and took off the tie and placed it on the settee, he looked at Jake. 'That's why I married your mother, she knows things.'

'OK, are we ready to go?' asked Jim.

And with that, they left the house and got into the car, it was only around the corner but they still preferred to drive, as did most of the people in America.

When they went to the restaurant, they were greeted by a waitress who was at the entrance door standing in front of a wooden pew. She was there to get people seated at the appropriate tables, she showed them to their table that was reserved and gave them a menu.

They were seated near the window which overlooked the car park and views of the mountains in the distance, it was getting dark as the sun started to set in the distance. The restaurant was full and it always helped with the atmosphere when there was a lot of people in the restaurant. It was a little noisy with the chatter amongst the tables and the clinking of glasses and cutlery but this added to the ambience.

As they were seated, Jake saw Corrine at the door along with her dad, she saw him and told the girl at the door that they were with that table.

Jake got up and gave Corrine a kiss and shook George's hand.

'Glad to see you,' said Jake.

'I'm glad to be here, Jake!'

'George! Come and sit here next to me,' said Debbie, so he did after shaking hands with Jim.

'Well, this is nice, we should do this more often' said George.

'That would be nice George, now that we know each other better, let's do that.'

Julia, the daughter of Antonio, approached the table with a notebook in her hand and with pen ready to go. Julia was 18 years old and went to the same college as Jake and Corrine.

'Hi Jake, Corrine, how are you guys doing?'

'Julia!' said Corrine, 'it's nice to see you, I didn't realise you worked here.'

'Yes unfortunately, but it's a good thing that I know the boss, are you guys celebrating graduating?' Julia asked.

'Yes, and also, Jake has asked me to marry him.'

'Wow!' She said, 'That's fantastic, you make a great couple,' she was so happy for them and a little bit jealous as well, she liked Jake but never told him. 'Have you decided what to order yet or shall I get your drinks first, Jake?'

'Yes, let's start with the drinks,' and he ordered some wine for the table and a Jack Daniels for his dad, and George, on the rocks, and a beer for himself.

They were celebrating after all, Julia went to the bar area and was talking to her father Antonio, he had a big smile on his face and decided to come to the table.

'And when were you going to tell me?' asked Antonio, Jim got up and reached out his hand to shake his hand.

'Antonio! Yes, it happened today, great news, isn't it?'

'I've known you kids since you were little, wow, how quickly they grow,' he said.

'Look, I am going to send some champagne, to celebrate.'

'You don't have to do that,' said Jim.

'No, I insist, it's not every day your friends get married,' and he went away to organise the drinks.

Julia had brought a bottle of champagne to the table and opened it, the plug popped into the air falling somewhere near the window. She filled their glasses and there was a little left in the bottle.

'Julia, here pour the rest into this glass and celebrate with us,' said Jake.

She was handed a glass from the table and she emptied the remainder of the champagne into the glass and raised her glass, she looked towards her father and he nodded.

'To Jake and Corrine, to the future,' said Julia.

And they all raised their glasses and joined in the toast. 'Dinner will be in twenty minutes, I will bring the drinks you ordered,' said Julia, as she walked away taking the empty bottle with her.

'That was nice,' said George. 'Have you guys decided on a date yet for the wedding?'

They looked at each other, and then looked at Jake and Corrine. 'No, not as yet.'

'We thought that we could discuss that over dinner,' said Debbie.

'How about a June wedding?' said Jake, out of the blue.

'Why, that is only six weeks away,' said Jim, you will need more time to organise, son.

'Why June?' said Debbie.

'Well, it's as good a day as any,' said Jake.

'How about you, George, are you happy with that date?' asked Debbie.

'I'm fine with that, are you going to have enough time to get everything arranged?' He asked.

'I should think so,' said Corrine.

'I think you two should give yourselves a little more time,' said Debbie.

'You're right, maybe July!' said Jake.

'That sounds better,' said Jim having just taken a sip of his champagne.

Just then Julia brought their drinks to the table and gave everyone their beverages. Then opened the bottle of wine and left it on the table for people to help themselves.

'How about church, which church do you think?' said Jim.

'The First Assembly of God church,' said Debbie. 'Well, we have been there a few times, and it looks quite nice, how about you, Corrine, what do you think?'

'That sounds good to me, they gave my mother a good service when she passed, so yeah, that's fine.'

So, the church was decided and the month was planned, the date would depend on the church. They would have to speak to the Pastor of the church and get that sorted, it was all going to plan, smoother than they thought.

Dinner arrived a few minutes later and Julia brought a trolley to the table and it smelt delicious, George ordered Chilli Con carne, Jim ordered chicken fajita with salad, Debbie and Corrine ordered the same, tacos and that came with a selection of goodies. When served onto the plates, the colours were rich, spread around the table, and all made fresh, they had built up an appetite after discussing the wedding. There was less talking while the food was being devoured. Julia checked on them from time to time, just to make sure they were OK, and to see if they required a top up on the drinks.

Once finished, they all sat back in their chairs and breathed a sigh of relief, 'Good food, good wine and good company, it doesn't get any better than that,' said George. 'I would just like to say, that I am really happy that Corrine got to know you guys, you are good people and I know she will be looked after if ever I'm not around.'

'What do you mean, Dad, why would you say that again today?'

'Well, I'm no spring chicken, and it's good to know there are people who will care for you, that's all I meant.'

'Dad, you will be around for a long time, I'll make sure of that.'

'Now who's for dessert!' Julia came over with the dessert menus.

'Can I recommend the Tres Leches cake, a three milks cake with condensed, evaporated and full cream cake, you will love it.'

They looked at each other, 'Let's go for that, we will all have the Tres Leches please, Julia,' said Debbie, and Julia smiled at her and left the table to get their cakes, this was a delicacy of this restaurant and went down well with the customers.

Cake soon arrived and it looked delicious. Julia also brought coffees for everyone. 'The coffee is on the house,' she said as she poured coffee into the cups already on the table. Their bodies would be heavy tomorrow, but as it is a work day they would probably burn most of that away, but for now, they were enjoying their dessert and coffee.

Tomorrow was another day, and a day to get some dates on the calendar and look to the future, Jake would have to choose a best man and Corrine, a maid of honour. As they didn't have a large group of friends, that task would be easier than most. He would also need a suit, he never owned a suit before so would have to buy one, they were not going to have a big wedding, so costs would not be high. As for the honeymoon, they would do that at a later date, there was no rush.

Chapter Eight

Monday started a little dull, Jake opened up his curtains in his bedroom to reveal a mist rising up from the river, the sunshine was hazy as it tried to burn its way through the cotton wool type of clouds that refused to burn away, allowing the sun to beam brightness onto the flowing river.

Eventually the sun would win but for now the cloud cover would be there for a little while yet, Debbie was already in the kitchen cooking breakfast. Scrambled eggs, bacon and biscuits, the biscuits was her mother's own recipe, was at the breakfast table when Jake came down, he sat at the table and started drinking the orange juice that was already poured into his glass.

'Just a little breakfast Mum, I am still trying to handle last night's dinner,' said Jake.

Corrine was going to work as well, Dalores had a few customers coming in that morning, Corrine liked her as a boss, she was understanding and kind and always looked after her. She had her regular customers who always asked for her. The salon was not far from her house so Corrine would always walk there, she liked the exercise, she would wear trainers to work and change into her shoes when she got there.

Jim had to sort out some stove orders from the sales last week, one order was for a quantity of stoves that he had to get delivered or shipped out by a carrier. He was going to advertise for an assistant because the work was getting too much for him and Jake, new blood was needed.

'You ready, Jake?' asked Jim.

'Yep! Let's go, shall I leave my car here?' asked Jake.

'You might as well, we have to organise the deliveries for the rest of the week, if you want you can do the smaller deliveries in your car once you have the dates.'

'That sounds like a plan,' said Jake. They both left the house and got into Jim's car and made their way to work. Jim was talking to Jake about hiring somebody and straight away a name came into his mind.

'Nathan! Is looking for a job, maybe we can get him in and talk to him,' said Jake.

'OK, son, get him to come in, it will save me advertising.'

It was too early to ring Nathan at the moment but he would ring him later that morning. They reached work within twenty minutes and Jim got out of the car to open the showroom doors, the warehouse was at the back of the unit, there were several units along that road all with large car parking spaces in front.

Jim had decorated the showroom with customers in mind, it was spacious yet had all the product displays on show. The majority of the displays were stoves as they were the bread and butter of the business. Jim had a lot of experience in that field and in the industry his name was up there with the best, good customer service is what he based his business on. The word soon got around and Jim's business was the go-to place for anyone who wanted to know about stoves, even builders big and small would contact him for advice. He always liked to help people sometimes too much, his wife would say, she was a shrewd business woman but Jim just liked to do business.

Debbie only came in to work two to three times a week, she was suffering an incurable disease called fibromyalgia, which attacked the nervous system and caused so much pain at times to her body. It was an illness that had doctors all over the world baffled, with its tenacity and not being able to find a cure.

Debbie had contracted the illness on a routine dental issue at the hospital, things went wrong and as a result the brain was activated into the fibromyalgia mode. To you and me, the person looked normal, but for the person, it's a living hell, the body feels bruised and the headaches and consistent pain from joints are relentless. It is said that if you can see a body on a screen with the afflictions that are suffered by the person, then you would see bruises all over the body, from head to toe.

Debbie used drugs now and then, but she didn't like to take them very often as it had after-effects, but women have a greater pain threshold than men and she found a way to live with this. Jim was in awe at the way she carried on day to day living with this affliction.

Jim put all the lights on and put the open sign on the entrance doors, they were open for business, Jake went into the warehouse and put the lights on, he went over to the truck and checked it over. Jim took out his folder and started to go through the orders, he passed over the deliveries that had to be arranged this week to Jake and his job would be to book them in and get the items delivered. This was where he would need help and it was then that he got his phone and gave Nathan a call.

Nathan's phone rang a few times before he answered it.

'Hello Nathan, it's Jake!'

'Hi Jake, to what do I owe the honour of this call.'

'Hi Nathan, look can you talk?'

'Yeah, what's up?'

'You looking for work?'

'Yeah, why?'

'Well, my dad's looking for help at the shop, are you interested?'

'Interested! When can I start?'

He was obviously very interested and Jake invited him to come to the shop later that morning. Jake had once delivered to Boulder Colorado with his dad, that was for a builder who was building off track lodges in the mountains. Geographically from Green River they had access to a lot of places of interest within their grasp in all directions.

Yellowstone Park was within a day's drive, Little BigHorn was the same distance, the Grand Canyon was two days away, Salt Lake City only a day's drive and lots of other famous places within that area. So, they were placed well and where they lived, long distance deliveries were a common in America because of the vastness of the land.

Maybe after they get married, their honeymoon could be in one of those places, Jake would have to wait and see. It would be a joint decision that the both of them would have to make. For now, he has to sort out work and get Nathan on board to help with the overflow at work and maybe long-term get him to go full time. This will free Jake to carry out some of his plans, Jake knew that his responsibilities lay with the business and his father was not going to be running the business forever, so he would have to juggle things around, to make it work.

Nathan arrived at the shop door and opened it then walked in.

'Hey Jake, Mr Rogers!'

Jim was at the counter with Jake and they looked up at him. 'Nathan! So nice of you to come down at short notice.'

'No problem, sir,' as he approached the desk. 'Pull up a stool and sit down,' said Jim.

After he sat down on the stool, Jake pulled a chair to the desk and sat down next to Nathan to keep him company.

'So, Nathan, I hear you are looking for work!'

'Yes, I am and thank you for this opportunity.'

'Well, we have a position in our showroom if you are interested,' said Jim.

'I sure am, Mr Rogers, Jake told me about it.' Nathan was very excited at getting his first job, he found it hard to contain his emotions.

'The job I have in mind is warehouse operative, which will include deliveries, obviously you don't drive yet, but maybe later we can get you lessons, you will also need to learn the products that we are selling and eventually learn the selling side of the job, what do you think?'

'I think I am going to enjoy working here, and I will learn fast and make you proud sir.'

'Well, the first thing I need you to do is fill out this form for me and then we can talk, OK?'

He handed him an application form and gave him a pen to fill it out with. Nathan took this and started filling it out on the counter, Jim looked at Jake and had a smile on his face, it was like watching a child get excited over a present that he was opening.

'Well, what do you think, Dad?'

'Son, I think it's up to us to mould him into what we want him to be, and I think he will do a good job.'

Nathan had completed the form and handed it to Jim, who took it and had a quick look at the form.

'So, Nathan, let me tell you a little bit about the job, come into my office,' Jim led Nathan into his office behind the counter.

Jake picked up some orders and put them in delivery date order, he would be calling the customers to book in the deliveries for later that week. As he was about to pick up the phone, the front door opened and a young girl came in with some flyers.

'Hi can I put a couple of these up in your window?' she asked.

'Let's have a look, what is it for?' asked Jake.

'It's for the state rodeo,' she said handing one over to Jake.

He looked at the poster and straight away got interested, he almost forgot about the girl being there. 'Yeah, sure, tell you what, just leave a couple here and I'll put them up for you.'

'Thanks mister.'

'No problem,' said Jake as he took the posters from her.

When she had left, Jake perused the poster closely, he always pictured himself riding in a rodeo. He had been to a few rodeos but this time his interest would be of a taking part basis, he was going to find out more about this rodeo, he had caught the bug!

The rodeo was to be held adjacent to the Wolves Stadium, which was used by the local college; it had been held there before on several occasions in the past. The organisers would be erecting a big top circus tent as this was not one of the biggest rodeo shows it didn't require a large stadium.

They would send a team of riggers a couple of days ahead of time to set everything up, and they would get some local people to help, to help with community spirit. It also served as a good public relations exercise which in turn helped to sell tickets.

Wyoming is the state rodeo capital and the Cody Centre in Newcastle is the biggest, named after Buffalo Bill Cody.

Jake thought to himself that he would make contact with the organisers and see if he could get involved, suddenly he had forgotten about the deliveries and was focussed on the rodeo. Jim had brought Nathan back to the front desk and had a smile on his face.

'Well Jake, put Nathan to work, he will help out today and start properly next Monday.'

'Jake! Are you with us!'

Jake took his eyes of the poster and looked up, he put his hand on the shoulder of Nathan. 'Welcome to the family.'

Jim saw the posters on the desk and went over to look at them, he had noticed Jake engrossed in them.

'It must be that time of the year already, my, time goes by so fast,' said Jim, at that time Debbie came into the showroom, Jim had called her and told her about Nathan joining the business.

'I just came over to say congratulations, Nathan, you will fit in just fine,' she said. 'Oh, the rodeo is in town, are we gonna go?' asked Debbie, 'Why not we do it every year.'

'Good, this year we can take along Corrine as well, as part of the family.'

Jim smiled as she went into the office, Debbie worked with the accounts and came in to carry out some work on the invoices that had to be paid. She didn't like to be behind on their payments, they had a good name in the business and she wanted to keep it that way. Jake had taken Nathan to his desk which was upstairs on the mezzanine that Jim had built when he first got the unit, he was going to show Nathan the ropes. Debbie was at her desk and turned on the computer ready to deal with the invoices. Jim was attending to a customer who had just walked in.

Jake and Nathan had finished the paperwork and went down to the ground floor. They were now going to be crating some wood burning stoves in the warehouse at the back of the showroom. Basically, they had to uncrate and check stoves that were delivered to them earlier, just make sure that they were not damaged. These were due to be delivered to customers once checked.

'Hey Nathan, Corrine and I are going down to the Red Feather bar tonight, she has to sort out some things for the wedding, you up for going?'

'Yeah, I'll be there, what time?'

'Be there for 7.30.'

'OK, no problem.'

Jake didn't drink too much, he just liked the company and a change of scenery is a good thing, especially when you are with friends. They carried on with the crating and then put the stoves away, the customers were contacted by Jake and delivery dates set. Their job was done and Jake moved on to other jobs that needed to be sorted out in the warehouse. It was nearly time to close the shop so Jim let Nathan go a little earlier, as this was his first day. Debbie and Jim were going to work a little late because she wanted to finish the payments, so Jake was closing the warehouse and getting ready to leave.

'OK, you guys, I'll see you later, and don't work too hard, OK!'

They waved to him and he closed the shop door and put the closed sign on, he was looking forward to going to meet up with his friends later.

Chapter Nine

Later that night, the Red Feather bar was busy for a Monday night, and there was a band booked for the evening. They were trying out a new resident rock band and wanted to see how they performed, music that attracted a younger audience.

Green River was not a huge town and was relatively quiet most of the time, but occasionally they would let their hair down. The college kids made up over half of the crowd, they were not particularly rowdy but alcohol changed that, nothing too serious to worry about, Sheriff Jones and his deputies had a relatively safe and danger-free job. Things got more hectic when they had concerts held at the bigger venues.

This night would see strangers at the bar, riggers from the upcoming rodeo were there, to have a drink and check out the locals. They were in their thirties and there were four men and one woman, she was the one in charge. This would also help with public relations for the rodeo show, they would be giving away some free tickets.

They sat at a table next to the bar and ordered their drinks. A couple of the men were looking at the college girls sitting with their boyfriends. They were smiling at the girls who in return smiled back, just being friendly.

But their boyfriends were not too happy with the attention that they were getting, and decided to look daggers at the riggers.

Rick was at the table, 'Look, guys, just ignore them OK!' But easier said than done, they didn't listen and kept looking in the rigger's direction. Just then Jake and Corrine walked in and the riggers at the table turned the other way to look at them.

There were smiles as they approached the table.

'Hi guys, what's up?'

'Hi Jake, Corrine,' said Rick.

'Oh, there's some guys at the other table who are not from here, I think they are something to do with the rodeo show, or something, and they are staring.'

Jake looked over at the table. 'Really! Cool, I might go over and talk to them.'

'Why?' said Rick.

'Well, its neighbourly, and I want to find out about the rodeo.'

'Yeah, but they were staring at the girls, and the guys didn't like them doing that.'

Jake looked over at them again. 'I'm sure they mean no harm.'

Nathan walked into the bar at this time, he had on a blue denim jacket and white jeans and was smiling, 'Hallelujah, the gang's here,' he thought to himself as he came up to the table and pulled up a chair.

'Hello, people, who wants a drink?' asked Nathan.

They gave him their orders in a heartbeat and Nathan was about to walk up to the bar.

'Hold up Nathan, I'm coming with you,' said Jake. He got up and walked up to Nathan, Corrine stayed seated and started talking to Tammy, her best friend.

'I guess you heard that I'm getting married to Jake, and I was wondering if you—'

But before she could finish, 'Yes! I'll do it!' She said.

'But you don't know what I was going to say!'

'It doesn't matter, I'll do it anyway,' said Tammy who was excited.

'Well, that's that then, you're my maid of honour!'

'Thank you, and I will look out for everything, don't worry!'

Jake and Nathan were at the bar and ordering their drinks, Jake put his arms on the bar counter and then leant over to look at the table with the riggers on.

He was curious and was thinking of a way he could introduce himself to them, this could be his way into the show, he thought to himself. But as he was about to pick up the drinks and take them to the table, two of the riggers got up and walked over to the friend's table. They were dressed in denim and cowboy boots; it looked like they had been drinking as they approached the table, they were looking at Corrine.

'Hey girl, my friend and I would like to buy you and your pretty little friend a drink.'

Corrine looked up at him. 'Thank you but we got drinks coming,' said Corrine.

'Well, how about we come over and sit down with you pretty girls,' said the taller of the two men, who got closer to Corrine, he was in his forties, unshaven with curly black hair.

'My boyfriend wouldn't be too happy about that, and he is bringing our drinks over now.' Corrine was looking towards Jake at the time, Jake approached the table and put the drinks down on the table.

'Is there a problem over here!' He asked as he looked at the two men.

'Well, you must be the boyfriend.'

'Yes, I am, so like I said, is there a problem?'

'Look, son, we were just asking the girls to have a drink with us, no harm in that is there!'

'Well, I think that you two guys should just go back to your table, the girls don't want to drink with you, OK!'

'Hey kid! We were just trying to be friendly, that's all.'

'Look, we are OK thanks, now if you don't mind. We would like to be left alone.'

Jake was a few feet in front of the taller one and could sense something was going to happen. 'Well, if that's the way you want to be, then.'

He clenched his fist and swung out at Jake, Jake moved his head and shoulder to one side and pushed the man over. He was drunk and not very stable on his feet so he went over very easily, his friend saw what happened and was about to attack Jake; when the woman from the rigger's table came over and grabbed the man and pulled him back.

'Sorry about the disturbance, you guys have a good time, they won't bother you again.' She dragged the man over to their table with the help from the rest of the crew, who had come over by now.

Jake sat down, and they picked up their drinks and Nathan made a speech.

'Here's to Jake and Corrine, here's to their future together, and from the way you handled yourself, a safe future, to Jake and Corrine.'

They raised their glasses and cans and toasted them; the scuffle had been forgotten and there were smiles all around as they all said 'Cheers.' Jake got up from his chair.

'I'm just going to speak to the lady from the other table before they leave.'

Corrine looked puzzled!

'Don't worry babe, I'm not going to start a fight, I just want to get some information about the rodeo.'

He went over to the other table and spoke to the woman, 'Hi, I'm Jake, I just wanted to apologise for earlier.'

'It wasn't your fault, sometimes drink gets the better of some of us,' said the woman.

'I'm Belinda and these guys are Buck, Dave and the inebriated one is Mike.'

Jake didn't sit down; he just wanted some information.

'Hi! Nice to meet you, I was wondering, how does someone get involved with the rodeo?'

Belinda looked at Jake, 'Well, you just turn up on the day and we can see what you are capable of,' she said.

'Are you there tomorrow?'

'Yes, we are there from daybreak, what did you have in mind?' said Belinda.

'I always had dreams of getting involved, I've seen a lot on TV and it looks like fun.'

'Well, it can be fun, but also dangerous! Can you ride?' asked Belinda.

'I sure can,' said Jake.

'Well, why don't you come down tomorrow at around 10am, and we can see what we can find for you.'

'That's great, I'll see you tomorrow.'

Jake left and Belinda and her crew were about to do the same, he went back to his table and sat down.

'Well, what did they say?' asked Corrine, who was intrigued.

'Well, I'm going to help out at the rodeo for a few days until opening on Saturday,' said Jake.

'What about work?' asked Corrine.

'Well, there are no deliveries tomorrow and Nathan is on board now, so Dad will be OK.'

'I gotta see what the rodeo is all about firsthand.'

'I've always wanted to get involved with something like this for a long time and now I get the chance.'

Corrine looked at Jake and paused for a moment. 'Well, don't forget not to get too carried away, you have responsibilities coming up.'

'I know babe, it's just something that I've gotta do.'

And with that they all got up, it was time to make their way home, Jake was a little bit happier even if Corrine wasn't. He would have to make it up to her and concentrate on the wedding once the rodeo was over, Jake never thought any further than the rodeo, what if he got the bug! What if he wanted more! He would not know until he actually got involved.

Time would tell, but for now he only had thoughts for the next few days, he would have to speak to his mother and father and run this by them first. Work had to come first, but because he was arranging the deliveries he had some control over his days off. Corrine had a slightly worried look on her face, what if Jake got too involved with the rodeo, where would she fit in! She would have to play this correctly, she loved Jake and wanted to make sure that he was happy in whatever he chose.

Chapter Ten

The next day Jake spoke to his parents and they were OK with him having some time off, but told him to exercise caution. He thanked them and got into his car and drove to the Wolves Stadium, where the rodeo was to take place. The big top was due to be erected and when filled it could hold around three to four hundred people and with plenty of room for the rodeo riders.

It was being set up on barren land, where they had held many shows over the years, the frame work was partly up and they were about to set the ring up. Jake parked his truck and walked over to where the crew were congregated and he saw Belinda and walked up to her. There were about a dozen people in the area mainly in their thirties and forties, riggers that were seasoned workers and lived their life on the road. Which meant, they didn't have permanent homes and the majority were not married, this is not a job for having a relationship, because of the hours they had to work. Not only that, but being on the road was normally six to eight months of the year of shows with not much time off.

Belinda saw Jake and smiled. 'Hey Jake, you look all set, ready for some hard work?'

Jake stood in front of her and he was wearing blue denim jeans and a checked shirt. 'I'm ready, what have you got for me?'

She pointed towards the ring that the crew were fencing; they were putting up steel tube fencing that was being supported by steel stakes into the ground.

'Can you work with that crew over there and help them get the perimeter fencing in place?'

'No problem,' said Jake.

'Report to that tall man with the black Stetson on, his name is Bill, he'll show you what to do.'

'Jake went towards the fencing crew, there were two men working on erecting the steel fence panels,' he reached them and called out to Bill who was just telling someone what to do. 'Hey, Bill! Belinda sent me to help out.'

Bill turned to Jake, and looked him up and down, 'Great! We can do with all the help we can get, there are some rigging gloves over there.'

Bill pointed to a bag on the ground and Jake grabbed a pair of gloves. They were all a similar size and fitted him well, he then went back to Bill and helped them to put up the steel fence panels.

They had to erect the panels in the shape of a large oval ring, this would protect the people in the crowd from getting too close to the horses and the bulls. This rodeo would not be using the more dangerous animals, for obvious reasons. Safety was a big factor at these shows but there had to be some element of danger. That is what the public pay for and it was the promoter's job to make sure the show was exciting but safe, that's why they only employ professional handlers.

The rodeo clowns were also a very big part of any rodeo, as they were the people who kept the riders safe and entertained the crowds at the same time. William F Cody (Buffalo Bill) created the first major rodeo and first Wild West show back in 1882, the show was in North Platte Nebraska. From there, he went on to organise his famous touring Wild West shows.

Other entrepreneurs started the rodeo shows after the great success of the Cody Show. The morning went well and the fencing was nearly completed, Belinda approached the crew working on the fence, 'Jake!' She called out. He turned to where the voice came from and could see Belinda walking towards him.

'I need some details for our records and for paying you.'

'You mean I get paid!' said Jake.

He didn't even find out about the money side of the position, he was thinking that this was just helping out, this got better he thought to himself. 'Yeah sure, what do you need from me?'

She gave him some papers to look at and a pen to sign when he had finished reading it. It didn't take him long to read the forms and he quickly signed the paperwork on the last page and handed it back to Belinda, 'There you go.'

She took the paperwork from Jake and walked away leaving Jake to get back to work. Once the inner ring fence was finished, they would concentrate on making an outer ring, this would be wide enough for staff to walk through, it was an escape route in case of any danger within the main ring. Bill was also the safety officer, it was his job to make sure the structure would be safe enough for all eventualities, people's lives depended on it. Double protection which was required from the regulations on setting up and running of these shows, nothing was left to chance.

Jake got a call from his father while he stopped to have a bite to eat, it was lunch anyway, 'Hey Dad, how are you managing at work?'

'Oh fine, son, I was just checking to see how you were getting on.'

'Yeah, it's great, just as I imagined, I'm just having lunch.'

'I have taken an order for a dozen stoves today and they want delivery next week, it's over in Fort Bridger, at the RV camp. They are building some lodges on the site to use as bed and breakfast facilities for campers. They are organising installation and don't require any flue systems.'

'That's great Dad, I can arrange a delivery once you have the stoves, have you got a date for the stoves yet?'

'Well, I have contacted the supplier and they will be with me by next Thursday.'

'The delivery will be a good experience for Nathan.'

'OK Dad, I'll see you later tonight, I should be finished here by five o'clock, what's for dinner?'

'Your mother is making meatloaf, is Corrine coming over?'

'No, she is doing stuff at home and her dad is cooking for her.'

'OK son, I'll see you later.'

Jake finished his sandwich that he got from the meal wagon, a mobile catering unit parked on the site where he was working. He was keen to get back to work, he really was enjoying himself, he went back and started to pick up the second row of fencing on his own.

'Jake!' A voice called out, it was Bill, 'You're keen. Leave some work for us!'

Jake laughed and carried on bringing the fence panels to where they were being erected. The day went so fast and before he knew, it was time to go home, the second row of fencing had been completed.

'Good job, Jake,' said Bill, 'Are you here tomorrow?'

'Yeah,' said Jake, 'if that's OK?'

'I will see you tomorrow then, Jake.'

Jake said bye to Bill and took off his gloves and put them back into the bag where he got them from and went to his truck, he called Corrine.

'Hey Corrine, it's me,' there was a pause.

'Yes, I know! Have you finished?'

'Yeah, and it went so quick, and guess what! I get paid for doing this work, can you believe it!' said Jake.

'Well, you didn't think they were going to work there for nothing, did you?'

'You know what, I never really gave it much thought.'

'How much are they paying you?' asked Corrine.

'$50 dollars a day.'

'Well, that's good, I suppose it's better than nothing.'

Jake started the engine while he was still on the phone.

'Look, what are you doing tomorrow night? I thought we could maybe go out and see a movie or something.'

'OK, let's see how you feel after you finish work and we will do something,' said Corrine.

Jake drove off as the evening grew dark and the sun was getting low in the sky, the evening skies glowed red and orange as the sun slowly diminished. Jake was only ten minutes from home, Green River was not the busiest town in the world, and people liked it like that. Unlike the bright lights of the cities and the relentless sound of traffic and pollution in the air, quiet towns were an attraction. Some people got fed up with the bright lights and were happy with the slower pace of life.

Jake arrived home and parked his car, he took out his keys from the ignition and looked in the rear-view mirror, he stopped for a moment to reflect on the day. He had a smile on his face as he got out of the truck and went inside the house.

Chapter Eleven

Tuesday morning started misty; a haze was forming above the short grass lawn leading to the trees at the back of the Rogers' garden. That guarded its path to the Green River beyond a wood fence. It was six o'clock in the morning and Jake was getting out of bed, he wore pyjama bottoms with a tee shirt and made his bed after getting up.

He was a little tired as he made his way to the bathroom to get a shower in preparation for the day's work at the rodeo. Jim was awake and already downstairs having a bowl of cereal and a cup of coffee. He was going to work and Nathan would join him there at 8am. Jake had got dressed after finishing in the bathroom and made his way downstairs to the smell of the coffee.

'Hey Dad, how are you?' Jim was at the breakfast bar in the kitchen finishing up his breakfast.

'Oh, I'm fine, you all ready for a hard day's work?'

'I think I am,' said Jake. 'Everything OK at work?'

'Everything is fine, all under control, we can sort out the delivery to Colorado when you are back at the end of the week.'

'Look, are you sure you will be alright at the shop without me this week, I feel guilty being away from work.'

Jim turned to him. 'Look son, don't you worry about work, Nathan and I have got everything covered, and if we do need help, your mother said she was working all this week.'

Just at that moment, Debbie had come down dressed for work. 'Is there any coffee in the pot?' Enquired Debbie.

Jake picked up the coffee pot and showed it to his mother. 'Let me pour you a cup,' said Jake.

She got a cup from the cupboard and gave it to Jake. 'Thanks son, how was the work.'

'It is good, hard work but it's different.'

'Mum, are you OK going to work? How are you feeling?'

'I'm fine son, I've taken my medication, I'll be OK, thanks for asking.'

The time was approaching seven thirty and Jim and Debbie were leaving the house together Jake would follow and they would be heading off in different directions.

Jake was only working at the rodeo till Thursday as he would have deliveries to carry out at the shop until the weekend.

He arrived at the showground and trailers had turned up during the night, these were some of the competitors and more help to raise the big top tent. This would be like a circus tent size, so would require a lot of people to support the super large canvas. The main wood poles were also a feat in itself to erect, they had to pile drive a couple more holes in the ground normally to take the weight of the timber poles. There were some holes made years ago but they would need a few more because this was a larger big top.

The rodeo site was coming together and the canvas was to be taken out of the large truck and laid out before it could be put up. There were separate sections of the canvas that had to be laid on the floor all around the poles. Then they would be secured to each pole and hoisted up section at a time, securing the canvas together with lacing straps. Like a giant shoe lace, these sections are lifted slowly using cranes hired for the day, until it forms the big top.

This normally took all day to erect and a steel fencing around the rodeo site has to be put up first, for security and to stop people from sneaking in without tickets. Jake would be on the outer perimeter fencing duty today and tomorrow he would be involved with the raising of the big top, which he was excited about.

The cranes were booked for Wednesday morning, so timing was very important, everything had to work like clockwork. There was a lot of work that went into staging a rodeo show, just like a circus, people don't realise just how much work is involved.

Jake would certainly not complain about the entrance fee in future, after working and seeing firsthand the work that's involved. The day was going well, Jake was having a break when his phone rang, it was Nathan ringing from the shop.

'Hi, Jake, sorry to trouble you, but I am missing an order for a customer.'

Jake sat down on the ground near to where he was working. 'Which customer is it?'

'It's a customer called Jacobs, they have a stove and flue system.'

Jake thought for a moment and then remembered something. 'Nathan, look in my desk top drawer, I put the paperwork in there because I was going to update it.'

'OK thanks, Jake, how is it going over there?'

'It's going well, I'll be at the shop on Thursday, if you get stuck in the meantime, you know where I am.'

Nathan thanked Jake and went to find the paperwork in the office, and later that evening. Jake arranged to meet his friends Rick and Nathan at the Red Feather bar; he was going to ask them to be his best men at the wedding. Corrine had already asked Tammy to be her maid of honour, she was super excited and couldn't wait for the wedding. Jake was otherwise engaged the last time they were at the bar, this time there would only be the three of them.

The day ended at around five thirty and Jake clocked off work and got in his car and made his way home to get changed. He told Corrine what he was going to do and she was OK with that, she had other things to organise. Jim and Debbie were at home after coming home from work and were ready for a relaxing evening, they knew that Jake was going out so it would be a quiet night in.

Jake got in and put his keys in the bowl near the door on a small table.

'Hi Mum and Dad.'

'Hi son,' said George. 'How was work?'

'Yeah good, big day tomorrow, the tent is going up.'

'That's a sight I would like to see,' said Jim.

'Why don't you come down, I can ring you when it's about to happen.'

Jim looked at Debbie and she gave him that look! Which said 'really!'

'Oh you boys, I don't see the fascination, but what the hell, we will all go.'

He smiled, and he looked at Jake and gave him the thumbs up. Jake smiled and went upstairs to get ready. Jim sat down on his sofa and put the television on.

'Drink dear,' said Debbie.

He looked at her and smiled, she knew that look and went to get him a beer from the fridge in the kitchen. Jim didn't normally drink too much but now and then he liked to kick back and relax, and this was one of those days. Jake was down within half an hour, he had a pair of denim jeans and tee shirt and was carrying his denim jacket over his shoulders. 'OK, I'll see you guys later,' he left the room, picked up his car keys and opened the door. The plan was coming together.

'Take care, son, and don't drink too much.'

Jim knew his son and he could trust him, but he just said it anyway, just in case. Jake had his head on his shoulders and was very responsible for his age. He had a clean boy image even at high school, and was ribbed quite a lot by the bully boy element. Jake soon reached the bar and parked in the car park; he waited a while to gather his thoughts before leaving the car.

Rick and Nathan were already in the bar, they grew up with Jake, they were very good friends and were inseparable. They would go down to the Green River and even learned to swim there. But kids grow up and eventually girls come along! They always planned things together when they were younger, they still have fun together now and then, but it's not the same especially when other interests come along.

Jake entered the bar and saw the two of them playing pool at the table by the far end of the room, he walked over to them and he passed the bar Kris (the owner) waved at him.

'Hey Jake, you OK?'

Jake turned towards him and waved back. 'Yeah, good, how is business?'

'Good, no complaints.'

'Can we have three beers at the table, Kris?'

'No problem, I'll send them over.'

Kris would get one of his waitresses to take the bottles of Budweiser over to Jake, likes Jake's father, he was not a drinker but liked a drink now and then. Kris knew Jake, Rick and Nathan because his son went to school with them. Kris was in his late forties and was well built and had a moustache with a beard, his hair was shoulder length and thick.

Jake went to the table where they were into a competitive game of pool, by the way they were concentrating on playing.

'How long have you guys been here?'

'Hey Jake!' said Rick.

'Only just got here,' said Nathan.

'Did you get a brewski?'

'Yeah, it's coming and I got you guys a top up,' said Jake.

'Look, I need to talk to you about something.'

'Yeah, we know,' said Nathan.

Jake looked puzzled. 'What do you know?'

Rick put his cue down and rested his hands on the table.

'We know everything that goes on in this town, a bird told us about the wedding, and we knew when you called us and told us to meet you here, what this was all about.'

'Yeah,' said Nathan.

'Well, it just goes to show,' said Jake, his drinks had arrived by way of a young waitress who gave one of the bottles of beer to Jake, and a smile too.

'OK, guys, well then you know that I want you two amigos to be my best men at the wedding.'

'We accept,' said Rick and Nathan.

Both of them were smiling and shook hands with Jake, he gave them the dates and chores that they had to do, and all was well as they enjoyed the drinks and played pool. Then from behind the bar the bell rang.

'People! Can I have your attention please, tonight we are celebrating a wedding, from one of our own.'

As he was speaking, the waitress brought more drinks for Jake, Rick and Nathan.

'Please raise your glasses and join me in a toast to Jake and Corrine.'

Kris raised his glass of wine into the air. 'To Jake and Corrine!' Everyone in the bar all raised their glasses and bottles of beer and cheered.

Jake was taken aback, he didn't expect that, he looked at Kris and gave him a stare, he looked at everyone and acknowledged them and raised his bottle of beer. Jake found out later that Tammy, Corrine's best friend, told them, Corrine obviously told her and it was a small town. The boys talked about the good old days and some of the things that they would get up to, and enjoyed each other's company. The evening was soon drawing to a close and Jake finished his beer and put his bottle down on the table next to the pool table.

'Well guys, it's time I was going, got to get up early tomorrow, raising the big top it's gonna be fun, you guys should come down.'

'Well, it depends on your father,' said Nathan.

'Dad is coming down; I'll see if I can persuade him to close the shop and let you come down as well,' said Jake.

'That would be cool,' said Nathan.

'Sorry, I can't make it, Jake, my boss is not so understanding,' Rick worked in the bank and would not be allowed to leave during the day.

'That's alright Rick, I'll record it for you,' said Nathan.

'Well, never mind, Rick it's my first time doing this, at least it will be recorded for all to see,' said Jake. 'Any way, see you guys soon, and I will update you on the wedding and the jobs that I need you to do, OK.'

They both nodded and waved at Jake as he left the bar, he waved at Kris and thanked him for the drinks.

'Thanks, Kris, for the toast,' Kris waved back.

'Congratulations,' he said as Jake left the bar.

It was pretty mild as the evening grew dark, but the bright moon lit up the streets as Jake drove home, the star-studded sky stood out like diamonds in the night sky. In this part of the country the sky was always gigantic, it took your breath away, no skyscrapers or bright lights to block out the view, like the big cities.

Chapter Twelve

The next day Jake had turned up to the rodeo site, he was early such was his excitement about the day. It was cool this morning but it was dry. He waited in his car while some of the riggers were stepping out of their mobile homes and being greeted by the morning sun. There was a kitchen set up for the staff and it was big! The kitchen staff were up at the break of dawn to prepare breakfast for the workers, the smell of cooked bacon and biscuits filled the air and pancakes were made in quantities.

You don't need alarm clocks when you work on the road, the smell of fresh cooked food is enough to get them up. Jake got out of his car and decided to go to the kitchen and join in, he didn't have breakfast at home, such was his rush to get to work. After breakfast, the crews started to go about their jobs for the day. The main centre poles were to be placed into position by way of using the crane. This had to be done before the canvass could be raised.

The cranes had woken up and the sound of the diesel engines filled the crisp hazy air, the noise was deafening as the great beasts got themselves into position. The operators inside the cabs within the mighty cranes operated them with great ease, experienced operators and they had to be, it can be a dangerous job in the wrong hands. The winds were mild and no sign of any storm as yet, but the weather has been unpredictable around the Midwest, tornadoes frequent the area now and then. Bill was looking at the sky and he didn't look happy; Belinda came over to him.

'What's the matter, Bill?'

'I'm not sure, but I don't like the look of that.'

He pointed up at the sky. 'I've seen this before.'

'Well, there have been no warnings by the weather department, so we will have to carry on. So work had to be carried out with military precision, the riggers and most of the riders were spilling out of the canteen and taking up positions in readiness to raise the huge tarpaulin covering which must have been at least 300 foot long and 150 foot wide.'

Jake was in his position; his job was to hold one of the dozen or so guide ropes that were to position the tent as it was being raised. The pressure on the guide ropes was going to be tremendous, it was not a job for a weak person.

Jim Rogers had pulled up into the car park away from the site of the tent erection and with him was Nathan and Debbie, they had decided that they would close the shop for the morning. They wanted to see this spectacle, as did many of the townspeople who had gathered a safe distance away. There were marshals patrolling the vicinity around the rodeo site, just to make sure the people were safe. The order was soon to be given to start the raising of the tent, but then suddenly the weather changed with the blink of an eye, the winds picked up and the sky grew darker. The foreman in charge was unsure as to what to do! If the raising started now and the winds grew stronger, there could be catastrophic repercussions as a result. The site foreman was Chuck Parker, a man in his late fifties, and a pro at this kind of work.

He had witnessed accidents that occurred while raising these large tents before, and even some fatalities, so he wasn't going to take any chances. He signalled for the work to stop and the cranes to be switched off, until he was sure the storm had passed. The people who came to watch looked uneasy as they too looked at the impending storm about to strike their town, some decided to get into their cars and wait it out, others thought it would be safer to leave the site and make their way back home. Jim was not sure what to do, just then Jake came over to them.

'Hey Dad, Mum I don't know what's going to happen, but I would say that nothing's going to happen for the next few hours.'

Nathan was in the car and got out when Jake arrived. 'Hey Jake, sorry about the weather, it does look bad.'

'It's not your fault bud, hey, I don't suppose you know of an ancestral dance that can help us out here do you?' said Jake.

'Jake! You can't say things like that to Nathan, it's not politically correct!' said Jim.

'I was only joking, Dad.'

'It's OK, Mrs Rogers, it was said in fun, I only know how to do war dances,' said Nathan with a smile on his face.

'Look, you guys had better get back home, I will call you when things get better out here,' said Jake, and with that they got back into their car and drove home. Jake took another look at the sky and it didn't look too good, he went back to the canteen which was inside a large tent and the wind was battering the tent.

It was fixed with steel poles and could hold up to most heavy winds, but it still did not feel safe. Just then, Belinda came up to Jake with Bill next to her, 'Hey Jake, are you OK?'

'Yeah, a little concerned about the weather, but otherwise fine.'

'Well, we don't know how this is going to play out, but we are telling everyone to go into the stadium until this storm passes,' said Belinda.

'The guys are making their way over now Jake, come with us and we will ride this out together,' said Bill.

They were about to make their way out of the canteen when all of a sudden heavy rain poured down on top of them and the wind picked up lifted half or the tent into the air. Tables were being tossed around inside the canteen and Jake was blown over along with Belinda and Bill, they were on the floor and surrounded by chairs and debris. There were people rushing around trying to help others and some trying to grab hold of the tent to try and fix it back into the ground. But it was pointless, the wind was relentless and kept pulling the tent back up again. The crowd who came to see the event had all evacuated by now and Jake's family were at home.

In the distance, Jake could see what looked like a funnel coming down from the sky, it was only a small funnel trying to form, this was a tornado! And there is nothing that can be done to try and save anything from its destructive path. Belinda was holding Bill's hand and they managed to get up and started making their way over to the stadium a few hundred yards away.

'Jake, you better come with us now.'

'I'll be there in a bit; I'm just going to check and make sure everyone is OK.'

Jake went back into the canteen and saw a couple of people on the floor next to the gas bottles that were used for cooking. He quickly turned them off to avoid any fires that may occur, Jake then went over to the injured lying on the floor, they were moving slowly.

'How are you guys doing?' asked Jake.

They shook their heads and raised up a thumb, to signal that they were OK. He helped them up and then helped them both towards the stadium, the site foreman was waiting at the stadium as Jake brought the two injured men over.

'I'm not sure that the main tent is going to survive,' he said, pointing to the large tent that was spread out over the floor in preparation for its raising.

There were weights already on the ends of the tent, but they were being pounded by the heavy rain and winds, and now the funnel had grown into a fully-fledged tornado! What started out as a happy ceremony to raise the tent was now a struggle for survival. Chuck asked for some volunteers to come with him to secure the tent ends, there were a few reluctant hands going up and Jake was standing next to Chuck.

'How many do you need?' asked Jake.

Chuck looked around at the handful of volunteers, and said, 'A lot more than this!' The volunteers came over to Chuck and waited for instruction, they would rather not go outside, but they also knew that if they didn't save the tent, then no one would be earning any money for a while.

'Right, I want to concentrate on the west side of the tent, get as many extra weights as you can and secure the tent, you three grab hold of the ropes and tie them off. The rest of you guys come with me.'

They went towards the wind and rain and were looking at the sky all the while, the funnel was about a mile away and depending on the wind direction, it would determine which way it was headed.

For now, they were safe but they still had to fight the heavy winds and rain, they reached the site and started to go about their business. Jake was with Chuck and followed everything that he would do. There were fifty-pound weights in one of the trucks and they were going to get them using a sack barrow and take them down to where they were needed.

The tents that were on the ground were being lifted and the existing weights were being moved around. Within a few minutes, Chuck had secured one of the tents, only had five more sections to go. After the others had secured the ropes, they went over to where Chuck was and helped to secure the rest of the tent. The wind had changed direction and it looked like it was moving away from them, the men had to avoid debris being picked up and hurtled towards them, one of the men got hit by a wooden pole and was knocked to the floor.

Jake went over and bent down to protect him from any more debris.

'Are you OK?' asked Jake.

'Yeah, I'm not too bad, just shaken a little.'

Jake helped him up, his head was bleeding.

'You better get back the stadium and get that cut seen to,' the injured man took his advice, he didn't need to be asked twice. They were near to the end of doing what they had come out to do and were about to make their way back.

'That was brave of you, son,' said Chuck, 'let's get back now, there not much more that we can do now.'

They were all in agreement there was nothing else that they could do and headed towards the stadium and to safety. It seemed the worst of the storm was going to miss them, but with tornadoes you could never be too sure of anything, and they were going to wait it out in the safety of the stadium.

Chapter Thirteen

Across town, Debbie was looking out of the lounge window with Nathan, who went home with them.

'Oh, I do hope that Jake is alright.' Jim came over to her and put his arm around her.

'He'll be fine, don't worry, I'm glad that the tornado has passed us, I was worried for a while,' said Jim.

'Hey look guys, it clearing up!' Nathan pointed to the sun pushing its way through the clouds like search lights beaming down from the heavens.

'We'll give it half an hour and then make our way back to see Jake,' said Jim as he walked back to the kitchen to get a cup of coffee.

'Do you want one, Nathan?' asked Jim.

'Yes please, Mr Rogers!'

'Don't call me mister Nathan, call me Jim.'

'OK Mr Rogers, I mean Jim.'

Jim smiled and poured Nathan a cup of coffee and they sat at the table to drink their beverage. Corrine was on the phone to Jake, she tried to ring him earlier but failed to get through. Jake didn't have his phone with him, as he was busy with other things.

'Hi, Corrine, are you OK?' asked Jake.

'Am I OK! How about you, I was worried out of my mind, not knowing what was happening to you.'

'Well, I was rather busy, but we are OK now, nothing to worry about.'

Jake walked into the foyer of the stadium where other people were talking to their loved ones.

'I'm glad that you are good, did you see the tornado! Wow, what a sight to behold.'

'I don't want to ever see that again,' said Corrine. She was worried and even wanted to go outside and make her way over to see Jake, but her father stopped her.

'Well, it's over now, do you want me to get Mum and Dad to pick you up, they will be coming back to see the tent being raised.'

'It's OK, Dad has to come down anyway, to check on a few things at the stadium, the only day he gets off and this happens.'

'Okay. I'll see you later,' said Jake, as he walked outside and into the sunshine.

Green River failed to become another statistic for the tornado, most other towns their size would be lucky if only half the town was damaged, such was the ferocity of nature's lethal weapon. They were lucky, but now the town would carry on as if nothing had happened.

The people started to arrive and this time it was to help clean the area of debris; such was the community spirit of the people in the town. By the time Jim and Debbie had arrived with Nathan, most of the debris had been removed and the raising of the tent was back on. Chuck had got the men to remove the weights from the tent ends and the cranes were powered up again and ready. Some of the riggers were helping the cowboys fix the canteen, after all, it was the most important place.

Chuck radioed to the crane operators and the countdown had begun to start the lifting, the eager crowd of onlookers all clapped their hands when the claxon sounded. The riggers were in place ready to help erect the tent and also to tie the laces together to secure all the joints. The tent was halfway up and everything was going according to plan, the laces were being tied and it was looking like a big top.

The day was getting darker and the floodlights were being put on, the big top was finally erected and being secured. Applause came from the crowd; they had come to see a spectacle and saw a little bit more than they expected. A day they will never forget, an eventful and yet exhilarating day in its finality. Soon the final stages of securing the big top was underway and Jake was standing back and admiring what he had helped create. Corrine came over to him with her dad by her side, he was going to check in with the staff at the stadium.

'Heck of a job, Jake,' said George.

As he passed Jake on his way to the stadium, Jake thanked him and then gave Corrine a big hug.

'What was that for?' She asked.

'Oh, I just realised how little we people are in the scope of things, and I am lucky to have you.'

Corrine smiled. 'You got yourself into some sort of trouble, knowing you, you're not the kind of person to stand back and watch, are you.'

'Well, there were some situations I could not avoid.' Just then, Belinda came up to Jake.

'You are a hero, Jake! Thank you, for helping out and saving those men in the canteen.'

Corrine looked on, as Belinda shook his hand and walked away, closely followed by the two men Jake helped. They also thanked him for his bravery, Corrine was looking at Jake with pride in her eyes. Just then Jim and Debbie came up to the two of them and gave Corrine a hug.

'We just spoke to the foreman, Jake, he said that you saved the day.'

'Yes, your son was being a hero,' said Corrine who was holding on to him.

'Well son, you made us proud, well done!' said Jim.

Nathan came over and asked them all to get together in front of the big top, so he could take a photo. They obliged and moved in front of the big top with its lights shining in all its glory, a picture to capture future memories and stories that would be told for many years to come.

The local press were down to talk to the people who witnessed the events that took place at the rodeo site. The Green River Star reporter, Bethany Roberts, a young nineteen-year-old, recently left college was asking the riggers. They all pointed towards Jake and so she headed towards his direction. Jake was still talking to Corrine and his mum and dad. She approached Jake along with her photographer, Pete Stalker, who was a bit older than Bethany.

'Hi Jake?' he turned around in her direction.

'Yes! That's me.'

'Hi, I'm Bethany Roberts from the Green River Star, I've been talking to some people who said that you helped a few people, even saved their lives! Can you tell me what happened.'

'Well, I just did what anyone else would have done, nothing brave in that.'

'You don't mind if we can take some pictures while we talk.'

Jake looked at the photographer, he was used to this.

'No, I don't mind, look this won't take long will it, I'm a little tired.' She put her tape recorder on, Corrine stood next to Jake.

'I'm here with Jake Rogers, hero of the Wolves Stadium, Jake can you describe in detail what happened here tonight?'

Jake went on to tell her the story of the events that took place, and went into great detail, Corrine was more amazed now that she was hearing all the truth that happened. She held onto him tighter, he was a hero, she thought to herself, and he's mine.

'Wow, Jake, that was mind blowing, and you still think that anyone else could have done what you did?'

Jake stood and thought for a moment at what he just told her and it brought some reality back to him.

'Thank you for your time, Jake, you will certainly be the news tomorrow, thanks again.'

She left the scene with her camera man and was happy with the story that she had and with so much material that the front page would be special tomorrow. Jim came over to Jake and Corrine.

'Well son, we're going home now, dinner will be in an hour or so, will you be coming for dinner, Corrine?'

She looked at Jake and smiled, 'No, Dad will be picking me up in a minute, he has prepared dinner before we came here, thanks anyway.'

'OK son, see you later.'

They left, leaving Jake to drive home in his car, bye to Corrine and her dad and headed to his car, as he was getting into his car, some people came over to him. And thanked him again for saving them, he smiled and started the engine and drove off.

The sky cleared up so fast and there was no sign of the storm, such was the speed of nature's silent killer, there were just a few white clouds lingering and the winds had died down. The evening seemed pleasantly calm, the site was now being locked up, everything was safely stored and ready for tomorrow's final preparation.

Jake would be back at his father's shop, and the rodeo would go through its final phase, the seats would be arranged and the horses and bulls would arrive. One day before the event, this would give them time to get over the travelling. There would be no need to promote the rodeo for Saturday, the weather did that for them and the press would give them more publicity that they could have hoped for.

Their advertising branch couldn't have planned it any better! Some good will come of the storm, you wouldn't have thought that a few hours ago.

Jake didn't know it yet, but he would be in the news, not only in Green River, but most of the Midwest. Jake had reached home and was ready for a shower and some good food and sleep. He certainly deserved this, he had gone through something that most people don't get to go through and survived to tell the story.

After his long awaited shower, he came downstairs and sat at the dining room table.

'Here you are, son, dinner.'

'Mum cooked you a pot roast.'

'Pot roast midweek! What's the occasion?'

Debbie sat down at the table and got ready to serve dinner.

'Son, we're so proud of you, you just eat up and enjoy, tomorrow you are staying in bed, you are taking the day off.'

'But I am fine to work tomorrow.'

'Not another word, we have spoken.' And with that, Jake didn't say anything, just smiled and ate his dinner, he was glad to be home and in the dry.

Jim was proud of his son, he raised him well, and was proud of that as well, he looked at Jake and wished that his father had done the same for him. His childhood was less instructional from his parents, he had to fend for himself and teach himself how to go through life, learn things that a parent should be teaching. His parents were not bad parents, they loved their kids, all four of them, but their main aim in life was to look after number one! First, hindsight was never their forte! His father was born in the depression during 1929 to 1941, the longest and deepest downturn in the history of the United States.

Strangely enough, it took a world war to end the depression, the war forced America to mobilise the economy and millions of men and women joined the armed forces, and even large numbers went to work in well-paying, defined jobs.

Jim was reminded now and then of how important it was to make sure his family didn't want for anything. He was focussed on life and would always make sure that Jake would be taken care of.

Chapter Fourteen

The next day started with a cloudy outlook, it was a little cooler than usual, that can sometimes happen when a storm has passed. Jim was in front of the television having a bowl of cereal for breakfast, the weather girl had just come on saying that today was going to be a clear sunny day and that the temperature was going to warm up. Then the local news came on, and Jake's picture was on the television. Jim sat up from his chair.

'Debbie! Jake's on the news! Come down quick.'

He quickly pressed the record button on the remote handset. 'Hurry quickly!'

He didn't know why he said that, after all he had just recorded the channel, Debbie came down she was on her way down anyway, as she was going in to work with Jim.

Jake had woken up and heard his dad shouting, so went down to investigate what the fuss was all about. Jake was in the front lounge and saw his parents sitting in front of the television.

'Jake, sit down, you are on TV,' said Jim.

Jim rewound the recording and played it to Jake. The news reporter Bethany Roberts came on. 'Well, I hope you are all in your seats because this next story is all about a local boy who became a hero overnight, yes folks, Jake Rogers saved a few lives last night in the tornado that struck Green River and nearly caused widespread damage, here are some people that Jake saved from near death! Jake Rogers saved some co-workers from death by risking his own life to drag these men to safety, just look at this footage.'

Then the channel played video footage, the footage was from the security cameras set up around the site, just before they too were blitzed out of action.

The cameras were focussed on the canteen area and caught the moment the tent was almost blown away. It was a little shaky after that but clearly caught Jake making his way over to the two injured men. Jake was actually being hit with debris as he fought his way to the injured men. After the video showed Jake with the two men and dragging them to safety, the video lost its connection. 'Well, there you are folks, A true hero and here's my interview with Jake.' The footage of Jake with Corrine at his side and Jim and Debbie in the background was being played, Jake's gaze was fixed to the screen, as was his parents.

'Wow,' said Debbie. 'Did you know that there was footage of you?'

The recording ended and Bethany closed, 'After watching that footage, how humble was that man, a true hero, Jake Rogers.'

Jim had a tear in his eye and he turned to Jake, he got up and went over to him and gave him a hug.

'I didn't realise how much danger you were in; it was a brave thing that you did son, well done.'

'There is not much more that I can say darling, but thank the lord for you,' said Debbie, who also had tears in her eyes, they never realised something could happen to their family, and she thanked God for keeping her son safe.

After the television was turned off, Jim and Debbie had to go to work, just as they were about to leave the phone rang, Jim answered it.

'Hello, Mr Rogers, are you the father of Jake Rogers?' The voice asked.

'Yes, I am, how can I help you?' asked Jim.

'Well sir, we are an advertising company and would love to use Jake's name for one of our products that we promote.'

'Hold on a minute, what are we talking about here?'

'Well sir, your son is famous and famous names sell products, and we can make your son rich.'

Jim didn't know what to say.

'Look, let me take your details and we will get back to you, OK! And Jim took down his details and put the phone down.'

They didn't expect this, and were not prepared for stardom. 'What do you think, Dad?' asked Jake.

'Well son, they say that they can make money off your name and they can make you rich.'

'I don't want to make money off what I did, it wouldn't be right and how would that look to the people that I helped.'

'I understand how you feel, son, but what about the money, now if someone is prepared to pay you just to use your name, isn't that worth thinking about!'

'I wouldn't feel right about that, Dad, let me talk to Corrine and see what she says.' And with that, they decided to wait until later that day. They left for work and left Jake to rest at home.

Corrine came over to Jake's house, Dalores had given her the day off, her father dropped her off and came to the door with her to say hello to Jake, Jake opened the door.

'Corrine! You're here! Oh hello, Mr Smith.'

'Hi Jake, I just came to say thank you for being there last night, and for what you did, I know that I don't have to worry about my daughter in the future.'

He shook Jake's hand and said goodbye. He was on his way to work as well, a lot to sort out before opening tomorrow.

Corrine came in and hugged Jake. 'Did you see the television, you looked great, how do you feel?'

Jake was about to close the door when he saw his neighbours wave to him, he waved back and then closed the door.

'To tell you the truth, I'm not sure what to think, this has all been a flash in my life and now I got an advertising company wanting to use my name on some kind of brand, and they want to pay me for doing it.'

'I don't know about that, making money off your name!' said Corrine.

'That's exactly what I said, who knew helping people could lead to this!'

'Just enjoy this for what it is, you saved some people and they thanked you for doing that, this will all blow over in a couple of days, you wait and see,' said Corrine.

'I certainly hope so, this is not what I expected.' They both went into the kitchen to get a cup of coffee and discuss this a little more.

The phone rang again. 'I don't know if I should answer it, it could be other people wanting to use my name.'

'Well, you can't hide from the phone every time it rings, just answer it!'

He picked up the phone, 'Hello, Jake speaking.'

'Young man, I just want to say thank you for saving my son, I am glad that there are people like you in this world, god bless you.'

One of the men he saved lived in Denver, he was given that information by Bethany who had got the stories about how they were rescued that night. 'There is no need for that but thank you, Mam!' said Jake, He put the phone down and looked at Corrine.

'Look, let's get out of here, away from the phone, it's a nice day let's go fishing, we haven't been for a while.'

'OK Jake, let's do that, let me see what's in the pantry and I'll make us some sandwiches to take along.'

'You do that and I will get my gear and some bait.'

Jake always used earthworms when he went fishing so he went into the garden to dig some up and get his fishing rods that were kept in the garage. Corrine had made sandwiches and took along some cans of coke and water. Jake made a gate by the back fence that would give him direct access to the river, and the fishing spot was ideal for the peace and tranquillity that the river would give them. And the good thing was, that it was within walking distance and Jake had everything that he needed for a relaxing day.

When they got to the spot where Jake and his dad frequented, he had brought two fold-up chairs so they could be comfortable. He got settled and got both rods set up ready for casting, Corrine was going to fish as well, even though she didn't like the cruelty to fish. Jake normally kept the fish they caught as they made good eating and it was fresh, nature's larder! It was a pleasant day as far as the weather was concerned and the river was quite clear and calm in places, which made it easier to see the float. No phone calls apart from the call Jake made to his dad to let him know where they were, so it was calm by the river. Maybe more people should take some time out and do something similar, just to get some free time without interruption by the phone.

After a few hours and a good collection of fish for the fridge, they decided that it was time to start packing up and make their way back home. Jake would have to gut and clean the trout which were brown trout, there were some white fish as well but he put those back into the river. Corrine washed her hands in the river and Jake emptied the rest of the bait into the water, to keep the fish happy. They made their way back and were hungry, so decided to have some lunch, Corrine saw to that while Jake took the fish out back to clean and then freeze them. The phone rang but Jake decided not to answer it, it was probably someone trying to use Jake's name to sell something. But it was Bandy who was trying to get hold of Jake, he wanted to meet him.

Chapter Fifteen

At the shop, Jim was talking to some customers, but it seemed that all folks wanted to talk about was the tornado and Jake's heroism! They got quite a few phone calls as well, again nothing to do with work. Nathan was in the warehouse sorting out the stock and putting away the morning's deliveries, he was kept pretty busy with checking in the goods and storing them in the right places.

Jim came over to Debbie in the office and opened the door, 'How are you doing?' asked Jim.

'I'm fine, I had to tell some people who called that Jake was not in the shop, they wanted to come down to see him.'

'Yeah, I know how you feel, who would have thought that doing a good deed would lead to all this,' said Jim. 'Maybe we should close the shop.'

'Look, I'm going to get something for lunch later, what do you want?'

'I'll have whatever you are having, dear.'

Jim went over to see Nathan and see what he wanted before going out. Just as he was going to leave the shop, Bethany from the press came in holding some copies of the newspaper.

'Hi, Mr Rogers, I brought you some copies of the newspaper, just in case you didn't get a chance to pick one up.'

'That's nice of you dear, we didn't know that so many people would react the way that they did.'

'Yes, I know, it's been pretty busy at the shop as well, phones have been ringing all morning.'

'I hope you don't mind, but we gave your number to the family of one of the men Jake saved, she was very persistent.'

'Oh that's alright dear, no harm done.'

Bethany gave Jim the bundle of newspapers. 'OK then, bye.' She left the shop and Jim took the papers and gave them to Debbie in her office.

'Right, I'm going to get lunch, see you later,' Jim left the shop and heard the phone ring as he left, he didn't want to answer it, he just wanted peace. He closed and left.

Chapter Sixteen

Over at the stadium, there was all sorts of clearing going on, the kitchen had been fixed and the tent housing the canteen was back to normal. This was just outside the stadium. George and his team were overseeing the trailers that were coming in thick and fast, riders who were going to be taking part in the rodeo were arriving.

They were running late because they were supposed to be at the venue last night, but the storm put paid to that. So hence the traffic, but George was used to this kind of mayhem, he'd seen it all before.

He arranged for some dump trucks from the municipal council to help clear away the debris from last night. There were a lot of branches from trees and parts of tin roof's that blew off the buildings, and wood splintered into large toothpick size chards of wood lying around on the ground which had to be cleaned up. Even the cowboys helped in the clear up, they wanted to make sure that the opening took place on time, they had a lot at stake and didn't mind helping.

It was a combined effort to get things ready for the opening tomorrow, and the rodeo still had to arrange the practice runs for the cowboys, they would normally need two days to get used to the animals and the surroundings. It was going to be tight, and they restricted the practice run to one per person, and that was going to continue into the night.

A black Chevrolet pick truck arrived at the venue, it was a Silverado 2500 and it belonged to Bandy, he was eager to see the aftermath of the tornado and as he got out of the vehicle and stepped onto the sandy forecourt with expensive cowboy boots. He had on a grey suit with a silk waistcoat, he was relieved to see the big top up and not too much damage was done. He got out and closed the door of his 4x4 and went over to Belinda, she worked for him along with her crew, he was also keen to meet up with Jake. Bandy had worked hard to run a successful company from almost nothing to his name, His past reputation helped him.

He was told about Jake by Belinda and she gave him glowing references, this interested Bandy as he was always on the lookout for new raw talent. After all, that was the business he was in and what he had heard about Jake, seemed like he might be persuaded to join his band of people. Bandy started out the same way, someone saw potential in him and led him to become a legend, maybe Jake was the next legend in the making, only time would tell. Bandy was in his sixties now and found a way to keep the rodeo clown in his blood, it wasn't easy but he managed it and became a successful entrepreneur in the process. Bandy would have to meet up with Jake and try and talk him into joining his band of workers. Belinda showed him the rest of the site and he thanked her.

'You have done well, Belinda, thank you!'

Chapter Seventeen

Back at the shop, Debbie was on the phone to Jim Maguire, from the Holiday Homes Group, he was about to put a large order their way. Jim had just come back from getting lunch and he saw Debbie waving at him, he knew Maguire very well and had taken orders from him before.

'Jim has just arrived, Mr Maguire, let me put him on to you, it's been nice talking to you,' said Debbie as she put the call through to Jim's phone.

'Jim! It's been a long time,' said Jim Rogers. 'How you doing?'

'I'm good,' replied Maguire.

'How can I help you today?'

'Well, I have some stoves that I'll be needing from you, it's for a site near the Rocky Mountain National Park, a place called Allens Park, there is going to be a development of a few lodges.'

'We need the usual spec.'

'I understand, and do you want me to supply the flue system as well?' replied Jim.'

'Yes, the full thing, but I'm going to need a good price from yer,' said Maguire.

'You always get good prices from me, Jim, you know that, what's the criteria for this job? What are they looking for exactly and have you got some schematics that you can send me.'

'I'll be sending them over to you as we speak, and I'm going to need this pretty quickly Jim, I am on a deadline.'

'Well, let me have a look and I'll get back to you tomorrow, is that OK?'

'That's fine, by the way, I've been hearing about a boy in your town, a hero they're calling him. No relation of yours, is he?'

'Actually, he's my son, Jake!'

'Well, isn't that a fine thing, good stock, good stock! Anyway, I'll be seeing you, ring me tomorrow.'

He put the phone down and Jim looked at his computer and waited for the email to come through. He wanted to see just how big this order was, the largest order that he has ever had from Maguire was eleven stoves with flue systems. That was a few years ago, while Jake was still at college.

He had a feeling that this was going to be bigger than that, he straight away started thinking about his stock of wood burning stoves and what he had to offer Jim, he was excited.

The email came through and Jim's face lit up. 'Dear, come and look at this!'

Debbie came over. 'What is it?' she said.

Jim printed off the email and took the paper from the printer. He put it on his desk and showed her, they both looked at the order, then they looked at each other. Nathan was just getting back into the showroom and noticed the two of them at the desk.

'You guys alright?' He asked.

Jim turned around and looked at Nathan. 'Er, yes, fine,' said Jim.

'Oh, Nathan, can you get me the latest stock report and let me know what stoves we have in stock please.'

'Sure thing,' said Nathan as he went to the stockroom.

'Do you realise what this means?' said Jim.

'Yes, but can we handle an order this big?' asked Debbie.

'Well! We will have to. I have to start thinking of shipping and the logistics alone will be huge, and I have to work out the flue system for each job.'

There were at least a dozen pages that he printed out and in total there were fifty plots, that's fifty stoves and flue systems to be worked out. Jim was going to be busy for a few days. He could probably get Jake involved, but then again, he was going to be tied up with the rodeo fresh on his mind. He would have to wait till the rodeo was finished at the week end, then Jake would have no distractions.

Jim didn't waste time. He gathered all the paperwork and went into Debbie's office.

'I'm gonna be in here for a little while, Deb, can you go through the stove manifest with Nathan and see what we have.'

Debbie said OK and waited for Nathan to get back and they would go through the manifest together.

A couple of hours passed and it was time to close the shop, time went by so quickly, especially as they were busy. Debbie went into the office to see how Jim was doing, he had the paperwork spread out over the desk and seemed to have the majority of the plots sorted in order.

'Well, so far, I've worked out the flue system alone and we are looking at well over $60,000 and I haven't worked on the stoves yet!'

'Well, that's nice, I hope we can handle this amount,' said Debbie.

'Don't you worry about that, we can handle this, we just got to get this right.'

'Well that goes without saying,' she said. 'Any way, it's time to make our way home and see what Jake has been up to.'

Before Jim could say anything, the phone rang, Debbie picked it up.

'Hi, Mum, I'm ordering in takeout tonight, I got a great deal on pizza, they want to give me this at no cost, all they want is to say that "Jake Rogers eats Giuseppe's Pizza" so I agreed.'

'Oh Jake, how could you!'

'It's only a pizza, Mum.'

'Look, we are on our way home and Dad's got some good news, see you in a little while.'

They left the shop and got into their car, the world seemed to be a better place and this order would give them plenty of breathing space. Nathan got on his bike and made his way home. The evening was warm and still, a stark contrast to nature's other side.

The pizza arrived and Jake opened the door, a delivery man had brought it on his scooter. 'Great timing,' said Jake as he took the boxes from the man.

'Enjoy your meal,' said the delivery man as he rode off out of the Rogers drive.

Jim had parked the car in the drive and he and Debbie went inside the house, it had been an eventful day, but a happy one. They all enjoyed the pizza and Jim told Jake about the large order and they were going to be busy for the next few months, in more ways than one.

Corrine got picked up by her dad a little later, he had finished for the day and the night shift had taken over at the stadium. They were all looking forward to the rodeo tomorrow, they had just about got everything together after the tornado's visit. This was a good example of a community coming together to get the job done, this is the sort of community spirit that should be evident in all towns and cities. Strange that it would take a disaster to get people together, and that is the case all over the world unfortunately!

Jim was going to open the shop only for half a day on Saturday, because the family were going to the rodeo later that evening. As they did every year, Jake was looking forward to it not only because he helped out in more ways than one. But he felt a rush whenever he was at a rodeo, the excitement and atmosphere was everything to him. Ever since he was a child and his father took him to see his first rodeo, he never forgot those days.

There was good weather planned for Saturday, although it didn't matter too much, as everything was under cover, but good weather always made people have a happy outlook on life. It was certainly going to be a wondrous day at Green River tomorrow. With all the press that was given to the rodeo, the turnout was expected to be big. Not only for the Green River residents, but also from neighbouring towns, as the news spread after the aftermath of the tornado. Jake didn't realise it, but he was fast becoming a celebrity and he would probably be better of wearing some sort of disguise. Bandy had underestimated how popular Jake had become, even more determination to try and recruit him into his organisation. He would wait till the rodeo had finished before contacting him, the rush of the rodeo will still be in his blood. He was quietly confident that Jake would come and work for him, so much so that he instructed Belinda to give Jake and his family executive tickets. This would give them prime seats and waitress service throughout the rodeo, he was going to call Jim Rogers and let him know.

'Hello, is that Jim Rogers?' asked Bandy.

'Yes, it is, who am I talking to?'

'My name is Bandy and I run the Green River rodeo, I just want to let you know that you and your family have got executive tickets for tomorrow's rodeo.'

'Why would that be?'

'Well, because of what your son, Jake, did the other day, it's the least that we can do for you, can you tell me how many of you are coming?'

'Well thank you very much, there will be five people.' Bandy thanked him and said that someone would greet them and show them their seats.

Chapter Eighteen

Rodeo day! Green River was waking up to excitement all over town, the rodeo was due to start at 12.00 noon, the first half would be more for the kids. There would be pony racing, roping competitions for the young, and the calf roping. The main events would start at 4pm and go through to 9pm, the bull riding being the main draw, this year there would be bigger bulls in the ring.

Jim Rogers had decided not to open the shop today, it would have been pointless, with most of the town going to the rodeo. He had to finish the quote for Maguire, so he would go into the shop in the morning and work till 1pm. Nathan was given the day off and he would be meeting up with Jake and Corrine at the rodeo later, George was working today as part of the stadium was going to be open, but he would be joining the Rogers during the rodeo. It was 9am and Jim was in the shop, he kept the open sign on the door, just in case there was someone who needed something, he always thought of other people.

He took out all the paperwork relating to the Maguire order and laid it out on his desk. He was going to draw the flue system freehand with a ruler and pencil the flue system. Jim always did it this way, he didn't like the computer version in his opinion, it took too long!

Jake was at home checking his car for oil and water, the hood was up and he took out the oil dipstick to check the oil. One of his neighbours came up to him, it was Mr Phillips, a man in his seventies and was wearing checked trousers and a short-sleeved light blue shirt.

'Hello Jake. How goes it?'

Jake put the dipstick back and turned around to Mr Phillips. 'Oh, hey Mr Phillips, just fine, thanks.'

'Checking the oil eh! It's nice to see young people who know what to do with vehicles, not many kids how to do that today.'

Jake smiled at him, 'I guess not.'

'It was a mighty brave thing you did the other night, Jake, I'm proud of you, son.'

He patted Jake on his arm, 'Be seeing you Jake,' and he walked away going on his daily walk, whistling a happy tune to show that he was in a good place.

Jake looked at him as he walked away and Debbie had come out by then, she came over to Jake his car was in the driveway by the garage.

'What did Mr Phillips want?'

'Oh, he just wanted to be friendly and congratulated me on yesterday.'

'That's nice, I suppose you got to get used to that now Jake, it's going to happen a lot.'

Debbie went back into the house; she was going to organise the laundry and carry out some house cleaning. Corrine arranged to meet Jake at her place at 3pm, he would pick her up on his way to the rodeo, his mum and dad would be going with them. It wasn't worth taking two vehicles such a short distance, the plan was to have lunch around 12.00noon and get dinner at the rodeo.

As Jake was closing the hood on his car, he noticed a black Chevrolet coming down the road towards where he was standing, the vehicle pulled up in front of his car and stopped, the engine was turned off and Bandy got out of the pickup.

'The very man I wanted to meet,' he said looking at Jake. He walked up to Jake with a slight limp, gained in the accident he had that put him out of the rodeo for good.

H reached out his hand to shake Jake's hand.

'My name is Bandy, and I have heard all about you, my boy.'

Jake shook his hand. 'I wanted to thank you for looking out for my workers the other night, it was a brave thing you did.'

'Thank you.'

'But it was nothing.'

'Nonsense! It was heroic! When it comes to pitch in or run, you pitched in, and I see in you someone who could have a career in this business, and that is what I have come over here to talk to you about.'

'Look, do you want to come into the house?' asked Jake closing the hood on his car.

Bandy looked at the house and then looked at Jake. 'Why not my boy, lead the way.'

Jake walked to the house and Debbie opened the door, she was watching through the window at this stranger talking to Jake.

They got inside and Bandy introduced himself to Debbie, she led him to the lounge and offered him a seat, he didn't have to be asked twice, he could only stand for so long, before his leg started hurting.

'Would you like a drink?'

'Yes, mam, water will be fine thanks.'

Debbie went to the kitchen to get his water, when she got back Jake was sitting on one the arms of the chair, she sat down on the chair across from Bandy.

'What exactly is it you want to discuss with my son? Mr Bandy, is it?'

'Well, mam, I was admiring his sense of duty and told him that men like your son Jake would go far in this industry, he has got the right stuff! For this business, Mrs Rogers.'

'Well, we know the potential for Jake, but he has a job in the family business, and he will take over the business one day.'

Jake was eager to hear more from Bandy, 'Let him speak, Mum.'

'You see, Mrs Rogers, there are some folks who know exactly why they were put on this earth to do, and Jake is one of them.'

Bandy got up, 'Well, thank you for the water and, Jake, I would like it very much if you come down tomorrow and see what the rodeo is all about.' Jake got up and walked Bandy to the front door.

'Come and see me tomorrow after the rodeo, at least see what this is all about and then you decide if it's for you or not, what can it hurt.' And with that, Bandy left limping towards hi pickup truck.

'I don't know, Jake, are you not happy with the shop?'

Jake turned to his mother. 'It's not that, Mum, it's just that I don't know, I'm not sure what I want.'

'Well don't forget that you are getting married soon, and you will need stability in your life for the both of you.'

Jake was watching through the window as Bandy drove off and he watched as the car faded at the end of the road and disappeared out of sight. What was he to do, sometimes his brain only sees what's in front of him and not the whole picture. He would need to talk to Corrine and work out in which direction he needed to go.

'Jake, when are you picking Corrine up?'

'I thought I would pick her up and bring her home for lunch, then we can all go together to the rodeo from here, what do you think?'

'That's a good idea, I'll make tacos, nothing too heavy, we'll probably get food at the rodeo, they make a good brisket!' said Debbie.

'I'm looking forward to that,' said Jake.

He phoned Corrine and arranged to pick her up in a little while, Jim would be home for lunch at 11.30, he had most of the paperwork finished and was ready to submit his quote. Jim closed the shop and drove home he got home just before 11.30am and he showed Debbie the quote for Maguire's.

'That's looking very good, have you gone through the supply prices and availability?' she asked, 'Yes dear, all sorted, so, with all the supply and taking into account the tax, we make a great profit.'

The total invoice came to $160,000, which include delivery by courier, by far the biggest sale they have had, and Jim was very confident of the supply, he had been in business too long to not check everything thoroughly. This would make them very secure and take some pressure off the business.

Working for yourself has its drawbacks, you have to make sure the company makes profit each year, it's in your hands. And when its good life is good, but when times are bad, it's up to you to sort it out. Jim was experienced and he knew exactly what was required to get his business to where he wanted it.

Chapter Nineteen

Debbie was just getting the food started and just then Jake and Corrine had arrived, Corrine came into the kitchen to help Debbie.

'Hello, dear, you look nice, is that a new top?'

Corrine looked down at her blue short-sleeve blouse which she wore with light blue jeans and cowboy boots.

'No, it's one of my mothers, I found it the other day.'

'It suits you, dear.'

'Can I give you a hand?' asked Corrine.

Debbie looked at the lettuce and tomatoes that she left on the preparation table.

'Yes, you can start the salad, if you don't mind.'

'Sure! No problem,' said Corrine.

Corrine started to sort out the salad and got a salad bowl and started cutting the tomatoes and lettuce.

'How do you want the salad made?' asked Corrine.

'Just like a Greek style salad without the Feta cheese, there is zucchini in the fridge if you want to add that, I know Jake likes that.'

Corrine got on with doing that while Jim had come down and got himself and Jake a beer.

'Corrine! Would you like a drink, some white wine?'

'That would be nice.'

Jim got her a glass of white wine and gave Debbie a glass as well, she had a sip and then carried on with lunch. They sat at the table when lunch was ready and enjoyed the food, Jake had told Jim about Bandy's visit and he told Jake about the executive tickets. Jake was happy about the tickets but unsure what to think.

After lunch, the family got ready to leave for the rodeo, it was nearly five o clock, Jim locked the front door and got everyone, into Jake's new car, because it had a lot more room. They set off and were looking forward to an evening of entertainment and with the weather holding and staying warm. It was going to be a pleasant evening without worry.

When they arrived at the rodeo, the car park was filling up, the people who came earlier stayed on for the evening's entertainment, but not the families who had children. The evening would be too much for them, Jake pulled into a parking spot, not too far from the big top. They all got out and walked towards the big top. Debbie had on a denim jean skirt and checked shirt and scarf around her neck. She was going to take her denim jacket as well because it could get chilly later.

Jim had on jeans as well and a cotton jacket with a light blue shirt, Jake and Corrine both wore denim as well, it was the choice of material for this kind of event. Jake was given five tickets as payment for his services and also for the recognition of what he did during the storm, Nathan would be waiting for them inside. It was a good crowd, it seemed that the whole town was here, which was good for the organisers. The family was met at the door by Belinda, she was all smiles as she called them over.

'Hi Jake, here are your tickets for the executive seating, if you follow, Tracy, she will take you to your seats.'

They got their seats which was in a sectioned area three rows up from the middle of the big top and there was waitress service available and the young waitress came over to them as soon as they were seated.

'Good afternoon, can I get you anything from the bar?'

There were some card menus on their seats and they were looking at these after they were seated, there was a selection of foods and drinks available. So, they all ordered drinks for now and would get food a little later.

There were some circus clowns in the ring trying to stir up the crowd with their antics, around half a dozen going around the ring throwing sweets towards the crowd and pretending to fall over at any given moment. These were not the rodeo clowns; these were the safe clowns whose only brush with death would be from some balloons or tripping up and hurting themselves. But they too had a job to do and they were doing well at the moment, the crowd were in good spirits, The Rogers family were now seated, they had found Nathan who was waiting for them at the entrance and they were joined by George. The show was due to start in half an hour, Jim had a program in his hand which he bought from the girl at the entrance. He opened it up to see the sequence of events, Debbie was looking through the program with him.

Jake was looking around to see if he could recognise any one, but with so many people still moving around, it was impossible. So, he just sat back in his chair and looked towards the ring area, at the far side of the ring Opposite him were the main gates where the horses and bulls would be let loose. There standing behind the gate was Bandy, he was giving orders to some of the people around him, getting his team ready for the rodeo to start. Jake thought that Bandy looked in his direction so he stood up and waved, but got no response.

'Who are waving to?' asked Corrine.

'Oh it's Bandy, he came over to the house earlier today.'

'What did he want?'

Jake sat down again and looked at Corrine. 'Oh, he wanted to talk to me about the rodeo and thank me for helping his men, he runs most of the people here you know.'

The drinks arrived and the waitress handed them out to Jim's party, once the drinks were handed out the show was about to start. Nathan wanted the men's room so he asked if Jake knew where it was, Jake stood up and went with Nathan to show him.

'Don't be too long, Jake, the show is about to start,' said Corrine.

'No problem, there will be some warm up acts first so we got time,' replied Jake. Jake took Nathan down to the toilets which were by the main entrance and by the beer tent and food halls.

'Sorry Jake, I should have gone before I left home, it must have been the Pepsi I had earlier.'

They had ten minutes to get back and get back into the seats before the show started, but Jake didn't need to rush, he knew he would have plenty of time. On their way back from the toilets a voice called out to him.

'Jake!'

He turned around to see who it was calling him, it was Belinda.

'Hi Jake, you better get back—they are about to start.'

'I'm working, but I'll probably catch up with you later, enjoy the show.'

He thanked her and had a few minutes to spare before the show started and he was seated and Corrine gave him his beer in a plastic tumbler.

'Well, cheers everyone,' he held his tumbler of beer up towards his family, and likewise, they did the same back to him.

The announcer on the tannoy system welcomed the audience and the show was declared open, within seconds the gates were opened and half a dozen horses with riders raced out into the ring. They were riding side saddles and unseating themselves and then getting back on while the horse was at full speed. Obviously trained riders, these were not the competitors, just paid entertainers who travelled the country performing, some worked in the film industry which was more lucrative. But only a selected few would be called upon regularly, most of the westerns or any movies which had horses, had these riders in the film.

This was the prelude to the main event, and the crowd loved it, there were smiles all around the big top as they wound down the performance. After they had finished, it was time for the rodeo clowns to be introduced to the audience.

'And now ladies and gentlemen, the people who keep the riders safe and without them there would be no rodeo.'

The rodeo clowns' music blared out from the tannoy to *Cowboy* from Garth Brooks, the rodeo clowns ran out tipping their hats as they circled around the area in front of the gates. They acknowledged the crowd as they all took off their hats and waved them as they made their way back behind the gates.

The show was about to start and first out was the bucking broncos, wild horses which had to be ridden for more than eight seconds. Doesn't sound that long, but on a horse weighing around 1500 pounds, and who didn't want anyone on its back, it was a lifetime.

There were six rodeo riders taking part and after every ride, the rodeo clowns made sure the riders were safe by distracting the wild horse away from the unseated rider. Even the ones who made the eight seconds, were in danger, they still had to get off the horse which didn't stop until it was back in the coral.

Two riders made it through to the final and the prize money was $5000, a very good payday indeed, there were also runner up prizes and every rider would get paid in some way. Next up was the most dangerous, the bull riding. The horses were dangerous, they had hooves that could cause damage, but bulls had horns and hooves and a lot of weight behind them. The rodeo clowns would have to be on their toes for this one, Bandy was always tense when the bull riding was about to start, he remembered how his career came to an end. Three of the cowboys who took part in the bronco riding, also were taking part in the next event, they would be joined by the professional bull riders. These were seasoned bull riders, some getting on and would probably be riding their last rodeo, it was difficult to let go of this lifestyle, especially when it's all you have known for most of your life.

A lot of them ended up with no money or prospects because they spent as fast as they earned, there was no retirement fund available for these men. People like Bandy, would be their only hope, and because he was one of them, he never let them worry about their future.

He would look out for them as long as he was able to.

After he was able to. [The bronco final had arrived and three riders were to contest the prize money, first up was Dusty. A cowboy from Denver Colorado, in his late thirties, ruggedly handsome, a 'ladies' man'. He was riding 'Amado' which translated means 'Gods Love' but he was not Godly at all. He sat on the horse and strapped his wrist to the saddle, the Penn gates opened and the horse bolted out and tried it's best to unseat his rider, Dusty was a seasoned rider, he held on for the full eight seconds and was helped off by the safety riders who came alongside on horseback.

The next rider, 'Slim' was mounted on 'Apollo' he was unseated within six seconds and picked himself up and dusted himself down. The final rider lasted seven seconds, so Dusty had won and threw hi Stetson in the air and 'Whooped' with celebration.

There was going to be break for thirty minutes before the main event, 'The Bull Riding' Jim had pre-ordered food for his party and happily eat this during the break with Country Music playing in the background.

The first bull rider was seated on his ride, Sirocco! A black and white a mixed breed from Brahman and Texas Longhorn. Certainly not the most dangerous, but enough to cause major damage. These bulls weighed from 1400 to 1600 pounds, imagine that monster running at you at speed.

It took three seconds for the first rider to be thrown and the rodeo clowns were quick to grab the attention of the bull, while the riders rode out to collect the bull rider and take him to safety. He wasn't badly hurt, just a couple of broken bones. He would get himself strapped up and get ready for his next ride. These guys were tough, their only aim was to get within reach of the prize money, they would nurse their bodies later.

The next rider stayed on for five seconds, he was very experienced and knew when to abandon ship and live to fight another day. His bull was Bushwacker! A well-known Piedmontese dark brown and fiery from head to toe, he was just mean.

He would be having a few more rides and would try to inflict as much damage as he could on the unlucky riders who were brave enough to ride him. At the end of the session, three riders remained, now the riders had to muster up all their strength for one last ride. The prize money was up to $10,000, Bandy was giving instructions to his men and they were ready for the last action of the day. He had so much tension on his face but he was calm with it, he had a good team working under him.

The first rider came blistering out on Bushwacker and was looking good until he made a mistake and lost control of his footing, he was dragged for a few yards until he was able to break free and fall to the ground. The crowd gasped and most of them stood up to get a better look.

He rolled away from the bull while the rodeo clowns distracted Bushwacker, the clowns were out quickly aware of the danger and tried to guide the fallen rider to safety. Once behind the gates, they knew that they were safe, they waited while the bull was distracted enough to get the bull back to its pen. Bushwacker hit one of the rodeo clowns but it wasn't serious, only enough to cause bruising in the next few days.

It was a close call but all were safe.

'And people do this for a living!' said Corrine who was holding on to Jake tightly.

Jake was having a great time, he wished that he was down there in amongst the action, though he never let Corrine know it. It was now the last ride of the night, and everyone in the audience was treated to a spectacular show. The last rider was about to get on top of Bushwacker, you would think that the bull would be tired by now, giving the rider a bit of a chance. But the bull had other ideas, he was trying to break the pen that he was held in and dismount the rider as well in the process. Hank Stevens, was a seasoned pro, he was going to ride this bull and stay the distance. This was his last ride before retiring from the circuit, he knew that if he didn't give his all, then he would have regrets. So, he was going to do whatever to stay on this bull, even his life depended on it.

The bell rang and the gates flung open, the bull was trying to leap and plunge downwards and leap and spin in order to dismount the rider. But he held on for dear life, could this be the only one to finish the eight seconds!

Two seconds to go and he was still on the bull, maybe Bushwacker was getting tired after all, he gave one almighty leap and spun around, the rider was hanging on for dear life. It was almost as if time slowed down just like slow motion in a movie, it seemed to go on forever. Finally, he gave one last grunt and yelled out to the bull, 'I beat you!'

The bell rang and he had done it, he had survived! The crowd cheered madly and favours were being thrown into the ring. It was almost like the scene of a Spanish bull fight, Bushwacker was led to safety away from Hank and he managed to bow to the crowd.

He was gonna be $10,000 richer tonight, he was a happy man. This elation was only felt on a few occasions but he was going to make the most of his time, no girl was safe tonight. He was given his trophy belt buckle, it was of a bull with long horns and a cheque for $10,000, he held the envelope to his lips and kissed it and let out a whoop!

The show was over and the crowd was not disappointed, it was a very successful show and all the tickets were sold out. The crowds started to make their way out of the big top and to their cars, some only had a short walk to their homes. The evening was still warm with a clear sky and the moon lighting up the town, like a giant torch! The organisers had done their jobs, everyone went home happy and didn't mind parting with their hard-earned money.

Jake followed his mum and dad out of the seated area with Corrine close behind him, Nathan had already left before them. He left his bike chained to a lamp post in the car park. As they were leaving the big top Bandy was waiting for them, he wanted to speak to Jake.

'Jake, my boy, how did you enjoy the show?'

Jim was behind Jake followed by Debbie and Nathan; Corrine was holding Jake's hand. Jake introduced Bandy.

'Corrine, this is the man who arranged the show, that's his workforce down there.'

Corrine held out her hand to shake Bandy's hand. 'Nice to meet you,' she said.

'You certainly run a tight ship around here.'

'Thanks, but the show almost didn't go on, but thanks to Jake here, well I guess you know!'

'Where do you go next?' asked Corrine.

'Oh, we got a couple of weeks to recuperate, and then on to Dallas.'

'You certainly get to see a lot of America, don't you!'

'It's my lifestyle, I couldn't live without it, you folks have a lovely evening,' as they were about to leave Bandy.

'Jake, could I see you for a moment?' Jake told Corrine to carry on and he would join them in a minute.

Corrine and the rest walked on to the car park leaving Jake to talk to Bandy.

'Jake, how would you like to take a chance on life?'

He looked a little puzzled, 'What do you mean?'

'I've heard a lot of good things about you, and I think that you are a natural. I can offer you a job as a rodeo clown, you have what it takes! Before you say anything, think about it and let me know, here's my card, call me when you have had a long hard think on it.'

He shook Jake's hand and walked away, back into the big top, Jake stood there and looked at the card and looked at Bandy as he walked away, then turned around and caught up with the others to the car.

'What did he want?' asked Corrine.

'Oh, he wanted to know if I wanted a job.'

'Really! You mean travelling around the country with his shows?'

'I guess so!'

'Well! I hope you told him that you are getting married and are settling down in Green River!' said Debbie who was standing next to Corrine.

Corrine agreed with her. 'Well, no not really, I think he wants me to try one show, you know, to see how it goes, I suppose!'

'I don't know if this is what I want, it's good that he offered anyway.'

No more was said as they got into the car and drove home, George was taking Corrine and dropping Nathan off as well. Corrine said bye to Jake and they kissed each other, he shook George's hand and told Nathan that he would see him on Monday.

A day of rest tomorrow, time to reflect for Jake, and he would have to think about the wedding as well, all these pressures building up. He would have to decide what he wanted to do, he didn't want to have regrets in his life, so he had to do the right thing and keep everyone happy. Bandy had planted a seed in Jake's mind and he knew what he was doing, he saw himself in Jake, and wanted to see if Jake would take the bait and come on board. Corrine will have to fight hard to keep Jake tied down to Green River, it wasn't going to be easy, but she believed their love will be enough.

Chapter Twenty

Sunday morning arrived and found the Rogers still in bed, it was 08.30 in the morning and the morning sun was stretching its rays over Green River. The leaves on the trees were stretching their young shoots using the sun's photosynthesis process to grow. Once the trees have a full house of leaves, the whole town seemed to change, it transformed life like magic.

Debbie was first to wake and she slowly went to the window and looked out onto her back yard, the plants were getting ready to expose their flowers. A couple more weeks and they would be in full bloom. She had a smile on her face and at that moment life seemed great, she turned around and looked at Jim who was just stirring from his bed.

'Hey sleepyhead, are you awake?'

'Yes, I'm awake, just enjoying the sleep in. It's amazing how time goes so quickly. If only I could invent a way to slow time down, I'd be a millionaire!' said Jim.

'That's never going to happen, so let's just enjoy the day, we will do things slowly today, how about that,' said Debbie.

Jake was also up and he looked out of his bedroom window, he looked out at Green River just past his yard. When the sun shone, it always made people look differently at life, the sunlight shining onto the water made it look like there was silver flowing. It just made you feel better.

It was BBQ weather and there was nothing better than a BBQ to get people hungry and gather round a flaming hot grill. Even the cooks who invariably get burnt in the process, enjoy the eating element of this ritual.

Jake was going over to Corrine's place for lunch, she wanted to cheer her father up, he was still feeling bad about a colleague who died at work a few days ago.

It was a man called Bob, he was getting on and was due to retire after working all his life, he had been working at the stadium for ten years now and was 70 years old. While he was unloading a delivery of timber boards which was going to be used as flooring for the rodeo, one of the straps got loose and the timber boards sprung free and landed on top of him.

If it was a younger man he would have moved out of the way, but Bob couldn't move that quickly and took the full force of the timber. His ribs were crushed and he died in hospital, he didn't have any next of kin, so there was no one to contact. He felt bad, and kept thinking about how it must feel to not have anyone in your life.

Of course, her dad would know having lost his wife himself, but he was lucky that he had Corrine, who looked after him. She had told Jake about this accident and even though Jake felt bad, she remembered how took the news. Jake paused for a moment, and thought about how life can just end at any moment, life was certainly too short, he thought to himself.

Sheriff Jones was called and he concluded that it was an accident, there was no malice involved and safety issues were looked at, so the case was closed. So that is why she arranged this lunch, to try and get his mind off the event at work, try and cheer him up.

Jim and Debbie wanted some time to themselves and could not make the BBQ, so Jake was going on his own, he was going to pick up some beer on the way. By the time Jake was ready, it was time to make his way to Corrine's. He came downstairs and got his denim jacket and said bye to his mum and dad as he left the house.

Jake was going to the gas station on the way to pick up the beer, when he reached Corrine's house he parked in the drive and went round the side of the house because he could smell the fire from outside. George was at the grill stoking it in readiness for the steaks. He was well known for his spice rub, even the neighbours wanted his recipe, so this would be the first time that Jake would taste the famous rub.

'Hi, Mr Smith,' said Jake.

George turned around towards Jake. 'Oh, hi Jake, and please call me George.'

'OK, I'll try, it just feels a little awkward.'

'Its fine, don't worry about it, you will get used to it.'

The steaks went onto the BBQ and straight away the smell wafted into the still summer air and the slight breeze blew the aroma towards Jake.

'Mmm, that smells amazing!'

'I told you; my dad makes the best steak in Green River.'

'I believe you!' said Jake.

After a few minutes, they were ready and George served Jake his steak with some potato salad, he had a drink already that Corrine gave him earlier.

'This is the best steak I have ever eaten, thank you.'

'That's OK Jake, it's nice to be appreciated.'

They sat down and were enjoying their meal and just for the afternoon George had forgotten all about work and enjoyed the company.

'Well, Jake, here's to you and Corrine, I am sure you will take care of my baby.'

'Dad! I'm not a baby.'

'You know what I mean, I'm glad Jake is in your life. You kids are going to be fine.' The lunch was going well and Jake wished that his mum and dad could have come, but just then he heard the side door open. It was Mum and Dad!

'What are you two doing here, I thought you had plans,' said Jake.

'Hi everyone, sorry to intrude but we could smell the steaks all the way from our house,' said Jim as they walked towards them.

'Hi George, are you OK if we encroach on your BBQ?'

'Hi, welcome, please come on in, we have plenty of food so don't worry about that, come and take a seat, I'm glad you could come.'

They sat down at the table and Corrine got up to get them some drinks, now it was really a happy table and the food went down well. A great way to spend a Sunday and still most of the evening left to go.

Chapter Twenty-One

The Monday morning mist rose slowly over the Green River and Jake was at his bedroom window watching it rise. The sun rays shone in patches through the trees and it made the river sparkle in places. The clouds were melting, breaking it up into clouds of white candy floss as it faded away into the morning daylight. The people of Green River would only get to enjoy a few more days of sunshine, there was rain and cloudy days forecast the following days to come.

Jake had a long delivery to do today and Nathan would be going with him, he had to go to Buffalo (Big Horn) country, a company called Bison Construction on Turkey Lane Buffalo.

This country was a bison migration trail before the settlers and the buffalo hunters came and almost wiped out the bison population. Greed for money made people not think about their actions, so thousands of bison carcases were strewn across vast valleys. The indigenous population were horrified at the waste and fought back to right a wrong, but we're outmanned and outgunned.

Although they had their victories, the battle of the Little BigHorn, being the most famous of their triumphs, General George Armstrong Custer became famous for that battle. Depicted in various movies, and told in different ways, but the indigenous tribe was always the bad guy! Hollywood had to sell seats in the movies and make the movie stars look good.

Yes, there was racism in those days, and by all accounts, it seemed like it all started in America, first with the indigenous people and later the black people. Imported from mainly Africa and other parts of the world, to be sold into slavery. And it is still happening even today!

Jake got dressed and made his way downstairs. He noticed that his mother was not downstairs, he saw his dad at the kitchen counter making a cup of coffee.

'Hey, Dad, is **Mum** OK? Only she is normally up before us.'

Jim turned to look at his son. 'She's got her Fibro back, the doc is coming over later, she has a few aches and pains and will be OK.'

96

'I hope so, I've heard a lot of bad things about that, anyway, I am on my way to get the van loaded for the delivery to Bison Construction, and I'll pick up Nathan on the way to the warehouse.'

'I'll meet you at the shop before you go, you will need some paperwork to give to the site office.'

'OK Dad, see you later.'

Jake left the house and Jim was thinking about Debbie, and had a worried look on his face, he had been alongside her since this Fibro started five years ago and knew what she was going through.

Jim sat down at the kitchen bar with his coffee, thinking to himself, with all the technology today, building satellites and launching them into space, they can't find a cure for a disease that attacks the brain.

Jake had picked up Nathan and was at the warehouse, he had to load five stoves and flue systems on the van for delivery, the company was building log cabins up in Big Horn Mountain Retreat off US 16 highway.

These cabins were for the rangers that worked in that location and also for the tourists, a place to rest and eat food, the stoves were for the colder part of the year. The cold weather can sometimes last for up to six months, hence the stoves.

'Jake! We need fuel,' said Nathan.

'Yeah, I know, we'll pick some up on the way at Rock Springs, there's a great breakfast diner over there.'

Nathan smiled, and got into the cab, Jake had closed the back sliding shutter of the van and got into the driver's side of the cab and closed the door. Jim had come to the shop just before Jake was about to drive off.

'You all set, Jake?'

'Yep, just got to get some fuel on the way?'

'OK, Jake, just take care and this is the prequel to the big delivery so, Nathan, you take care and I'll see guys when you get back.'

Jim gave Jake the collection notes and then they left. Jake said bye and with that they set off for Rock Springs. Back at the house Dr Sanjay Patel was knocking at the door, a man in his late fifties, he had lived in Green River for the last ten years after immigrating from England. He lived with his wife and daughter, his wife was also a doctor and worked at the same surgery. His daughter had finished school and was a pharmacist, she had the pharmacy next door to the surgery. Debbie made her way to the door, still a little dazed and in her dressing gown.

'Oh, hello Dr Patel, thank you for coming this early.'

'That's OK, I was on my way to surgery anyway and it made sense to see you on the way in.' She opened the door wider.

'Come in please.'

He walked in with his black leather doctor's bag, which he carried everywhere with him. Debbie showed him to the settee and asked him to have a seat. He opened his bag and took out Debbie's records, it was a grey folder with various papers in it. 'Right, what seems to be the problem?'

'It's the Fibro again, but this time I have really bad headaches and have to tie a bandana around my head to take some of the pressure off.'

He reached out to Debbie to hold her wrist, he wanted to check her pulse.

'I will just take your pulse, Debbie, and then we will take your temperature.'

After doing that, he wrote some notes in his paperwork. 'So Debbie, you are taking one codeine twice a day, is this still the case?'

'Well! I find that if I take them regularly, I get some symptoms like tiredness and I need to be awake to do my accounting paperwork, so I only take them when I need them.' He made more notes.

'I know it's difficult with this, Fibro, and there is no cure that I know of, all we can do is to try and take some of the pain away to give you some rest, have you thought of alternative medicine?'

'What do you mean?' asked Debbie.

'Well, I have heard of some patients who have had physiotherapy, and in some cases, the patient felt a little better. Now I'm not saying that this will cure you, but it may be worth a try!'

She looked at him. 'You mean a workout sort of thing?'

'Yes, something like that.'

'I don't know, I will have to talk to Jim about it and let you know.'

'OK, in the meantime, drink some ginger tea, this will help with the headaches and take a codeine tablet if the pain gets too bad, I'm sorry that I don't have a cure for you, well you take care.'

He put his paperwork in his bag and got up. 'Please call me if you get any problems, and let me know about the therapy option, OK?'

'Sure thing, doc,' said Debbie, showing him the way out.

Dr Patel got into his car and drove off, Debbie closed the door and took a deep breath, then walked to the kitchen to get a glass of water. She took a tablet and then decided to get ready for work, it was time she got her mind on something else. She had got used to fibromyalgia and had lived with it for a few years now. It didn't get any easier and some days were just better staying in bed, Debbie was a strong-willed woman and her pain threshold was high. Even so she would rather not have this affliction, maybe one day they will come up with a cure, there was always hope.

Chapter Twenty-Two

Jake was on his way to the highway, Nathan was excited, his first working trip, the skies were looking a little grey and the sun was fading in and out of the clouds. Jake was going to Rock Springs on the way to put some fuel in the van and have breakfast before the long journey to Buffalo, it should take him two hours to get there and if all goes well, they would be back by 3pm. It all depended on the road being clear and how quickly they could unload the stoves.

They were approaching Rock Springs, famous for one of its residents, Butch Cassidy who worked and lived in Rock Springs. Before he got involved with outlaws and became a folklore legend, when he teamed up with the Sundance Kid. Their main target was the Union Pacific railroad, which they robbed more than a few times. Their hideout was the infamous hole in the wall, which was situated in the Big Horn Mountains, in Georgeson County Wyoming.

The movie featured Paul Newman and Robert Redford, who looked pretty close to the original outlaws. Blairtown was an offshoot to Rock Springs, a staging point for the Union Pacific during its early Pioneer days when the west was first opened up. The coal mine there employed mainly white Americans but because of costs, the railroad board of directors started bringing in Chinese immigrants into the country and using them as cheap labour to work on the railroads. This brought a lot of animosity from the white workforce, and tensions grew so much that one night in 1882 the white workers went on a rampage, burning down tents that were housing the Chinese workers, some had their families inside at the time, women and children.

28 Chinese people were murdered, including some children and some women, eventually this was all put behind them when the railroad owners decided to give everyone a raise and eventually there was harmony in the workforce.

After Jake and Nathan had finished breakfast, they got back into the van and continued their journey to Buffalo, they should reach their destination by the early afternoon, if all went well on the road. Their journey would take them to Walcott and from there onto the I-30 highway on to Medicine Bow, set in the Seminoe Mountains, a beautiful landscape of lakes and winding rivers, some fast flowing. A fisherman's paradise with over 300 trout streams, Medicine Bow is famous for Irwin Wista.

In 1885, he came across the town and decided to stay, in his next fifteen years he would encounter events that would be documented within his diary. Accounts of his encounters with Red Indians, outlaws, cattle barons and cowboys, which later encouraged him to pen the novel 'The Virginian', which, in the sixties turned into a series for television, a western with James Drury playing the lead role along with Doug McClure as Trampas, and Lee J Cobb playing the Colonel.

Also known for its Palaeontological Paradise, for its discoveries of dinosaur fossils, a museum was built in 1913, to house the numerous bones found in its locality. It's hard to imagine dinosaurs walking the land, the sheer size of these monsters, and think of the damage they could do to the infrastructure of today. There just would be no way that they would fit in living side by side with humans, it's still amazing how they survived for millions of years. We have barely been on this earth for less than three thousand years and look at the damage we have already caused to the planet.

Chapter Twenty-Three

Time was going by slowly on the road, because of its vastness the motorway seemed endless, such were the roads filled with vast open spaces with just mountains and open land as company. The occasional town would creep up and with a blink of an eye be gone, Jake kept the vehicle at a steady 70 mph eating up the miles. He thought to himself, maybe next time he would have to arrange for delivery through a carrier, much as he liked driving, there were limits!

Debbie had packed lunch for Jake and Nathan, roast beef sandwiches and two flasks of coffee. It was fast approaching lunchtime and Jake had to find a place to pull over for a rest and a bite to eat. There was clearing further ahead, a lay by, he was near Walcott in Carbon County, ahead lay open land for miles with sandstone mountains populating the desert in the far distance. Scenery that you would see in the westerns made by Hollywood and other movie companies, John Ford made a lot of his westerns with this landscape. There were a few trucks on the road spread out along the highway into the horizon fading out of sight as they grew further away. He stopped the van on the layby, stretched his back and moved his neck from side to side to relieve the stiffness that he felt.

'Are you OK?' asked Nathan. 'Yeah, just a little stiff.' He opened the door and got down and stood on the red sandy layby, and breathed in the mountain air. Nathan got out as well and took in the air.

'Wow, take a look at that scenery, it makes you feel very small, doesn't it?'

'The big country! This why it's great to be alive, just look at this, the people living in the big cities just need to come out here and take it all in.'

They got back into the truck and got ready to have their lunch, Jake had told Nathan that his mum had made sandwiches for them. Jake took out the plastic lunch box that Debbie put his lunch in and opened it.

'Here you are, Nathan. Lunch!' He handed him a sandwich wrapped in paper.

'It's beef, are you OK with beef?'

Nathan reached out to take the sandwich, 'Thanks, Jake, your mum thinks of everything, she looks after you, doesn't she?'

Jake took out his sandwich and opened it. 'Yes, she does.'

They ate their lunch looking out at the open land scenery that surrounded them, it was a beautiful sight but also a reminder of the distance they had to clear just to get onto the next phase of their journey. But for now, they were just enjoying their lunch and the rest bite from the road. They probably had an hour of driving left and it was looking more likely that that they would be back a little later. Jake hadn't quite decided yet whether to drive back after the delivery, he would have to see how he felt, he wanted to make sure that he would be able to drive back safely. He had to look out for Nathan as well, so more responsibilities for him to consider before making his decision.

Jake's phone rang, he picked it up and answered it.

'Hi Jake, how are you doing?'

It was Corrine, she was having her lunch break as well and thought to see how he was. 'I was going to ring you, I'm glad you rang, it's nice to hear your voice, I'm not saying that Nathan's voice is bad or anything, but I like the sound of your voice.'

'Thank you dear, anyway, are you two OK?'

'Yes, we're fine, just having a rest and a bite to eat.'

'How much further have you got to go?'

'I think we will be at Buffalo by 1.30 and then I will see if we need to stay over or drive back and get back late.'

'Well, you make sure that you are not too tired to drive back, I want you back in one piece,' said Corrine.

'OK, babe, I will ring you when I am at Buffalo OK?' And with that, Corrine agreed and finished the conversation.

Chapter Twenty-Four

The final journey into Buffalo was in sight and the weather had changed dramatically, the rains had come down with a vengeance making the driving harder. Jake had put on the windscreen wipers to maximum speed and even then, couldn't see clearly, so he slowed down and was debating stopping. The next turn off was at south main street, the highway was a little busier on this stretch as they got nearer to their destination. Jake decided to stay on the highway, it was probably safer in the long run, he only had a couple of miles left to go albeit slowly with the weather conditions being what they were.

He eventually came off the highway and made his way to North Main Street at the junction, he turned right and was five minutes from his drop on McKinney Street. There was a sign for Bison Construction, Jake slowed down and pulled into the car park, there was a worker outside the warehouse signalling for him to park outside the warehouse doors. He stopped the van and pulled down his window, the warehouseman came out to meet him.

'Hi there, you made good time.'

'Yeah, would have been here earlier if it wasn't for the weather,' replied Jake.

'Just pull your truck inside the warehouse and park over on the right and we'll get you unloaded,' said the warehouseman.

Jake pulled the van inside out of the rain, and parked to where he was instructed to stop. He got out of the truck and Nathan followed him and stretched his legs and arms, the rain was slowing down and not as heavy as it was earlier. They both went into the warehouse, there was an office on the left-hand side and there was a young girl sitting behind a desk inside the office. Light brown hair and very attractive, must have been in her late teens, she wore a cotton floral dress knee length with short sleeves. Jake walked in through the door and approached the desk.

'Hi there,' said Jake to the young girl.

She turned to him. 'Hi, how can I help you?'

'I'm Jake and this is Nathan, we've got a delivery for you from Green River, for Jim Maguire.'

'That's great, you got here then!'

He didn't know what she meant by that, but just smiled at her.

'Would you like a coffee while you wait?'

'Yeah sure, that would be great thanks.'

Nathan was staring at the girl, Jake looked at him and could see that he was infatuated with her. She asked if they wanted sugar and milk in their coffee, they both nodded yes and she went to get their coffee.

'You fancy her don't you?' asked Jake.

Nathan blushed a little and smiled at Jake. 'She's nice, and very pretty. Well, if you like her, say something, and you do know that we are only here for today, and it's a long way to come if you start a relationship.'

'Yeah, I know, but there's no harm in being friendly,' said Nathan. By then, she had come back with their coffee and handed them their drinks.

'Here you go, is there anything else you need.'

'My friend here wants to know your name,' said Jake.

Nathan punched Jake on the arm lightly, she looked at Nathan.

'My name is Sally.'

'Nice to meet you, Sally,' said Nathan.

At that moment, Jim Maguire came into the warehouse and walked into the office. 'Jake!' said Jim.

Jake turned around. 'Yes, that's me.'

Jim reached out his hand to Jake, Jake shook his hand. 'It's nice to meet you, and put a face to the voice,' said Jake.

'I know your father well, he and I go back a ways, and I've just sent him a huge order for a site we are installing, will you be delivering those?'

'No, Dad's got a transport company covering that order, it's too big for our truck.'

'You got my stoves, that's great, I told your dad to send them by carrier, to save you a trip.'

'I wanted to drive and deliver them myself, but I think that if there is a next time, I will send them by carrier,' said Jake.

'Are you staying over or driving back today?' asked Jim.

'Well, we made it in good time, so I think that I will drive back today.'

'That's a shame, I could have taken you guys out for a meal if you were staying over, along with my daughter, Sally here, have you met?'

They both looked at each other, then at Sally. 'Er, yes sir, we have,' said Nathan in a withdrawn manner of speech; he obviously didn't know that Sally was Jim Maguire's daughter.

'Thank you for that, but I think we should be OK driving back,' said Jake.

'Well before you go back fill up your van from our fuel tank over there, it's the least that I can do for you,' said Jim.

Jake looked to where Jim was pointing at the fuel tank.

'Thanks, that would be appreciated.'

The warehouseman came into the office with the paperwork.

'All unloaded, Mr Maguire, here's the paperwork for your signature.'

He handed Jim the delivery note and Jim took it to the desk and picked up a pen and signed it. He took one copy and gave the other to Jake.

'There you go, Jake, and give my best to your dad, tell him that I will pop down and see him sometime soon.'

Nathan's eyes lit up with the thought that he may bring Sally down with him. 'Will do, thank you again for the fuel.' He said goodbye to Jim and Sally and left the office towards the van, he got Nathan to check the back of the truck to make sure everything was in place and tightened down.

Jake got to the van and filled up the tank with the diesel and closed the cap when it was full. He got back in the truck drove out of the warehouse and out of the yard, he then pulled up on the road just past the warehouse.

'I forgot to ring Corrine.' So, he got his phone and called her and let her know that they were on their way back home and they should get home by 8pm allowing for a stop on the way. Jake took a drink of water from his bottle and stowed it in the side of his door. 'You ready for the drive home?'

'Are you sure you feel up to it, Jake, you have driven all day!'

Jake looked at Nathan. 'I'll be OK, I just want to get home and sleep in my own bed tonight,' and with that he put the truck into gear and drove off.

Chapter Twenty-Five

The Rogers were getting ready to prepare the evening meal and would keep Jake's dinner in the oven for when he returned home. Jim was going to give Jake the day off tomorrow because he would be pretty tired from the long drive home. He would also let Nathan take the day off. He was only a passenger but he was still important in his role as co-driver (even though he couldn't drive) and he would keep Jake from falling asleep at the wheel. A lot of people who make long journeys by road, think that they can drive for hours without rest, but most end up in an accident.

So, it was important to have someone next to you to keep you on your toes, and he had to be vigilant and not fall asleep through boredom. So, deserving of a day off, Debbie was going to bake a steak pie and have some potatoes with carrots, she didn't make the pie from scratch, it was bought from the local store.

Jim was in charge of the vegetables and gravy, he was proud of his gravy, and this was made fresh, from a recipe given to him by his grandmother. Jim rang Jake and told him that the two of them were going to have the day off to relax, so there was no need to rush home. Nathan was happy and knew what he was going to do with his time off, sleep!

Jake would take it easy and maybe do some fishing in the river behind where he lived, he could try another spot by Expedition Island, he had seen a spot by the bridge, where he could protect himself from the sun if it got too hot. He sent a message to Corrine to say what he was going to do and she would meet him there after work and bring him some lunch, as she was only working half day tomorrow. Debbie would go into work with Jim and finalise the quote, so everyone was aware of the plan, Jim was putting the finishing touches to his gravy in the kitchen.

'This gravy is the best one yet!' said Jim.

Debbie looked at him and smiled. 'You say that every time.'

They sat down at the table and served themselves.

'It's a shame Jake is not here, I miss him,' said Debbie.

They sat in silence the rest of the meal; they were still thinking about Jake driving home. He would be home in a couple of hours then things could go back to normal.

Later that night Jake had finally got back to the warehouse and Nathan collected his bike and made his way home, Jake parked the truck and got into his car. He called Corrine on his phone to let her know that he was back and would see her tomorrow, before driving home. He checked to make sure that the warehouse was locked tiredness can make you forget things. He sat for a while, tired from the trip but glad to be home. Never again.

Chapter Twenty-Six

Tuesday started dull and overcast and a little cooler, that's because of the cloud cover, but the good news was that would only last during the morning.

Corrine was on her way to work as usual; the time was 08.45 and she walked to work, not because she didn't drive or have a vehicle, but because she liked the exercise. It was a little cooler than normal because of the overcast skies, but the weather was due to get better later in the day. It was Dalores' birthday today and Corrine was going to go to the pastry shop to surprise her with a cream cake. She loved fresh cream cakes.

When questioned about her love of cream cakes, she replied, 'You don't get a voluptuous body like mine without a little wicked craving.' Obviously meaning the cakes!

Jake was in the garage getting his fishing equipment together, the garage was very well organised, Jim liked to see everything neatly arranged so it was easy to find things. Moving house taught him always to run a tidy ship, all his tools were neatly placed on hooks lined up on the wall and electric tools stored in cupboards, the floor was spotless.

He had dug up some worms earlier in the morning. The best time to dig up earthworms was before it got too bright and too hot, he had a trick that his grandad had taught him. The trick is to place a damp piece of carpet or blanket over a portion of soil the night before, this would trick the earthworms into thinking the sun hadn't come up and draw them to the surface. It always worked, so he was all set to go fishing, his mother had made him a flask of coffee and some snacks, she knew that Corrine was going to bring him some lunch so she never packed that for him. He walked to the back of his garden to a gate that he had made specifically to get access to the river, he turned right outside the gate and closed it behind him, then walked the short distance to the bridge.

The river always looked good no matter what the weather, he put his bag down and took out his folding chair and opened it and placed it in position to where he was going to be fishing. He tried not to go too near the edge of the river, in case of scaring off the fish. Jake sat down on his fold-up chair and then picked up his carbon fibre fishing rod and set it up, he opened the bait box and put a worm on the hook then cast it into the river. The water was flowing steadily and he cast his float into a still section of the river, this was referred to as an eddy! This was caused by water being forced around a rock or rocks shaping the water in a type of whirlpool. Thus, creating a still section of water, this would stop the float from being dragged down the flow of the river.

He sat there staring at his orange tipped float and waiting for a bite from a fish, coarse anglers loved this part of fishing, trying to outwit the fish, trout were plentiful, brown and rainbow, also Whitefish with the occasional catfish and even Burbot. There was some Salmon caught there too, but it was normally seasonal. While he was sitting waiting, he couldn't help thinking about the rodeo and Bandy, was this something that he was seriously thinking about. What would Corrine do if he did go down this route, he probably knew the answer to that question already. His float had been dragged under and he had a fish on, he got up and was holding his fishing rod then started reeling the fish in. It was a trout, and not a bad size either, Jake was happy and was smiling widely. He pulled the fish up out of the water and brought it to him. He sat down in his chair and picked up a damp cloth that he had in a plastic bowl, he placed the cloth around the fish and then took out the hook from its mouth. The trout was of a good size and could be kept for eating, so he humanely hit it on the head and put it into a box that he had brought, in case he caught some good fish.

After all, it was free food!

Jake then put fresh bait on his hook and cast out into the same spot where he caught the fish and within seconds, the float was taken under again. Another trout, he couldn't believe his luck, he had never had this kind of luck before. He kept catching fish with every cast and soon had five trout in his box, some that he caught were too small and they were released back into the river. These were the rules of fishing, so that order was maintained in the rivers and lakes in America.

Before he knew it, lunchtime approached and with it the sun rose for the first time today, he got a call from Corrine to say that she was on her way to him and she wanted to make sure that he was where he told her he was going to be. Within a few minutes, Jake could see her in the distance walking towards him, she was going to get a shock when she saw what he had caught.

'Hi Jake.'

He looked at her and had a big smile on his face.

'You look happy, you must have caught a fish.'

'Wait till you see, guess what we are having for dinner tonight?'

He opened the box with the fish in and waited to see Corrine's face. 'Wow, you caught all those!'

'Yes, I couldn't believe it either, and I have a feeling there's more out there to be caught.'

'Well, be careful you don't catch too much, don't forget the fish we caught the other day that you put in the freezer.'

'Of course, I forgot about that, anyway there doesn't look like you've got enough room in the box for any more.'

'Then I can go home with the box, put the fish in the freezer and come back with an empty box.'

'That's a good idea, Jake, I can look after your fishing rod while you go home.'

So that's what Jake did, he picked up the box and told Corrine that if she caught any more fish to put them in the plastic bag, until he got back. Corrine was now in the chair looking at the float, but there was no movement, just the water moving the float. So, she had her lunch while looking at the float in the water.

About half an hour later, Jake got back and was ready to take over, he had a bottle of beer in his hand that he had been drinking. Corrine got up from the chair and put the rod on its rod rest.

'You eat your lunch first, Jake before you start fishing again, I got you a steak sandwich and a piece of birthday cake.'

'Whose birthday was it?'

'It was Dalores, I got her a cake this morning on my way to work you better eat quickly or the cream will spoil,' said Corrine. She sat on the bank to finish her lunch while Jake sat back in his chair and opened his sandwich, Corrine was due to go back to work so she kissed Jake and left and told him not to be too late. He finished his lunch and carried on with the fishing, he took a couple of swigs of his beer and refreshed the bait on the fishing rod and continued. He was probably only going to be at the river for another hour or so before packing up and making his way back home. As he was about to pack up, Corrine rang him.

'Jake, there isn't a lot happening at the salon so Dalores said that I can finish early, so I am going to pop over to give you a hand and then I thought that we could cook the fish at your place tonight, what do you think?'

'That sounds like a plan, I will let Mum and Dad know I'm sure they will be happy about that.'

Later, Corrine met up with Jake and she helped him to pack up and they made their way back home, Jake had a great day and washed the long day's driving out of his system. He was ready for work tomorrow and planning the wedding together, he had no thoughts at all about the rodeo.

Chapter Twenty-Seven

The evening was drawing in closer and Jim lit the BBQ, Jake had cleaned the fish and Debbie was going to wrap them in tin foil, she would put herbs inside with a cube of butter.

'You will have to take some home to your dad, I know he likes trout,' said Debbie.

'Good idea Mum, I'll wrap up a few and take them to him when I drop Corrine off.'

Debbie put the ready to cook fish on a table next to the BBQ Jake was going to cook them and give his mum and dad a breather. Even though Debbie prepared the food, he let them know that he and Corrine were making dinner tonight. So, Debbie didn't have to worry, they had a busy day at work and didn't really want to start dinner, so she was happy. Debbie wanted to talk about the wedding plans, as it wasn't too far away, there were lots of things to sort out, so they were going to be busy tonight.

'What time is your dad working tonight, Corrine?' asked Debbie.

'I think he is working till 10pm tonight because there was an upcoming concert at the stadium and it's a rock band.'

'Rock band! Who is it, do you know?'

'Not yet, but I will find out, they normally advertise the even weeks in advance so it's really strange that a concert is planned so quickly. I think this what they call a 'Lost Leader.' This a PR stunt that normally gets more publicity for the band.'

'Do you think we should make extra food and take some home for your dad, I'm sure he won't have time to cook dinner when he gets home?' asked Debbie. 'That's a great idea, why didn't I think of that!' said Corrine.

Jake had set aside a few trout for Corrine to take home as well as dinner for tonight, her father would appreciate this. He was working late tonight and would be having a rest the following day, George had planned on going to the cemetery to see his wife, Corrine was going with him, she had taken the day off at the salon. Jake went into the house to get cleaned up after cleaning the fish, he was going to cook the fish and dinner would not take long. Corrine was in the kitchen making the fries, the salad was already prepared earlier by Debbie. By the time Debbie and Jim had come down dressed for dinner, dinner was ready and Corrine had set the table on the patio in the garden.

'Hi kids, mmm, that smells wonderful,' said Debbie.

'Yes, I certainly am looking forward to dinner tonight,' said Jim.

'You guys are in for a treat, thanks to Mum preparing the trout, the dinner is going to be delicious.'

'I thought we could eat out here, if that's alright with you guys,' asked Jake. 'As it's not so cold.'

'That's a great idea,' said Debbie.

As they sat down at the table ready for dinner, Jim decided to say grace for the first time.

'I think because of all the good things that has happened to our family this year and the inclusion of a new family member.' He looked at Corrine and smiled, she smiled back.

'Our lives have been made richer and now is the time to thank God, now you know that I am not a religious person, but there is no other explanation for it! So please close your eyes. Thank you, Lord, for the food on our table, good wine and the prosperity of our family, Amen.'

The food was served at the table and they all were enjoying the food.

'So, Jake, you had a good day fishing I hear,' said Jim.

'You should have been there, Dad, I just got lucky I suppose.'

'That's impressive son, what bait did you use?'

'Oh, just earthworms.'

'I don't believe it, just earthworms?' said Jim.

'Well dinner is really tasty son, thank you.' Jim poured wine for himself and Debbie and asked Corrine if she wanted any, which she did.

Jake picked up his glass of wine and proposed a toast.

'To fine food and fine company and to our upcoming wedding, cheers.'

They all raised their glasses and said cheers together, then sat down to finish dinner. 'We will have to talk about the wedding plans after dinner, Corrine,' said Debbie.

'It's getting close and we have a lot to organise.'

'Yes, I wanted to talk to you about that.'

'There is plenty of time for that, let's enjoy this lovely meal first,' said Jim.

They all nodded and enjoyed the meal. Because the dinner was cooked on the BBQ, there were less pots and pans to clean. So, it wasn't long before they were putting plates away and sitting down in the lounge. Debbie had a notebook with her and a pen to make notes regarding the wedding.

'I have spoken to Pastor George at the First Assembly of God Church and he has space for a wedding in the next few weeks.'

'That's great,' said Corrine.

'Hold on a moment,' said Jake. 'Isn't that a little fast, I mean, there's lots to plan, isn't there?'

'It's not going to be a big wedding, so there shouldn't be that much to organise,' said Jim.

'You'll be surprised, it's not just a matter of turning up and saying your vows, there's the dress to consider, and the bridesmaids and their dresses, and what about your suit Jake. Have you thought about that?' asked Debbie, Jake scratched his head and looked at his dad.

'Well, no, not really.'

'So that's the first thing we need to address,' said Debbie. They looked at each other and Debbie made some notes in the book.

'I looked into some venues to hold the reception, and the church hall seems to be the best so far,' said Jim.

Debbie looked surprised that he would do that on his own initiative. 'You have been busy,' said Debbie.

'Oh, I have my uses,' replied Jim.

'Right, so we have the church, we have the venue, we just need to know how many people are coming and sort out the food situation,' said Jake.

Things were going well and plans were put in place, at that moment the front door bell rang, Jim went to open it, it was George, Corrine's Father, Debbie had rung him earlier knowing that they were going to make wedding plans at the house. He walked into the room with Jim.

'Dad!'

Corrine was all smiles, 'I thought that you were working late!'

'I was, but when Debbie rang me, I knew that the planning was important, so I pulled a few strings, and here I am.'

Debbie had got George a plate of food that they saved for him and gave it to him, which he was happy to receive.

'What kind of father would miss out on his daughter's wedding planning, thanks for the food, I'm famished.'

George sat down next to Corrine at the kitchen table, and Jake had brought a drink for him. 'Here you go, George, Debbie will bring you up to speed on events so far,' said Jim.

'Oh, and by the way, that dinner on your plate, Jake caught it from the river earlier today.'

'A man of many talents,' said George as he tucked into his food.

After explaining what was discussed so far, George mentioned that he knew the manager at the Hilton Inn and that he would get the best deal at a good price.

'I want to pay for this, as my treat, and I don't want any discussion on that, please.'

They all agreed as this venue is better that the church hall and the reception venue was put to bed. The plan was now for Corrine and Jake to get a list together of all the friends they wanted to attend the wedding, and Jim would get a list of any family that would be invited. They all agreed that the wedding would take place at the First Assembly of God Church on Saturday, 10 June at 2pm. That was the time that Pastor George had pencilled into his diary, when Debbie saw him. They could sit back and relax now and enjoy the rest of the evening together, it was like a big weight had been lifted and everyone was breathing easier.

'Well, you two seem to know what you are both getting involved with and I think that you both will make each other very happy, I'm happy for the both of you,' said George.

'Yes, and the both of us and George will be here for you, in case you need any help along the way,' said Jim. Debbie was alongside him and all smiles.

'You have made us very happy,' said Debbie. The evening was at an end and all sorted.

Chapter Twenty-Eight

The next day Debbie had arranged for Corrine and her to go shopping for a wedding dress, they booked an appointment at the wedding dress boutique on Wilkes Drive in Green River, Celebrations was the only wedding dress boutique available. They arrived at 10am and were met by Vickie, the owner.

'Good morning, Corrine.'

'Yes, good morning and this is Debbie, my mother-in-law to be.'

'They entered the boutique which was very cool and bright, with lots of light colours adorning the walls and somehow bringing out the white wedding dresses, almost like a bright light. Designed with that purpose in mind, the dress was the important factor!'

'Dalores told me to take care of you as you are very important to her.'

'You know Dalores?'

'Yes, we go back a long way, so I had better do my job and look after you.'

After two hours in the boutique, Corrine had chosen her dress, and Debbie was going to pay for the dress that had been arranged back at the house. The dress cost $2000, which seemed a lot when you consider it was only worn once, unless it was handed down to a daughter. It does bring into question why wedding dresses are so expensive considering that fact! Weddings on the whole were big business, the average wedding could cost anything from $10,000 up to $50,000, and that's just the average. The rich and famous spend an average of $250,000 up to infinity, one always trying to outdo the other, it's all about bragging rights.

Stupidity would be a better word for it, but then, hey, people have to make a living I suppose.

Next port of call was the flower shop a few doors down but before that Corrine was told that Debbie must have rest and subsistence and she was not to be tired out. This was because of her fibromyalgia.

'Let's have a drink and some food, all that waiting has made me feel hungry.'

'If you're sure, then why not,' said Debbie. They walked into a McDonalds a few hundred yards away, once inside Corrine told Debbie to find a seat and that she would get the food and drinks, Debbie had told her what she wanted and she then found a table next to a window. The restaurant was getting busy as it was lunchtime, a fact about McDonalds is that nobody knows exactly how much the chain is worth. It's mainly because the operating company set up by Ray Krock who made it his job by popularising the McDonald's name, bought the land that each McDonald's was built on. Making it the largest landowner in the world, and because land prices are never stable it is impossible to say how much they are worth. So, it is estimated that they are worth around $195 billion dollars. Ray Krock himself would have been worth $18 billion, but he donated a lot of his money to charities, God love him!

After lunch, they set off again refreshed from the break and sustenance and were ready to tackle the flowers, this should be less time consuming as it was a straightforward matter of choosing a bouquet to match the dress and what the bridesmaids should be wearing. The bridesmaids' dresses were also chosen when the wedding dress was purchased, they were going to be powder blue dresses.

So armed with that information and some material samples given by Vickie at the boutique, their job would be easier. It's amazing how thighs just turn out to be so true to form, the bouquet was chosen in less than half an hour and the bridesmaids' flowers would be worn on the wrist, so they didn't have to carry them.

'Job done, let's go home and see how the men have done,' said Debbie, as they made their way to the car. Debbie rang Jim and found out that they were on their way to sort out their suits for the wedding.

'Well! This should be fun, they are going to choose their wedding suits,' said Debbie.

'Oh, maybe we should have gone with them.'

'The good thing with shopping, is that you can always take things back and change them.' She winked at Corrine as they decide to make their way home.

Chapter Twenty-Nine

Jim and Jake were just leaving the shop. They were letting Nathan hold the fort with strict instructions to only answer the phone and that they could be contacted by phone in emergencies. They were off to the menswear department at the local Moll, there were several menswear shops to choose from. Jake was told that he had to get a suit for himself and the best men, and that was Nathan and Rick.

He had arranged for Rick to meet them there, that would only mean that Nathan would be required to go back and try on his suit once it was chosen. The Moll was unusually busy as they entered the first menswear shop and looked around at some of the designs. Rick had seen them and entered the same shop; an assistant had come over to them by now.

'Are you guys OK, or do you need some help?' Jim turned to the assistant, who was a teenager who recently left school.

'Are these all the suits that you have on display?'

'Yes sir, have you seen any that you like?'

'Not yet but we will let you know when we do,' said Jim.

'Jake!' called Rick. He had caught up with them.

'Hey Rick, you made it then.'

'Told you I would, well what are we doing?'

'Glad you could make it; you know my dad.'

'Sure do, hi Mr Rogers.'

They exchanged pleasantries and got on with looking at the suits on the racks and nothing caught their eye. After twenty minutes, they decided that there was nothing special at this shop and decided to move on to the next shop. After they had been to the last shop, Jake finally decided on the suit and after trying it on said that he was happy with it and Jim agreed. They found an assistant and got him to find a suit in a different colour to Jake's but the same design, for Rick and Nathan. Jake's suit would be in a grey colour and the best men would wear a matching colour. The suits were chosen and Rick's suit had some alterations to be carried out because he was a little more portly in his appearance, he wasn't fat, just enjoyed his food.

The shoes had also been chosen and ties to go with the suits, Jim had agreed to pay for these items, so that was ticked off the list of things to do. It was going well and Jim was wondering how well the girls were doing as he paid for the goods and arranged for Nathan to come to the store later that afternoon. He was going to ring Debbie but at that moment, Jake's phone rang.

'Hi darling, are you OK?'

'Yes thanks, how did you get on with the dress?'

'Well, we got the dress and the flowers sorted and we are at home, how did you get on?'

'Oh just fine, suits sorted, shoes sorted and just got to get Nathan to try out his suit later then were done for today.'

'Great, we will have dinner ready for you when you get back home later.'

'OK, that's great, we will see you later, just got to pick up Nathan and get him to try out his suit, then we will see you at home.'

They made their way back to the shop and Jake picked Nathan up and drove him back to the menswear shop to try on his suit. Jim stayed at the shop he was going to close the shop and he would see Jake at home later. At the store, Jake had got Nathan to try on his suit. It was lucky that his suit didn't need any adjusting.

'It fitted perfectly job done!' said Jake to himself as they agreed to collect all the suits and shoes once the alterations were completed on Rick's suit. Jim and George were wearing suits that they already had which were going to be suitable for the wedding, so there was no need for them to buy new suits.

Jim closed the shop at 5pm and headed home, Nathan was dropped home and Jake was on his way back as well, the day had gone according to plan. Jake had erased the rodeo from his mind during the wedding plans, his mind focussed on one thing, Corrine. He had to keep his focus on the things that were real in his life at the moment. George would meet up at the Rogers' home to see how the day went, he had been in touch with the manager at the Hilton Inn and he was going to see him at the weekend. He had reserved a venue for him and needed to discuss the sit-down meal, George had to find out how many people were to attend. Everyone was at the Rogers' home and dinner was about to be served, tonight was chicken night, prepared by Corrine and Debbie. The table was set and they sat down to eat.

'I would like to say, thanks to everyone for making this day go so well, and here's to the future, may it go the same way,' said Jim.

They all raised their glasses and dinner was enjoyed by all, a happy family united by love and friendship. After dinner was done and the plates washed up and put away, they sat down in the lounge for coffee, they discussed what each had done and the next question was what was next on the list.

'Corrine, do you know how many people will be coming to the wedding?' asked Debbie.

'Well, I am only inviting half a dozen of my friends from college and Dalores and her boyfriend.'

'And likewise, but I will be inviting Antonio and Julia, oh and Miguel from the coffee shop,' said Jake.

'How about you Jim, do you know which family members will be coming?' asked George.

'Well, I've spoken to my sister from Dakota, and Jill will be coming with her husband and three kids, and I spoke to Ted, my brother, he and his wife will be coming with their three kids and Debbie's folks are in New York so we haven't heard back from them yet.'

'How many in New York, Debbie?' asked George.

'There will probably only be two, my brother and his wife.'

'Well that makes 30 people so far, so I think it will be safe to assume that 40 places should be fine, in case of any additions, at least it gives me something to work with,' said George, who took control of the numbers, someone had to.

'Well, it's just a matter of sending out the invitations and then we will get a better head count for sure,' said Jim.

And the evening came to a close, George and Corrine went home and a new day was to beckon the Rogers. Debbie came over to Jake, who was reflecting on the conversation.

'What are you thinking about, Jake?'

'Oh, I was just thinking how quick all this is happening, I just need time to digest all this.'

'You are not having second thoughts, are you?'

'No, Mum, I love Corrine and want to be with her.'

'Then everything will be fine, don't worry, we are here for you.'

Chapter Thirty

Debbie Rogers had spoken to the Pastor from the church and arranged for Corrine and Jake to meet with him to discuss the ceremony. The appointment was made for Friday evening after service. The Pastor invited them to sit in on the service that evening, it would give them an insight as to the type of service that is used at the church. It was another way of the Pastor trying to recruit new blood to his church, the American people favoured religion highly and it took over towns in some areas of the country. Religion is a very lucrative business in America and its followers pay a fortune to their so-called saviours, so much so that these so-called 'Messiahs' have expensive homes and cars and some even have private planes. All paid for by their congregation. This is so that they can travel to places quicker to bring the word of God to more people.

Gullible! That's the word you would have to use, the word of God has been lost in translation and unscrupulous people have taken over and are cashing in on the sheep that seem to follow without hesitation.

Jake had some concerns on why there were so many churches, and some with different beliefs! In Green River alone, there were The Emmanuel Lutheran, the Hilltop Baptiste, The Living Hope, The United Pentecostal and the Nazarene Church.

Anyway, they were just going to get married in the church only once and religion had no part to play in that as far as he was concerned. So they would go and sit in on the Pastors service and then meet with him after and go through the ceremony procedure. Debbie was at home and decide to ring George to remind him of the appointment on Friday evening.

'Hi George, its Debbie here, are you OK?'

'Hi, Debbie, yes I'm fine, thanks for asking, how can I help you?'

'It's just to remind you about the marriage ceremony at the church tomorrow night, do you want us to pick you up?'

'No, that's OK, Corrine and I will meet you there, it's at seven pm, isn't it?'

'Yes, that's right.'

'OK then we'll see you there, have a good day.'

She put the phone down and got on with the invitations. Debbie was addressing the envelopes to all the people on the list, she would also send emails to speed things up, there wasn't that much time to the wedding. Contingency plans had to be made to contact them by phone after the letters and emails were sent out. This would make sure of the numbers, so they would wait till a few days before ringing people, give them time to get the mail. Corrine had already taken the invite for Dalores to give it to her by hand as she worked for her, and Jake was going to give invitations to Antonio and Miguel. This was part of the discussions that took place.

Jim spoke to his sister Jill from the shop this morning and she has confirmed that she will attend the wedding, so even though most of the people were to be contacted either verbally or by email Debbie still liked to send the invites in the post. It made it more personal, she didn't agree with the texting and email culture today, she understood that it is needed to survive in the world that we live in today. But she didn't have to like it. This tech caused kids to cheat on their assignments given at school, because they download everything from the internet! How was that learning? The good old days are gone forever unless a Third World War were to happen, then there would be no tech because all the satellites would cause mayhem around the world, trying to knock out the enemy's source of communication.

So, the world would have to start all over again and learn the old ways of communicating and living, how ironic!

Chapter Thirty-One

Friday was upon both families—like anything to do with time, it went too fast and before you knew it Friday would be over and the weekend was upon you. It's strange, Monday starts slow and Tuesday just as slow and you are wishing that the weekend would hurry up and get here, but you then want to slow down time. Because the weekend arrives too quickly, maybe there's a message there for us, don't wish for time to go quickly at the beginning of the week.

Debbie had sent all the invites and contacted all the people on the list that she had to deal with. George and Jake were both at work and Corrine was at the salon.

'Corrine, it's your wedding practice tonight, isn't it?' asked Dalores. She turned around from washing a client's hair in the sink.

'Yes, it is, I hope it goes well.'

'Don't be silly, there's nothing to it, you will get through it with no problem.'

There were two middle aged women clients in the salon both listening in on the conversation. Like most salons and barbers, that's where people go to talk and hear gossip, more so with the salon's, women love to talk.

'Well keep calm and don't try and take everything in all at once, it will come to you, believe me, I should know, I've been married twice!'

'OK, I'll try,' said Corrine. She got on with washing the lady's hair.

'I couldn't but overhear dear ooh, it's exciting isn't it, you make sure you enjoy every minute of it, you know when I got married things were different then. When I think of the cost of things today, I worry how the younger people can manage.'

'Thank you, Mrs Wilson, I will.'

Dalores laughed and carried on styling the other ladies hair. The ladies were both in their late sixties and were regular customers. Ladies at their age didn't have much to look forward to, both lost their husbands and most of their relatives don't keep in touch. It's sad but a fact of life, these women have a wealth of knowledge locked up in their minds that never see the light of day. Maybe they should invent a computer that can absorb these memories from people and then store it somewhere, to be called upon when needed. Jim had a plan to take the wedding party to dinner after the church practice, only for beer and burgers, nothing too posh. He contacted Kris at the Redfeather Bar.

'Hi Kris, it's Jim Rogers, Jake's dad.'

'Oh, hi, Mr Rogers, how can I help you?'

'Well, I'd like to book a table for tonight for a meal and drinks, around eight pm.'

'That's fine, I'll arrange a good table away from the noise, there is a country band on tonight, you sure it won't be too noisy for you?'

'No, that's fine, I'm sure we can cope with that, country music has to be loud.'

'What's the occasion?' asked Kris.

'Oh, Jake and Corrine are having a wedding rehearsal at the church and I thought it would be nice if we ate out instead of cooking, you know what Jake has put you down on his list of people he would like to be at the wedding, how about it, are you free on Saturday, 10 July?'

'Well, that's real nice of you, Mr Rogers and I am graciously going to accept your invitation, you let me know if you want me to bring any drinks or food, it will be on the house.'

'That won't be necessary, Kris, we are having the reception at the Hilton, and, please call me, Jim.'

'Okay, then Jim, I look forward to the wedding, and tonight's dinner is on me, on this I must insist.'

Jim didn't know what to say, 'Thank you Kris, we will see you tonight.' Jim put the phone down and went over to Debbie who was in the office.

'Kris has told me that dinner's on him tonight, isn't that amazing!'

'Well, that's nice of him, are you sure he said all of us?'

Jim looked puzzled, 'I'm not sure that I told him how many people were going.'

'I'll talk to him when we get there tonight, oh, and there's a band on tonight, a country band!'

'Oh, that will be nice, I don't think I could put up with a Pop or Rock band,' said Debbie.

'Yeah, I know what you mean.'

Chapter Thirty-Two

Later that day, Jim was at the shop just getting ready to go to lunch when he got a phone call from Jim Maguire the builder from Buffalo.

'Jim! How are you doing?'

'Oh, I'm fine, is everything OK, I was going to call you next week, did you get my quotation?'

'That's what I wanted to talk to you about, is that the best you can do on the final price?'

Jim thought for a moment, 'I'm afraid so, Jim, I tried every way to reduce the figures as best as I could, you know I always do my best for you.'

'That's OK, look, the people that are funding this project have accepted my quote and that means that your quote is good.'

'That's good news!'

'Congratulations Jim, I'm glad that I could give you this order, you earned it.' Jim was elated, he thanked Jim Maguire and immediately. 'Oh hey! I almost forgot, you know my son is getting married soon, how would you like to come to the wedding?'

'Well, that's nice of you to think about me, you know, I can do with a trip down to your end of town, yes! I will take you up on that invitation Jim, thank you. Oh, and bring your daughter if she wants to come, how is she doing?'

'She thinks that she is running the business, tells me what to do, very bossy!' Jim laughed.

'Anyway, you take care, and I will send you the details of the wedding and thanks again.'

He went into the office. 'Deb, guess what?'

'What dear! I thought you were getting lunch?'

'We got the Maguire job! He spoke to me a little while ago, it's all good.'

Debbie felt relieved, with all the money they have been spending recently, it made a dent in their bank account. This was a 'God send' and she was all smiles.

'Thats fantastic, Jim, when do we start the job?'

'Soon as possible, he said he's ready when we are, he has already started the land clearance and can store the stoves and flue system on site.'

'Well, I think that we should start the job after the wedding.'

'No! We have time before the wedding, it won't take long to get the stoves ordered I have already got the proforma from the supplier and they said that they can ship the stoves within the week.'

'On Monday, we will spend all our time on that job,' said Debbie.

'I agree, we will go down that route, look I can finish early tonight and maybe you and I can go for a drink, would you like that?'

'That sounds like a good idea, but you are forgetting about the wedding practice later, plenty of time to have that drink after.'

Jim then rang Jake.

'Hi, Jake, what you up to?'

'We are on our way back from the delivery to Mr Jones, everything went fine and he was happy, gave us a $10 tip.'

'That's great, listen I have something to tell when you get back.'

'Tell me now.'

'No, it can wait, I'll see you when you get back.'

Ten minutes later, Jake and Nathan had parked the truck and walked in through the warehouse doors. 'Dad, we're back.'

Jim was just pouring himself a cup of coffee by the kitchen. 'In here, son.'

Jake walked over to the kitchen. 'Don't mind if I do.'

Jim poured Jake a cup of coffee and also one for Nathan who was with Jake.

'Thanks, Mr Rogers,' said Nathan as he took his drink.

'Look guys, I might as well tell you both, we have the quote from Maguire's and he has accepted my quote and we have the construction job!'

'Why that's great news, Dad.'

Nathan was not aware of the quote. 'What does that mean exactly?' asked Nathan.

'What it means, is that we have a big order to fulfil and we will have to make sure it all gets sorted with no room for mistake,' said Jim.

'How many stoves are we talking about?' asked Jake.

'Fifty stoves and twin wall flue systems.'

'Well, we had better check if our warehouse can handle that amount, what about delivery?' asked Nathan.

'This one is going by freight carrier, the price has been factored in, we just have to store the stoves in the warehouse for a couple of days until we arrange for the courier to collect them.' Jake lifted his cup of coffee and said cheers, they did the same and smiles were abundant. 'Listen, Jake, me and your mother are going to for a quick drink to celebrate, do you think that you and Nathan can close up later.'

'Sure thing, Dad. No problem.'

'We will see you later and don't drink too much, remember you are both getting older!'

Jake laughed and Jim also had a laugh with him, he then went over to Debbie and asked to finish earlier, they are going to have that drink after all. So, everything was set for the evening and the Rogers family were in a happier place, the business was going to be OK for the rest of the year thanks to this order. The pressure was off the shop, so that meant they could relax a little bit more, but sales are still sales, and Jim wasn't going to take his foot off the throttle just yet.

Jim and Debbie left the shop and left Jake with Nathan to work the next two hours. They drove to Don Pedro's restaurant. They had a bar area attached to the restaurant. Jim parked the car and they both went into the bar.

'Well, this is different,' said Debbie, 'It's not every day we get to do this, it's a rest bite from work and family,' replied Jim.

Antonio was at the bar and looked surprised when they both walked in.

'And to what do we owe this honour!' He said.

'Hello Antonio, we just came for a quiet drink' said Jim.

'It's always nice to see you two even if it's only every blue moon!'

'Well maybe we can make this into a habit,' said Debbie.

They both walked up to the bar and sat on the bar stools. 'What can I get you?'

They both looked at the selection of drinks at the bar and said, 'I'll have a Jim Beam on the rocks.'

'Are you sure dear?'

'Yes, quite sure.'

'And you Debbie, what can I get you?' asked Antonio. 'I think that I will have a martini please.'

Antonio got Jim's drink and placed it in front of him at the bar he then went to get Debbie's drink and within a couple of minutes he had her drink on the bar as well.

'Enjoy,' he said as he went back to the restaurant side.

'Well dear, here's looking at you, kid.'

Debbie smiled at him, 'That's a good Humphrey Boghart, dear.' They both smiled and sipped their drinks.

'You know we should get out more, I like this, it feels right, why didn't we ever do this before,' said Jim.

Debbie looked at Jim and took another sip of her drink. 'Well, the business and raising Jake sort have has taken a big chunk of our lives I suppose,' 'You know what, from now on we will make a promise to live a little more and spend more time together. After all, we have worked hard and I think we deserve this.'

Jim agreed and knocked back his whiskey, he put his glass on the counter and Debbie did the same and they signalled to Antonio. He saw them and came over. 'You guys ready for another?'

'Yes please, and get yourself one as well.'

'Thanks, I will join you with a beer, if you don't mind?'

'Not at all, please feel free,' said Jim.

Antonio brought back their drinks and joined them, he had a bottle of Coors and toasted them both, and the afternoon went well. 'You know, I heard that your son was getting married.'

'Yes, he's getting married to Jackie Smith, they went to college together.'

'George's daughter, well that's nice, congratulations to you both and this drink is on me.'

They both looked at each other and clinked glasses and sipped their drinks.

'Thank you for that Antonio, and good health to you,' said Jim as they drank up and decided to call it a day, even though they were both having a good time.

Chapter Thirty-Three

The Rogers family arrived at the church and were ready for the next chapter in their lives, Jim parked the car and was about to get out when he noticed George's car arriving. They waited for them to arrive before they went into the church, which was very modern looking from the outside.

The congregation in the church was near to capacity when they walked into the church, they were met by white walls and oak Pews either side. Leading up to a back lit cross above a blue carpeted Vestry or Sacristy which was very clean. They were ushered to some seats towards the back of the church, the Pastor was in his pulpit and was welcoming everybody.

'And a special welcome to the Rogers family and the Smith family. First timers at our sanctum.'

Then he went on about the lives of families and how family life had changed, today with the onslaught of technology families were segregated, privacy was more important. 'We need to bring back the family life to our community, we need to stop the progress of the big brother situation, and yes, it is a situation. That has grown out of control, we need to slow things down and remember who we are, remember life as it used to be before the internet and the mobile phone took over.'

The Pastor was right in what he was saying, but how do you stop progress! After the sermon the congregation were given a couple of songs to sing and then the sermon concluded and it was over. After everyone had left the church, Pastor George came over to both families.

'Thank you for attending our church, what did you think of the topic today?'

'Well, you were correct about technology, but it's an uphill battle to convince people to use less of it,' said George.

'Yes, I know, but it's my battle and there's only one way forward for me and the church, right, shall we get on with the rehearsal?'

They were taken to the pulpit at the Vestry area of the church and the Pastor got out his book on the wedding ceremonies and opened the book. He read through the relevant section and made sure that Jake and Corrine knew what was going to happen, and were ready to take the wedding vows and adhere to them. Nathan and Rick were then showed their roles in the ceremony and understood what had to be done. They both nodded their heads in agreement and that was mainly it, the rehearsal went well and everyone knew their places and what to do on the big day.

They left the church and Jim told them that he had booked dinner at the Redfeather bar and they should drive there and talk about how the rehearsal went. It was agreed and they got into their cars and drove off in the direction of the bar, it wouldn't take long to get there as it was only a small town.

When they arrived at the car park and got out of their cars, Jim got them together before going inside, there was music that could be heard from the car park.

'They got a band in tonight?' asked George.

'Yeah, it's a country band that they are trying out,' said Jim.

'Sounds good,' said George.

As they entered the bar the music was louder and they were met by a waitress. 'Hi, are you the Rogers family?' She asked.

'Yes, and the Smiths as well, how did you know?' asked Jim.

'I was told to expect you around this time, please follow me.' She led them to a table near a window and not too near the band. She got their drinks order and left to get their drinks from the bar.

'Why have we never come here before to eat?' asked Debbie.

Jim looked puzzled, 'I'm not sure, maybe because we thought it was a bar and not a restaurant,' he said.

The waitress returned with their drinks and put the tray on the table, after handing everyone their drinks she asked for their food order. They had a quick look through the menu and ordered, Jim and Debbie ordered burgers with fries and a salad.

'I think Corrine and I will have the same, how about you, George?'

'You know what, I will have the same as well.'

Food was ordered and they were listening to the band who were covering some George Strait songs.

'You know, they are not bad' said George. 'I've got some of these songs at home, I'm a big fan of George Strait,' he said.

'I must say, they are good,' said Debbie. After a few minutes, the food arrived and it actually looked like the menu.

'You know the fast-food sector can learn a few things from places like this, serve you food that looks like the picture,' said Jim.

'It's so annoying when you pick something from the picture on the board and when it arrives it looks flat and nothing like the photo.'

He was moaning, but it was a valid point, and they all agreed before eating their food. There was quiet for a few minutes while they savoured the burgers.

'Well, son, did you listen to the Pastor at the church, and are you OK with what's going to happen?'

'I think we are both happy, it's not rocket science, so yeah, we're fine.'

'It was pretty quick, not at all what I expected,' said Corrine.

'It's not what it used to be like when we got married,' said Debbie.

'Churches have changed from traditional services to more modern ones I suppose, so long as they keep the correct wording in,' said Jim.

So, the ceremony was discussed and dinner was enjoyed by everyone.

'We must do this again, this was enjoyable, I didn't realise how much I missed this,' said George.

There were smiles all round, and Corrine looked at her dad with saddened eyes, remembering her mother and how they used to be so happy together.

'Don't worry Dad, we will, I promise.'

She reached over to hold her dad's hand on the table and they looked at each other and smiled. Kris came over, after they finished the meal.

'Everything OK, folks?'

Jake replied, 'Yes thanks, Kris, it was as pictured.'

They all laughed but Kris was a little puzzled. 'What we mean is, that you get exactly what you see on the picture, we compare that to the fast-food joints,' said Jim.

'Oh, I get it now, well that's how we do things here, maybe they should learn from us,' they laughed again at his comment.

'Anyway, what I came over for was to say that tonight's dinner was on the house, an early wedding present.'

'You don't have to do that, Kris,' said Jake.

'It's the least I can do Jake, you're a hero around here after what you did the other night.'

'Look, anyone could have done the same thing,' said Jake.

'Don't sell yourself short, Jake, when push comes to shove the true heroes step up.'

They thanked Kris and got ready to sit back and enjoy the music for a little while, the waitress cleared the table and just left the wood table with a candle in a vase after wiping it down. They were left with just their drinks and time to sit back and take in the atmosphere.

'Well! Jim, how do you feel?' asked Debbie.

'I'm happy, our son is getting married, we couldn't ask for a better daughter in law and what is there to go wrong!'

Debbie held his hand and looked happy as they sat and watched the band play one of George's favourite George Strait song 'Got to Get to You.'

Jim and Jake were going to work on Saturday, but they opening the shop at 10am to give them a little time to recover from tonight. Nathan didn't work on Saturday's as yet because he was still on trial, but Jim saw that he learned very quickly. Nathan was happy at the shop and saw a career in this business, and he enjoyed working with Jake and his family. Jim had decided that if Nathan was serious about making a career working for him, that he would send him to evening classes and learn more about business studies. Then he and Debbie would be able to take more time off work, giving them more time to spend together. Once Nathan had proved himself, he would sit down and talk to him about his future.

Chapter Thirty-Four

Corrine woke up at 8am and thought that she would go to see Jake, sitting on the edge of her bed she reflected on her mother, and wished that she was here now. She would have loved her mother to be with her to see the wedding, a sadness fell over her and her eyes welled up. She got up and walked to the window and looked out at the sun shining through her net curtains and sighed. George was in the dining room drinking a cup of coffee and had taken a paracetamol tablet as he was feeling a little pain on his chest. Corinne saw him take the tablet while she walked into the room.

'You OK Dad?'

'Yes dear, just got a slight headache.' He lied to her because he didn't want to her to worry about his health.

'Well, you take care and drive slowly if you are not feeling well, I'm going over to see Jake in a little while sot out final preparations.'

'OK, dear, I will see you later, I should be done at work by 2pm, I'll call you and maybe we can go out for dinner tonight.'

'OK Dad, see you later, and be careful.'

He left the house and waved to Corrine before driving off. After breakfast, she went to see Jake at his home. When she got there and was at the door, she thought to herself, 'What a fool. Jake was at work today.' She forgot; Debbie opened the door.

'I thought it was you,' she said. 'Sorry, I forgot that it was Saturday and Jake is at work.'

'That's OK, come in and we can have a coffee.'

Corrine went inside and Debbie went into the kitchen and got a cup to pour Corrine a cup of coffee. 'Here you go dear,' Corrine took the cup and sipped it straight away. 'Thanks!'

'Look Corrine, we were meaning to talk to you and Jake, regarding after the wedding, have you thought of where you would like to live, I mean we would love for the both of you to move in with us, but there is your dad to consider. I don't know if he is expecting you to move in with him.'

'We have thought about it, Dad would be on his own and I think he was expecting us to move in with him.'

'That's fine, if that's what you two want, I mean you are only ten minutes down the road, it's not that you are miles away from us.'

They finished their coffee and smiled at each other, 'I wish my mum was here to see all this, she would have been in her element,' said Corrine with a tear in her eye. Debbie went over to her and put her arm around her to console her.

'I know how you feel dear, I know that I can never replace your mother, but you are like a daughter to me, and I'm here if ever you need anything.'

They hugged for a little while and even Debbie had a tear in her eye.

'Hey! I have an idea, as she left the embrace. Let's go shopping,' said Debbie.

Corrine wiped the tears from her eyes, 'Are you sure?'

'Yes, I don't have a lot to do at the moment, so yeah! And with that, they got their things and left the house to hit the shops for some girl time.'

While in the car, Corrine was telling Debbie about her dad. 'You know, he will be so happy when we tell him that we are moving in with him, it will seem like a family in the house again.'

'You should tell him when he gets home later today, what time is he working till?'

'I think he is working till 2pm today, there is a function on, probably around eight pm, but he has people to cover for him.'

'I have an idea, what's his favourite dish?'

'I know he likes a good Italian dish, spaghetti and meatballs, but I have never made that before.'

'Don't worry, we will cook it together at your place.'

'Well, I know what we are going shopping for then,' said Corrine.

She couldn't ring her dad but he would certainly be surprised when he got home.

'Why don't you guys come over for dinner tonight, Jake would like that, wouldn't he?'

'If that's what you want, Corrine, then it's a deal.'

Debbie would tell Jim about dinner plans and Jake too, Corrine cheered up and the tears had long dried up but not forgotten, as they drove off to the shops.

There were a lot of people shopping in Green River, the sun brought out the shopaholics in their droves and the retailers appreciated the business. After visiting a few dress shops and purchasing some items, Corrine decided to give Jake a call.

'Hi Jake.'

'Corrine! What are you up to?'

'Oh, I am shopping with your mum and we are going to make dinner for my father tonight, are you busy at work?'

'It's not that busy but we have had a few people in this morning, listen, do you want to meet up for lunch?'

'We'll see how the shopping goes. I will call you later OK!'

'All right, see you then, I love you!'

'Love you too babe!'

Chapter Thirty-Five

George was on his way to work and was on Astle Avenue when he started feeling a pain in his chest again. His first reaction was to massage his left side of his chest to relieve the pain, he thought it was indigestion, but as he got further, the pain got worse. He pulled over to one side of the road and stopped the car, he was sweating a little now and the pain wasn't letting up. He started to get worried so he got his phone and called Dr Adams, who was a friend of his, and looked after his wife during her last days.

'Hi Doc, it's George Smith.'

'Oh, hi George, I was just thinking about you, isn't that strange.'

'Doc, I got a bad pain in my chest and I'm sweating real bad.'

'Where are you, George?'

'I'm on Astle Avenue by the river, I've pulled over to the side of the road.'

'How is your breathing, George?'

'Difficult, I'm struggling to catch my breath.'

'OK George, look, I'm gonna make my way over to you, just loosen your shirt around your neck and try and relax, I'll be with you in ten minutes.'

The doctor called the hospital and told them to get an ambulance over to Astle Avenue as soon as possible, there was a potential heart attack in progress.

George was finding it difficult to breathe and started to panic, he put the air conditioning on full blast to try and stop the sweating but was getting hazy vision now, he could feel his left side of his body start to go numb. He tried to dial Corrine's number and found it difficult but managed to ring her number, she picked it up, she was at the Moll with Debbie.

'Hi Dad, what's up?'

'He could barely speak, he muttered her name and then said nothing, all she could hear was hoarse breathing.'

'Dad! Are you alright, where are you, are you at work?'

'What's the matter, Corrine?' asked Debbie.

'It's Dad, I think he is in trouble, he can hardly speak!'

She was getting a little panicked and Debbie was trying to calm her down.

'Where is he?' asked Debbie.

'I don't know, I thought he was at work.'

'Dad! Can you hear me?'

Her voice was getting louder. All she could hear was silent breathing. He was trying to get some words out but was struggling to actually speak.

'Keep him on the phone, Corrine, I will ring Jim to let him know. Maybe Jake can trace George's route to work and see if he is somewhere along the route.' Debbie rang Jim.

'Hi dear, there's a problem with George, he rang Corrine and he doesn't sound so good, can you ring his work and see if he is there?'

'I will get Jake to do that but I will call sheriff Jones as well he might be able to help.' Meanwhile, the ambulance was near to where George said he was and Dr Adams was in sight of George's car. He pulled up behind the car took his bag and got out of the car and rushed over to see George.

When he reached the car, he opened the door and George was slouched in the seat, he felt his pulse and it was very weak. The ambulance pulled up next to the car and two of the Paramedics got out and came to where the doctor was.

'How's he doing, Doc?' asked one of them.

'Not good, he has a weak pulse, we need to get him in the ambulance and get him breathing.'

They went back to the ambulance and got the stretcher, and within minutes, George was lifted onto the stretcher and placed in the back of the ambulance.

The paramedic put the oxygen mask on him and administered the air, Dr Adams put his stethoscope on and placed it on George's chest, he looked concerned, 'Get the defibrillator, he is not breathing!'

Within seconds, they opened his shirt and placed the pads on his chest. One of them shouted, 'Clear!' and administered a charge, his body lifted and then dropped, nothing happened.

'Again!' said Dr Adams.

His body lifted and dropped again, there was a weak heartbeat. The ambulance driver had the sirens on as they sped to the hospital, they were only minutes from there. They were trying to save George.

'What's our ETA?' asked Dr Adams.

'Should be there in three minutes, the sirens were loud and lights flashing as the ambulance sped down the road towards the hospital. The roads were pretty clear of traffic so there would be no hold ups on the way. Dr Adams left his car with George's car because he needed to be in the ambulance with him, he got his phone and rang Debbie, they had been good friends ever since they first came to Green River.'

'Hello Debbie, it's Dr Adams, I'm here in the ambulance with George Smith, he's having a heart attack.'

'Thank you for calling, Doc, Corrine's going out of her mind with worry, how is he doing.'

'He is not doing too well, listen we are taking him to Castle Rock Medical Centre and we should be there in a couple of minutes, can you bring Corrine there as soon as possible?'

'Yes, Doc, we're on our way.'

The ambulance reached the hospital and there were hospital staff waiting with the trolley to take George in to the emergency unit where they were waiting for him. Built only a few years ago at the end of Uinta Drive, it has top of the range medical equipment and has plenty of parking spaces. The medical staff came out to the ambulance and wheeled George into the emergency ward, where he would be attended to by a heart surgeon Narinda Patel, he was installed at the hospital two years ago. He straight away looked at George and checked his pulse.

'We gave him CPR in the ambulance to keep his blood flowing and administered aspirin,' said Dr Adams.

'Thank you for doing that, doctor, we'll take it from here.'

Dr Patel ordered his team to take George straight to the 'Cath lab' this is where they will use a procedure called percutaneous coronary intervention (PCI) this was to restore blood flow; the doctor suspected a blockage of the coronary artery. This was dangerous for George and they would have to act fast to restore his heartbeat. George was in the 'Cath lab' and Dr Adams went to see the family, who were now at the hospital.

Debbie and Corrine were at the reception area waiting by the chairs, they didn't want to sit down because of the urgency, Corrine was welling up and Debbie was doing her best to keep her calm. Jim and Jake came through the doors and saw Debbie and Corrine and went towards them, Jake rushed straight over to Corrine and hugged her.

'How is he?' asked Jake.

'I don't know, we are still waiting for the doctor to see us, I'm worried, Jake.'

Jake held her hand, 'He will be OK, he is strong.'

Dr Adams came out and walked to where the family were congregated and spoke to them, 'Hi Corrine, sorry to meet under these circumstances, your dad is being looked at by a leading heart specialist, they are doing everything they can for him.'

'Can I go and see him?'

'It's best that you stay here, they won't let you see him anyway.'

'George has the best people looking out for him, the surgeon will be out to see you as soon as he can.'

Just as he said that, Narinda Patel came over to the family, and gathered that Corrine was the daughter. He went over to her and introduced himself.

'Hello, I am Dr Narinda Patel and I will be looking after your father, he is in good hands and we will do our best for him.'

'What's wrong with him?'

'He has a blockage in one of the arteries, and suffered a STEMI, which is a myocardial infarction, we have to try and unblock this as soon as possible. He is being prepped as we speak for surgery. I will update you as soon as I can.'

He left to go to the operating theatre and a nurse came over to the family and asked them to wait in the waiting area which was near the front of the hospital. The full glass windows showed the rugged mountains in the distance, they sat by a round table on some chairs and the nurse said that she would get them some water.

When she returned, she brought some paperwork for Corrine to fill in, they needed George's medical details and insurance details. She left the jug of water with some plastic cups on the table, and said that she would pick up the paperwork in a few minutes. They were anxious to find out how George was, Jake was consoling Corrine and he poured her some water in a cup.

'Do you want a coffee?' She looked at him.

'Water will be fine, thanks Jake.' She took a sip and held the cup in her hands looking towards the reception. Debbie came over to Corrine.

'We had better get these forms filled in Corrine, they will need this back today.'

Corrine picked up the pen the nurse had left on the table and proceeded to fill the form; Jake was with her as she did so. The operating room was busy with everyone trying to save George's life, the surgeon wore glasses and they were getting steamed up because of the surgical mask that he wore and the nurse had to keep wiping his glasses when asked. He was worried because he could not restore the flow of blood to the right artery. George was growing weaker and the fight in him was gone.

The surgeon had done everything he could to save his life, but it wasn't enough, he halted the surgery after the machine flatlined for more than a minute. There was nothing left for him to do but surrender to the fact that George Smith had passed away, at least George had died without any pain, but that didn't make the surgeon any happier.

The sun was beating down relentlessly and it was unusual for this time of the year, Narinder Patel came through the double doors into the reception area a few minutes later and looked dejected, he. Approached the family. He was not looking very positive.

'I'm sorry, but I tried all that I could to save your father but there wasn't any fight left in him. He passed five minutes ago.'

Corrine broke down and was crying. 'No! No, he must be just resting, please try again, he is strong, please try again.' She begged and Jake held on to her, he also had tears in his eyes. Jim went over to Narinda, and shook his hand.

'I'm sure you did everything you could, thank you for trying…would it be OK for Corrine to see her father?'

Debbie came over to and gave him a hug. 'Oh Jim, what are we to do?'

'We do what we always do, we stick together like a family and see this through, we go on to make sure George is never forgotten.'

'Can I see my father please?' asked Corrine, there was a nurse with the doctor.

'The nurse will take you to see your father, are you sure you want to do this? Just give her a few minutes to get the room set up for you.'

George's body was taken to the aftercare room, the nurse will bring Corrine and Jake first of all to identify the body and then give her bereavement advice before George's body is taken to the mortuary for final preparation. The hospital guidelines had to be followed, a few minutes later, Corrine and Jake were taken to see George. Debbie and Jim stayed in the reception area, working out what to do next.

George's body was placed in a hospital bed in the room, as they walked in Corrine took one look at the bed and broke down again. Jake held her tight.

'I'm right here with you, come on.' He helped her walk towards the bed. George's face was looking peaceful, like he was sleeping, she was expecting him to wake up at any moment.

Corrine got to the bed and sat on the chairs placed near to the edge of the bed, the white cotton sheet covered his body, just his face was exposed. She took hold of his hand and held in her hands.

'Oh Dad, what am I going to do now without you?' She put her head down on the sheet next to his shoulders and the tears kept flowing down her face and dropping onto the sheet. After ten minutes, the nurse came in to the room.

'Sorry, Corrine, but we have to get your father ready for the final stages,' said the nurse.

Corrine took one last look at her dad, and got up with help from Jake and walked away. As she left the room she turned one last time, to see her father, the finality was apparent and she turned and walked away back to the reception area.

George's body would now be taken to the morgue, and from there to the funeral home where the body will be washed and drained of blood then embalming fluid will be injected into the body via the carotid artery, this is done to preserve and sanitise the body. Corrine was not in a fit state of mind to arrange any funeral arrangements. So, Jim and Debbie were going to handle that, Jake took Corrine out of the hospital and put her into his car. His mum and dad would stay at the hospital to make all the arrangements for George's final resting place and sort out the death certificate. Dr Adams was with Jim and Debbie.

'I'll get the death certificate released Jim, can you drop me to my car on your way home, I left it next to George's car. I have his keys; you will have to pick his car as well and drop it home.'

Jim took George's keys off him and looked at them for a few seconds.

'I know, I've seen this too many times, to a lot of good people, the next few days will be difficult but I'm sure you two can handle it.' He left them to go and sort out the death certificate, Jim hugged Debbie and they just looked around at the hospital in silence and sadness.

Chapter Thirty-Six

Jake had taken Corrine back to his house and made her a cup of coffee, her eyes were red and swollen from all the crying, he sat her down on the couch while he got her the coffee. She looked at him.

'I have no more tears; I have used up all my tears and can't cry anymore.'

He came over to her to try and console her.

'Here drink this, I will get you some paracetamol, it will help, you need to try and get some sleep later.'

'Thanks for being there, Jake, I don't know what I would have done without you and your family being there.'

'I'll always be there for you, and we will get through this, I don't want you to worry about a thing OK.'

She looked at him and sipped her coffee, Jake came and sat next to her on the couch, they just sat and stared at the switched off the television.

Half an hour had passed when Jim and Debbie came into the house, Debbie had dropped Dr Adams to collect his car and Jim took George's car and dropped it at George's house. He kept George's keys in case Corrine forgot her keys.

'How are you doing Corrine?'

'I'll be OK, just need time to try and make sense of all this.'

'Well, you are not to worry about anything, Jim and I will take care of all the funeral details.'

Corrine found some tears again. Jake held on to her. 'We'll get through this,' said Jake.

Jim didn't say anything to Corrine about dropping George's car to the house in case it upset her.

'Well, I'm going to make some lunch, none of us had a chance to eat anything, so I'll make something light, OK?'

Corrine nodded and Jake smiled at his mother.

'Corrine, is there anyone that you would like us to call, any family you want to tell?'

Corrine wiped her tears with a hanky that Jake had given her.

'My grandmother and Dad's brother, I've got their phone numbers in my diary in my bag.'

Corrine took out her address book and gave Debbie the two phone numbers. 'I'll give them a call and let them know what happened, do you want to say anything to them?' asked Debbie.

'I'm not ready to talk to my family yet, can you please do that for me?'

'No problem, dear.'

Debbie went into the kitchen and used the phone there and contacted Corrine's grandmother first and told her the bad news, she was heartbroken, Debbie had told her that she would let them know when the funeral was and if she could contact any other members of the family it would help. The grandmother agreed and Debbie then rang George's brother.

'Hello, is that David Smith?'

'Yes, who is this?'

'You don't know me but my son is getting married to Corrine, I'm Debbie Rogers. Well, I have some bad news to tell you, your brother George passed away earlier today.'

'What!'

'Yes, he had a heart attack and was taken to hospital, Corrine was with him and Jim and I are sorting out the burial details, to help Corrine out.'

'I can't believe it, I thought he was quite fit, what with his job and all!'

'I don't know what to say, how is Corrine doing?'

'She is taking it hard, that's why I am ringing you and not her.'

'Well, thank you for all that you are doing, do you need any help with anything, I still can't believe it.'

'I will send you details of the funeral and if you want to see George, there is an open casket viewing in two days time at the funeral hall.'

'Yes, I will want to come down and pay my respects, can you do me a favour and find me some hotel numbers please.'

'No need for that, you can stay with us or at George's house.'

'Please send me details and thank you for what you are doing.'

Debbie was going to send them details once she and Jim got everything together. They finished lunch and then Corrine said that she wanted to lie down for a little while, Jake took her to his room and told her to sleep in his bed, he would help his mum and dad to get all the details for the funeral.

The day went by quickly and everything was arranged and Debbie sent details to Corrine's family. The wedding was on the back burner at the moment. They were not sure if there would still be a wedding, time is a healer but how long? One thing at a time, thought Debbie to herself.

Debbie took George's keys from Jim; they would have to go to his house to get one of his suits and shirt and tie for the undertaker. George's body had to be dressed for the viewing. Jim and Debbie left the house and told Jake to keep an eye on Corrine, while they went to George's house, the day was going quickly and it would soon be evening. They would need to take the suit tomorrow morning to the undertaker and then speak to the town hall to get the burial booked in. This was moving very quickly, these procedures normally take longer, but this was a straight forward heart attack, and Dr Adams sped up the process.

George had a shared plot with his wife at the River View Cemetery which they kept spotless. George would be buried alongside his wife, that was something that he always wanted. The next job would be to sort out a solicitor for the will reading, Corrine would have to arrange that, Jim and Debbie were not family. That wasn't going to happen until she was ready, that would be a job to discuss with Corrine tomorrow. Corrine was out for the count. Jake stayed in the bedroom until she fell asleep, then came downstairs, he wasn't very hungry and Jim and Debbie didn't have much of an appetite either.

'How is she doing?' asked Debbie.

'She's fast asleep. I think she's all cried out, it's best we let her sleep, it will do her good,' said Jake.

'Do you want some dinner, Jake?' asked Jim.

'I'll get something a little later. I'm not that hungry.'

'I know how you feel, we lost a good friend today, and it's going to take some time to get over this.'

Jim went into the kitchen, and looked around trying to get some sort of enthusiasm to move forward.

'Well, I'm going to make myself a snack, do you want anything dear?' asked Jim. Debbie nodded.

'I'll have a ham sandwich please dear, there's some cut slices of ham in the fridge.'

'You sure you won't have anything, Jake?' asked Debbie.

'Since you are in the kitchen, why not!'

Jake went to help his father make the sandwiches while Debbie put on the coffee, there was silence in the Rogers household as they sat down to eat their food. There was reflection all around on the day's events, tomorrow would be a busy day, Jim would have to go to the shop and leave Debbie to handle Corrine, he had no choice but he would only work half day.

'I have made an extra sandwich and left it in the fridge, in case Corrine gets up later,' said Jim.

'Thanks, Dad, I appreciate all you guys are doing for Corrine.'

'We are family, Jake, that's what we do, everything will be alright don't worry, son.'

Chapter Thirty-Seven

The next morning, the breakfast table was set, Debbie had got up earlier to get breakfast ready, the smell of bacon cooking would certainly get the rest of the family up. Corrine was up and was staring out of Jake's bedroom window, looking at the river and beyond. Sunlight reflecting of the river made it looked that there were diamonds floating on the water. Thinking of her father and mother both gone, but she knew that they would always be with her and she would never forget them. Jake came into the room; he slept downstairs because he wanted to give her time to herself.

'Hi, babe, are you feeling better this morning?' She turned to him and rushed towards him, then hugged him.

'Oh Jake, tell me everything is going to be alright.'

'As long as I am here, you have nothing to be scared off, you're part of this family now, Corrine.'

They both went downstairs the smell of bacon was too much to resist, she was feeling a lot better and coming to terms with her loss.

'Good morning, dear, you are looking much better, come and sit down, you must be hungry,' said Debbie.

'Yes, I am a little hungry, thank you for taking care of things, I'm really grateful.'

Jim was already at the table just about to eat his breakfast, there was scrambled egg, biscuits, bacon and pancakes on the table. Debbie had brought a fresh pot of coffee and placed it on the table.

'You must think that I am a burden, I've just dumped myself on you.'

'Certainly not, don't you ever think that Corrine, we are family and you will always be part of us,' said Jim.

They sat down at the table and enjoyed breakfast; Corrine certainly had an appetite after missing dinner yesterday.

'I think that I would like to go home after breakfast, I need to get used to living there without Dad, it will feel strange, you know, expecting him to be there and all.'

'You will have to take it one day at a time Corrine, and we think that Jake should stay there with you,' said Debbie.

Jake got the car ready and Corrine picked up her handbag and went to the front door.

'Take care, dear,' said Debbie.

Corrine walked towards the car and then got in. Debbie closed the door and turned to Jim, 'I hope she will be alright; it's going to be tough walking through that front door.'

'Jake will be with her, they will be fine,' said Jim.

Jake and Corrine arrived at her home and Corrine was taken aback at seeing her dad's car in the drive, she thought for a moment that all this was a dream. But reality hit home as soon as she got out of the car and a cool breeze touched her face, it woke her up and she realised the situation. From a moment of exhilaration to sadness, her face changed, Jake took her by the hand and walked her to the front door, she took out her keys and opened the door. The house was in darkness so she opened up the front room curtains and then the patio curtains, the light was instant into the room, she felt a little chill as she looked around.

'Let me put the coffee on, it will make you feel better,' said Jake.

'Thanks Jake and thanks again for being here.'

'Look, enough with the thanks, you don't have to do that all the time, I'm not going anyway and you and I, were together, we will get through this OK!'

Corrine looked at him and smiled a little then looked around the room again and then went upstairs to her dad's room first and opened the door. The curtains were open and the room was neat and tidy, George always kept a tight ship, that was his Navy training, once installed it barely left him. She went over to his dressing table and saw her mother's picture in a silver frame taking pride of place, he never remarried or even saw another woman after she died. She picked up the picture and held it to her chest.

'Oh Mum, keep him safe.' A teardrop rolled down her cheek and she held onto the picture for a few moments.

'Corrine, coffee's ready!' said Jake.

She seemed to wake up, as if she were asleep. 'Coming!' She replied putting the picture back on the dressing table. She came downstairs and went over to Jake.

'I don't know if I will be able stay here on my own, I miss my dad so much.'

'Look Corrine, you can stay with us if you want, or I can move in with you.' He gave her a cup of coffee and he had one as well.

'We have the rest of Sunday to sort out what you want to do, either way, you will be fine, trust me!' Jake sipped his coffee and smiled at her. Jake asked her if she wanted to go down to the river, to a place they went frequently when they wanted some alone time, a place to think. She agreed and they left the house and got into the car, the drive was only ten minutes away and the fresh air would probably do her a lot of good. Jake parked the car when he reached their destination, they walked the short walk to the river to where a bench was placed, for people to rest and look at the beauty around them. Jake walked over the bench and Corrine was behind him, when all of a sudden, she felt a cool wind rush through her. She caught her breath for a moment.

'Oh my god, Jake! It felt like my father's spirit just went through me, my god what was that?'

'It's just a wind the indigenous people call "Chaparral". It means wind of the spirits, they believed in the afterlife, they would bury their loved ones high on stilts. This would give their spirit a better chance of reaching the heavens. That's amazing, it felt so weird though.'

They sat down on the bench and stared at the river with its relentless flowing silky waves and the calming sound of the water as it navigated its flow around the rocks in the riverbed. This was certainly working as they just sat and reflected on life, she was in a happy place.

Chapter Thirty-Eight

The week went by so quickly, Jim and Debbie had arranged everything for the funeral on Friday noon, Pastor Taylor would be presiding and there were around twenty people who would be attending. The funeral service was to be held at the church and then on to Riverview Cemetery where Corrine's mother was buried. The cemetery was like an oasis in the middle of the desert, a patch of green intended to initially be a park when first created in 1944. Adorned by Elm and Maple trees, it was paradise amidst a rocky outcrop of land with rugged mountains for a backdrop.

The arrangement was for the hearse to collect George's body from the funeral parlour, then on to Corrine's house with two other limousines. They were for the immediate relatives, and close friends, they would then would be driven on to the church. After the church service the procession would then leave from there to River View Cemetery.

On the day of the funeral, Corrine was getting ready in her bedroom, Jake had been staying with her during the week. His parents would meet up with them at Corrine's house and George's brother and his wife were due to arrive anytime soon. They were flying in from Syracuse in Kansas and were staying with Jim and Debbie, they would fly back to Kansas on Saturday. Gerald, George's brother, and his wife, Julia had moved to Siracuse in the nineties, he was the older brother and only surviving relative. George never had a close relationship with him and they grew distant over the years.

The time was approaching eleven o' clock and the hearse pulled slowly into Corrine's drive, Jake was looking out of the lounge window.

'The hearse is here, Corrine and Mum and Dad are here as well with your uncle and aunt.' She was downstairs just sorting her bag out.

'OK, I'm ready.' She looked at herself in the long mirror by the front door, she was wearing a black knee length dress and waist jacket. Jake opened the front door as the hearse came to a standstill. Just then, Debbie, Jim with Gerald and

Julia arrived by car. They got out and paid their respect to George's coffin draped in the American flag before going into the house. Gerald came over to Corrine.

'Hi Corrine, I'm, your uncle Gerald and this is your aunt Julia, we're sorry to meet under these circumstances.'

Corrine shook his hand and then went over to hug Julia.

'Nice to meet you, it's nice to finally put faces to the names.'

'My, you've grown so much, the last time I saw you was when you were in diapers.' Corrine smiled at her and then pulled away.

'I have seen pictures of the two of you, that Dad used to show me I'm glad you came.'

The funeral director came up to them who were standing at the door. 'Good morning, let me know when you are ready and then we can proceed to the church.' They were all dressed in black, the driver of the hearse as well as the director, Jake had on a black suit as did Jim, Debbie had on a grey dress with black knotted crescent shaped fascinator hat, the weather was good, slightly windy, but not raining. They got into the limos and the sign was given to the funeral director to carry on. The hearse slowly made its way out of the drive followed by the two limo's, Corrine and Jake's friends were going to meet them at the church as were Dalores Jackson and Dr Adams.

They made their way to the church and Pastor Taylor was waiting at the doors and he would walk in front of the coffin to the catafalque. A moveable platform where George's coffin would be rested, then the ceremony would begin. The church was filled with the friends of George and Corrine, there were about thirty people seated, the organist played how great thou art as the pallbearers brought the coffin in slowly. Jake and Rick were supporting the coffin at the rear, Corrine and Debbie along with Jim and George's brother and wife followed behind. Heads bowed with the odd sniffling along the way, when they reached the catafalque, they gently laid the coffin down and then moved away. The Pastor came up to the coffin and sprinkled holy water onto George's coffin.

'In the name of Christ,' he said loudly and then walked to the pulpit to deliver his sermon. Corrine was in tears and Jake was comforting her with his arm around her, they were seated in the front.

Midway through the sermon, the Pastor called to Jim to deliver the eulogy, Jim arranged to do this because there was nobody else who knew George that well. Corrine wanted Jim to do this gesture, he got up to the pulpit and took out a sheet of paper from his inside jacket pocket to read to the congregation.

'I have had the pleasure of knowing George for just a little while, and I wished I had known him longer, George was the kind of man who would do anything for you. He always thought about others before himself, he will be missed by me, my wife, Debbie and all who knew him. He leaves behind Corrine, who we have grown to love as our own, and will always be part of our family. Please say with me the Lord's Prayer as we say goodbye to a dear friend.'

The Lord's Prayer was read out loud and everyone was in fine voice, the funeral service came to an end and the pall bearers took up their places by the coffin. George's coffin was raised again and onto its final resting place at River View Cemetery, Jake and Rick were again called to help with the coffin. The organist played Amazing Grace as they slowly walked through the church and to the awaiting hearse. The rest of the congregation got up from their seats and followed George's coffin.

The hearse slowly pulled out of the church grounds followed by the family and then friends. There were some members of the public waiting along the road outside the church, workers that worked with George and just some passers by paying their respects.

The mood was sombre as they entered River View Cemetery, the large elm trees lined the way to where the final resting place was to be. Their green leaves rustled in the wind and except for the sound of the vehicles, that was the only sound in the cemetery, it was a calm serene morning. Dr Adams had picked up Nathan and Rick; they would also follow the line of cars to the final resting place for George Smith.

Sheriff Jones followed up behind in his police car, he was good friends with George and he was shocked when he heard that George had passed. George was always a strong person and was never ill. The hearse pulled up alongside the plot where George was to be buried, the other cars pulled into the car park. And when the vehicles had stopped, they all got out and walked towards where the burial was to take place. The funeral director had four men with him who were there to lower the coffin into the ready dug grave. They needed two more people to help carry the coffin and Jake and Rick volunteered, the back doors were opened to reveal the stars and stripes draped over the coffin. The coffin was brought out and then raised, Jake and Rick placed their shoulders under the coffin and they were ready.

The walk began towards the grave site and the people took up positions around the already dug grave, there was green astroturf carpet draped over the soil and two sets of ropes which were to be used to lower the coffin. Pastor Taylor was standing by the grave with his prayer book in his hand, the coffin was brought to where it was going to be rested, the last farewell from all his friends as they stood waiting to say goodbye!

'O God, by whose mercy the faithful departed, find rest, bless this grave and send your holy angel to watch over George Alexander Smith. As we bury the body of our brother, deliver his soul from every bond of sin that he may rejoice in you with your saints for ever. We ask this through Christ our Lord, Amen.'

The four pallbearers gently lowered the coffin by using the ropes slowly into the grave, Corrine had tears in her eyes, consoled by Jake who was by her side. When the coffin was laid to rest, Corrine walked up to the grave and picked up a handful of soil and gently threw it onto the coffin.

'Goodbye Dad, I will miss you.'

One by one, the mourners came to the grave to throw in some soil and pay their respects. Corrine stared at her dad's grave and turned and walked away with Jake, she was saddened and now had to start a new chapter in her life. Memories are a wonderful thing; she will have enough to last her a lifetime.

Chapter Thirty-Nine

Antonio Garcia from Don Pedro's restaurant had arranged for his restaurant to be open just for the funeral procession and closed to the public until the afternoon. Everyone made their way there and there was food laid on by Antonio, he didn't want any payment for that. The Pastor was there, Dr Adams, the sheriff and all who attended the church service. The Rogers family and George's brother and wife sat at one table. The men got up to get some food for the girls. There was some easy listening music being played in the background to try and ease the day away, Corrine and Jake got up and wanted to thank the people for their support. So, they went to each table to speak to everyone in turn, then returned to the table.

'Corrine, eat something, you did a great job today!' said Debbie.

'I'll have a little bit to eat, and thank you both for arranging all this, I would have never got through this without you.'

Antonio came over to the table. 'You guys doing OK?'

They stopped eating, Corrine got up and went over to him and gave him a hug.

'You are a wonderful man, thank you for this.'

She was referring to the use of the restaurant and not wanting any payment. 'George was a good person, and I will miss him so don't mention it.'

'It was my pleasure.' She sat back down and Antonio went to speak to the other people, to make sure everyone had food. The afternoon was drawing to close and people were making their way home, they came to the Rogers table on their way out to commiserate with Corrine. It was finally the turn for them to leave and they thanked Antonio again, Rick and Nathan were going to stay behind to help Antonio clear up.

Jake was going to stay with Corrine at her house and it looked like this was going to be permanent because she did not want to be alone. Jim and Debbie took Gerald and Julia home. They would be flying back home on Saturday afternoon.

Debbie was going to take them to the airport as Jim would be at work. When they got inside Debbie made a start on the coffee, they sat down and reflected on the day's events.

'Listen Jim, I want to thank you again, I know I've said it before, but honestly, you have done more for George than I could ever do, so thank you, and you must let me pay towards the cost of everything. These things are not cheap, and he was my brother so I insist on paying something towards the cost.'

'Happy to help, and I meant what I said about your brother, he was a great guy, and I know you won't take no for an answer, so I will email you when you get back and we can work something out, OK!'

Gerald agreed and left it at that, Jim would work out what he had paid out and then send Gerald an amount to pay. They sat down on the couch and each had a cup of coffee and were just going to sit and relax. Julia wanted to thank Debbie for her hospitality.

'Debbie, it is really nice of you to put us up and pick us up from the airport, you two will have to come over to us, you know once everything has settled down.'

'Don't mention it, and thanks for the offer, we can certainly do with a break.'

'We were happy to help, and don't worry about Corrine, she is part of our family now.'

'I know, we could see how she is cared for by you guys, well, if you ever need anything please let me know.'

Later that evening the Rogers would be having a takeout meal, they had had a good meal at Antonio's so they decided on just a light meal. Jim was ordering in a pizza; they couldn't be bothered to cook. The time was approaching 8pm when the pizza arrived and they all sat back and enjoyed the food, Jim asked Jake and Corrine, but she still needed some time to get over today. Jim put a movie on, so that for a little while their minds would be elsewhere.

Saturday morning started with Debbie making breakfast for the four of them, it was early and they would have plenty of time before they had to drop them to the airport. After breakfast, Gerald went upstairs to get their suitcases and bring them down.

Jim had got his car keys and he and Gerald put the suitcases in the car, Debbie and Julia followed them into the car. Jim was going to work so he said goodbye and got into his car and drove to work. Debbie set off to Corrine's house so that Gerald and Julia can say goodbye to the both of them before going to the airport.

Jake was up and was just making breakfast for himself and Corrine, when he heard a car pull up into the drive. He saw who it was and called up to Corrine.

'Corrine, your aunt and uncle are here, probably to say goodbye.'

'OK, I'll be down in a sec.' He opened the front door and waited for them while they got out of the car.

'Morning,' said Jake. 'Corrine's just coming down.'

Debbie got out of the car and smiled at him, 'Morning son, Gerald and Julia are on their way to the airport and wanted to say bye to Corrine.'

'Corrine's just getting ready, come in.'

They reached the front door and entered the house.

'I can't remember the last time I came here,' said Julia.

'Corrine was just a baby then,' said Gerald.

Corrine had come down by now and walked towards them, she went over to Gerald and hugged him.

'Thanks for coming down,' and then went over to Julia and hugged her as well.

Julia was welling up and got a tissue from her bag.

'You've grown so much, I was telling them, the last time I saw you was when you were just a baby,' she blew her nose in the tissue and tried to pass it off as hay fever.

'Well young lady, you know where we are, take care of yourself, and don't be a stranger,' said Gerald.

'We have to dash if we're going to catch our plane, but we will see you again and spend more time together.'

'Yes, we will be in touch,' said Corrine.

'Jake, you take good care of her, I can see that you two are good together, take care.' He shook Jake's hand and then they left for the airport. Jake and Corrine waved them off from outside the front door and saw them drive away out of the drive.

Chapter Forty

Green River had grown over time from only six thousand inhabitants to over twenty thousand in the space of ten years. And with the growth, there was expansion and business, Jim's business was a niche market and the more houses that got built, was an opportunity for a sale. Jim always wanted to work for himself, he liked to have his own fate in his hands, his business was built on trust and expertise, his customers liked him for that.

He had a great knowledge of the industry that he was in, and with that came experience and with experience came calm in front of customers. That's why selling came very easy to him. Obviously, he didn't want to be too big where he was not in control and couldn't meet demands, so he had to stayed a small business. Jim always started the business to pass it down to Jake, that's what family was all about, in his mind.

He was hoping that Jake would want to take over the business, but he hadn't really sat down and talked to him about it. Jim would have to wait until after the wedding and then approach and sit down with Jake and Corrine and discuss their future.

Debbie got back home from dropping Gerald and Julia to the airport and decided to have a lazy day and not plan any activities for the day, Debbie gave Corrine a call.

'Hi Corrine, how are you feeling today, I didn't have much time to talk to you earlier.'

'I'm fine, thanks for asking, what are you guys doing today?'

'Well Jim is at the shop and I was just going to chill and not do too much.'

'How about you?'

'Well, I know we have to sort out the wedding and I am OK with doing that, so if you have time today maybe we can pop over and go through some things!'

'Are you sure dear, we didn't want to put this on you at this time, we even thought of moving the wedding date. I mean everybody will understand.'

'No, I think Jake and I want to get this done, Dad wouldn't want us to put this off.'

'OK, then, why don't you and Jake come over and we can have lunch and then go through the wedding plans.'

'That's great, I'll tell Jake and we will see you later.'

'Debbie rang Jim and told him what was going to happen later today.'

'Do you think it's a good idea to put this on Corrine so soon?' asked Jim.

'The wedding is only weeks away, and we have no other choice, otherwise we will have to cancel the wedding and wait later in the year,' replied Debbie.

Debbie got Jim's approval and then said bye, she got up from the settee and walked into the kitchen.

'I had better think about making lunch, I hope they will be OK with chicken?' She said to herself. Debbie was going to make chicken salad, a light dish and not too difficult so she got on with that, she was thinking about Corrine as well and wondering if she really was OK. Debbie couldn't help thinking about George, so much had happened in a short space of time. Jim surprised her when he walked into the house, he had finished early and put a sign up at the shop that they were closed for lunch.

'What are you doing back, I thought you were at work!'

'He came over to her.'

'I need to be here when Corrine comes over, this is more important after all, so! What do you want me to do?'

'But what about the shop?'

'Don't worry, I put a 'Closed for Lunch' sign on the door, I will go back after lunch and open up again, all under control.'

When Jim came into the house, he noticed an envelope on the floor by the door and picked it up and while talking to Debbie, he opened it.

'Hey! Look at this, Jake is to get an award.' Debbie rushed over to Jim.

'Let me see,' she sat down next to Jim and held one page of the letter.

'Oh my god, yes he is, but they are supposed to contact Jake first, aren't they?'

'You would have thought so.'

They carried on reading through the paragraph intensely, 'Let's wait till they come over and we can tell him,' said Jim.

At that precise moment, the front door opened and Jake walked in with Corrine right behind him.

'We're here!' said Jake.

'Hi son, hi Corrine, lunch will be ready in half an hour.'

'How are you, Corrine?' asked Jim.

'Yes dear, how are you, did you get some sleep this time?'

Corrine came to the lounge and sat down on the settee. 'Yes thanks, I feel much better having slept in my house. I feel that I can stay there and know that Dad is always going to be there, he has never really gone.'

Debbie had a sad moment and wiped her eyes, then put on a little smile. 'Oh Jake, Dad has something to show you.'

Jake came over to where Jim was sitting and sat down next to Corrine on the settee, Jim picked up the letter and found the page where Jake was to receive an award.

'Look at this son, the town council are to give you a bravery award next Friday at the town hall for your part in saving lives at the rodeo.'

'What!' said Jake as he reached over to receive the letter from his dad.

'Why! I don't really want or deserve that,' he said.

'It's their way of showing their appreciation for what you did, son,' said Jim.

'I know Dad, but really, anyone would have done the same faced with the same situation.'

'Don't short change yourself, not everyone would have the courage to do what you did, you should be proud, son.'

Corrine held his hand. 'Face it, Jake, you're a hero in this town! So just accept it and smile when they give you the award.'

And with that, they put the letter down and started to talk about the wedding, but they would have to eat first. Debbie was putting the finishing touches to the lunch and called them over to the dining table.

'We can discuss the wedding once lunch is over.' Lunch consisted of fried chicken, potato salad, green salad and biscuits. They sat down and enjoyed their food and once that was over it was down to the serious talk about the wedding plans.

Chapter Forty-One

It was Monday morning and Jake was at the shop along with Nathan, Jim was going to come in a little later. As it was his business, he decided to let Jake handle the shop, get him used to doing things related to work on his own. He was showing Nathan how to prepare the paperwork for the new orders when the shop door opened, it was Bandy.

'Hey Jake my boy, good to see you again.'

Jake was surprised and paused for a moment before saying anything.

'Bandy! Great to see you, what brings you to this part of town?'

He walked to where Jake was and leant on the counter. 'I heard about your girlfriend's father, how is she doing?'

'Yeah! She is getting over it slowly, it takes time.'

'I'm sorry for her loss, I met him briefly, he was a good man, sad loss.'

Just then, Jim had come in and saw Bandy at the counter, he thought for a moment as he looked familiar, Jake called out to his father. 'Dad, look who's here!'

Jim was still trying to think who this man was.

'It's Bandy, he organised the rodeo and came over to talk to us after.'

'Ah, yes, now I know, how are you?'

Jim reached out his hand to shake Bandy's hand.

'Glad to meet you properly this time, so what brings you to this part of town?'

'I was about to let Jake know that there is a big rodeo coming up, it's at the Weston County Fair in Newcastle. I was kinda hoping that Jake could be persuaded to be part of the set up over there, he would get paid real well.'

Jake looked at Bandy and then at his dad, and wasn't quite sure what to say.

'What do you mean, be a part of it?' said Jim.

'Well after Jake's heroics, his name has spread around the counties.'

'I think that Jake is a natural and the rodeo is in his blood.' Jake was looking confused.

'I'm getting married in a couple of weeks, I'm not sure this would be a good time.'

'Oh no, it's not for a month yet, so you see, you have time.'

'What about the shop? Dad's depending on me to eventually take over the business.'

'Don't get me wrong, I would love you to be part of any rodeo.'

'It doesn't have to get in the way, think of it as a side business, you can still run the business side by side.'

'That's not a good idea, this business needs a lot of time spent on it,' said Jake.

'But I'm not thinking of retiring anytime soon, maybe you should think about this son,' said Jim.

'Well, I thought that I would let you know, the rest is up to you.'

Bandy put his hand on Jake's shoulder. 'You are a natural, son, think about it and here, take my card, ring me once you have decided.' Bandy said goodbye and walked towards the door and opened the door, he turned to Jake. 'I'm staying at the Travelodge, ring me and maybe you can meet me for breakfast tomorrow, oh and by the way, congratulations on your wedding, give Corrine my love.'

He closed the behind him and walked away.

'You need to think about this, Jake, think about Corrine.'

'Yeah, I know Dad, but the temptation is so great.'

'Yes, I know, look you will have to weigh this up long and hard, the business will always be here for you no matter what.'

Jake looked at the business card that Bandy gave him and then put it in his pocket. 'Well, it won't hurt to find out more about this, and think of the extra money.'

Jake was going to think about it and speak to Corrine, in his mind, he had already made up his mind, it was going to be Corrine who would decide their future. Nathan was in the background listening to everything that went on, Jim went into his office and closed the door.

'Hey Jake, he's right, you know, you are a different person, and the rodeo is exciting! I wish I had it in me, otherwise I wouldn't hesitate, I'd be gone.'

That didn't help the situation. Jake picked up some orders and went with Nathan to find the goods to mark them up with customers' names. This would take his mind off the rodeo for now, well until he got home anyway. Corrine was spending time with Debbie today, they were at Corrine's house and it was laundry day, this involved taking down the curtains and washing them. She had a laundry room at the back of the house and plenty of drying space on the washing line in the garden.

Corrine was going to cook dinner for Jake later when he got home later, Debbie had agreed to help her. Keeping busy was the best way to cope with grieving and Debbie was going to make sure that she kept her mind occupied, but in a good way.

As time passed, they were getting through the work fast and they put up the last curtain.

'There, doesn't that look better?' asked Debbie.

'The house feels brighter and smells linen fresh, thank you for so much for your help!'

'Don't mention it, what are mothers-in-laws for!'

They both laughed and Debbie could see that Corrine was in a happier place, it was time for her to go home, they hugged and she said goodbye. Corrine had to get on with dinner, Jake would be back soon.

Chapter Forty-Two

Later that night Jake had got home, Corrine had not gone back to work at the salon yet, and Dalores had told her to take the week off. She had made dinner for the two of them, steak and potatoes with green beans, Jake entered the house and closed the door behind him.

'Hey Corrine, I'm home.'

'Yes, I can see that you are, go wash up dinner is ready.'

'I could get used to this.'

'For this week you can but when I am back at work, we will both chip in.'

Jake looked at her and smiled. 'Of course, that goes without saying, I won't be long.'

He went upstairs to wash up and change into his house clothes, Corrine set the table and started to serve the food. A few moments later, Jake had come down and went into the kitchen.

'Do you need help?'

She turned to him, 'No, you sit down, we are having steak and potatoes, you OK with that?'

'Mmm, sounds and smells nice, I could eat a horse.'

He looked at her sheepishly! 'Corrine, I met up with Bandy this morning.'

'Oh yes, and what did he have to say?'

He fumbled with his steak with his fork, moving the potatoes around his plate, 'Well, he offered me a job, actually.'

'But you have a job.'

'Yes, I know, but this is in the rodeo and it's not really a job, more a try-out and the money is really good, it will only be on a Saturday.'

There was silence for a moment, she looked at him, 'Jake! You know I don't like you doing that, it's dangerous, and what about us, and the wedding.'

'Look. Corrine, I just feel that I should at least try it, if anything, to get it out of my system.' They both took a bite of their steak and there was quiet for a little while. An uneasy silence hovered above the both of them.

'Look Jake, this is what we will do, let's get the wedding done and give ourselves some time, after that we can sort out what you want to do, and if you feel that you still want to give the rodeo a try, well, then, give it a go.'

Jake looked at her, 'OK, let's do that.'

There wasn't much more to say after that, so they carried on with dinner and gave each other unsure looks in between.

'The steak is nice,' said Jake, Corrine shook her head and smiled.

'I think that I am ready to go back to work, I spoke to Dalores earlier today and she said that it might be a good idea to come back. Take my mind off things, a busy mind and all that!'

'Are you sure you are ready? If you are sure, then it will probably help, it will help.'

After dinner Corrine was in the kitchen cleaning up, Jake was washing the dishes, they worked as a team to get the jobs done. The days of the sixties and seventies, where women were expected to look after the cooking and cleaning and the men were the earners, bringing in the wages and leading a life of male dominance, had long gone. That's in the western world of course! Other countries have different outlooks on male women relationships, and women still struggling to gain independence and be free to live to their potential.

Corrine decided to go get her clothes ready for work tomorrow, the uncomfortable silence between conversations told its own story.

'Right, I'm going to get my things ready for tomorrow, what are you going to do?'

'I thought that I might play a little guitar and chill out, do you need any help with anything?'

'I don't think so, I'm pretty sure that I can manage, just one thing!'

'What's that?'

'Your guitar is at the other house!'

Jake sighed and said to himself, 'Silly boy! Oh well, I guess I'll just watch some tv then.' Jake was going to meet Bandy tomorrow for breakfast before he went to work, he rang his dad to let him know what he was doing, his dad reluctantly agreed. The wedding plans were all finished with. It was just a matter of turning up at the church and taking the vows, the timing of Bandy turning up was ill timed. But then he was only thinking of business, getting Jake would get him a lot of kudos in the rodeo circuit, Jake's exploits were well documented throughout the rodeo industry.

Bandy had a reputation and was under pressure to get Jake on board, so this was his chance to strike, he knew that Corrine had recently lost her father. Jake didn't know it yet but Bandy was on a mission and resistance was futile. He already had Jake hooked and just had to reel him in.

Chapter Forty-Three

The next morning Corrine got up and was just getting a drink of orange juice before going to work, she was looking forward to meeting other people again and getting back into the swing of things. Jake was also up and didn't have breakfast as he was meeting up with Bandy.

'OK, Jake, I'm off to work, now don't go promising him anything, speak to me first.'

'Yeah, OK, you have a good day at work, do you want me to pick you up after?'

'No. I'll be OK to walk home, the weather looks to be fine, see you later.' She then left the house and made her way to the salon Jake offered to give her a lift, but she was adamant that she wanted to take her time and walk.

Bandy was in the restaurant at the Travelodge Motel and was getting ready to sit down to have his breakfast, he had yesterday's newspaper in his hand. Jake entered the motel and was directed to where Bandy was sitting, Bandy waved to him and Jake waved back and made his way to him. There were a few people having breakfast, mostly sales people who travel and live in hotels most of their life.

'Jake, glad you made it, sit down I was just about to order what do you want.'
He shook Bandy's hand and sat down.

'Just eggs and bacon please.' The waitress was at their table, Bandy ordered breakfast with toast and coffee, and Jake's as well. The waitress took the order and left them to talk. The restaurant was fitted out in a sixties style breakfast bar with racing red leather seat stools and stainless-steel legs along the bar and red chairs around tables elsewhere in the restaurant.

'Well, are you ready to join me and make yourself a lot of money?' asked Bandy.

'I'm going to think about it and wait till after I get married, before committing myself.'

'That's fine, my boy, you take your time. I said that there was no rush, I understand everything, and there is no problem.'

Breakfast was served and they both started eating. 'If I wasn't getting married and was single, I would have no hesitation in signing up, it's what I have always wanted to do.'

Bandy had a smile on his face, he knew that Jake was more or less hooked and it was just a matter of time when he would get him to sign on the dotted line. Bandy gave Jake a flyer on the Weston County Fair where the rodeo was to be held, it had the address on and a map of how to get there.

'I will be there three days before the show and if you were to join then you would need to be there at least two days before. For training and the heads up of what to expect.'

Jake took the flyer and looked at it. 'I'm not promising anything, but I will be in touch,' said Jake.

He then got up and thanked Bandy for the breakfast and made his way out of the restaurant and out into the sunshine and the car park. He got into his car and closed the door and again looked at the flyer, Bandy was at the hotel lounge window looking at Jake in his car. He had a cigar in his hand and put it to his mouth and smiled as he took a puff. Jake drove off and was on his way to the shop where his dad and Nathan were, he put the flyer on the passenger seat and concentrated on the road.

On the way back home, Jake was travelling down Shoshone Avenue and as he was driving past the State Bank, he noticed something that didn't look right. He noticed a black Camaro with its engine running and emitting a lot of exhaust fumes and there was a young a man sitting in the driver's seat wearing a bandana over his mouth. He drove past and then further up turned the car round to take another look. Jake drove past and then pulled up past the bank and stopped, he picked up his phone and called Sheriff Jones.

'Hi Sheriff Jones, this is Jake, this may not be nothing, but there is a suspicions car outside the State Bank and the driver is wearing a bandana over his mouth.'

'Hi Jake, where exactly are you?'

'I pulled up just past the bank and I am parked.'

'Look Jake, don't do anything foolish, just stay in your car, we are on our way, now promise me that you will stay in your car!'

'Sure thing,' said Jake as he put down his phone.

But Jake was curious and didn't listen to the voice of reason, he got out of his car and walked towards the bank, he was going to go into the bank. He thought that he would pretend to be a customer, there was a man by the doors of the small bank and he didn't look like he worked there. Jake opened the door and walked in. The man at the door had on a bandana as well and had a gun in his right hand, he signalled Jake to go over to where three other customers were sitting on the floor. Jake saw another man by the desk pointing a gun at the assistant behind the desk, she was looking very nervous as she was filling up a bag with notes.

Jake knew that the police were on their way he just had to try and stall proceedings, the bank robber at the desk took the filled bag of money and turned to his partner by the door. 'OK, let's get going, nobody get up and don't try and be a hero, we have guns.'

He waved his gun in the air to show them that he had a gun, Jake had to do something, he was a few feet from the bank robber at the desk so he decided that he would make his move. He got up and rushed the bank robber inflicting a football tackle on him, throwing him to the ground. The bank robber was taken by surprise and lost his gun in the process, the man at the door panicked and ran out of the bank. But Sheriff Jones and his deputies were already on the scene and had arrested the getaway driver in the car, the bank robber dropped his gun on the floor and raised his hands in the air. Inside the bank, Jake had got up and as the other bank robber was on his feet Jake threw an almighty punch and caught him on the chin. He was knocked onto the floor and by then the deputies had entered the bank, and pointed their guns at the man on the floor.

It was all over and the man got up slowly and raised his hands, he looked at Jake with disbelief in his eyes. Sheriff Jones came over to him and put handcuffs on him.

'You are under arrest; the deputy will read you your rights.'

Then he turned to look at Jake and shook his head. 'Jake! Is that you over there, I thought that you were going to stay in your car.'

The other customers got up by now and were clapping Jake and cheering, the bank manager came out from behind the desk to show his thanks as well. He was in his late fifties and wore a dark grey suit and tie.

'Young man, thank you, thank you for showing such courage and saving the day, the bank will be in touch, what's your name, son?'

Jake told him and the bank manager raised his eyebrows.

'The same Jake Rogers from the rodeo storm?'

'Yes sir, look, I don't want a lot of fuss over this, I don't want my parents to know that I acted so recklessly.'

'Look son, you have just stopped a bank robbery and no matter what I say it's gonna be out there, so you had better get used to the adoration, you are a hero!'

He shook Jake's hand and thanked him again and the went to speak to his staff holding the bag of money retrieved from the floor. The would-be bank robbers were all inside the police cars and on their way to the cells, Sheriff Jones came over to Jake and put his hand on his shoulder.

'Jake, what am I going to do with you! I have to say, in my opinion, you are a hero, but you have to let me do my job in the future, I don't want you to get hurt. These guys are dangerous, you were lucky this time, you make your way home and I'll catch up later.'

Jake left the bank to applause and turned and waved to them apologetically, he was humbled and did not glorify his bravery. Thats what this was, bravery! And he was fast getting a reputation that he probably didn't want; he was just in the wrong place at the right time. What was he going to tell his parents and Corrine, he decided to go home to see his mum first and explain his story.

It took him ten minutes to reach work and after parking the car he went into the shop and was greeted by his dad.

'Well, how did the meeting go?' asked Jim.

Jake came over to him.

'It went well, it's what I expected, and I told him that the wedding comes first, and that I would think about it after that.'

'That's a step in the right direction son, now we have some orders to sort out and Nathan has a great idea on how to make more space upstairs.'

'Dad, I gotta tell you something, no doubt you're going to hear about it anyway from Sheriff Jones.'

'What is it, Jake, what have you done?'

'Well on my way back to work, I sort of got involved in a bank robbery!'

'What!' said Jim.

'Now don't get angry, but I noticed that something was wrong so I called the sheriff and ended up in the bank at the same time and intervened sort of!'

Nathan had come down by now and was all ears.

'Go on Jake, tell us more.' Jim looked at Nathan and sighed. 'So, you got involved.'

'So, you got involved, didn't you?'

'Well, I couldn't just stand by and do nothing, so yes I got involved.'

Just as he was about to tell his dad everything the phone rang, Nathan answered it. 'It's Sheriff Jones, Mr Rogers!'

Jim went over to speak to the sheriff, 'I'm not done with you yet!' He said to Jake.

'Hello sheriff, I suppose you are going to tell me about my son!'

'Hi Jim, and yes, I was, look don't be hard on him, he just can't stop being a hero, there was nothing I could have done, I told him to sit still, but you know your son!'

'Yes, I know!'

'Look the bank are gonna be sending Jake a thank you of some sort, you know to say thank you for what he did.'

'Were there any weapons involved' asked Jim.

'They had guns, but none were fired and to tell you the truth, the guns were not loaded, but Jake didn't know that, neither did anyone else! So, take it easy on him, you've got a good one there Jim, see you later.'

Jim put the phone down and looked over at Jake who was talking to Nathan, explaining what happened and Nathan watching in awe. He went over to them.

'OK, Jake, there is a problem, you seem to attract danger, but not in a bad way, I don't know quite what to do with you. But you have to be more careful, the bank robbers had guns you know.'

'Yes, I know.'

'It's a good thing that their guns were not loaded.'

Jake looked shocked. 'Well, I didn't know that, boy, that was a bit of luck!'

'Luck had nothing to do with it, just remember in future, be careful son, now you are gonna have to explain all this to Corrine. Before she finds out from someone else, it won't take long before that happens, this is a small town.'

Nathan was standing at the bottom of the stairs to the mezzanine and looking at Jake with a grin on his face. Jim looked at him and told him to get back to work, Nathan waved at Jake and went back up to the mezzanine. He decided to ring Corrine, 'I'm just going to ring Corrine, Dad.'

'She is at home isn't she?' asked Jim.

'No, she decided that she wanted to go back to work, to get her mind occupied.'

Jake went into Jim's office and made the phone call there, it was a little more private. The phone rang and Dalores picked up the phone.

'Hi, this is Jake.'

Before he could say anything else she interrupted, 'Hello Jake, it's Dalores, Corrine said that you would ring, she is just finishing with a client, she won't be long.'

'How is she getting on?' asked Jake.

'She is doing fine, sometimes it's better to get back into the swing of things and keep yourself busy, how are you doing?'

'Oh I'm fine, so much happening in my life at the moment.'

'Yes, I saw the newspaper yesterday, congratulations on getting a medal, did you know about this before it was printed in the paper?'

'No, it came out of the blue,' said Jake.

'Well, you take care Jake, Corrine is here now.'

She gave the phone over to Corrine. 'Jake! How did the meeting go?'

'Never mind the meeting, how are you, are you feeling?'

'Yes, I'm fine, I'm glad that I came back to work, I feel a little better about everything.'

'That's good, I just got say something before you hear it from some else.'

'What is it Jake, you are worrying me now!'

'I was involved in a bank robbery earlier and I sort of got involved and helped the police out.'

'Jake! How does this happen to you, are you alright?'

'Yes I'm fine, there is no need to worry now, look everything was OK the bank got their money back and the robbers got arrested. So, all is good!'

'I don't know what to say, why does this happen to you? I suppose this is going to be on the news and in the papers, you are making a name for yourself in this town. Well, I'm glad that you are OK and I'll see you after work.'

'Now let me get back to work and I'll see you at five.'

Corrine put the phone down and carried on with her work, Jake was going to pick her up after work and he was feeling a little happier. For now, he was concentrating on the wedding and other matters regarding the wedding.

Mrs Conzalez, a regular customer, came in for her 2pm appointment. She always had Corrine fix her hair and was excited to see her in the salon.

'Oh Corrine, you're here, I am sorry to hear about your father, I didn't expect you back at work so soon. Are you alright, dear?'

Corrine turned to her and smiled. 'Yes, I'm fine, Mrs Conzalez.'

'Oh, call me Connie dear, Mrs, makes me feel old.'

'OK, Connie, why don't you take a seat over here.'

Connie followed her to a chair by a sink and sat down in the black leather chair.

'So how was your trip to Tucson?' asked Corrine.

She shook her head and looked at Corrine. 'A big mistake!' She said, 'I should never have gone there with that man, he left me for a younger woman. And after all that money I spent on him.'

'Oh, I'm sorry to hear that, anyway you are back home now, and with friends,' said Corrine.

'I know dear, it's so comforting to know that you are here, can I have the usual please Corrine.'

Mrs Conzalez was a Spanish lady who came to Green River from Tucson when she was in her fifties, she married a man younger than her by fifteen years. She was well off as a result from her last marriage, her husband was a lawyer and left her a small fortune when he died at an early age. Corrine got the young assistant to make Connie a cup of coffee while she got her settled in the chair.

'How are you coping dear, I know what it's like to lose someone.'

'Oh, I'm fine, I don't know what I would have done if it wasn't for Jake and his mum and dad, they have been a great help to me.'

After talking and fixing Connie's hair, she was looking like a different woman, she showed Connie the mirror from the front and sides.

'Well, what do you think?'

'As usual, a great job, thank you dear.'

She got up from her chair and the assistant brought Connie's coat and Corrine took the coat and put it around Connie.

'There you go, Connie, you're good to go, going clubbing tonight?'

She laughed. 'The only clubbing I'll be doing is to the chicken that I'm going to cook later!'

They all laughed at the salon. After paying her bill, Connie gave Corrine a large tip, it was fifty dollars.

'No, I can't accept this, Connie, that's way too much.'

'Don't be silly dear, it's a wedding present as well, I know you and Jake are going to be good together, take care dear.'

She left the shop leaving Corrine with a big smile as she put the money in her jeans pocket, Dalores came over to Corrine.

'I couldn't overhear your conversation with Jake, what happened?'

'Oh, he got involved in another situation, this time at the bank, something to do with a bank robbery.'

'My god, he sounded fine when I was talking to him.'

'He is OK, trouble just seems to follow him around,' said Corrine.

'Yes, you had better keep an eye on him, what's it like to live with a hero?'

Corrine smiled and went back to tidy up her area where she worked earlier, she still had Jake on her mind and was worried about him.

Chapter Forty-Four

Jake was parked outside the salon. The time was approaching five o' clock and he could see Corrine heading towards the door of the salon. She waved at him and opened the door and walked into the street and over to where Jake was waiting in his car.

'Hi Jake!' said Corrine, she got into the car. She then reached over to give him a kiss on the lips.

'I've missed that all day,' said Jake.

She smiled back at him.

'How about we go get some food at Verizon, instead of cooking tonight!' said Jake.

Corrine thought about it for a moment. 'OK, let's do that, I don't feel like cooking tonight, you can tell me all about your day.'

Verizon was only a short walk away but they had a car parking space outside the restaurant, so Jake decided to drive the short distance and park outside. Jake told her exactly what happened on the way, she didn't know what to say, just hugged him and accepted that her husband to be was a hero.

The Verizon was an older style restaurant with rustic Wild West furniture tables and chairs, it had wooden floors and a bar which resembled a Wild West saloon bar. The owner was Miguel Lopez, again another person from Mexico who settled in Green River fifteen years ago. As they entered, they heard a voice.

'Hi Corrine, Jake, come in.'

Jake acknowledged him and walked into the bar room.

'Hi Miguel, how you doing?'

'I'm fine, sorry to hear about George, Corrine, he was a good customer.'

Corrine had a sad face for a second or two and then looked up at Miguel and gave a little smile.

'I'm fine, thanks for asking.'

'Are you staying for food?'

'Yes,' said Jake. 'What's good tonight?'

'We always have good food here, just like mama used to cook!'

'Great, we will have what you recommend, Miguel.'

'Take a seat and I will bring it over to you, what will you have to drink?'

'I'll just have a beer and Corrine, what do you want?'

She looked at the drinks on the shelves behind the bar for a few seconds, 'I think I'll just have a white wine spritzer, Miguel please.'

'No problem, I'll bring them over to your table.'

They went over to the table by the window and sat down, the evening was still bright outside as people were making their way home from work, traffic normally built up around this time. There was a jug of water on the table with some glasses around it. Jake picked up two glasses and poured some water into the glasses. He gave one to Corrine and one for himself. There is something about clear cool water in a glass jug that makes you want to just drink it all down.

'Well, this is nice, no washing up to do,' said Jake.

She smiled at him, 'Don't get used to this, we still have to manage our money.'

Now, he smiled. 'We're fine, babe, we have all that we want, I can't wait for the wedding and to start our lives as Mr and Mrs Rogers.'

Miguel brought their drinks over to them and dinner was not far behind, 'I heard that the State Bank got robbed and the police were there and apprehended the culprits, I also heard that you were there Jake, you are getting a rep, I'm proud to have you in my bar, Jake.'

One of the waitresses brought the food over to the table that Miguel had recommended. He brought them the house special, which was chicken enchilada, his chef that cooked for him was an authentic Mexican cook, and this was his mother's recipe.

'Tell me what you think after, you will be amazed, enjoy!'

He walked back to the kitchen and Jake and Corrine tucked into the food. Jake took the first bite; he closed his eyes and the enjoyment was on his face for all to see. He smiled.

'Oh, this is amazing, he was right.'

Corrine took her first bite, and the same expression was on her face. 'Wow! I'm glad we came out to eat.'

Miguel was behind the bar now and looked across at them. Jake stuck his right thumb up in his direction to indicate satisfaction, Miguel smiled and carried on with his work. They both finished dinner and ordered coffees, it was getting on for seven and they were in no rush to go home just yet. Jake knew that he would have to see mother later and explain again what happened to her. They talked for a while about the wedding and if they should go on a honeymoon.

'Your mum told me to tell you not to book anything.'

'Why didn't they say anything to me!'

'They probably didn't have time to tell you, anyway, they have something planned.'

'I wonder what it is!' said Jake as he sipped his coffee.

After paying the bill, they waved goodbye to Miguel as they left the restaurant to go home. The wedding was two weeks away and they were counting down the days. Jake had to go and see his parents now and then would go home to Corrine's house.

Chapter Forty-Five

Time passed quickly, and there were only two days left until the big day, Corrine was in her room trying on her wedding dress. Debbie was with her to help out.

'Wow Corrine, I feel so proud, just look at you, the dress fits really well.'

Corrine got choked up and her eyes welled up, she came over to Debbie and hugged her, 'Corrine, be careful, your dress!'

Corrine hugged anyway. 'It's only a dress! I feel like I have another mother.'

Debbie put her arms around Corrine. 'And I have a daughter,' she said.

She let go and took a step back and looked at Corrine, 'You are going to fit right in with our family, I'm so glad you two are together.'

Jake was downstairs trying on his suit, and again it fitted perfectly. Jim was helping him with his tie, he didn't like wearing ties so wasn't good at doing them up.

'Well Jake, you will be a different man come Saturday, and your mother and me, well we have something to tell the both of you.'

Debbie and Corrine came downstairs, Jim looked at them coming down the stairs, 'That's good timing.'

When they were all together Jim and Debbie stood together and looked at the both of them, 'Your mother and me have bought you two a honeymoon, now don't go getting too excited, it's not a trip to Europe or anything, but it is a week in Flaming Gorge Resort.' Corrine held Jake's hand.

'That's so thoughtful of you both, but you shouldn't have, but thank you so much,' said Corrine. Jake looked at the both of them.

'Thanks, Mum, thanks Dad.' This is fantastic!

Jake smiled and gave them both a hug. 'I wanted to send the two of you to Niagara Falls, but your father decided on this other place.'

'Anyway, the two of you have two days left and you had better get your bag packed for the honeymoon, your mother and I have been to Flaming Gorge before, a long time ago and you will love it there, take your fishing gear, Jake, the trout there are gigantic.'

Corrine looked at Jake sternly.

'You are not going there to do any fishing, Jake Rogers, you are going to spoil me something rotten, and then some.'

Jake looked at her. 'Of course, dear.'

They all had a laugh and Debbie wanted to go through the wedding plans again, just to make sure that everything was going to go well on Saturday. Jim was closing the shop on Saturday to make sure they had more time for the wedding, he was considering closing on Friday as well but he had some customers coming in to place orders. Corrine was given the week off by Dalores in preparation for the big day, so everything was set for their big day, the last day of being single and the first day of the rest of their lives.

Chapter Forty-Six

The big day had arrived, the skies were a little overcast at first but the forecast was for a sunny day albeit a little colder than normal. Corrine had booked Dalores to come to the house and style her hair, Dalores didn't need to be asked twice, she was excited and jumped at the chance.

Corrine's friend, Tammy and her friend, Beverley were also going to meet up at the house, to help Corrine get ready. Jake was staying at his house, because Corrine didn't want him to see her dress, tradition still holds well, even in Green River. The time was approaching 8am and there was a knock on the front door. Dalores went to answer the door with a drink in her hand.

'Hello girls, come on in,' Tammy and Beverley walked in.

'So, you started early,' said Tammy.

Dalores closed the door behind them. 'It's a great excuse to start early, you don't get married every day, put your stuff down by the table and relax, Corrine will be down in a second,' said Dalores as she went to the kitchen to get the girls a drink, champagne was the drink for today. Dalores brought a couple of bottles with her.

'This is so exciting!' said Beverley as she took a glass of champagne from Dalores. 'I shouldn't really, but like you said, it's not every day you have a wedding to go to.'

Tammy gave in and accepted a glass as well; Corrine came down the stairs.

'I thought I heard you guys, thank you for coming over, I would be struggling on my own.' Another knock on the door and Tammy opened the door, Debbie had arrived with yet more drink, this time a bottle of wine.

'Good morning girls!' She said as she walked in.

Corrine was all smiles. 'Hi Mum!'

The girls looked at her when she said that.

'It's about time you called me that,' said Debbie.

'Now, what's happening with you?'

'Well, Dalores, is going to sort my hair and makeup out Tammy is doing my nails and you are my dress queen.'

'Right the first thing is, to slow down on the drinks and let's get going. We have two hours to get you to the church.'

And with that, they got themselves organised and Dalores sat Corrine in the chair and Tammy pulled up a small table to where Corrine was sitting and put Corrine's hands on a towel on the arm of the chair. Her nails wouldn't take very long because Beverley was working on the other hand. Things were now running smoothly and over in the Rogers household they were just eating breakfast.

'How are we doing for time, Dad?'

Jim looked at his watch.

'We have time, how do you feel son, are you ready for this?'

Jake put his coffee down and looked up at his dad who had finished eating. 'You know, I'm fine, I really thought that marriage would scare me, I mean, with the commitment and all that.' He then picked up his coffee, 'I'm happy, Dad, really happy.'

Jim smiled, 'I'm glad son, now finish your breakfast, now where is Nathan and Rick, I told them to be here in plenty of time.'

'Don't worry, Dad, they will be here.'

As they were clearing up, there was a knock on the door, Jim went to the door and opened it. 'Well! You two are going to live a long time, we were just talking about you, come on in boys, better late than never.'

He closed the door and they had their bags with them. 'Where are your suits?' asked Jake, 'Oh, they are in the car,' said Rick.

'He's only joking they are in the bag.'

'Well, you better get dressed, we need to be at the church in 45 minutes,' said Jim. Rick took out their suits, they had been pressed at the shop before they were delivered to them. Jim told them to go to Jake's room to get dressed, Jake and his dad were already dressed and just had to put on their jackets. Jim tied Jake's tie; Jake wasn't good at that.

'There you go, son, let me look at you,' Jim stood back and took a long look at Jake, 'I'm proud of you, son.'

He was about to well up but Jake saw what he was about to do.

'Don't go crying on me now, Dad. Mum will not be happy if you get your suit wet.'

Jim smiled and put his hand on Jake's arm, 'Let's go, son.' And with that they all left the house, Rick and Nathan hitched a ride with Jake and his dad. Rick had tied a white ribbon on Jake's car before they came into the house, Jake had a big smile when he came outside and saw his car.

Both cars made their way out of the drive and on to the church, they had to get there before Corrine and the girls to get everyone in their right seats.

A limousine had been ordered by Jim for the girls, he wanted them to arrive in style. The girls had had a few drinks, but they were jolly and not drunk, Debbie saw to that. She checked that they had everything before they left the house and once in the limousine, she tidied Corrine's wedding dress to make sure it didn't get creased. The limousine pulled away and they were on their way and any last-minute nerves were dispelled and left in the house. Corrine was happy but she glanced behind as the limousine pulled away from the house. She stared at the house and thought about her dad, a moment of sadness came upon her at that moment.

'Are you OK dear?' asked Debbie, she turned to her and brought a smile to her face.

'Yes, I'm fine now,' they looked at each other, Debbie knew that Corrine was thinking about George, she missed him as well.

Chapter Forty-Seven

Jake was at the church in the front seats with his best men, his dad was across the aisle where he would wait for the nod that the bride had arrived. His job was to walk Corrine down the aisle, he would replace George. Corrine had asked him to do this. The two best men were sitting next to Jake and Nathan was just checking to make sure he had the rings. He was nervous, but reassured when he found them in his waistcoat pocket.

Pastor George Taylor was getting ready at the altar and he signalled over to Jim, which meant that they were here and his cue to get up and get ready to walk Corrine down the aisle. The family and friends were all seated and looking towards the entrance in anticipation of the bride walking down. Jim was in position and he nodded to the Pastor who signalled the organist to start playing the wedding march. Debbie had already made her way to the front seat; she would wait for Jim after he had finished walking Corrine down the aisle. The organist started playing and Corrine walked slowly to meet up with Jim with the bridesmaids behind her, he took her hand and smiled at her.

'Are you ready, dear?'

Corrine looked at him, 'Yes, I think I am.'

They walked towards the altar, the friends and family all looked toward Corrine, cameras were clicking and there were smiles all around. Corrine was making her way to Jake who was standing in front of the altar, he turned to her as she stood alongside him. When she reached the altar, Jim let go of her hand and went to sit down with Debbie, Jake reached out his hand and held Corrine's hand. The Pastor asked them to come forward to the altar and then he spoke.

'Dearly beloved, we are gathered here in the sight of God, to bring together these two people. Jake and Corrine, who are ready to start their journey together in life by getting married, in God's house.'

Jim held Debbie's hand and looked at her with love in his eyes, they were transported for a moment to when they got married. The wedding service went on till it was time for the rings to be exchanged, Nathan got up and walked towards the two of them. He gave the rings to the Pastor who put them on a velvet small cushion, he then asked Jake to hold Corrine's hand and asked him to repeat after him.

'Corrine, I give you this ring as a symbol of my love for you, I will always be there for you and you will never walk through life alone.' Jake repeated word for word and then it was Corrine's turn, she did the same, she started a little jittery, but thought of her dad and got through it.

'Jake and Corrine, you have both made your commitments to each other in the presence of God, and if there is anyone here today who questions these vows, please stand up and speak or forever hold your peace.' He turned to the people briefly and then back to the couple, with the authority vested in me and under the laws of the land, I now pronounce you, husband and wife, please go in peace.

They kissed each other to a loud cheer from the guests, and turned to walk back to the desk where they had to sign the register. Jim and Gerald were going to be witnesses, when that was finished the newly married couple walked down the aisle as husband and wife, hand in hand. When the music started, everyone started laughing, Nathan had arranged for a Johnny Cash song to be played, 'A Thing Called Love' and Jake looked around to see who put the song on. Nathan raised his hand sheepishly as he looked at Jake, who laughed and carried on walking with Corrine out through the doors.

When they got outside, the sun was shining and there were people lining the front of the church, ready to throw confetti, the photographer was taking pictures as were some of the guests. The photographer gave the signal when Jake and Corrine were in range and the confetti rained from above, their aim was very good and most of the confetti hit the target. The both of them got into the limousine after taking photos outside the church, first with Jim and Debbie, then with family members, and finally with friends. Once inside the limousine, they were to be taken to the hotel where the dinner and entertainment were to be held, at the Hampton Inn. This venue was booked by George shortly before he died, a legacy left for them to remember him by.

Chapter Forty-Eight

The party arrived at the hotel and were shown to the hall where the dinner was to be held. The bride and groom were shown their table which was centred in front of the main dance floor area. The tables had a floral display in the middle, chosen by Corrine and on the bride and groom's table a floral arrangement which was stunning. Debbie had arranged the flowers, some of Corrine's favourite, she didn't want Corrine to know about, as it was a surprise. The white linen covered tables were adorned with fine china plates and gleaming silver service cutlery. The hotel manager was with them as they were seated at the table.

'Is this OK for you?' He asked.

'Perfect, you have outdone yourselves, thank you,' said Jake.

There was now a wedding cake brought to them and put onto a table in front of them, this was a present from Miguel, it was three tiered and decorated with swirls around the sides and two models of a man and a woman atop the cake.

'Oh, Jake, the cake is beautiful,' said Corrine.

Debbie sat them down next to each other. 'It's from Miguel, isn't it wonderful!' said Debbie, Corrine was so happy at this moment, she sat down and felt that she belonged at last in her life. The guests were all seated by now, there were eight people at a table and there were five tables around the bride and groom's table. Rick stood up and picked up a glass of champagne, he picked up a dinner knife and tapped the glass.

'Listen everybody, can I have your attention please.'

There was quiet in the room apart from the clinking of glasses as everyone picked up their glasses, a foregone conclusion by the guests, they knew what was about to happen.

'I was going to say can you raise your glasses, but looking around, I can see you've done this before, please raise your glasses, a toast to the bride and groom, Jake and Corrine Rogers, cheers!'

They all said cheers and consumed the champagne.

'Please take your seats, I don't mean literally! Haha.'

He was expecting more laughter but tumbleweed could have swept through the room at that moment.

'Anyway, the best men are now going to read some telegrams and cards and then after some shaming, I'm sure we can get Jake to say a few words.'

The guests were seated again and getting their glasses topped up, the lunch would be served directly after the speeches. Nathan who was sitting at the table next to the bride and groom moved his chair back and stood up. He was holding some cards in his hand and a telegram.

'I would like to firstly say, congratulations to Jake and Corrine, and get right into reading some telegrams and cards from people who couldn't make it today.'

He took the telegram first and put down the other cards on the table, he opened the telegram and read it out.

'This telegram is from Jake's uncle from Australia! Wow, I didn't know you had relatives down there! Anyway, it reads, "Congratulations, Jake. I'm sorry I couldn't make it to your wedding, but from the pictures that Jim sent me, you have a wonderful partner, take care and lots of love, signed Andy Rogers".'

There was applause from the guests, Nathan then gave the telegram to Jake and came back to his table and picked up the cards, he read through from well-wishers who again could not make the reception and then it was back to Rick.

'OK you guys, before we sit down to a great lunch which I did not prepare! I have a little speech that I did prepare earlier. Well, I've known Jake since he first arrived in Green River, and through school and finally college. He has always been there for me and anyone who needed help, and he displayed this kind of help when he saved those people in the tornado. Not caring for his own safety, he just dove in and did what came naturally to him. And not to be out done, he even saved the bank from being robbed, what a guy! The people all clapped and cheered Jake.'

'That's the kind of guy Jake is! Corrine, has always been a methodical kind of person and weighs things up before she commits, Jake will need this kind of support and she will keep him in check. So again, I raise my glass to the two of you and wish you the best for the future.'

Jake then got up to applause and moved his chair back to give himself some room, he looked at Rick and Nathan.

'Thanks guys, you did your jobs well, where do I start? As you can see, I didn't prepare a speech so I'm just going to say what I mean. Thank you all for your support in the past few weeks, especially after George was taken from us so suddenly.' He raised his glass into the air and looked up, 'This is for you George, thank you for Corrine, I will look after her for as long as I may live.'

Corrine looked up at Jake and smiled a sad smile.

'To my beautiful wife, just saying that word makes me feel whole! Thanks to Mum and Dad for all the support, through all your hard work you have built a future for me, and now Corrine. Well, I am thankful for all the people who helped us through this journey. And Miguel, fantastic cake, thank you.'

He raised his glass and put it aloft, 'To all of you, cheers.'

He got thunderous applause from the guests and some wolf whistles from the usual suspects. Jake sat down and gave the nod for lunch to be served. Almost immediately the staff were bringing food to the tables, starting with the bride and grooms table first. The menu was a three-course starting with options of soup of the day, battered mushrooms or egg salad. The main course was chicken in sauce served with new potatoes and broccoli and a side salad. The other option was fish with sauteed potatoes, greens and sauce.

The food was being enjoyed by all Jim and Debbie ordered more wine for their table and made sure that everybody had plenty of drinks. There was music being played in the background, Jake had arranged for a DJ for later.

'How are you doing, Corrine?' asked Jake as he was cutting his chicken.

'I'm fine, the food is good and I'm so happy right now, I don't want this to end.'

'There's more to come later,' said Jake.

At that precise moment, Bandy had walked into the hall, he was holding a present for the bride and groom, Jake saw him approach their table. Corrine looked up and was a little uneasy, she still wasn't sure about him and the effect that he was having on Jake.

'Jake, my boy! I'm sorry I missed the church, got held up on the road, but I'm here now, congratulations to both of you.'

He put the present on the table and took a step back, Jim saw him and told Debbie he got up and went over to Bandy.

'It's nice to see you again, let's find you a seat at one of the tables, you are staying, aren't you?'

'If I'm not intruding,' said Bandy.

'OK then, I can see a space on table six, let's get you seated and lunch has just been served, I'll get you some food to start with.'

Jim led Bandy to table six, where Miguel and his wife were seated along with Dalores, who took a shine to Bandy.

'He can sit next to me,' she said.

As she pulled out the chair next to her, Bandy went over and sat down. Jim ushered a waiter to come over and sorted out lunch for Bandy, Dalores was halfway through her lunch but she slowed down so that she could chat to him.

'So, how do you know Jake?' She asked.

'Oh, I ran the rodeo that Jake was helping out on, and because of his heroics, well, let's just say that he got my attention.'

'By the way, my name is Les, but people call me Bandy!'

'Oh, and why is that?' She asked.

'I think it goes back to my younger days, there was a song on the jukebox called 'Bandy the rodeo clown' and it was playing while I was doing my act as a rodeo clown in the ring, so it stuck ever since then.'

'And what is your name?'

She put down her fork and held out her hand to shake his.

'I am Dalores Conzales, and I own the hair salon in Green River.'

'It's nice to meet you, Dalores, and may I say, you are looking stunning.'

She blushed and smiled at him.

'Why, thank you,' his lunch had arrived and he was having the chicken as was Dalores.

They seemed to get on well and carried on with the questions to each other, after lunch had finished the dessert was served, everyone was engrossed with the food. Even Miguel was impressed, 'This food is made very well, almost as good as my food at the restaurant,' he said with a cheeky smile on his face, to which the guests at the table laughed.

Once the three-course meal was finished and the waiting staff had cleared away the plates and cutlery, it would take half an hour to get the music set up for the after party. The assistant manager came over the bride and groom's table and was doing to inform them that their room was ready for them to change before the evening entertainment was due to start.

'Your suite is ready for you, if you would like to go and freshen up while we clear away the room ready for later.'

The porter was in his forties dressed in a blue tunic and black trousers.

'If you follow me please,' he led them to the lifts and entered the open lift and took them to the bridal suite.

When they got to the door, he opened the door and gave Jake the key, Jake gave him a ten-dollar tip and took the key. 'Thank you, sir.'

He then left and Jake opened the door and picked up Corrine in his arms and carried her through the threshold. He closed the door behind him and went straight to the bedroom and placed Corrine on the floral cover duvet covered with red rose petals. There was also a champagne bottle in a silver ice bucket waiting for them, he got off the bed and opened the bottle. The cork flew across the room, to which they laughed at. He then poured two glasses half full and gave one to Corrine.

'Here you are, Mrs Rogers.'

She took the glass. 'Why, thank you Mr Rogers.'

They both sipped the drink. Corrine's wedding dress was a conversion dress which transformed into an evening dress. So, she got off the bed and started to take her dress off, Jake's eyes lit up, she looked at him.

'Don't get any ideas, I don't want to ruin my make up until after the dinner,' Jake sipped his drink and sat on the edge of the bed and watched her.

'Do you need any help?'

'Of course silly, the dress won't take itself off!'

He jumped up off the bed and went to her, he unzipped the back of the dress to reveal a white bra strap and slim soft skin naked back, he was getting aroused. Maybe it was the champagne but he found it difficult to keep his hands off her.

'Jake! Remember what I told you.'

'Yes, I know, but you haven't got make up down here.'

He was referring to her lower back and the top of her underwear.

'Jake Rogers, you will refrain from your actions and wait till tonight, do you understand?'

He backed off and she got undressed and separated her dress to turn it into an evening dress, which she then put back on. He reluctantly zipped her back up and they were ready to go down to the reception. She could see that Jake was a little deflated as he showed his puppy dog eyes. She sat him down on the bed and knelt down in front of him.

'Let's get rid of this tension, shall we?' She undid his zip on his trousers.

'What are you doing?' asked Jake.

'Relieving some stress from your body,' she replied. She began to perform fellatio on Jake, this was not the first time she had performed this with Jake, they had a healthy sex life while they were going out with each other.

The couple came out of the hotel room refreshed, well certainly Jake was, and made their way down to the reception hall. Corrine's dress was long white silk with short sleeves and a comfortable neck line. When they reached the hall, the attendants opened the double doors to a noisy room filled with people, suddenly there was quiet and Rick picked up the microphone from the stage and said, 'Ladies and gentlemen, I give you Mr and Mrs Jake and Corrine Rogers.'

Background music played as they walked into the hall to applause and more clicking of cameras, both smiling hand in hand and heading for the bridal table.

The waiting staff had their orders to move the tables around the polished light oak wood rectangle dance floor to D J was getting ready with his play list and as always, the first dance was to go to the bride and groom.

The song chosen for them by the best men was 'I Got you Babe', a song by Sonny and Cher. They thought it would get everyone in a happy mood by playing this song. Well, they were right, there were smiles from all the guests as Jake got up and reached out his hand to Corrine.

She held his hand and got up gracefully, 'Can I have this dance, babe!'

She replied, 'Of course.'

They walked to the dance floor while everyone else turned to watch. When they were on the dance floor Jake said, 'This is the first day for the rest of our lives.' Corrine was touched and gazed at him with a smile that really didn't need words to express how she felt for him.

He put his hand around her waist and pulled her towards his body and started dancing. They were not professional dancers, but they did OK as they swept around the dance floor. The rest of the guests were invited onto the dance floor by the DJ and they were all up and dancing around Corrine and Jake. Even Bandy was on the dance floor with Dalores, the evening was going well considering this wedding was organised so quickly.

Chapter Forty-Nine

The next morning, Jake and Corrine were woken by the alarm on Jake's phone, the time was approaching 8am. The sunlight shone through the curtained windows brightening the room as they were slowly getting out of bed. There was no duvet, only sheets, they could not sleep with the duvet on, it was too warm in the room. Corrine had the air conditioning on all night, they had to catch the river taxi by 10am, to start their four-day honeymoon. He turned to her and said, 'Hello beautifully.'

She smiled at him. 'How did you sleep?' asked Corrine.

'I slept well, our first night together as husband and wife, I'm hungry, are you?'

'Let's order room service,' said Corrine.

'Why not?'

Jake picked up the bedside phone and dialled the lobby and ordered breakfast. Corrine got out of bed and headed for the shower, as she reached the bathroom door, she turned to look at Jake with a naughty smile on her face.

'You coming? I might need by back scrubbed.'

And she then turned and walked into the bathroom leaving the door open, he didn't need asking twice, Jake was up and joined her in the shower. It was a spacious shower room with double glass doors, the mist from the shower soon filled the room, they embraced and started to make love in the shower. After the lovemaking, they soaped each other and started to laugh a little.

'Still trying to comprehend that we are actually married now, wow! I am so happy right now; I never want to let this go.'

There was a knock on their hotel room door, it was room service with their breakfast, the waiter had to knock a few times before they heard him. 'Just a minute!' said Jake as he grabbed a white towel robe from behind the bathroom door, he hurried towards the door and opened it.

'Hi!' said Jake.

'Room service sir, shall I bring it in?'

Jake opened the door wider and ushered the waiter into the room. 'Just leave it on the table please.'

The waiter did as he was told and then looked at Jake, probably for a tip. Jake looked at him for a second and then the penny dropped. 'Oh, sorry, hang on for a moment.'

He went to his wardrobe and opened the door, then took out his wallet, he took out ten dollars to give to the waiter; who thanked him and then left the room closing the door behind him, at this moment Corrine came out of the bathroom with no robe on. Jake looked at her. 'Well, shall we have breakfast later,' he said in a suggestive tone.

'No, I am famished,' as she put on a white cotton robe and made her way to the table and to the bacon, eggs, biscuits and pancakes breakfast. They both tucked in and it didn't take long to polish it off, they sat back in their chairs and looked at each other. Both had smiles on their faces.

'I think we had better get ready, we have about half an hour before we have to be collected outside the hotel,' said Jake.

And with that they both got dressed and packed their suitcase in readiness for their honeymoon.

When they were ready, they made their way to the lift and down to the reception to hand in their keys and pay their bill. Unbeknown to them, Jim had already arranged to pay for the hotel, as they found out when they were at the desk. They were given their receipt for the hotel stay and made their way to the awaiting river taxi, waiting at the jetty on the river. It was a short walk to the jetty from the hotel, so they didn't need a taxi. The exercise is something that they both could do after the night they both had. The midday sun was making its way to the noon slot in the sky, it was getting warmer as they reached the jetty to find their boat ready and waiting for them.

There were a few other people on the boat travelling with them, there were other stops along the way for people to get on and off, this was a taxi after all. They were ready to start their journey to their holiday destination at Flaming Gorge Resort. Jake held Corrine's hand and smiled at her. She smiled back and hugged him.

'I love you, Jake Rogers!'

'Ditto!' said Jake as the boat moved off and onward to their honeymoon.

Chapter Fifty

At the Rogers household Jim was getting ready to start making lunch, it was his turn today, Debbie was having a work free day today. He was in the kitchen getting the ingredients for his interpretation of a chicken curry, he found this recipe on line and decided to try it out. Debbie was aware of what he was about to make and she was going to just keep an eye on him, just to make sure he didn't spice it up too much.

'Jake called me and said that they were on the river boat and to thank us for paying for the hotel, he was not happy that we are paying for everything.'

'Oh, we can talk to him when he gets back, it's not every day your son gets married, were they OK?'

'He seemed fine and he said not to worry, he will take good care of Corrine.'

'I'm so happy for the two of them, I just wish George could have been here to see this, I do miss him,' said Debbie.

While Jim was getting ready to start his curry, there was a knock at the door, 'I'll go, you carry on with your curry,' said Debbie.

She got to the door and opened it.

'Hey Mrs Rogers,' it was Nathan, 'Is Mr Rogers in?'

'Yes, he is, come on in.'

Nathan entered the house and saw Jim in the open plan kitchen.

'Hey Mrs Rogers, sorry to disturb your day, I can see you are busy cooking, what are you making?'

Jim turned to Nathan, 'It's a curry, well, what brings you here on a non-work day! I just wanted to talk to you, if you had time.'

'Well, I am in the middle of making a dish that I have never tried before and I will need a lot of concentration, by the way what are you doing for dinner?'

Nathan wasn't expecting to be asked for dinner, he was a little taken aback. 'Er, no plans as yet.'

'Good! Deb, set another plate at the table, Nathan is going to have the privilege of tasting my curry.'

'Curry!' said Nathan, 'Well, I'm not sure, have you ever made this dish before?'

'Don't worry my boy, you just get yourself a drink and we can have a talk while I'm cooking.'

Nathan was shown the fridge and he opened the door and took out a coke, he was not a beer man, he closed the fridge and went over to Jim. Debbie let them get on with the cooking as she got on with setting the table, she was going to make a dessert to counteract the effect the curry, just in case, as a standby!

Jim was just getting ready to cover the dish and let it simmer. Then he would have time to talk to Nathan, he didn't know what the conversation would be about as he was busy with the recipe.

'OK, what did you want to talk about.'

'Well, I don't know how to tell you but, I was wondering if there would be any chance of a pay increase, I know I have only been there a few weeks, and I really didn't want to have this conversation. But the situation at home is strained, you know my father left us last year, and well, my mother is struggling to make ends meet.'

'I didn't know that; Jake didn't say anything!'

'No, he wouldn't, he is a good friend.'

'Well, Nathan, is your mother working at the moment?'

'She was working full time until last week, when she got bad, and her health has made her only able to work part time.'

'I am sorry for asking you this and I will fully understand if you say no, but I had to ask.'

Jim looked a little sad, Debbie had heard what Nathan had said. She came into the kitchen.

'I couldn't help overhearing Nathan, I'm sorry to hear that, what is wrong with your mother?'

'Well, she never really recovered when Dad left us, but she started taking some tablets, she was given them by her doctor to help with her depression, but she carried on taking them and now she can't go a day without taking them.'

Jim came to Nathan and put his hand on his shoulder. 'Come and sit down at the table, and we can talk a little more.'

They sat down at the table and Debbie turned the gas down to very low while they talked. 'Look Nathan, we can certainly do something about your wages, but I'm more concerned about your mother, has she sought medical advice?'

'She won't, she thinks that everything is OK, she is blinkered and I don't know what to do.'

Nathan had a tear in his eye and he reached his finger to wipe the tear away, Debbie put her hand on his shoulder.

'You are not to worry about anything, we will sort this matter out. I'm glad you told us about this, this is something you can't bottle up will talk to Dr Adams, he will be able to help, I'm sure of it!'

'And as for work, leave it with me, now it's time to start dinner, everything will be fine, now get ready to test your taste buds,' said Jim as he got up and went to the kitchen to put the finishing touches to his curry. He served the food into their plates; each was looking at each other to see who would be the first to taste the curry, Jim was being brave and looked at his plate. 'Mmm, this looks nice.'

And then he took a spoonful and tasted it, they both looked on and could see that his face hadn't changed, in fact he smiled, so they took that as a sign and started to eat. The meal was enjoyed and Debbie even put some food in a Tupperware dish for Nathan's mother, she might like it. Nathan thanked the both of them for dinner and the talk as he was waved off. He left the house a happier person. He was glad that he came and spoke to the Rogers and hopefully things were going to look up, Debbie closed the door and breathed a sigh of relief.

'What are we going to do, Jim?'

'Well, you speak to Dr Adams on Monday, I will sort out the money side of things, we are fine financially, I just didn't know that Nathan was going through this, it just goes to show, you just never know.'

Chapter Fifty-One

Jake and Corrine were well into their journey along the Green River, enjoying the cool wind from around the river as their boat powers its way through the rivers current, the river is quite deep in places and the skipper has to be weary of shallow parts of the riverbed, only experienced skippers navigate this river with a motorised boat. It is mainly used by smaller motorised boats and canoes, used by avid fishermen and women. There's good eating fish from the river as the water is so clean and fresh, the lush greenery surrounding the river all the way during its winding route is a stark contrast from the barren lands further away, this due mainly to the heat from the desert like conditions from the mountains in some parts of the terrain.

'Did you know, Jake, that there is some history to the Green River?'

Jake turned around from looking at the riverbank.

'What history is that, dear?'

'Well in 1869, Major Wesley Powell led a landmark expedition from Expedition Island, with a group of nine men and set course to the Colorado River and the Grand Canyon.'

'In 1868, the Union Pacific reached the City of Green River and that had a major impact on the area. Settlers who didn't want to go any further to Oregon stayed in towns along the river and settled down there. And did you know Jake, that during 1941 to 1945 during the world war over 1000 trains passed through Green River.'

'Well, your history certainly came in handy, and no I didn't know all that, that's impressive!'

'We should be at the resort in half an hour, are you happy, Corrine?'

She held his hand and smiled at him.

'What's not to like? I am with the man of my dreams, going to a beautiful place for our honeymoon; it doesn't get any better than that.'

They both sat back and enjoyed the mesmeric scenery as the weather stayed bright and warm along the river, the waves from the boat lapped across the bank as the boat neared the last bend before reaching Flaming Gorge Holiday Resort.

This scenery made you think that all was well with the world! But Man was ruining the planet with his greed, polluting the atmosphere with gases all for the sake of a 'Better life,' sorry, I'm digressing from the story.

Before they knew it, they were pulling up to the jetty and getting ready to disembark, the jetty was made of lumber from the forest and was over a hundred feet long. Every timber building was made from the forest, recycling at its best, they even grew their own fruit and vegetables and had a chicken farm attached. Self-sufficient as described in their brochure, The resort had its own vineyard as well, not very big but good enough for its clients.

They were met at the jetty by a holiday representative, a lady in her forties, dark haired and of Cheyenne descent; there were quite a few indigenous people working at the resort. There were six people on the boat with Jake and Corrine, two other couples a little older than them.

'Welcome to Flaming Gorge Holiday Resort, my name is Kaya Roberts and I'm a full blown Cheyenne Indian, I work here at the resort as do a lot of other tribe members. If you follow me, I will take you to get you checked in at the lodge, and then you will officially start your dream stay at Flaming Gorge Holiday Resort.'

She got them off the boat and then turned and walked along the jetty towards and on to the sandy path leading to the main lodge. The other guests followed and Jake and Corrine were at the rear of the party. The lodge was very large a typical settler style log cabin. They arrived at the lodge and walked in through the door, Kaya got them all together.

'If I can get you to check in here.' She pointed to the check in desk where there were two members of staff waiting. A young man in his twenties with blonde short blonde hair, white college student, working through the holiday.

'If I can get Mr and Mrs Whittaker up first please to check in.'

They came forward and approached the desk, a couple in their fifties.

'Good day to you, my name is Tyrone and I will be looking after you all during your stay here, if I can get you to sign in the register, please.'

They are a married couple that have been coming to this resort for the last four years and would love to live at the resort if they could, they love it so much. After they signed, they were given keys and was then led off to their cabin. The other two guests were checked in and it was Jake and Corrine who were the last to check in.

'Mr and Mrs Rogers! Welcome to Flaming Gorge, newlyweds! Thank you for booking with us, you have lodge number 13, and Tanya over there will show you to your lodge.'

Tanya, a descendant from the Crow tribe stepped out from behind the desk and approached them.

'If you follow me please, I'll show you to your lodge.'

She was in her late twenties, tall around 5'9 and very pretty. Corrine looked at Jake when she asked them to follow her, but he only had eyes for Corrine, but it was difficult not to look! They stepped out of the main lodge and followed Tanya along a gravel path that led to a row of lodges along the banks of the lake, protected by some Quaking Aspen trees which sheltered the lodges from the lake. They reached lodge 13 and Tanya took the key that she had in her hand and opened the oak door, she then walked in and when Jake and Corrine were inside, she gave the door key to Jake.

'Here you go, sir, you'll find details of all the facilities in your lodge, have a wonderful stay.' She then stepped out of the lodge and walked back to the main lodge.

'Well! She was nice, don't you think?' said Corrine.

Jake looked at her, 'Are you jealous, dear?'

She looked at Jake, 'Don't be silly! Of course not!' She took her suitcase and went into the bedroom.

The lodge had three rooms, a bathroom that had a shower and toilet next to a wash basin and a table with mirror, the other room was a large bedroom with a double bed and wardrobe with a dressing table. The window had a spectacular view of the lake.

'Jake, come and take a look at this. It's amazing.'

Jake walked over to her by the window. 'Wow! This is fantastic, I'm going to enjoy this place, let's unpack then go for a walk.'

Corrine agreed and they got their suitcase opened on the bed and unpacked. Once unpacked they left the lodge and went back to the main lodge to get a map of the resort and ask for details of events. They bumped into Tanya, who was just coming out of the lodge.

'Mr and Mrs Rogers, do you need any help?'

Jake stopped in front of her with Corrine at his side. She then held his hand, to show that he was her man. 'Hi, yeah, we were thinking of going for a walk around the complex and wondered if you had a map!'

'Yes, of course, follow me.' She turned and walked back into the lodge through the opened door, and they followed her in. Tanya went up to the desk and picked up a couple of two-page flyers, one was a map of the resort and the other events that were due to take place over the next few days.

'Here you are.' She handed the flyers to Jake and he thanked her, 'Oh and before I forget there is a BBQ tonight by the lake, it's on the flyer, we have a famous country star performing as well, it should be exciting.'

Tanya then went back out of the lodge to see other residents who had some things that needed sorting out. That was one of her job titles, Liaison Officer, Jake had a quick look at the map and looked at Corrine.

'Are you ready?'

'Ready when you are.'

And they left hand in hand out through the lodge door and headed towards the lake. The afternoon was heating up with the sun shining bright and the lake which was actually a section of the river that was wider in some parts forming a series of lakes. The part of the lake they were heading towards was placid just right for canoeing, as they headed towards the jetty area where they could see about a dozen canoes tied up by the jetty. The canoes were yellow in colour, so not difficult to miss when out on the lake, there were around half a dozen canoes already out on the lake, mainly couples, but a few family canoes as well.

Jake and Corrine were shown to a canoe and given brief instructions on safety and had to put on life jackets which were a requirement, they were also in yellow. Jake felt a bit silly putting these on, didn't make him feel manly! But rules were rules and they had to be obeyed.

Corrine had a paddle as well and the both of them pushed away from the shore and gently paddled out into the lake, it was a little cooler out in the water with a gentle breeze blowing in their hair. The wind had a cooling effect.

'You should be wearing a hat,' said Corrine.

'Yeah, should have brought my Stetson, could have played the part then.' They laughed and carried on paddling.

They paused now and then to take photos of the breathtaking scenery; Jake was looking forward to the BBQ tonight.

'Hey, I wonder who the country singer is?'

'Well, we will find out tonight,' said Corrine.

They had spent an hour out on the lake before turning back towards the jetty, they were still a little tired from the wedding night and decided to get a little rest before attending the BBQ. Once back on dry land, they made their way to the lodge, Jake opened the door and went inside Corrine followed him in.

'I'm going to take a shower and then get some rest for a couple of hours,' said Corrine.

Jake had a smile on his face. 'You know what, I think I'll join you.'

She smiled back and they both knew what they were going to do and showering was part of it.

Later that evening they got up from an afternoon nap and started to get ready for the BBQ, Jake was going to wear jeans and a denim shirt, Corrine was also wearing jeans and a cowgirl shirt that she wore from time to time. Both ready and looking forward to the show, Jake opened the lodge door and could see other people heading in the direction of the BBQ. Everybody looked happy, probably because they were hungry. There was a strong smell of the BBQ and it made them feel more hungry, they heard some people talking and found out that the artist tonight was George Strait, he was Jake's favourite singer so he was very happy.

'George Strait! Do you know who he is?' Corrine looked at him.

'My dad used to listen to his music at the house and in the car, so yes, I do know his music but this will be the first time seeing him.'

'Well, this is just the icing on the cake, this evening just got even better.'

They walked hand in hand towards the event and the weather also didn't disappoint, the evening was going to be dry.

Chapter Fifty-Two

As evening approached in Green River, the Rogers were getting ready for bed, it was a work day tomorrow and they decided to have an early night when the phone rang.

'Who can that be?' said Jim.

'You better answer it, dear.'

He went over to the phone. 'Hello,' said Jim There was a pause from the caller.

'Oh, hi, Mr Rogers, it's Nathan.'

'Nathan! Are you OK?' There was another pause.

'Er, yes, sort of!'

'How can I help you, Nathan?'

'It's Mum, she has overdosed again, I called the ambulance and they have taken her to Castle Rock Medical Centre.'

'Why aren't you with your mother?' asked Jim.

'She doesn't have medical insurance; it was never renewed and I don't know what to do.'

'I don't want to bother you with my family problems, but I have no one else I can talk to.' Debbie was listening in on the conversation. 'Hello, Nathan, it's Mrs Rogers, I couldn't help but listen to the conversation, tell us what the problem is and how can we help?'

'The hospital is asking for $5,000 dollars just to get her back to being healthy, and I don't have that kind of money, I was wondering if I could borrow the money and pay it back to you in stages.'

Jim thought hard for a few moments. 'What about her doctor, have you tried to contact him to see if he can persuade the hospital to do something?'

'She stopped seeing him months ago.'

Debbie was in her night gown as she came down the stairs. 'Jim, get dressed, you and I are going to the hospital,' Jim always did as he was told so he went

200

back upstairs to get dressed, Nathan had made his way to their house and Jim let him in, 'Nathan, take a seat and we will go to the hospital with you and sort this out for your mother.'

'Thank you, Mrs Rogers,' he sat down on the dining table chair and waited for them to get ready. Nathan hated relying on other people, but in this instance, he had no choice, and he was lucky there were still good people around to help. A few minutes later, the Rogers were down stairs and Jim went to get his car keys from the glass bowl in the kitchen table counter.

'OK, let's go,' said Jim, he opened the front door and they left the house and got into Jim's car, he started the engine and drove towards the hospital.

'Mum has been having problems with depression ever since my father left us and went away to start a new life, well, she has been taking antidepressants to help, but she has got addicted to them and she is finding it hard to stop taking them.'

'How is she getting these tablets?' asked Debbie. 'The doctor keeps giving her a new prescription each time she goes to see him.'

Debbie was in shock. 'Surely, he has to evaluate her first before prescribing medication, who is her doctor?'

'I'm not really sure, I don't go with her to the medical centre.'

'You are saying now that she does not have a doctor, is that right?'

'So how is she getting the prescription renewed?'

Nathan was puzzled and showed a blank expression on his face, all he ever wanted, was a simple life but he got stuck with this one.

'Thanks Mr and Mrs Rogers for doing this, it's not something I wanted to burden anyone else with. I thought she was getting better.'

'Look, Nathan, you know you can always come and speak to us whenever you want.'

'That's great to know, sir, and thank you for helping.'

'Don't mention it, son, we are here for you.'

Nathan was relieved he felt that a lot of pressure had been taken off his shoulders. A problem shared is a problem halved, that saying always rings true. Jim had phoned Dr Adams while he was upstairs getting ready and asked him if he could meet him at the hospital. Doc and Jim were good friends and he arranged to meet them there. They reached the hospital and after parking the car went into the hospital and up to the information desk.

'What's your mother's name, Nathan?'

'It's Carmilla Vasquez Jones!' said Nathan.

Jim spoke to the girl at the desk. 'Good evening, I understand that this boy's mother is at this hospital, her name is Carmilla Vasquez Jones, can you let me know what ward she has been taken to, please?'

'Certainly sir, are you a relative?'

'No, this is her son and we are here to sort out the medical insurance.'

'I will just see where they have put her sir, give me a couple of minutes.'

She had a look at her computer screen and punched in Nathan's mother's name. 'It looks like they have taken her to the ICU ward for immediate attention, if you would like to wait in the seating area, I will get the hospital administrator to come and see you.'

'I thought they weren't going to see her because of the insurance!'

Just then a voice from behind spoke to Jim. 'I have insisted that she be seen straight away, Jim.'

He turned around and saw Dr Adams standing in front of him. Jim reached out his hand to Dr Adams.

'Thanks, for doing that, Pete, I can't believe that it's come down to this, where you can only get treated if you can afford to pay for it, it's crazy.'

'Did you know that the US is the only developed nation without a system of universal healthcare, a lot of healthcare facilities are run by the private sector. And only 21% of hospitals are government owned, 27 million people in the US don't have insurance.'

'Just find this extraordinary, I had no idea that the scale was so big.'

'It's ironic that America is a global leader in medical innovation, measured either in terms of revenue or the number of new drugs and devices introduced.'

A few moments later as they were seated in the waiting area, the hospital administrator approached them, he was a tall white man in his late forties and wearing a white hospital coat, 'Good evening, are you here for, Mrs Jones?'

'Yes, how is she doing?'

He looked at his notepad and turned a page. 'Well, she is comfortable and is in a ward, we had to pump the drugs out of her and she is currently on a drip.'

'What's her blood pressure and do you know the substance that was ingested?' asked Dr Adams.

'You must be Dr Adams, thank you for your assistance earlier, it was Sertraline and there was a lot of it in her bloodstream, we are still trying to find out where she got these from.'

'What is sertraline, Pete?'

'It's known better by Zoloft, it's used for mental health and mood disorders, unfortunately there are some unscrupulous people selling this on the black market.'

'I have some forms for you to fill in, is it Mr Rogers?'

'Yes, that's me and this is her son, Nathan, show me the forms so that we can get this sorted out quickly so that we can get some sleep tonight.'

Jim went to the desk with the administrator leaving Debbie with Dr Adams with Nathan. After ten minutes Jim came back towards Debbie and Nathan, Dr Adams was saying goodbye to them and met Jim halfway.

'OK, Jim, I need to get home, I think they will keep her in for tonight, you should get home and get some sleep.'

'Thanks for all your help, Pete, I owe you!'

He smiled and shook Jim's hand, 'See you later' and walked towards the exit doors.

'Well, that's all taken care of, your mother is well and is sleeping it off, she will be staying here tonight, you are welcome to stay at our place tonight, it's getting late and you can borrow some of Jake's pyjamas. I'm sure he won't mind.'

Nathan was beholding to them. 'If you don't mind, I don't think that I can stay at home without my mother there.'

'That's settled then, right let's go home,' said Jim.

Chapter Fifty-Three

The evening was going according to plan as far the camp was concerned, the BBQ was in full swing and the beef joint was cooking nicely. There were chairs set out in rows around the stage area, there were around 150 people expected and the sound checks were taking place. George Strait had his backing band with him and his sound engineers were checking the microphones for sound levels. Jake and Corrine sat near to the stage and Jake couldn't believe that he was going to be so close to his idol.

The rest of the holiday makers had taken their seats and there was a hum of noise hovering over the concert air. A noise of people talking in trepidation of what was to come, they didn't have to wait too long. The band got on stage to applause and was ready to introduce the main act for the evening, George Strait's band was on stage and was testing their instruments.

'Ladies and gentlemen, welcome to the Flaming Gorge Concert, and without further ado, please make welcome the legend that is George Strait!'

The audience clapped and cheered, almost drowning out the band. George Strait walked onto the stage, he was wearing denim light blue jeans with a cowboy style shirt which had patterns on the front and back of his shirt. He raised his right hand to acknowledge the fans and then reached the mike stand and picked up the guitar that was in a guitar stand next to the mike. He put the strap around his neck and got ready to sing, he adjusted the height of the microphone and looked again at the audience and smiled. The evening sky was conjuring up a spectacular early sunset and the winds were light as George introduced himself to the audience and then began to sing some of his 80 top hits. He could not sing all of them or they could be there for a week.

'Are you happy?' shouted Corrine.

Jake turned to her and said, 'What! You bet!' This has made this trip even more memorable.

Corrine smiled and continued watching the show tapping her feet on the firm ground. The evening was turning out to be everything they expected and more, Jake held Corrine's hand as he submersed himself in the music, also tapping his feet. After the first session which lasted about 45 minutes, they announced that the BBQ was now being served. There was a selection of side dishes laid out and even the band were tucking into the famous Flaming Gorge BBQ and they were enjoying it tremendously. With their stomachs full and drinks in hand, the audience were seated and ready for the second half of entertainment. After the band had started playing, George Strait came out to more applause, some of the audience decided to get up and dance in the aisles; they were soon followed by more. Corrine turned to Jake.

'Shall we?' Jake looked at her. 'Are you sure!' said Jake. She started to get up and held out her hand to Jake. 'Yeah! You only live once.'

Reluctantly he got up and looked at the other members who were dancing and held Corrine and started dancing. The music was infectious, but then George Strait's music did that to you.

As the evening was coming to an end and the last song was being played, after the song he thanked the audience and waved them goodnight, he got a standing ovation as he melted into the stage background slowly followed by his band. Jake put his arm around Corrine and gave her a kiss on the lips, she hugged him back and they walked out of the concert grounds heading towards the lodge. They had planned a walking day tomorrow through the grounds of the resort which extended far along the borders where the mountains hugged the tree lined resort and along the lake shore. Corrine had pre-ordered a picnic from the main lodge that they could collect early in the morning. There was no rushing on this holiday, Jake was not going to be bothered by work and his mother and father made sure of that.

Corrine woke up with the sun shining through the net curtains from her bedroom window, she smiled and brushed her hair from her face. She looked at Jake lying in the bed half covered by the cotton sheet, 'My husband,' she said to herself, she still found it hard to believe that they were married, she smiled as she looked at him. Then decided to wake him up, but then thought to let him sleep while she ordered breakfast for the two of them. Breakfast was served between 07.30 and 09.30 in the cafeteria but she would get it delivered to the cabin instead. It was going to be 10 to 15 minutes before they delivered the breakfast, which would give Jake plenty of time to get up. She went back into the bedroom and sat down next to Jake and pushed him a couple of times, he stirred and saw her at the corner of his eye.

'Morning beautiful, you look totally radiant!' The sun lit up behind her cotton night dress and showed her slim torso and outlining her figure.

'I know what you are thinking!' She said smiling.

'We've only been married a day and you already know me, that was fast, do they teach you that in college?'

'No silly, it's just that I know you, they say that you always know the one you love, and that's true. Anyway, breakfast will be here in 10 minutes, so get ready.'

Jake didn't need telling twice, he jumped out of bed and raced into the shower while Corrine was getting ready. Breakfast arrived a few minutes later and they sat at the table and enjoyed the eggs and bacon with sausage and biscuits. They would need a walk to remove the calories from this food.

It was 10am when they started their walk, the picnic basket was delivered to the cabin along with the breakfast. Flaming Gorge Resort was not fenced in and so they shared the open space with the forest animals. Jake was given information about the possible wild animals they could encounter. Grizzly bears, mountain lions, bobcats and coyotes, they were fortunate to be in area where these animals were seldom seen. But caution was always advised and if required, guides could be hired, but Jake didn't see the need for that.

They had been walking for an hour and the heat was having an effect on Corrine, she had to rest, they stopped in a shaded spot to get out of the sun.

'Here's a good spot, we will have rest for a few minutes and then take a look at the map,' said Jake.

Jackie found a smooth rock to sit on and breathed a sigh of relief as she took the weight off her feet. Jake came over to her and opened the picnic basket and got a drink for her, it was water and she opened the bottle and took a sip.

'That's better, I guess I'm not used to walking.'

'Its fine, we haven't done something like this for a long time, we will take it easy until you feel better, you'll be OK!'

They approached a narrow valley covered by some trees and shrubs; it was beautiful when Corrine heard a noise. 'Jake! What's that noise?'

'What noise?'

'Listen!' They looked towards the end of the track ahead. It was quiet and then there was a sound, it sounded like a big animal.

'Shall we go back?' asked Corrine, Jake waited for a moment, then there was a growling sound, and a shape appeared from behind a large bush. It was a big bear, the bear was on all fours and it saw them, it stopped for a look and Jake was staring at the bear. He didn't know what to do, but he knew that he had to keep Corrine safe he told her to stay behind a rock that was nearby.

'But what about you, what are you going to do?'

'I'm not really sure, but I know that you better stay behind this rock and try and climb up to a safe height.'

'I'm not going anywhere without you Jake!' He turned to her and put his hands on her shoulders, 'Look, the bear has seen us he will probably try and attack us, you have a phone, call the lodge and tell them where we are, I will try and get the bear to follow me away from you. Don't worry, I will be OK, just ring the lodge.'

Jake waited till Corrine was safe behind the rock and then moved towards the bear but kept a safe distance, the bear watched him and made some threatening thumping sounds, Jake climbed up a little higher, he could see a path that would take him and the bear away from Corrine. The bear started to follow him, it was working, he started to run a little faster and moved further away, this bear would not let go he was getting closer to Jake, but he climbed even higher and got onto a tree which was overhanging the rock. He climbed up as far as he could so that the bear could not follow, and it worked. It was a big bear but too fat to climb, he tried to climb the tree but was not successful. So, after a few minutes he lost interest and decided to go back the way he came, he waited for a few moments until he could see the bear was out of range and started to climb down and get back to Corrine. He got to where she was hiding and called her name, Corrine came out and saw him standing there.

'Didn't I say it would be OK!' She ran towards him and hugged him. 'Let's get back to the lodge, I have had enough of nature for one day.'

They set off back towards the lodge and when they were ten minutes out two rangers from the resort met them.

'Are you OK? We got a call from the lodge; they said you had bear problem.'

'Yes, we did, but its OK now my husband led the bear away and we are safe now.'

'That's good, it's unusual for them to attack like that maybe it had young cubs, anyway we are going to look further and make sure that the bear is away from this area. You make your way back to the lodge; you have a brave man here!'

Corrine smiled at the ranger. 'Yes I know,' and they made their way back. It was an eventful day.

The next few days were very enjoyable and Jake had forgotten all about the rodeo and Bandy, he tried to contact Jake through Jim, but was told that they were not to be disturbed on their honeymoon. Bandy has something cooking and he was trying to get Jake involved. Jake and Corrine were getting ready to spend their last night in the lodge, they had amassed so many memories in the short space of time and had enjoyed their time there. They would soon be back at Green River and back at work and their pace of life would change, but they knew that and were prepared for the rest of their lives. The next morning, they said goodbye to the Flaming Gorge Resort and boarded the river taxi which would take them back to the hotel, they looked back at the resort as the boat pulled away and the outboard engines kicked in and white water spurted from the back of the boat's motors. As it roared away with speed along the river banked by beautiful scenery on both sides, truly a memorable time in their lives to cherish. One day, they will be back and maybe with a young family only time will tell.

Chapter Fifty-Four

The honeymoon was coming to an end and they had spent quality time together, they were now ready to face anything. As they left the resort behind them, the sun was just coming through some clouds, which were being burnt away. The forecast for today was cloudy with a chance of rain later in the day, they picked the right day to leave.

Jake was not working today and the same went for Corrine. So they had another stress-free day to look forward to. Corrine had to decide whether she wanted herself and Jake to live in her father's house, she still hasn't got used to living there without her dad. But Jake being there helped her to get through the stay and now after the honeymoon the relationship was cemented.

'Jake, I've decided that I want the two of us to live at my house, are you happy to do that?'

He turned to her from his seat on the boat, 'If you are happy, then I'm happy, we will let Mum and Dad know when we get back.'

She had a smile of relief on her face as she shuffled up to Jake and put her arms around him, they were nearly at their destination and Jake called his dad to let him know they were on their way home.

They would be staying with them for tonight and would move to Corrine's house the next day, Jim was at work with Nathan going through some routine work when Jake rang. They were coping quite well but were looking forward to Jake getting back to work, they did miss him. They had reached their destination and Jake helped Corrine out of the boat and they walked towards the car park at the hotel. Jake carried Corrine's suitcase, he just had his rucksack, he had put some of his things in her suitcase. When they got to the car, he took out his keys and opened the car doors and put the suitcase in the trunk, then got into the car and once Corrine was in and secured, he started the engine.

'Well, are you ready to go home?' said Jake.

Corrine turned to him, 'Why not, let's go home.'

They made their way home to Jake's house; Debbie was at home cooking lunch for them. Jim was closing the shop early today to have lunch together at the house, he was excited to see the both of them.

'Say hi to Jake for me,' said Nathan as he mounted his push bike ready to head on home. 'I will, you take care, and remember what we said to you about your mother.'

'Sure thing, Mr Rogers.' Nathan then rode his bike off the sidewalk and onto the road, homeward bound. Jim got into his car and he too made his way home, normal service would be resumed once Jake and Corrine get back into the swing of things.

Back at the Rogers' household, Debbie had finished lunch and was setting the dining table in readiness for their arrival. You would think that Jake and Corrine had gone away for weeks the way that Jim and Debbie were fussing over them. But it's not every day your son gets married and although the circumstances were not the best, with the loss of Corrine's father, George, they all pulled together to make the occasion memorable.

Jim had arrived home and was just coming in through the front door when Jake and Corrine had pulled up in the drive alongside him. Jake got out of the car.

'Hey Dad, how are you, it's good to see you.'

'Hi son, come inside and we will talk about your honeymoon.'

Corrine got out as well, 'Hi Dad,' she had a smile on her face and closed the car door behind her.

'You both look well, the lake must have agreed with you, come on in, Jake and I will get the bags later.'

Jim opened the front door wider to let them both into the house, 'Look what I found outside,' said Jim.

Debbie turned around and smiled widely, then walked over to both of them. She hugged Corrine. 'Oh it's so good to have you both back home,' she then held Corrine's hand and led her to the dining table.

'Lunch will be five minutes, why don't the two of you go and get washed up ready to eat.'

They both went upstairs to Jake's room to do just that. Debbie started to put the plates onto the table, 'Jim, why don't you take the wine and the glasses, I think this calls for a celebration.'

He did as he was told and went to the fridge to take out a bottle of Liebfraumilch German white wine, he loved this wine, he was introduced to it when he served in Germany for 12 months. The Germans loved their wines and beers and Jim got hooked, he wasn't a big drinker, but occasionally liked to get a little dizzy (he called the expression) which after a few glasses of wine, gave you that feeling. After a few minutes, Jake and Corrine were both downstairs and ready for lunch. He gave them both a glass of wine each, the wine was chilled from being in the fridge, they sat down next to each other at the table, Jim sat at the head of the table and Jake and Corrine sat opposite each other. Debbie had brought out the main dish of chicken curry and accompanied it with some basmati white rice, there was salad as well and some chutney for added taste.

'Wow! You made a curry,' said Jake. 'It's your dad who made the curry last night, we had it a yesterday and Nathan was here but that's another storey, and well, he is hooked on it.' After Debbie had served them the food, Corrine was apprehensive, 'I've not had a curry before, I've heard that they are usually very hot.'

'It's alright dear, he didn't make it very hot, try a little first,' said Debbie.

Jake had already started eating and was enjoying the food, 'It's good, Corrine, and not too hot.'

She took a small spoonful and started eating it with apprehension, then after chewing and tasting the spices she had a smile starting, 'Wow, it's so nice, you must give me the recipe?' asked Corrine.

They all laughed and got on with eating. Jim picked up his glass of wine, and raised it, 'A toast to Jake and Corrine, welcome home.' The wine went down well with the curry and the meal was thoroughly enjoyed by all.

Jake and Corrine showed the pictures of the honeymoon and Corrine explained how Jake was a hero again with the escapade surrounding the bear. Jim was jealous that they saw George Strait, it was his favourite country star as well, they were happy that they enjoyed they time together away. Debbie told Jake that the reporter from the newspaper came round and wants to write a story about Jake and the hero of the State Bank, she will be back no doubt.

Chapter Fifty-Five

The next day Jake was taking the morning off to help Corrine move back into her house, they didn't have a lot of things to move, so the move was not going to take long. They would have to get most of Jake's belongings and get some groceries for the week, Corrine was going to invite Jim and Debbie over for dinner once they settled in.

It was stock taking at the shop, and Debbie was going into work to help out as well. Once Jake had loaded all the cases and boxes into the car he called out to Corrine, she came out of the house and waved goodbye to Debbie. Jim had already gone to work and Jake told his mother that he would see her at work after lunch.

Jim and Nathan were well into the stocktaking and Nathan had certainly found his feet while Jake was away. It put more pressure on him having to cope with situations on his own, that's probably the best way to learn.

'Nathan, can you let me have the sheets that you have completed so that I can get an idea of how far we have got please.'

'Sure thing, Mr Rogers. And I want to thank you for helping my mother at the hospital. I am going to collect her this evening.'

'That's great news, Nathan, how are you going to pick her up, you only have a bicycle!'

Nathan thought for a moment, 'Well, I could get a taxi.'

'Nonsense! Let me know what time you are going and I will get Jake to take you to pick up your mother, and I will not have any arguments about the matter!'

Nathan was dumbstruck, he didn't want to upset Jim, but he also didn't want to behold to him as he had done so much already.

'I just don't know what to say, Mr Rogers, you have done so much for us already. If Jake is OK with doing this then, yes please.'

'That's settled then, now, let's have the sheets that you have completed?' asked Jim and Nathan took out the completed sheets from his clipboard and gave them to Jim.

As Jim was walking towards his desk, the door of the shop opened and Bandy entered the shop, 'Jim! Nice to see you again, how have you been?'

Jim was startled at first and realised who it was, 'Oh it's you, I suppose you have come to see Jake?'

Bandy walked closer to Jim, 'Is he back from his honeymoon yet?'

'Yes, he came back yesterday.'

'I don't suppose I could talk to him?'

'Well, he is not at work till later this afternoon, perhaps you can call back then!'

'That sounds good to me, I'm staying over tonight, so I'll call back around 2pm see you guys later.' He then left the shop and closed the door behind him.

'Wonder what he wants with Jake?' asked Nathan, 'Ah! He wants Jake to join one of his rodeo shows, he thinks that Jake is a natural, I don't know, Jake has a job and now a wife, I hope he doesn't get tempted to join the rodeo.'

'Jake likes his life too much here, and now with Corrine, I don't think he will,' said Nathan.

A few minutes after Bandy had left, Debbie came to the shop, 'Hi dear, how is it going?'

Jim came out of the office and looked at Debbie, 'Going well, by the way, we had a visitor.'

'Who was that?' Bandy popped in, looking for Jake.

'Oh dear, what does he want now?'

'Probably to join him at the next rodeo knowing him.'

'Well, we will just have to wait and see, I hope Jake has more sense than to get involved with the rodeo.'

'He will be alright, Mr Rogers, Jake will get his priorities in order,' said Nathan, Debbie looked out of the shop window at the high street making sure that Bandy had gone.

'It's up to Jake now, but whatever he decides, we must not question him.'

They all looked at each other and went about their business and finished the stock taking, Jake would be coming in after lunch to help with the heavy stock.

Debbie had promised Corrine that she would swing by later today to help out and take Corrine shopping to stock up on food. As soon as Jake got to the shop, Debbie would leave and meet up with Corrine.

The stocktaking was all but over and it was just the stoves and pipes to count, Nathan went to make tea for everyone at Jim's request and the rest would be well earned. Jake had arrived at the shop and opened the door, 'I'm here!' They all looked at him.

'How did it go at Corrine's?' asked Jim.

'It's looking like home,' said Jake as he walked in and closed the door behind him.

'Right, well I'll leave you guys to get on with the rest of the work, while I take Corrine shopping. I think she's worked hard enough today,' said Debbie.

She collected her bag and left the shop. 'Well, that means she will be spending money, ah well, let's get on with the paperwork and we might get to finish early today,' said Jim and after drinking the tea, they got on with the work.

'You know Dad, I must have done something right to have all this luck, everything seems to be falling into place.'

The door opened and in walked Bethany Roberts from the Green River Star, 'Hi, Jake, I'm. Glad that you are here, can I talk to you?'

Jake looked at her and was caught by surprise, 'Oh hi, what can I do for you?'

'I got the story from the sheriff and I was wondering if I could get your side of the story.' He looked at his dad to ask for time out. Jim nodded and Jake showed Bethany to Jim's office, once inside he closed the door.

'Right, I just wanted to help out at the bank, I saw that something wasn't right so I called the sheriff and yes, he told me to wait in the car. But I just couldn't just sit there, so I went into the bank and well, things just happened!'

'Jake, this is twice now that you have done something heroic, what is it about you, were always this way?'

'I have always wanted to do the right thing and I guess luck has been on my side.'

'You know that you are going to get a bravery award from the mayor, well, I think they might even give you the key to the town at this rate.' Jake grinned and looked at his dad, Bethany said bye and left the shop, off to write another hit story about a local hero.

Chapter Fifty-Six

Later that day Jim was getting ready to close the shop, the shop door opened, it was Bandy! He walked in and immediately saw Jake and smiled at him.

'Jake my boy!' He said loudly and with a wry smile on his face.

Jim turned around and his face dropped. 'Oh no, what does he want,' he said to himself, Jake went over to Bandy and shook his hand.

'I didn't know you were in town, when did you get in?'

'I swung by earlier but you were not here, how was your honeymoon?'

Bandy closed the door and they went over to the desk. 'It was great, I saw George Strait, he was performing there.'

'That's fantastic, I like his music, down to earth and not like the new country singers, who all sound the same and there are so many of them now. You know, I went to Nashville once, wanted to go to the Country Music Hall of Fame, it was fantastic, I even went into Johnny Cash's dressing room. But I noticed, that nearly every young person was carrying a guitar case. All trying to make it big, it's a tough business.'

'Hi Jim,' Bandy waved over to him who was in his office with the door open. He acknowledged him and waved back. Jim forced a little smile on his face.

'Look, Jake, I need a favour, I've got this gig at the Weston County Fair and I'm short a handler, I know it's short notice but I am desperate, what do ya say?'

Jake thought a little, 'You know that I just came back from my honeymoon, and I would love to help out.'

Bandy put his hand to his face and held his chin, 'Did I mention that the pay is good!'

Jake's eyebrows lifted, 'How much are we talking about?'

Bandy looked into Jake's eyes and put his right hand onto Jake's right shoulder, 'Well normally the job would pay $100 but seeing as it's you and it is short notice, $250!'

Jake stood up straight. '$250 dollars!'

'Yes, that's right, one night's work, but it will be a long day.'

Jim came out of the office; he had heard the amount in question. 'What has he gotta do for that kind of money, he hasn't got to ride a wild bull, has he?'

'No, not at all, he will be helping out the rodeo clowns, you know just making sure that the riders are protected.'

'But doesn't that involve getting close to the animals and is that not dangerous?' asked Jim.

'Well, yes, it can be, but he will be working with experienced people and safety is our primary concern, he will be safe.' Bandy almost sounded genuine.

'I don't know,' said Jim. 'Dad, it should be safe, well look what I did at the rodeo, these are professional people, I'm sure they know what they are doing.'

'Let me speak to Corrine tonight and I will give you my answer tomorrow morning. Where are you staying?'

'I'm staying at the Hampton Inn, I do hope you say yes, the show needs you my boy,' he shook Jake's hand and said bye to Jim and left the shop.

'I'm not so sure that you should do this Jake, I have a bad feeling about this.'

'I know Dad, but at least I could try and see if this what I want to do, I mean the money is good.'

'You had better run this by Corrine and see what she says.'

And with that he turned the lights out and after Nathan and Jake were outside the shop, he closed the door. 'I almost forgot, Jake, I told Nathan that you would give him a lift to the hospital to collect his mother and drop her home.'

'I hope you don't mind.' Jake looked at Nathan, 'I didn't know your mother was in the hospital, what happened to her?'

'It's a long story, your dad will explain everything, but I need to pick her up and take her back home, are you OK with that?'

'Hey! No problem, what time do you want to go?'

'Now, if you are free.'

'I'll just ring Corrine and let her know, here take my keys and let yourself in.' He gave Nathan his car keys and took his phone out of his blue denim jacket pocket Jake rang Corrine.

'Hi Jake, are you OK?'

'Yes, I'm just going to take Nathan to the hospital.'

She interrupted, 'Hospital! What happened to him!'

'No, nothing has happened to him, it's his mother, he has to take her home, she was at the hospital.'

'Well. What's wrong with her, nothing serious, I hope!'

'Mum and Dad will explain everything later but I won't be long.'

'OK, well take your time, your mother is staying to help me with dinner so if you want to bring your dad over later when you get back, that will save him driving.'

'OK babe, see you later, oh, and I need to talk to you about Bandy, he came by the shop earlier.'

As Corrine was about to say something, Jake hung up. She had that look on her face, the same look that Jim had back at the shop, she obviously knew that Bandy was after Jake to hook him up with his rodeo shows. But that was something that she would discuss with Jake later.

'Was that Jake?' asked Debbie.

Corrine turned to her, 'Yes, he and Nathan are going to pick up Nathan's mother at the hospital and he bumped into Bandy.'

'Oh no! What did he want?'

'I don't know, but I bet it's got something to do with the rodeo.' They looked at each other. 'Look, dear, you are going to have to play this one safe, if Jake wants to get involved with the rodeo, then let him try it out and see if he likes it. You must give him some slack, he's not silly, he will do the right thing.'

Corrine looked pensive as she thought about the future, what was she to do? She decided that she would let Jake do what he wanted to do and time would tell if she was doing the right thing. After all, she had a good job and she was married to the man she has known for a long time. She would play the waiting game and see how it turned out.

Over at Corrine's house, Debbie was helping in the kitchen with the dinner, Corrine decided to have Mexican tonight, she had bought some readymade tortillas she wasn't going to attempt to make them from scratch like her mother used to do.

'Just the salad left to do, Corrine, we should probably wait until they arrive before we make it, it might spoil otherwise,' said Debbie.

'Good idea, well, I think this calls for a drink,' said Corrine, she went over to the fridge and opened it, got out a bottle of white wine and showed it to Debbie. 'What do you think?'

Corrine had a smile on her face, and so did Debbie, 'Where are the glasses?' asked Debbie. Corrine pointed to the cupboard above the sink and Debbie went over to get two wine glasses for the two of them.

Jim and Jake would go home after work and then come over to Corrine's house, even though Jake was now living at Corrine's he still had some clothes in his old room to change into.

The evening grew closer as the wind blew a slight chill around Green River; some evenings could be quite cold, even in the summer months. Jake put on a cardigan with jeans and Jim had on black trousers and a white shirt, he took a jacket with him just in case it turned colder later. He also took a jumper for Debbie; he knew she would want to wrap up later.

'THESE are things you find out about each other when you have been together for some time,' said Jim. Jake just nodded and opened the front door, they both left in Jake's car, Jim would be coming home with Debbie in her car, he locked the front door and they both got into Jake's car and drove off.

The evening meal went well and once they had finished and everything was cleaned up, they sat down on the couch and Corrine made coffee for everyone. 'Jake, Mum said that Bandy came into the shop earlier today, what did he want?'

Jake swallowed his coffee which was a little hot but took like a man and didn't make a fuss. 'Er, well, he was asking me if I would like to go to the rodeo at the Weston County Fair over in Newcastle. He wants me to be part of the show and help out, sort of!'

'What exactly does that mean?'

'Well, you know help out, with the rodeo clowns and things like that, I said that I would speak to you first, you know to see what you thought about it.'

Corrine looked at him with serious eyes, he looked uneasy as he put down his cup. 'Well, I want you to try it out and see what you think, give it a go and then decide what you want to do, you know, I'm fine with that. But I want to be there too, after all we are married and my place is with you.'

Jake was surprised and so was Jim, there was a look of disbelief on his face, but then a smile. He knew that Debbie had probably spoken to her. Jake went into another room and called Bandy and told him the good news, the evening went well after that. Everyone had got the white elephant in the room out of the way. Corrine took a deep breath and hoped that she had done the right thing. Jim and Debbie got up and got their things, they were a little tired. Debbie had taken extra medication to get through the evening, she was ready to call it a day and had a bath and bed that had her name on it.

'Thanks for a wonderful evening, Corrine, the food was great but now I must go home and get some rest,' said Debbie.

'Ditto!' said Jim, 'it was wonderful, you kids enjoy the rest of the evening, and I'll see you at work tomorrow, Jake.'

And with that they left the house to head on home, Corrine and Jake waved them off and then closed the door, 'Let's get an early night, Jake,' she had a smile on her face and a certain look in her eyes. Jake got the message and didn't argue, that's twice now that she has surprised him. He locked the front door and turned off the lights downstairs and followed Corrine upstairs to the bedroom.

Chapter Fifty-Seven

Over at the Weston County Fair ground, Bandy was out in the ring inspecting the surface of the ground, they had machines that dragged a kind of rake behind it. This was used to pick up any objects that would cause damage to any rider that could fall onto it, also to prevent damage to the livestock. But Bandy was old school and wanted to inspect the ground for himself. He wasn't going to inspect the whole ground, just around the release area, after all, this was his show.

He stopped and thought for a moment and his mind gazed back to when he was younger and getting into the rodeo circuit for the first time. He was thinking about Jake and what he was asking him to do, he leant up against the gate and rested his arms on top of the gate. He too was once married; his wife was someone he grew up with and very similar to Jake and Corrine. Bandy was hooked big time on the rodeo circuit and was blinkered to anything else around him. It wasn't long before he spent more time away from his wife, and as time went on, she started to see other people and soon got to like hanging around with other men. Bandy wasn't there to object and she also forgot about the love they once shared and grew further apart. It all came to a head when one evening while attending a rock concert in Dakota, she was allowed backstage to meet the band. Handpicked by the bouncers to supply women for the band, and she didn't know it at the time. She thought she was going to meet the lead singer alone. Well things turned out bad for her and became one of the groupies that followed the band around to various gigs, and was treated to a concoction of alcohol and drugs. She lost all track of time and was on a downward spiral of life.

Bandy on a rare occasion came home only to find that the mortgaged house was closed with an eviction notice stapled to it. His key did not fit the lock so he picked up a rock from the front garden border and smashed the glass in the door and put his hand inside to open the door to let himself in. He was only inside the house for a few minutes when he heard sirens from the local police station. They had got a call from a neighbour, obviously a diligent neighbourhood watch observer. So, he was taken to the local sheriff's office and locked up for the night, he was released after paying for the damage and was asked not to go back to the house. After that Bandy had realised that his marriage was over and it was his fault, he tried to find his wife but gave up after a few days.

From then on, he went downhill with his life and ended up homeless and took to the bottle, he would join a band of hobos who rode the freight trains for free. Their lifestyle was rugged and they lived mainly outdoors, some would get jobs in the towns that they ended up in. Others would turn to a life of crime and steal. He was depressed and would reflect on life while sitting around a campfire with a can of whisky in his hand, still thinking of the mess he had made of his life.

A few years later, he decided to get his life together and make something of himself. It took a few years, but he clawed his way out of the hobo lifestyle and made it where he is now. He was interrupted while in thought by one of the ground staff who wanted to know if he could exercise the rodeo stallions.

'Take them out one at a time and let them run around, oh and Miguel, play the music loud, get them used to the noise.'

'Si senor, He went away to get the horses along with a couple of handlers, this would give the horses some needed free time with no pressure. Get them used to the ring and the noise around them, the horses would still be wild because they have never been broken.'

Bandy lost a good man in the ring at the last show, unfortunately he died from his injuries, a fact that he forgot to tell Jake about, or his family. He did feel guilty about that, but life has made him hard and bad thoughts just fade into the back his mind.

He would have to try and get Jake a few days earlier to the show, to get him trained up to what he was really going to be doing. Jake would get paid a lot for the show and Bandy was putting a lot of faith in him, he had a feeling that Jake would do fine, he was a natural. Normally it would take three months of training for a rodeo clown before he could be allowed into the ring, Jake had three days!

There was another first as well, the bull that was going to be used was the notorious El Toro! This bull had caused more injuries to man than any other bull throughout the circuit. The most famous of the rodeo bulls weighing a massive 1,900 pounds was Cat Ballou from Weatherford Texas.

The most dangerous part of the bull is his hooves, one kick from them and you can say bye-bye! His record is one complete ride out of eighteen. El Toro had the same reputation, so this information has been kept away from Jake, and for good reason. He just would not turn up; he would ring Jake and ask him to come up earlier.

Bandy walked over to where El Toro was being kept, the bull was in a pen by himself, he didn't like to share his space with any other animal. He approached the pen. The bull sensed him and stared at him with his cold dark eyes, if looks could kill! Bandy stopped just short of him and looked in his eyes.

'Well! Are you gonna behave yourself?'

The bull just stared and then grunted at him, the bull had a job to do and that's why he was always in demand. Bandy was thinking to himself, if he was twenty years younger, he would have no problem handling this bull, he would have to give Jake all the experience that he had learned and hope that it was going to be enough. He dialled the number and Corrine picked up the phone.

'Hello,' he knew that it wasn't Jake. 'Oh, hi is that, Corrine? It's Bandy, is Jake there?'

She had that look on her face, 'Hang on I'll get him for you,' she called out to Jake who was just coming down the stairs, he was in a happy mood. Corrine gave him the phone, 'Hi, Bandy, how's it going?'

'Oh, just fine my boy, listen Jake the reason I called is that I'm gonna need you up here three days before the show, is that something you can do?'

'I'm not sure, I will have to see the work situation and get back to you, I should know later today.' Bandy sounded relieved and guilty at the same time. 'That's great my boy, ring me later, you take care now and give Corrine my love.'

She came up to Jake, 'Well! what did he want?' asked Corrine.

Jake put the phone on the table, 'He's alright he just wants me to come up a few days earlier, something about extra training.'

'What exactly will you be doing at this show?' asked Corrine. Jake was edging, 'I'll be helping out the rodeo clowns, you know making sure that everything runs smoothly.'

'That can be dangerous, Jake! I hope he knows that you are not a professional.'

'Look, there's nothing to worry about, I'll be fine.'

They looked at each other and then switched on the television, there was nothing much to watch, it was just a distraction from the conversation. Then the news channel came on and Jake's face was on it. 'I don't believe it! What are they doing to me.'

'Jake, you should be proud, I certainly am.'

'I know, but there is no need for this, I thought she was just going to put it in the papers.'

'Well, you can't do much about it now, so get used to it, hero!' She smiled and punched him on the arm in a playful way.

Chapter Fifty-Eight

The week went fast and it was soon Tuesday, Jim and Jake were at the shop and he had spoken to his father and was given the all clear to go Newcastle three days earlier. The proviso was that Corrine and Debbie were going to meet up with Jake the Friday before the show. Jake was actually glad that they were coming. Jim had to stay because he had some people coming in on the Saturday in question, work had to come first. Bethany entered the shop.

'Hi Mr Rogers, hi Jake. Did you see the news report the other day, sorry I couldn't give you the heads up, but I didn't know they were going to run the feed that quickly.'

'Hi Bethany, come in, would you like a drink?'

'No thank you, Mr Rogers. I just came over to let you know that the State Bank are going to give Jake a reward for foiling the bank robbery.'

Jake's ears perked up. 'Reward! Why would they do that?' asked Jake.

'Well, you stopped the bank from being robbed and like any other bank, they offer a reward, if the bank robbers had got away with the money, the bank would still offer e reward for getting their money back. So, you got their money back!'

'When is this supposed to happen?' asked Jim. 'Oh, they are going to be there when Jake receives his bravery award tonight.'

'Tonight!' said Jake. 'Why is everything so quick, they haven't said anything to me!'

'Well, that's why I'm here, to give you and your family the official invite.' She handed Jake a letter in a white envelope, 'Here you are, Jake, I will see you there tonight at seven o'clock, dress nice. There will be pictures.'

Bethany said bye and left the shop, 'I'd better let your mother know, she will, she will want to look her best, you let Corrine know and we will see you at the town hall later.'

The day went by without any problems and Jim took a few orders and was ready to close up, Jake had plans to invite his parents over for a BBQ, a dinner before he has to go away to Newcastle. But that was before the award ceremony came up, so now they would have to get something to eat after the ceremony. Jake called Corrine and told her to forget the dinner plans and told her about the award tonight. She asked the same question, why so soon! Lack of communication from the governor's office said Corrine, but she accepted that she had to go.

It was 6.30pm and Jake and Corrine was at the town hall, Jim had pulled up and parked the car, he saw Jake outside waiting on the steps leading up to the entrance door. They met up and were met at the door by the town clerk, 'Mr Rogers!' They both answered together, the clerk looked confused.

'Er Mr Jake Rogers!'

Jim looked at Jake and said, 'That's him.' Pointing at Jake, 'If you follow me sir and I'll take you where the ceremony is to take place.'

They followed him into the town hall and up some stairs to one of the main halls, there were a lot of dignitaries seated behind a long desk, the mayor was seated in the middle of them. Jake was taken to the table and the mayor got up and walked around the table to the front of the desk.

'Ah, Jake, I've heard so much about you.' He reached out his hand and Jake obliged, 'Thank you for coming at short notice, it's a pleasure to give you this award.' The clerk came over with green velvet cushion with a gold key placed on top of it, the mayor reached out to pick up the key.'

The press was there taking pictures, 'It gives me great pleasure to give you the key to the town, for your undoubted courage in the face of danger. Not only during the tornado that nearly destroyed this town buy also to save the bank from being robbed. I can't think of anyone better to give this award to.'

He gave Jake the key and waited for the press to take photographs, this was also an endorsement for himself, voting was soon approaching for the mayor's office. One of the directors of the State Bank was also in attendance and he was waiting for the mayor to finish before approaching Jake.

The mayor stood back and introduced him, 'Jake as a result of your bravery in the face adversity the State Bank is giving you a reward for your efforts.' He moved out of the way and Frederick James, one of the board of directors stepped forward and gave Jake a cheque.

He held the cheque while Jake got hold of it and waited for the press to take photographs before releasing it to Jake. He was in his sixties and was smiling as he spoke to Jake, 'Young man, you are made of the stuff that made this country what it is today. This country could learn a thing or two from your example, it's an honour to meet you, son.'

They shook hands and more photos were taken. After the ceremony had finished, Jake went to his family, Bethany came over.

'Congratulations Jake, we will leave you alone now until the next time!' She smiled and shook his hand and left the family.

Corrine came over to Jake and gave him a hug. 'How do you feel?'

'Well, I'm glad it's all over.' Jake took a look at the cheque that was handed to him, he didn't even get a chance to look at it before.

His face dropped. 'Are you OK son?' said Debbie, he handed the cheque over to his dad.

Jim stared at it for a few seconds, 'It's a cheque for the amount of $10,000,' said Jim. They were all silent for a moment. He gave the cheque back to Jake. 'Well, you deserve it, son, you make us proud, now let's go and get something to eat.'

Later that evening they walked into Don Pedro's restaurant. Pepe looked shocked to see them. 'Good evening, you guys, to what do I owe this honour?'

'Hi Pepe, we just like your food so much,' said Jim.

They were taken to a table by the window and once seated drinks were brought over. 'We haven't ordered drinks yet,' said Jake.

'He said you would like these,' said the waitress. It was champagne. Pepe looked over at them and raised his thumb in the air and smiled at them.

Jake sat down and took a sip of his drink, 'Well, there isn't much to get ready really, but I'm all packed and I plan to leave in the morning tomorrow, so I better not drink too much.'

'I don't understand why Bandy decided to get you to go up earlier.3 something just doesn't seem right to me, and just exactly is he expecting you to do?' said Jim, 'It's fine Dad, there's no problem, everything will be just fine.'

Pepe came over to their table. 'Jake, would it be OK if I can have a picture with you, just to put up the wall behind the bar.' Pepe had various pictures of celebrities that he dedicates a wall space behind the bar. He has collected quite a few over the years. 'You sure you want to take a picture of me, I'm not really a celebrity!'

'Nonsense! To all the folk in this town, you are!' Jake got up and stood next to Peppe and the waitress took their picture.

After dinner, Jake went to call Bandy to get final details on where to meet and to book a room for his mother and Corrine was going to be in Jake's room. 'Hello, Jake my boy, nice to hear from you at this late hour. And congratulations on your award.'

'You ringing to find out where to meet up, I have booked you in at the Sundowner Inn, which is off West Main Street, I'll send you details of how to get there.'

'I need you to book another room for my mum, and Corrine will be coming too,' Bandy was a little hesitant. 'Oh! Are they coming with you?'

'No, they will be coming up on Friday.'

'That's fine, my boy, I'll book another room for Debbie and Corrine can bunk with you, not a problem.' He said goodbye to Bandy and made his way back to the table where they were clearing the table. 'Well, that's all sorted, you guys are booked in for Friday at the Sundowner Inn, just outside Newcastle.'

'I have arranged to take this Friday off at short notice, Dalores was very understanding,' said Corrine.

'That's good dear, now I thought that we could leave Friday morning, it's a three-hour drive so if we aim to get there for lunchtime, it will give us some shopping time,' said Debbie.

'Oh boy! There's that word again, how you women like to spend hours just shopping is beyond me.'

'Well, it's not a man's delight, I think if you spent more time looking around and taking your time, you will appreciate shopping.'

'Well, time is something that we don't have, there's always something that needs doing. I can't explain it, perhaps it's because we have our own business.'

'That explains a lot,' said Debbie.

'We had better get going, Jake has to get an early night.' They said goodbye and left the restaurant, Jim would be OK at work. There were no deliveries and Nathan was up to speed, so they were covered, less pressure on Jake so he could concentrate on the rodeo.

'Are you sure you OK to work in the rodeo? I don't want you to get hurt, I've heard so many bad things about people who work for the rodeo.' He smiled at her and held her hand, 'Look, I'll be fine.'

'Bandy will look after me and you will be there to see me on Saturday, so don't worry, now let's go to bed.' And with that, Jake turned off the light downstairs and they both walked up the staircase to go to bed.

As he walked upstairs, he was thinking to himself, 'I hope it all goes well.'

Chapter Fifty-Nine

Wednesday morning started with the sun rising over Green River, it was a little misty but that wouldn't last too long, it was going to be another fine day. Jake put his bag into the car and Corrine was at the door of the house in her dressing gown waving him off, she was going back to bed as she didn't start work till 9am.

'Now don't forget to ring me when you get there, I love you.' Jake looked at her and smiled, 'Love you too,' he got into the car and closed the car door and started the engine. He looked at Corrine again and waved at her while pulling away from the drive.

She waved back and then went inside the house closing the door behind her. She leant her back against the front door and looked up at the ceiling. 'Please look after him,' she said to herself and then went towards the stairs and back to bed.

Jake rang his dad to say that he was leaving and his mother was standing next to Jim, 'You take care son and we'll see you on Friday.'

Jake was soon at Interstate 80 and on his way to Newcastle, he took a sip of coffee from his flask that Corrine had prepared for him. There wasn't much traffic on the Interstate so he had much of the road to himself. The Interstate is named after Dwight D Eisenhower who was a military officer and served as the 34th President of the United States. Eisenhower planned and supervised two of the most consequential military campaigns of World War II. Operation Torch in the North Africa campaign in 1942–1943 and the D-Day invasion of Normandy in 1944, during the second world war.

Eisenhower started his military career in 1915, after graduating from Westpoint he served under Sam Houston throughout World War I. He ended the war as the commander. Later, he would be first supreme commander of NATO, he then won a landslide victory to become President in 1956. He was involved with the development and construction of the interstate highway which remains the largest construction of roadways in American history. In 1957, he created NASA and forced Russia to up their game in the space race, he has always been in the upper tier of American presidents.

Jake was travelling to Rawlins where he would need to come off the Interstate 80 and join the South Higley Boulevard. He would stop over at Rawlins and rest before getting back on the road again.

The drive had taken just under two hours when he got into the town, he made his way to the Country Pride restaurant where he ordered two omelette and chicken fried steak with pancakes This place was recommended by Bandy. It was opposite the Conoco petrol station, so he would top up his fuel while he was there. It was busy but there was a place at the counter to sit and eat. After having his lunch, he took a couple of deep breaths to let the food digest.

The waitress behind the bar looked at him. 'How was the food?'

'Well ma'am, it's the best chicken and omelette that I have had.'

'Thank you.' He left the restaurant and got into his car and drove across the road to the gas station and put some gas in his car. He was then ready to move on to 3rd street and catch Highway 287. This would take him on to three forks where he would join the 220, he would then join up with Highway 25 and onward to Newcastle. He was tired but wanted to push all the way to the Sundowner Inn, total time would be close to four hours. Bandy had arranged with Jake to meet up in the evening on the day of his arrival.

Jake phoned Corrine. 'Hi babe, well I'm halfway there, what you up to?'

'I am at work, you know, what most of us do during the day, unlike some people who just drive around all day.'

'Haha funny, I miss you too, look I will ring you when I get to the hotel OK!'

'OK babe, take care and drive safely.' Jake got a call from his dad just as he finished with Corrine.

'Hi Jake, how you doing?'

'Just fine Dad, had some lunch and boy! What a lunch, I think I over eat!'

'Well, you take care and drive safe and I'll ring you later.' He got back into his car and headed for the highway, he was contented and relaxed, ready for the drive.

Chapter Sixty

Later that day the weather turned a little dull and there were grey clouds sweeping across the highway, Jake was nearly at his destination and only had a couple of miles left to go. The Sundowner Inn was outside Newcastle, he pulled off the highway and along a smaller road that would take him to the Sundowner Inn, there was not a lot of greenery around, just patches here and there. He could see in the distance a white clad building; it had a grass lawn in the front of the motel which stood out like a cactus flower in the desert.

As he pulled into the entrance, he was greeted by a porch in the front decorated with hanging baskets all around. It certainly made you feel like coming home. He rang Corrine and told her that he had arrived and that he was going to freshen up and relax for a while before meeting up with Bandy.

Jake parked the car near the motel got his bag and got out of the car, after closing the door he walked on the gravel and sand path to the entrance through the porch. It was very quaint! Leather chairs were on either side of the carpeted lobby floor, there was a fireplace with an open basket fire, not in use at the moment. There were American flags adorned around the brick fireplace, in case you forgot what country you were in!

The family that ran the inn had a reputation for being friendly.

'Howdy!' said the man behind the desk.

'Hi, my name is Jake Rogers and I believe you have a room booked for me.'

The clerk looked at his register, 'Sure do, can you just sign the register and we can get your room sorted out for you.'

He turned the book around so that Jake could sign it. He gave Jake his pen, there should be another room for my mother who will be here on Saturday. My wife will be coming as well, it should be booked already.

'Sure thing, Mr Rogers, let me just have a look and see what rooms are free.'

'We are not too busy this time of the year, but with the rodeo in town, it can be hectic! Bandy said you would be coming in, how do you know him? Jake explained how they met and that he was looking forward to the rodeo.'

'So, how do you know him?' asked Jake.

'Well! He is kind of a legend around here, known him for years.'

'My name is Jed Pickens, related to the actor Slim Pickens, you know, on my wife's side. I am the owner of this establishment, Bandy was right, he said that you were a nice feller.' He opened his drawer under the desk counter and saw that there were three room keys available. 'OK! You can have room 9 your mother's room is 10 which is one room away from your room.'

'That will be fine,' said Jake. 'I just need to take some details for the room, can you fill in the parts marked with an x.'

Jake took the form that he put in front of him and filled in his mother's details then passed it back when he had finished.

'OK then, that will be $45.00 are you paying by cash or plastic?'

Jake took out his wallet. 'Cash please,' he gave Jed the cash and got the key for his room. 'It's down the hall on your left, I hope you enjoy your stay.'

'Thanks, I'm sure I will.'

Jake picked up his bag and walked towards the direction of his room, the hall was brightly decorated with patterned carpet on the floor and pictures of scenery from around Newcastle hung on the walls. Jake recalled the motel sign outside saying 'Just like home' and it certainly felt like that. He opened his room door and was greeted by more patterned carpet and more pictures on the walls, there was even a desk and settee there. He smiled and put his bag on the bed, he got his phone and decided to ring his parents, he rang his mum's phone.

'Hi Jake, how is everything?'

'Fine Mum, it's like being at home.'

'Well, that's nice, did you sort out a room for Saturday?'

'Yes, that's done, you are one door down the hall from me.'

'I'm going to have a little sleep and Bandy is coming here later to pick me up for dinner, I think there are some people he wants me to meet.'

'Well, you take care and don't promise anyone anything, I know you!' She said.

'No Mum, I won't, well I'm going to unpack and I will call you tomorrow OK.'

'That's fine, son, you make sure you get some rest, we love you.' He closed the phone and unpacked and then got ready for a shower and a quick nap.

After waking up, it was time for Jake to meet Bandy in the lobby, he had left his room and walked towards the lobby. He could hear Bandy's voice and as he entered, he saw Bandy talking to Jed, both laughing and talking about the good old days. Bandy turned towards Jake, 'Jake my boy!'

He was holding a drink in his hand, a glass of what looked like whisky, Jed was also holding the same.

Jake smiled and came over to shake Bandy's hand. 'I hope you had a good rest; we are gonna meet a couple of people who want to meet you.'

'I thought we were just going for dinner.'

'Well, yes, we are, but these guy's pay the rent, so to speak. It will just take a few minutes.'

Jed interjected, 'Like the last time you had one of your dinners, remember, the next morning they were still drinking.' Jed was looking at Jake and smiled.

'Yeah, but that was when I was a lot younger,' said Bandy.

'Well, some things just don't change,' said Jed.

'Just give the boy a drink, Jed and then we will make a move.' Jed went to get Jake a glass when Jake stopped him, 'Just a coke if you have one, it's a bit early for me.' Bandy nodded his head towards Jed to approve Jake's decision, there were a few other guests in the lobby waiting to hit the town, they were also here for the rodeo.

Sponsorship was big business in the rodeo game and it could make or break companies. Jake was not aware of the plans that Bandy had for him, plans that could cause problems for Jake's home life and marriage. Bandy saw himself as a Colonel Tom Parker, who made Elvis Presley a legend and then proceeded to destroy him with his greed for money and gambling took over his life. Before they were to leave, Jake rang Corrine to let her know that he was about to head out for the evening, she told him not to overdo things and she would call him tomorrow. They left the Sundowner and headed to Bandy's pickup truck and they headed for the city centre on Interstate 16, to Newcastle.

'We are going to the West End Bar and Grill,' said Bandy. 'I've been going there on a regular basis, hell, I've got my own table there.'

He laughed as they drove a little faster. Jake noticed that he had sped up a bit so thought he would talk him into slowing down. 'So how long have you been coming to Newcastle?'

'Oh, I've been coming here for nigh on twenty years, there's no place like it.'

'So, it's kind of like your home in a way then?' Bandy turned to him briefly, 'Yep! You could say that.'

'I never really thought about it that way before,' he had slowed down a little, so the talking worked.

'You know something Jake, this place has so much history, a couple of hours east of here and you will find where Custer had his so-called last stand, at the Little BigHorn.' You know, when you stand on the land there, you get this uneasy feeling, that you are being watched, give me the heebie-jeebies!

'You know I learned all about the American Midwest history when I was at college, a lot of history in a short space of time.'

'Did you know that Custer was 37 years old when he died, he was born in Rumley Ohio and he was buried at West Point Cemetery in 1877. The Native Americans won that day, but their struggle was hopeless against the tide of civilisation. They were later described as "An obstacle to progress", they had their day, but the odds were too great against them.'

'You really know your stuff Jake, I'm impressed.'

They had arrived at the place and Bandy pulled off the highway and towards a long drive, they could see the West End Bar and Grill in the distance all lit up, it was on a slight hill and stood out like a roman candle in the middle of the desert. There were plenty of cars in the car park as they approached the car park, Bandy found a spot and parked the car. They got out and headed for the entrance, they were met by a lady in a red skirt and white blouse revealing some cleavage, she was pretty and welcomed them in.

A waitress came up to them and Bandy told her who he was and she acknowledged him and they followed her to a table to one side of the room. After sitting them down, she said that a waitress would come over and take their order, a few minutes later, a waitress did arrive at the table.

'Hi, my name is Tammy and I am your waitress for tonight.' She was also pretty and had the same uniform as the lady at the door, 'Can I take your drinks order first and then when I get back, I can then take your food order.'

Bandy ordered a whiskey and Jake ordered a beer; Tammy went off to get their drinks. 'Well, what do you think, nice place?'

Jake looked around, 'Yeah, not bad, very busy.'

'The guys meeting us here later, are the sponsors, and if it wasn't for them, the shows would not go on, they put a lot of money into this business.'

Tammy had brought their drinks to the table, 'Here you are gents, have you decided on your food?' Bandy had a quick look at the menu and looked at Jake, 'Let me suggest the Texan Burger with fries, you'll thank me later for this,' he looked up at Tammy, 'Two Texan Burgers and fries darlin, thank you.'

Tammy smiled 'Good choice,' and she left to get their order.

Tammy was in her late teens and had just finished college and was in between jobs at the moment. 'Hey Jake! What do you think of her,' winking at Jake and moving his head to point towards Tammy.

Jake turned to look and then turned back to Bandy, 'Are you crazy, I am married you know.'

'Yeah, but you're a long way from home,' Jake picked up his drink and sipped the glass. 'I'm fine thanks, anyway, Corrine will be here on Friday.'

'You're alright Jake, just testing you, good boy!'

Bandy was about to say something to Jake when he was interrupted, two men in their late fifties approached their table and one of them stood behind Bandy's right-hand side. Bandy turned around, 'Ah Blake, you made it,' Bandy got up from the table and faced him to shake his hand. 'Take a seat, we have just ordered food, what can I get you.'

'Look if you don't mind, we will just have drinks, we had a heavy lunch earlier. Oh, and this is David Jones, he's a promoter, I thought it would be nice to get his input, hope you don't mind.'

'The more the merrier,' said Bandy as the two men sat down at the table, Tammy had just reached their table with their food which was on a tray.

'Good evening will you be having a meal as well?' asked Tammy.

'No, but we will have some drinks please,' replied Blake.

'Certainly sir, what would you like?'

'Two whisky and sodas please.'

'Thank you, I will be back shortly,' said Tammy as she went to get their drinks.

'Nice girl,' remarked David, who was dressed in a grey suit and black shirt with no tie, Blake was dressed in a black suit with white shirt and tie, very business-like.

'Well, is this the young man we have been hearing great things about?' asked Blake.

Bandy turned to Jake who wasn't sure what all the fuss was about, 'Yes! This is Jake Rogers, and I am expecting great things from this boy.'

Blake reached across the table to shake Jake's hand, 'Nice to meet you Jake, I guess this man hasn't told you a lot about us and what we do has he?'

Jake was just about to put a piece of food in his mouth but stopped to reply, 'Not exactly,' said Jake. 'Well! Jake, we are part of a team that promotes events like the rodeo and its stars. We get paid by advertising companies who pay for the privilege of putting your face on their products.'

Jake was eating and quickly chewed and swallowed his food, 'But I'm a nobody, I mean I'm not famous, so why me?'

'That's the beauty of all this, it's our job to make you somebody! And we know talent when we see it.'

David then spoke, 'Jake, we read the newspapers and from what Bandy has told us about you, well, let's just say that we are very interested in promoting you.'

Bandy was well into his food and encouraged Jake to eat up, Tammy had arrived back at their table, 'Here you are gentlemen, two whisky sodas, can I get you any more drinks,' she was looking at Jake.

'I'll have a top up how about you, Jake?'

'No, I'm fine, thanks.' Tammy went to get Bandy another Jack Daniels on the rocks.

Jake was halfway through his food when Bandy spoke, 'You see my boy, these men know talent and you are going all the way up, but we need commitment from you, I know it's difficult to take all this all in at the moment. But it will make you rich.'

Jake nodded towards Bandy, 'Well! I hope I don't let you down, but you will have to explain to me exactly what it is that I have to do.'

'You leave that to me Jake, I will take real good care of you, my boy.' Jake finished his burger and Bandy was talking shop with the other two, Tammy had come back to clear the table.

'Was everything alright?' Jake looked up at her, 'You were right, the burger was great.'

She looked at his plate. 'You didn't finish it, are sure it was OK?' He looked at his plate, 'I had a big breakfast this morning so couldn't finish it, I'm sorry!'

'That's OK, would you like a coffee?'

'No. I'm OK thanks.'

'What about you gentlemen, would you like coffees?'

'No darling, we are fine and thank you for your service, can I have the bill please?' asked Bandy.

'No problem, I'll get it for you.' She left their table and headed for the kitchen. Jake was thinking about his role in all this. Well one thing for sure, he was going to find out exactly his role once the training starts.

Chapter Sixty-One

Thursday morning started fresh with a slight overcast sky over Green River, the forecast was for sunshine to bring brighter spells later in the afternoon. Over at the Rogers household, Jim was getting ready to go to work and Debbie had arranged to go shopping later with Corrine, who had asked Dalores for the morning off work.

There was not too much to do at the salon today so Dalores was able to cope, Corrine was well loved there and great with customers.

After he had left for work Debbie decided to ring Jake, just to make sure he didn't sleep in and to make sure that she knew what Bandy had planned for him. She called his number and looked at her watch just to make sure it wasn't too early to call him, it was 08.30am so she didn't think that was early.

'Hello Jake, it's Mum.'

Jake was in bed and when he answered the phone. 'Hi, Mum, you're early, are you OK?'

'Yes of course, I just wanted to make sure that you were awake and find out what Bandy had planned for you today.'

'Why?'

'Well, we are worried about you and we don't want him to take advantage of your good nature.'

'I think that I would know if that was going to happen, look don't worry, all is fine, where is Corrine, is she with you?'

'No, I'm going to pick her up later, we are going shopping for the trip to come and see you tomorrow.'

'So, what have you got to do today?'

'Well, today I am going to get acquainted with El Toro! The bull Bandy says that I have to show the bull no fear.'

'Well, you take care and don't get too close to that critter.'

'OK, Mum, I will call you guys later, say hello to Corrine for me I am running a little late so won't have time to ring her.'

'OK, dear, will do.'

'Well, how was he?' said Jim. Debbie picked up her cup of coffee and came over to him who was putting his shoes on while sitting on a chair next to the coat rack. 'He seems OK, but I'm worried about him, he's all on his own.'

Jim smiled, 'He knows what to do, just enjoy yourself shopping today, I'm off to work, I will see you later,' he got up and gave Debbie a kiss on the lips and left the house.

Just at that moment, Debbie's phone rang, it was Corrine, 'Hi, Mum, have you heard from Jake, I tried ringing him but he didn't answer.'

'He's fine. I spoke to him a couple of minutes ago, he was late and told me to tell you that.'

'How did he sound to you.'

'He went out for a meal last night.'

'I hope Bandy didn't get him drunk.'

'We are talking about Jake aren't we, he is fine, he didn't sound like he had a hangover. What time do you want me to pick you up?'

'Is 9.30 OK?'

'Yes, that's fine, I'll see you later.'

Jim had opened the shop and Nathan had just arrived on his bike. 'Morning, Mr Rogers.'

'Morning Nathan, how are you this morning?'

'Good thanks, did you get to speak to Jake yesterday?'

'Yes, we did, and he is doing fine, Debbie and Corrine are going tomorrow morning to meet up with him.'

'I bet Jake is looking forward to seeing them.'

'Yes, no doubt. Before we start work why don't you go and get us both a cup of coffee from the coffee shop, I don't like the taste of the coffee that we have,' he gave Nathan ten dollars from his wallet and Nathan put his bike away and then walked to the coffee shop which was a few doors down the street.

Debbie had arrived at Corrine's house and beeped the horn, Corrine opened her net curtains and waved at Debbie who was looking up from her car window. A few moments later, Corrine was closing her front door and walking towards the car, Debbie opened the passenger door from the inside and Corrine got in and closed the door.

'Are you ready to spend some money!' Corrine smiled and Debbie drove off towards the Moll, they were going to get some clothes for the trip and have lunch as well. It was just an excuse to get Corrine out and take her mind off things, she has been through a lot recently. They will still keep the memory of George alive but for now, Corrine was the one they were concentrating on.

'Can you drop me to the bank, Mum? I have to deposit Jake's cheque, he asked me to bank it.'

'No problem, dear we can park there and visit some shops nearby.'

Bethany came to the Jim's shop to drop some photos off for the family, she was hoping to see Jake but Jim told her that Jake was going to be working at the Weston County Rodeo.

'That would have been a great chance for our paper to get some pictures and it would make a great story,' said Bethany, 'Well the rodeo is on Saturday, maybe you can get the paper to pay for you to cover it!'

'Well, there's no harm in trying, I suppose, well here are the pictures for the awards, these are for you to keep.' Jim thanked her and she left the shop, he called Nathan over to look at the pictures. 'If Jake carries on like this, he will be running for mayor one day!'

Jim looked at him and reflected for a moment and then carried on looking at the pictures.

Chapter Sixty-Two

Jake was on his way to the Four Seasons Arena, to meet up with Bandy, after driving for ten minutes he drove into the car park and looked for the staff car park. Bandy had told him to park there, he went to the staff entrance and opened the door. There was a security guard inside sitting behind a desk with a brown uniform on. 'Good morning, can I help you?'

'Er, yes I'm here to see Bandy, my name is Jake Rogers.'

'He's been expecting you; can you sign in this book please,' he showed him the book on his desk in front of the guard and gave Jake a pen. The guard then opened the drawer to his right and took out a badge with a lanyard on it and once Jake had finished signing the book gave him the lanyard.

'Take a right down the hall and follow the passage to the end, then turn left and his office is on the right.'

'Thank you,' said Jake as he set off.

After walking for what seemed like ages, he arrived at Bandy's office, he could see him sitting behind his desk through the glass panel in the door. Jake knocked on the door and Bandy looked up at Jake and smiled, he waved him in and Jake opened the door and walked in.

'Jake, my boy! Come on in and help yourself to a cup of coffee,' he pointed to the table in the corner of his spacious office. There was light blue carpet on the floor and the furniture was in mahogany, there was a walnut wooden cupboard to one side near to his large desk and a Chesterfield rich brown leather settee on the other side, there were two wooden upholstered chairs in front of his desk. Jake went over to get a coffee as he left the motel in a hurry, 'Do you want one?' asked Jake.

'No, you carry on and come and sit here when you are ready.'

Jake brought his coffee in a mug and sat in one of the upholstered chairs, 'impressive office,' Bandy smiled.

'I worked hard for these pleasures,' he said. Jake sipped his coffee.

'As we have a lot to get through today, Jake, I'm sorry but you will probably be late home today, I hope you don't mind.'

'It's what I expected, anyway I have nothing to rush home to as I'm staying at a motel.'

'Well finish your coffee and we will go and meet some of the men you will be working with.'

First of all, we need to get you legal, he took out a folder with Jake's name on it and opened it, he then took out a contract for Jake to sign. 'I will just need your signature on this form Jake and then we will be able to pay you.'

Jake had to put his bank details down on the form so that the company can pay him. 'Your salary for the Saturday will be $350.00, Jake and we will keep the contract on an open basis, what that means, is that it's open ended. You still work for me but only when you want to, if you get my drift.'

'I think so, but I thought you said back in Green River that it was $250.00.'

Bandy smiled at him with a poker stare into his eyes, 'that's right, but after last night the board had agreed to increase your money, now that's done let's go meet the people. Exactly what is it that I am going to be doing in this rodeo.'

'You, my boy are going to be the star of the show, you are the rodeo clown, along with a few others, your job will be to keep the cowboys safe. From the bull's hooves and horns and wild horses kicking out in anger.'

'That sounds dangerous.'

'Not really, once you get the hang of things you will have nothing to fear, I have faith in you Jake, and I'm not normally wrong.' Jake was thinking to himself, 'what have I let myself in for,' he was going to see what else was involved with this job and evaluate later.

They approached the main arena and it was huge, it had sturdy wood fencing all around and double gates leading to another arena where the animals were kept. There were holding pens where the bulls were kept just before being released in the main arena. It was an impressive set up and safety was the primary concern, Jake felt a little more at ease as he followed Bandy to meet some of the other hands who were going to work with Jake.

They walked towards the pens and there were four men working some horses, 'Hey Bob, come over here and meet Jake! Bob was the main guy who looked after the other hands, it was his job to keep everyone on track, a kind of foreman and father figure. He was in his late fifties but still played an active part in the show, he had a slight limp from an incident with El Toro!'

'Bob, meet Jake, my replacement.'

Bob looked at Bandy surprised, 'Replacement! But you retired a while ago.'

'Yes, I know but this is the new me, Jake is a natural, put him through his paces and don't hold back.'

Bob looked at Jake. 'Well, if Bandy sees something in you, then he is not often wrong, let's hope he is right, we desperately need some new blood in this industry.' Jake was taken to meet the rest of the hands and would be learning everything from roping to learning all the tricks of bull dodging!

Jake was going to go through intense training because his life would depend on it, and Bandy knew that he was taking a chance with him. But he had no choice, his empire was falling down around him, he needed young blood to take over. There were not enough younger people wanting to learn the art of the rodeo clown, too many accidents and not enough limelight. Bandy was hoping that Jake was going to change all that, he was praying that Jake was going to be the one!

Chapter Sixty-Three

Corrine had stayed over the night before at the Rogers house she stayed in Jake's room, it made sense because they were travelling together on the long drive to Newcastle in the morning. Debbie was awake early getting breakfast ready and making sandwiches for the journey, Jim was up as well even though it was earlier than he would normally get up.

'Do you want me to start putting your bags in the car?' asked Jim.

Debbie was in the kitchen just taking a sip of coffee, 'Yes please dear. She came out of the kitchen and walked up to him before he could pick up the bags and kissed him on the cheek.'

'What was that for?' asked Jim.

'Oh, no reason just felt like doing it' said Debbie in a happy mood.

Jim smiled at her and picked up the two leather bags with their clothes and toiletries in and took them to the car. Debbie's car was a little older, but it ran well and was regularly maintained by Jim, he was good at that sort of thing. It was time to hit the road and Corrine was ready and waiting by the door, she was wearing light blue jeans and a waist length checked shirt. Debbie had on jeans as well but with a tucked in short sleeved blouse, Jim was at the door ready to see them off.

'Well! Are you girls ready to go?'

'Yes, we are,' said Corrine as they approached Jim, he opened the door and stood by the side to shepherd them out. 'Now you take care of yourself and make sure you eat properly,' said Debbie as she leant over to kiss him on the lips, 'Yes dear and you take care driving, don't forget to rest now and then.'

'Yes darling, I will ring you when I get there,' they both left the house and got into the car, Debbie started the car and pulled away waving to Jim as they left the driveway and onto the road. Jim waved back and was wishing that he could have gone with them, but work was important and with Jake away someone had to make sure that the ship was steadied.

The highway was a little busier than normal being a Friday, but the weather was nice and once they had Green River behind them all that lay ahead was grassy plains, dry prairies dotted with shrub-stepped sagebrush and ephemeral wetland. Rocky, jagged formations rising from the desert, some mountains were majestic in their appearance.

A poet once said of Wyoming, Bluffs. Buttes, mesas, and mountain ranges, thick forests, colours that blend one into the other in every imaginable shade of green-emerald. Chartreuse, silver-grey, sage, vibrant teal turquoise and deep forest green. This is my Wyoming, my lasting impression of a vast, open, unspoiled land with few people, abundant wildlife, stunning views, and a definite western flavour. This is my Wyoming.

'I can never get enough of this scenery, we should drive out more often,' said Debbie.

'I know, it's beautiful,' replied Corrine as she opened the passenger side window and lay back in her seat, slight overtones of 'Thelma and Louise' possibly. They were well on their way and Corrine was wondering what Jake was doing, she was concerned about him and hoped that he was alright.

Chapter Sixty-Four

The training was going well and they were all impressed with Jake, how he adapted to all situations as if he had been doing this forever. Bob came over to Bandy who had made his way down to the arena, he stood by the gates and rested both arms on the gate, 'You were not wrong, that fella is a natural, I've never seen anything like it, are you sure he has not done anything like this before?'

Bandy laughed, 'No siree! He's the real deal alright, just got to convince him to stay.'

'Well, if it's in his blood, then he ain't gonna need convincing,' said Bob, Bandy stared at Jake as he was practising with the lasso throwing it around a wooden bull placed in the arena for practising. A thought suddenly occurred while watching him.

Bandy signalled over to Jake with his hand, waving it in the air, Jake looked over eventually and acknowledged him, he had a smile on his face. Jake was enjoying himself and made his way towards Bandy who was still waiting by the gate.

'Hey Jake! You look like you're having a good time, they tell me that you are quite capable out there, how do you feel?'

'I feel great, so far so good, when do I get to meet the bull?'

'Well, there is someone you will have to meet first.' Bandy put his hand on Jake's shoulder and steered him towards the door. 'Jake. My boy, let me introduce you to "the bull".' They walked to the entrance of the arena and into the foyer, it was a large expanse where the customers entered through the ticketing booths and there were refreshment counters towards the back just before the entrance. There were large video screens up above the refreshment stands showing forthcoming attractions. And there with pride of place was a mechanical rodeo bull.

It was protected with large leather cushions all around for the unfortunate riders who fell off the bull. Jake smiled and looked at Bandy, 'You are kidding right!' They approached the bull and Bandy stood by the mahogany and white patched bull with a saddle on its back, 'All joking aside, this is not just a toy, many a cowboy has been thrown by this machine, we like to call it "The Bronco Buster".'

Jake was encouraged to get on board, he approached the bull and put his left foot into the stirrup and climbed aboard, he then put his right foot into the other stirrup, there were reins made of leather and he took hold. Bandy took out a pair of leather wrangler gloves from his back pocket and handed them to Jake, 'These have been with me a long time,' and Jake took them and put them on.

Bandy picked up the remote-control box. 'Well, are you ready?'

Jake nodded, and Bandy started the ride, he turned it on to the first setting, this was used for the children, it moved slowly in a backward and forward motion and started spinning around slowly. Jake thought that he looked silly sitting on this bull, he increased the bull straight to the third setting, this was for the adults and budding cowboys. Jake was very comfortable.

Bandy set it to number five, and this was in the territory of the more experienced riders, this didn't seem to bother Jake as he still looked at ease. Jake was starting to get an audience who could see that this could be worth watching, Bandy looked at Bob who was impressed with Jake's ease of riding. He increased to number six and smiled at Bob, thinking that this will test Jake. This setting was for the rodeo rider's level and Jake still looked comfortable. More onlookers arrived. He was gathering quite a crowd even some rodeo riders were among the crowd anxious to see this green horn. There was cheering from some parts of the crowd. Bandy went up another notch to experienced level. Jake was a little unsettled but adjusted his stance and held on tighter. The cheering got louder and Bandy looked at Bob again.

'Didn't I tell you this kid is the one! Bob could not believe what he was seeing, only a handful of experienced rodeo riders would be able to stay on at this pace.'

There were two more settings and Bandy put the next level on, Jake was struggling a little but was still holding on, just. There was disbelief in the crowd, they could sense something special here and cheered Jake on further, this level has only been reached by few experienced riders, the bull was kicking up and down and tilting further forward and backwards, Jake had banged his head on the neck of the bull a couple of times but was still holding on for dear life.

Bandy clicked on to the last level and two other riders had achieved this level and they were legends. Jake held on for a few seconds and then lost control of his hands and slipped off the mechanical bull and landed on the leather cushions on the floor. There was clapping and whistling and the crowd went up to Jake to see who this kid was. Bob went over to help him up, he received handshakes and pats on the back, Bandy turned off the bull and went over to Jake who was taking off the gloves that Bandy gave him.

'Jake! Are you alright?'

Jake was a little dizzy but acknowledged Bandy. 'I knew it! I knew you had it in you, consider this your final part of your training. This will give you the edge you need when you are in the ring.' The onlookers slowly dispersed, still talking about the green horn who broke the bull.

You take yourself a break and give your wife a call, they should be coming over today, then after lunch we will introduce you to El Toro! Jake smiled and made his way to the canteen. Once he was there, he grabbed himself a tray and went up to where the food was being dished out, the canteen was quite large and could cater for up to five hundred people. He helped himself to a steak and potatoes and green beans, he got a drink from the dispenser, sprite was his choice, he needed something refreshing after building up a sweat. He sat down at one of the tables and took out his phone.

He rang Corrine to find out how far they were, the phone was ringing, 'Hi Jake! I knew you would ring, how are you?'

'I'm fine, how are you doing, and how far are you from Newcastle?'

'Well, I think that we are about an hour away, maybe a little less, I'll ring you when we get to the inn.'

'OK, is Mum OK with the driving?'

Debbie could hear the conversation, 'I'm fine son, can't wait to see you, we'll talk more then.'

'OK, I'm just having some lunch and will get to meet El Toro! Later.'

'Just be careful Jake, please.'

'Don't worry about me, I'm fine, I'll see you later, take care.' Jake carried on with his lunch, he wanted to finish lunch quickly, he was anxious to meet the bull. Jake still didn't understand exactly what he had to do in the rodeo, but was quite confident he could cope. A few people came up to him while he was eating to congratulate him on the bull ride. His quick lunch was going to take a little longer.

After lunch, Jake went to Bandy's office and knocked on the door, a voice called out to him, 'Come in Jake.' He opened the door and walked in. Bob was in the office sitting on the leather couch.

'How was lunch?' asked Bandy.

'Great thanks, steak was big!' said Jake.

Bandy smiled. 'Only the best for our boys,' he said.

'I think you are ready to meet our star attraction,' said Bandy.

'OK I'm ready,' replied Jake.

'You are in for a treat,' said Bob. Bandy got up and moved from behind his desk and walked up to Jake, he put his right hand on Jake's right shoulder, 'Let's go and meet El Toro!' Bob opened the office door and they all left the office Bob following from the back.

They went to the holding pens which were near the main gates, the musty smell of animals was apparent as they neared the bull enclosure. There in front of them in a pen was a huge mass of black and fawn-coloured bull. The bull turned his head as they approached the gate and stared at them.

His cold dark eyes transfixed on Jake, he seemed to know that Jake was the newbie. 'He has seen you, Jake, now he is trying to weigh you up.'

Jake couldn't take his eyes off the bull, it was almost as if the bull was trying to hypnotise him. Jake shook his head and blinked a couple of times and then looked at Bandy, 'So long as I don't have to ride him, I think I will be fine.'

'But don't take anything for granted Jake, he is as quick as lightning and can turn on a sixpence.'

'We'll help you out as much as we can Jake, we have a good team,' said Bob. As they were about to turn away from the pen, El Toro snorted and stamped his feet on the ground and gave the action of trying to charge, the ground shook with the weight of the bull as he thumped the ground. Jake stood there and stared at the bull and tried not to blink, he was making the bull know that he was not scared of him and would not let the bull intimidate him. They walked away from the pen and Jake turned to look at the bull as they walked.

'I'll be seeing you,' Jake thought to himself. Bob took Jake back to the arena for more training, a few more hours would be needed to get Jake up to speed. He was then going to meet his mother and Corrine for dinner later.

Chapter Sixty-Five

It was approaching mid-afternoon. Debbie and Corrine were approaching the outskirts of Newcastle; they turned off at the next junction and headed towards the Sundowner Inn. Corrine was anxious and couldn't wait to meet up with Jake, she missed him while he was away.

Debbie pulled the car into the car park at the inn and parked just outside the inn entrance, she looked around at the area surrounding the inn. She got out of the car and stretched. 'Mmm, just smell that mountain air,' Corrine smiled, 'Why would you want to live in a city when you can have this.'

After taking out the luggage they entered through the front door and were greeted by Jed, 'Good afternoon, you must be Jake's mum?'

Debbie looked a little taken back, she wasn't sure that she was that well known, maybe they didn't get that many guests. She smiled at him, 'Yes, that I am, but how did you know?' she said as she walked up to the desk with Corrine next to her. 'And you must be Corrine!'

'Yes, but how did you know?'

'We have been expecting you, Jake has told us all about you.'

She felt a little surprised but managed to smile and take it in her stride, 'If you can both sign the register then I can show you to your rooms,' said Jed, after signing he took two keys from under the counter and stepped out from behind the desk.

'If you would follow me, please,' they picked up their bags and walked behind Jed to Debbie's room, he gave her the key and then he gave Corrine the key to Jake's room. Debbie told Corrine that she would knock on her door a little later to go shopping if she was up to it, Corrine agreed but first a shower and freshen up after the long drive.

An hour later, Debbie came out of her room and went to Corrine's room, it was only next door and knocked on the door. Corrine opened it, 'Come on in,' she said. 'I'm just finishing my hair.'

'It's a nice room, very homely,' said Debbie. 'Yeah! Just something about this place makes you feel like your own place.'

When Corrine was ready, they both left the room and went to the front desk. 'Oh, Mrs Rogers, Jake asked me to give you a map of the area.' She took the map from him and quickly looked at it.

'Thank you, we are just going to drive into the town and explore a little.'

'Well, you have a good day, and if you want anything, just let me know,' said Jed. Jake had called Corrine and arranged to meet up with them around six o'clock so that they could have dinner together. Debbie got into the car and took and opened the map, 'Right, let's see where we are going to go.'

There was a main road through town and shops dotted along either side, they decided to just drive into the town, park the car and walk around the town. After crossing the railway tracks entering the town they saw the Weston County Home Centre, which was like a department store with concession shops inside, ranging from antique shops to menswear. It wasn't overly large, just big enough for its inhabitants. They found a place to park the car and got out to enjoy the fresh mountain air which this area was famed for.

Corrine got out of the car and as she stood up, 'Just smell that air, it's wonderful,' Debbie got out of the car and closed the door and took a deep breath. 'You're right, it is different, really clean and crisp.' They walked to the shop's window shopping at first and would then go into the shopping centre.

Jake was coming to the end of his training and was on his way back to the locker room when he saw Bandy walking towards him. 'Jake! Hold up,' he stopped in front of Jake. 'You done well my boy, I knew you had it in you.'

'You know something, if I ever wanted a son, I couldn't be more proud of him being like you, Jake!' He felt a little emotional and looked at Bandy, 'Thanks, that means a lot to me.'

'Look, I'll see tomorrow morning at 10am, now you go and spend some time with your wife and mother.'

Corrine and Debbie were inside the shopping centre and looking into the many shops within. Debbie had already had a couple of bags from the shops that they had visited, Corrine's phone rang and she took it out of her hand bag. 'Hi hun! We are shopping at the moment at the Weston Home Centre.'

'That's great, look I should be with you in about half an hour, don't spend too much, only joking! I'll see you later.'

Corrine smiled and said goodbye to Jake. 'What is he doing? Is he going to meet us soon?' asked Debbie.

'Yes, he said that he will be about half an hour.' They were almost finished and decided to go and get a cold drink. They walked into the ice cream parlour and ordered a couple of soft drinks and found a table in the corner of the room so that they could sit down.

Jake saw his mother's car in the car park and pulled up next to it and got out of the car, he made his way into the store. As he was passing the ice cream parlour, he noticed Corrine and his mother sitting at a table, he walked into the room and was noticed straight away.

Jake pulled out a chair and sat down at the table 'Fancy meeting you here! He said, they looked at him and laughed, 'Do you want a drink?' He looked at their drinks and said, 'No, I think I'll wait till we get to the restaurant; I could kill a beer!'

'Right, we will just drink these quickly and go,' said Debbie as they were only drinking soft drinks, it didn't take long and they got up and left the ice cream parlour. Corrine got up a little too quick and she held her head, 'Head freeze!' She said.

'Just take a second,' said Debbie, as they waited for her to get over it.

They headed towards Isabellas, a restaurant that Bandy had recommended to Jake, it wasn't far, just a couple of hundred yards up the high street. The restaurant was set back from the high street and stood alone with a car park at its side, there were tables set outside with parasol umbrellas above each one. As it was a sunny day and quite warm, they would be sitting outside.

'You guys sit at a table and I will get some menus,' said Jake as he walked towards the entrance of the restaurant.

There were a handful of people already sitting at tables outside but Debbie had found one and put her bag on one of the chairs. 'This looks fine!' She said and Corrine agreed as they both pulled out the wooden chairs and sat down. The tables were wood as well, made out of locally sourced Montana pine. Jake was inside the restaurant and walked up to the bar. There were tall wooden stools placed along the length of the bar, which was made of solid pine polished to a gloss finish. A typical western bar, pretty commonplace as this area was historical. The Black Hills were on the border and that was famed for the Battle of Little BigHorn. Where General George Armstrong Custer led his infamous 7th Cavalry into legendary status, many cattle towns sprung up along the trails and some turned into larger cities. Deadwood, Rapid City, Sturgis, Sundance and many others, some wagon trains followed the cattle route as well, and a few families stayed put at one of the towns, not wishing to go any further. Those were hard times but without them there would be no west!

Inside the restaurant there were two young girls and a man in his forties, who looked like he was in charge, serving behind the bar. Jake stood by the bar, one of the girls came up to him and smiled, 'Hi, there, how can I help you?'

'Hi, can I get a couple of menus please.'

'Sure thing,' she said with a smile and got some menus from behind the bar and gave them to Jake. He took two of the menus.

'Do I order in here?' asked Jake. 'Are you sitting outside?'

'Yes, there are three of us.'

'That's fine I'll be right out to get your drinks order and your mains.'

'Thanks,' said Jake as he took the menus and went outside, once at the table he gave one to his mother and the other to Corrine. 'The waitress will be out in a bit to take our orders, so choose!' said Jake. They looked through and didn't take long to decide what they wanted.

The girl from the bar was making her way towards Jake and was coming to take their orders, she approached the table and smiled. She was in her early twenties and pretty with long auburn hair. 'Hi there, how you guys doing?' She asked. They smiled and Corrine noticed that she was looking more at Jake than the two of them. She took out her little notebook and was ready to write down their orders, 'My name is Becky and I will be serving your table today, have you decided what to order?'

'Well,' said Debbie. 'There is so much choice, but I will have the Custer burger with fries and salad please, how about you, Corrine?'

'That actually looks good, I will have the same; tell you what, make those three Custer burgers, and I will have a beer, what about you two?' asked Jake.

'I will have a tall coke with ice,' said Corrine.

'And I will have a white wine spritzer,' said Debbie.

'That's great, I highly recommend the burgers, I will be back shortly with your drinks,' said Becky as she headed back to the restaurant.

'Well, this is nice,' said Jake. 'Yes, it is and I still can't get over the fresh air, I thought Green River had the cleanest air!'

Corrine looked at Jake. 'Well it looks like you have an admirer.'

Jake looked at her, 'No, she is just doing her job.'

'I'm sure they all talk like that around here.'

He thought it best not to elaborate any further. 'Well, I don't know about you but I'm hungry, it must have been all the walking we did while shopping, it's amazing how time flies when you are having fun,' said Debbie. 'So, I have to tell you guys something, about tomorrow.'

'What do you mean?' said Corrine. 'Well, I don't want you to get worried or anything, but I will be a rodeo clown tomorrow.'

Corrine looked surprised and Debbie looked a little puzzled, 'But I thought that you were just there to help in the background?' asked Debbie. 'Well, that was how it started but they are short staffed and it's very safe, I have had a lot of training, and they are paying me a lot for just one day's work.'

'I knew that Bandy was up to no good,' said Debbie. 'Wait till I see him again!'

'Look, it's not his fault, he sees something in me and to tell the truth, I feel good about this!' Corrine looked at Debbie, 'So what's the future going to bring Jake, is this your new path?' asked Corrine.

He looked a little puzzled, 'What do you mean?'

'Well! What happens after this show, will there be another? And is this going to be your future! Have you ever considered us in all this!' said Corrine a little upset.

'No! I mean, I don't know! It feels right and I'm sorry that I was not thinking any further about the future, I suppose I was just caught up in the moment!' Jake reached out to put his hand on Corrine's hand. 'I'm sorry babe, I wasn't thinking! After the show I will tell Bandy that this is a one off and then we can go back to Green River,' Corrine held his hand, 'I just don't want anything to happen to you Jake, you are my life now, I have nothing else!'

At that moment Becky had arrived with their drinks, 'White wine spritzer for you, cola and ice for you,' as she passed Corrine's drink to her. 'And one beer for you,' she opened the bottle and gave it to Jake with a smile aimed directly at him. Corrine was staring daggers at Jake. He caught her eye staring at him as he smiled back at Becky.

'I'll be back with your burgers shortly,' she said as she departed.

Debbie raised her glass, 'Cheers! And let's just enjoy the day and think about the show later.' A little motherly advice as she could see an argument stirring.

The burgers arrived and they looked delicious and big, served with fries, 'Well, I'm looking forward to this,' said Jake, they tucked in to the food and not much more was said about the show for the moment.

After lunch, they got up and Jake went back into the restaurant to pay the bill, Debbie and Corrine walked back to where they parked the car. Corrine decided that she would ride back to the Sundowner with Jake and she waited by his car. Jake arrived and opened the car door for Corrine to get in. 'Well did you give her a tip?'

'It is customary to tip around here, so yes, I did,' he got into the car and they set off with Debbie following behind.

When they got back to the inn, Jake said goodnight to his mother and went to his room. Corrine decided to have an early night as well. Debbie was going to the bar at the inn and have a night cap, she sat down at one of the four stools by the bar. Jed came over to attend to her, 'On your own tonight?'

'Yes, I thought that I would have a drink before hitting the hay!'

'What will it be?' He asked. After looking at the drinks, she asked for a gin and tonic with ice and a slice of lemon.

Jake took a shower and Corrine followed him in and they made up for the days they were apart, she had forgiven him for earlier at the restaurant. Although it was strictly not his fault, he was just returning a gesture.

Chapter Sixty-Six

It was the day of the rodeo and it started with an overcast open sky, Jake was up early as he had to be at the arena a couple of hours before the first show started at twelve noon, Corrine was awake as he leant over to kiss her goodbye, he left the room at 9am. He had on a tee shirt and denim jacket with blue jeans as he got into his car and drove out towards the arena.

The roads were damp from the early mist but that would soon evaporate with the impending sun on its way. He put the radio on and as usual country music was playing and it made him happy listening to that type of music, he liked other genres of music but preferred country. He reached the arena within half an hour and pulled up into the employees' car park, Jake got out and entered the building, he had been given a badge by Bandy to wear on a lanyard around his neck. The security guard smiled at Jake. He was in the crowd that saw Jake on the mechanical bull.

'Unbelievable ride, Jake,' he said as he let Jake through. 'Thanks,' said Jake walking towards the locker room.

The members of his team were there just putting their things away before going to have breakfast in the canteen. 'Hey Jake,' said one of them as he walked in.

Jake smiled, 'You guys ready for today?'

'Yeah,' they said collectively, Bandy walked in with a cup of coffee in his hand.

'Morning everyone! Just here to say this is it! We need to give them a great show today, and I will see you later after breakfast at 11am in the meeting room.' They all made their way out of the locker room and towards the canteen, Bandy looked at Jake, 'You OK?'

Jake smiled back at him, 'I'm ready.' The canteen was alive with the sound of clanging steel pots and crockery, the strong smell of steaks cooking filled the air in the room, it made you feel hungry.

Breakfast was steak and eggs with biscuits and gravy, the staple diet of any rodeo worker, there was an endless supply of fresh coffee at hand.

The smell of fresh coffee wafted around the canteen as they tucked into their breakfast, Bob sat next to Jake, 'I'll be working with you, Jake, on the south side of the arena, and don't worry, after what I saw of your training, you will be alright.'

It was coming up to 10.30 and breakfast was nearly over, one by one they made their way to the meeting room where Bandy would go through the events happening today. But first they would have to change into their uniforms, they each had individual outfits, just like performing clowns they had a registered outfit that belonged to them. Jake had given to him Bandy's colours, black and white striped trousers with yellow braces and red shirt and fedora brown hat. The footwear was optional, they could wear whatever they wanted so long as it met safety standards. Once dressed, they entered the meeting room which was a short walk from the locker room.

Bandy was at the desk in front of a large black board. 'Settle down, people, we have fifteen minutes before we get set up out there, now you all know where and who you are working with, I don't have to tell you that safety is key our success and I don't want to see any fuck ups out there! The members of the public, who pay your wages, want a stress-free show. So, let's give them what they have paid for and make it look good and take care out there.'

They collectively shouted, 'Yes sir!' And left the room.

Once dispersed Bandy came to Jake, 'Well Jake, its time, show them who you are, my boy!' The meeting room was empty and Bandy was left alone staring at the empty chairs, he looked around the room and slowly closed the door behind him, he stood in the hallway 'Lord keep them safe.'

The arena was filling up with members of the public, the noon show brought mainly families together and the show catered for the younger audience. The scary stuff came later for the evening show, today's programme featured pony wrangling calf steer roping and clowns performing. There were also going to be the young rider's bronco horse trials, these riders would go on to become experienced rodeo riders, this was a training prequel to the real thing. Jake and Bob were ringside, this event was not going to be as dangerous as the evening show but they still had to be alert to prevent any accidents from happening.

Debbie and Corrine were going to be attending both shows, they were here mainly to see Jake so it was going to be a long day for them, country music filled the arena as the show was about to get going, the PRCA rodeo announcer started to speak, his job was to bring enthusiasm to the show. He began as a contestant many years ago and gained an insight into the sport. His job is to make the audience part of the show and part of each performance.

Whether its wild and western or polished and professional, it's excitement at its best, 'Good day to you one and all, and welcome to the Weston County Fair Rodeo, now folks you are going to have a great time today, we have the pony club finals with the top ten junior riders competing, boys and gals. We have little bull wrangling and bucking bronco teenage style.'

The arena music was turned up as the clowns entered the arena, there were half a dozen clowns running and stumbling on the sandy floor followed by a couple of clown cars with special wheels on to cope with the sandy floor.

The audience was cheering and clapping to the music, the announcer was speaking trying to get the crowd involved, after ten minutes the clowns left through the gates and it was the turn of the junior pony riders. The hurdles were being set up for the ponies to jump over by a dozen hands who practise this on a regular basis, the stage was set for the first of the juniors to ride out into the arena, this competition was against the clock, they had to jump six fences of different styles and sizes, and the best time wins.

Debbie and Corrine had good seats, four up from the front middle section which were right in front of the main gates of the rodeo entrants. They each had a cup of coffee in a disposable cup and were enjoying the show so far, Corrine waved out to Jake because he was to her right on the arena floor and saw them both as they sat down.

They were not going to get too much involved in this show but will be required for the calf roping and bronco riding later, for now they just helped with the running of the ponies. The winner of the show jumping against the clock was won by a girl, she is the current state champion in this event, so no surprise there then. It was now the turn of the roping of the calves, three calves were let loose into the arena and the competitors from the pony riding were let in and the first to rope a calf would win. It was pretty exciting and the speed of these ponies was something else. The crowd was cheering on the kids and eventually there was a winner, a boy this time. Jake and Bob had to round up the calves that didn't want to go back into their pens, they wanted to stay out in the arena, it seemed they liked the crowds. Jake was on horseback as he guided the calves towards the gates where Bob was waiting. Corrine liked the idea of Jake on horseback, apart from the clown outfit, it made him look sexy in her eyes.

'Okay folks, we will be setting up for the main event, the bronco competition, this event is for 16 years and under, and let me tell you there are some competitive riders taking part in this.' The horses taking part were not fully grown and could still cause a lot of damage, that is why only the best riders can take part in this. Jake would be on foot in this part of the show as the dedicated show riders would be taking part in this. Their job is to make sure the riders are safe from the broncos; they would ride up alongside to prevent any unfortunate accidents. Jake and Bob would see the broncos out of the ring by taking the attention off the rider, for this part of the show it would be less troublesome.

The winner was announced and the first part of the show was coming to an end, it was approaching 2pm and Debbie and Corrine would make their way back to the Sundowner for a little rest and get ready for the evening show. 'Well Corrine, that wasn't that bad and I think Jake did very well.'

'Yes, but that was the family part, the test will come for the main event, and the bull riding, I am so scared for him.'

'Jake will have his wits about him, if I know my son.'

They were out in the car park looking for their car when Jake caught up with them, 'Mum!'

They turned around to see a clown running towards them, 'It's Jake,' said Corine, he caught up to them and took his red nose off. Debbie laughed and Corrine couldn't help but laugh as well.

'Well! What did you think?' He said. 'Darling you were looking good out there, so far so good.'

'Just be careful for the next event, and keep a safe distance from the bull please,' said Corrine. 'Don't worry, I have a good team that have my back, look I will see you back at the inn, just need to take off my outfit and make up.'

'Well, at least you will get an idea what we have to go through every day,' said Corrine.

'Look, why don't we wait for you, it seems silly to use two vehicles when we have to come back anyway,' said Debbie. They agreed to wait for him and they can drive back together.

Chapter Sixty-Seven

The evening came quickly and they were back at the arena, it seemed like it was only a few moments ago that they left, the time had passed so quickly. Jake left them at the entrance and went off to get dressed into his outfit the other crew members were there already waiting by the gates for the second half of the show. He would have to be on his game and alert to the situation ahead. Jake and Bob were wearing headsets so that they could talk to each other. Amidst the overwhelming noise from the arena, they would be able to hear each other.

Debbie was frantically waving at Jake but he didn't see her straight away because he was looking towards the gates. Eventually he turned to where they were sitting and waved at them, the show was about to start, and the announcer was about to speak.

'Well ladies and gentlemen, the time has come, are you ready?'

The response from the crowd was loud, 'Okay then please get ready to be thrilled and enjoy the show.' The bucking bronco riders were getting ready in the chutes, the first horse was looking down and snorting, shaking left to right and stamping its feet. 'Let's start the show, give a big hand to Dusty Springer riding Sallamar, a colt as wild as my wife, no, not really folks, give it up for Dusty!'

The gates were opened and the chestnut mare bolted out of the chute bucking wildly trying to dislodge its rider, he had to stay on for as long as he could, the qualifying time was six seconds. The crowd were cheering loudly and Dusty was holding on for dear life, the buzzer sounded after six seconds and he had qualified. Two riders rode alongside him as he was helped onto one of the horses, this was practised for hours and these riders were professional. The loose horse was directed back towards the gates by the rodeo clowns. Jake was on one side and Bob on the other. It went smoothly without a hitch, the two men seemed to understand each other and worked as a team.

The bucking horse is basically any breed of horse with a propensity to buck when made angry. The bronco was one of many names given to these horses, they can weigh anything from 1200 pounds to 1500 pounds. A kick from these horses could seriously injure or even kill you, that's why safety is key and this is where the rodeo clowns earn their keep.

The next horse was announced as wildfire ridden by Buck Harris from Tulsa, a pro rider and well known throughout the state. He was one of the top earners in the country, and he made this seem easy, that's what experience can do. The chute gate opened and wildfire jumped out all four feet off the ground, he hit the woodwork on his way out and Buck's leg was pressed against the gate. He grimaced in pain as he struggled to stay on, he tightened his grip on the rope and in there, it seemed to take forever but the buzzer sounded and he gladly accepted a lift off the horse. Jake and Bob were out again along with one of the riders helping drive wildfire back. Buck was in a lot of pain and was holding his leg as he sat behind the rider and once he was dropped off to safety the doctor on hand rushed over to see him.

There was a cubicle set up for this type of injury. He administered a hydrocortisone injection into Buck's leg, this was steroid medicine that took care of the pain and would enable the rider to continue to ride, but too much could be harmful to the body. Buck was no stranger to this type of drug. He was still going to take part in the competition, he needed the money, even though he is one of the top riders, money was important to him because of his lifestyle. Buck liked the women and booze and would spend on some occasions, all of his winnings in one night. After four more rides, the bronco was at the next session and this time it was the riders who qualified and that turned out to be four riders. They now had to ride for position and the rider to last the longest would win the prize money of $5000 dollars, that's why Buck does what he does!

This time they were drawn with different horses, chosen for their meanness, Buck had to go first and he was drawn by a horse called rocket, this horse has a reputation for being unreliable. He shot out of the gates and just leapt into the air, all four feet off the ground at the same time causing the rider to lean back as far as he could. The rider has no time to think once on the horse, just has to take a deep breath when he can and hope he doesn't black out. The rider is thrown around like a rag doll, the ferocity is relentless. This is not a sport for any ageing rodeo rider, only the lonely are brave! Buck was thrown off after seven seconds, not a bad time but something for the other riders to aim for. After the other two riders had been dislodged within five seconds. It was the turn of the last rider and so far, Buck was still in the lead.

Dusty was drawn on wildfire who weighed 1400 pounds and was as mean looking as the day is long. The gate opened and he seemed slow to come out which gave the rider a false sense of security, then within a click he went into a frenzy Dusty held on but was losing his grip, his feet were bouncing in the air with every leap the horse made, five seconds went by and he was hanging by the side of the horse and then he was on the floor, 6.2 seconds was his time. Buck had won he had gone up some steps to receive his prize money, but as he went up to collect his prize money he was limping badly, the steroid was wearing off.

The announcer was speaking again, 'Wow! Wasn't that fantastic!' He said, give it up again for Buck Harris. After that, I think I need a drink, you have fifteen minutes to get yourself down the refreshment hall before the next competition starts, the rope a steer contest, followed by the one you have been waiting for, the bucking bull! See you in fifteen!

He switched off his mic and took a drink of Jim Beam. Country music was on full blast, it even got some people dancing in the aisles, Corrine and Debbie were buzzing with excitement, they had seen rodeo's before but never as big as this one. The atmosphere was electric! They stood up and decided not to go for a drink, they still had drinks in their bottles and they were not that hungry, they would just stretch their legs and wait for the next part of the show. Debbie hated queuing; it was safer to stay put. Corrine looked for Jake but he was called in by Bandy to have a rest and a drink. Jake was kept busy but he was handling it well, but the test was yet to come.

It was time for the show to start, the audience were returning to their seats with their drinks and food, the music was loud during the interval and the announcer was back in action. The outside temperature was cool, but inside the arena the temperature was hot! Expectations were high for this final part of the show. Bandy was giving Jake his advice and told him to be careful and remember there was a team behind him. Jake went to his position and Bob was next to him.

'Well Jake, this is it, get through this and you will know why they pay you well.'

Jake smiled at him uneasily. 'Thanks!' He said as he looked towards the arena gates and the first bull rider. The rope a steer competition was pretty tame compared to the bull riding, and was over in less than an hour.

The main event was about to start and the seats filled up, people who were still getting drinks quickly moved back into their seats.

Buck Harris was just about to mount the bull, Patch was a 1500 lb all American bronco bull, not quite the reputation of El Toro! But still able to cause a lot of pain to its rider. He was lowered on to the bull's saddle and put his right hand on the reins, still in a lot of pain he was clenching his teeth and he would need all his strength to pull this off. He placed his left foot into the stirrup and then the right, the bull was uneasy and let his rider know it. Patch snorted and started jumping up and down and his rump was banging against the chute's timber sidings, causing a thumping sound. Buck wound the reins tightly around his hand and was going to use his left hand to steady himself once the bull was released, the bell sounded and the gates were opened. The bull dashed out forcing Buck's head and body to be pushed backwards almost hitting the rump of the bull with the back of his head.

The announcer was building up the crowd, but they didn't need prompting, they were loud vocally. Buck was holding on gamely as Patch tried its best to unseat its rider, all four feet were high off the ground on one leap and Buck winced in pain as he could feel his bones being rattled with each jolt. Eight seconds and the buzzer sounded for the end of the ride, the clowns moved in and raced to distract the bull as they skilfully managed to catch Buck as he was loosening his grip of the reins. The bull carried on bucking without its rider and the clowns were sent into the ring to take its mind off the rider while he was taken to safety. Jake was on one side and Bob on the other, waving their red bandanas and managed to catch the bull's eyes. They were now the target. First Bob was chased towards the side of the ring and was only a matter of feet away from the bull's horns before he leapt to safety over the fence. Jake waved frantically at Patch calling his name loudly to attract his attention, the bull turned to Jake and stopped, he stamped his hooves into the ground and galloped towards him, the crowd were shouting to Jake to get out of the ring.

Bob had jumped back into the ring and was waving his bandana to attract the bull's attention, Jake ran to one side and then changed direction causing the bull to put on its brakes. But when 1500 lbs of beef stopped, its momentum takes it a good 20 feet further from when it stopped, giving Jake time to run in another direction. The crowd were loving it and cheered for Jake, Bandy had a tear in his eye, his boy was doing good and he was recognised by them. Bob had now stood alongside Jake and they had their backs to the main gates which opened. They had to get the bull to run towards them and move out of the way at precisely the right moment so that the bull went past the gates and into the escape chute.

Timing was the key and Bob had done this many times, he would let Jake know when to move out of the way. The bull charged at them and when it was fifteen feet from them the signal was given and the both of them moved in either direction causing the bull to run straight past the gates as it tried to slow down. Once the gates were shut Jake and Bob waved to the crowd, the first act was a success Corrine stood up, she was at the edge of her seat during the stunt, the applause was deafening. Debbie stood up and put her arm around Corrine, she looked at her and smiled, He did good! They carried on clapping until the sound slowly faded as they were getting ready for the next rider.

The next rider was Cody White, he was drawn to ride War Paint, a 1850 lb bull, sometimes the sheer weight of the bull made it cumbersome and if the muscle content was lacking then it made it easier to ride. Although still very dangerous, to an experienced rider, this was in the bag. And so, it proved, as he came through relatively unscathed and even the clowns had an easy time rounding the bull who basically gave up and surrendered without a fight. The bulls are marked on their performance and this bull was marked down on points, which meant that it probably would go to a stud farm for retirement. The semen alone from these bulls were worth their weight in gold. Bushwacker was probably the greatest bull of all time, his semen was estimated at over $100,000 dollars, so there was big money in this game. After the next bull, rides a couple of riders retired with broken bones. It was left to just three riders to compete for the prizes and the next bull was in the chute getting ready.

Buck again was first up, he was nursing a strained back and was bandaged around his rib cage, he was taking no chances, Silverado was in the chute waiting for its rider to mount, it was unusually quiet and the handlers were looking at each other wondering what was going on! Buck didn't care, he just wanted to take this opportunity to mount the bull and get settled in for the ride. The gates were opened and then all hell broke loose. The bull was frantic as he leapt off the ground and caused Buck to wince even more catching his breath, which was a bad sign. He lasted four seconds before he was thrown off and as he fell was caught with one of the hooves which cracked a couple of his ribs. He was quickly helped out of the ring, this time there were five helpers at hand. Buck was not going to be riding anymore tonight.

It was now time for the event that everyone had come here to see, the 2000-pound black bull 'El Toro,' the Mexicans called the bull, El Diablo, 'The Devil' The unlucky rider was Tex Marinello, he was in his thirties and a pro of the circuit. He was from Waco in Texas and was suntanned and a ladies' man, another rider that lived for the day and the fame.

The announcer spoke, 'This is the big one, this is the moment you have been waiting for, the meanest bull since Bodacious.' The bull was in the chute snorting and stomping his hooves in the dust, Tex looked a little nervous as he was helped onto the bull. El Toro's cold black eyes stared at him as he mounted.

'I give you El Toro!' Once he was tied on, the gates opened and the bull shot out into the arena, Tex was shaken up and was already sliding onto the side of the bull. The bull knew the rider was in trouble and jumped a little higher. Five seconds and Tex was in trouble he was thrown at the next jump and the bull wanted blood, he turned on a sixpence and charged the unmounted rider. Jake was quick off the mark and was behind the bull and could see what was about to happen, he hit the bull on the rump hard to get his attention and then wished that he hadn't. In the meantime, Tex was helped out of the arena, the bull had now set its sights on Jake. Corrine was screaming out to Jake but her screams were lost amongst the crowd's screams and whistling, she was worried and so was Debbie, they both looked concerned for him. Jake was a few feet from the gates and ran towards it with the bull on his heels, Bob jumped into the arena and was frantically waving his bandana, the bull was honed in on Jake and managed to hit his heels with its horns. Jake tripped but managed to jump high enough to get out of harm's way. The bull hit the gates and broke one of the cross sections.

The crowd gasped and Corrine was almost in tears. 'What is he trying to do to me,' she said to herself. The bull now turned around and saw Bob and two other clowns near to him, he put his huge head down and stamped his hooves into the sand, then without warning charged at Bob. Bob was caught out and he was signalling to Jake to ask if he was alright and forgot the rule of make sure you are out of danger first.

He was too far from the gates or fence; the other clowns were trying to get the bull's attention but it was too late. Bob was knocked out of the way by El Toro's head and was lucky the horns only grazed him. Still, it was enough to knock the wind out of Bob as he lay motionless on the floor. Jake instinctively jumped back into the arena and ran towards Bob, he saw the bull look at him, Bob showed some sign of movement and Jake knew that he had to get the bull away from Bob so that he could get help. He signalled to the other clowns and then ran away from Bob hoping the bull would chase him, it looked like suicide and Bandy watched from the sidelines with great apprehension.

'Oh! Jake, what are you doing!' He said out loud, the bull took the bait and gave charge. While this was happening, Bob was being helped out of the arena as quickly as possible.

Jake's plan was working and the gates were flung open in readiness for the bull to be herded back to its pen, the only problem was that he was chasing and gaining on Jake. Corrine and Debbie were holding each other in sheer panic, there was nothing that they could do but pray that Jake would be safe. Jake was about to try and fool the bull by changing direction by dropping his shoulder and turning to his left. As he did, he tripped over his own foot and fell onto the floor. Luckily for him, the bull's momentum took him past Jake and Jake quickly got to his feet and made a dash for the gates. The bull had now come to stop and was looking a little tired, but not tired enough, he was ready to give chase again after Jake.

Even the attention of the other clowns could not deter the bull, he wanted blood! Jake was ten yards from the gate and he was being signalled by the hands to jump over the side fence and let the bull run through the gates. He could feel the breath of El Toro behind him and with an almighty leap jumped into the air and landed onto the fence next to the gates, his legs were still hanging down but he lifted them up in time with some help from the hands. The bull ran straight through the gates and was now running into the pens. The crowd cheered so loud that the roof was in danger of being blown off! A new hero was made, Jake had won the attention of everyone in the arena, and there was a relieved Corrine and Debbie in the stands.

Bandy had tears in his eyes as he listened to the applause for Jake. Bob was hurt and had a broken leg, but he was alive. Bandy went over to see Jake who was being patted on the back by everyone.

'Jake my boy! You were amazing, reminds me of me!' He said.

Jake took a few breaths. 'That was a close one, how is the bull?' Bandy couldn't believe that he was interested in the health of the animal that tried to kill him. The show was over after the awards were handed out. Tex had won by point five of a second and Jake had finished his shift, Bandy gave him an envelope and thanked him for taking part. All Jake wanted to do now was to see his wife and mother, and get back and have a well-earned bath and rest. Corrine was speechless, she was shaking with fear and excitement, she could not sit through another show with her husband in, it was too much for her. They exited the arena and made their way to where Jake was and waited outside the doors. Debbie had asked the security guard to get Jake and he made a call to Bandy.

He came to the doors when he heard that Jake's mum was there, 'Debbie! Come on in, hi Corrine, please come in, Jake will be here in a moment. Did he do well or what!' said Bandy.

Jake had just arrived and was high on energy, 'Did you see!'

'Yes, we did,' said Corrine. 'And it scared me to death, how are you?'

'I am over the moon, on a high, I'm still pumped.'

'Corrine will ride with you in your car and I will follow you back to the inn, Bandy, thank you for giving Jake this chance, keep in touch.' They said goodbye and left.

Back at the Sundowner, Jake was in the shower soaping himself when the shower door opened and Corrine slipped in, there was a lot of steam inside but not enough to hide her nakedness. 'Here, let me soap your back' she said taking the sponge from him, Jake didn't argue. 'You looked so sexy out there in the arena and I see you are still excited as she looked down at his torso.' One thing led to another and one thing for sure, he was going to get a good night's sleep tonight.

The next morning, they got their things together and went to have breakfast before checking out.

Debbie had arranged that Corrine would drive home with Jake and she would follow them on the road home. And after breakfast, they were getting ready to leave the Sundowner, Jed came up to Jake who had his bag in his hand.

'Jake! I want to shake your hand son,' Jake put his bag down and shook his hand, 'You have made a lot of people happy, and it's been a privilege to have had you as my guest.'

Jake thanked him and they got into their cars and set off home.

Chapter Sixty-Eight

Jim Rogers was getting lunch ready at home, he was glad that his family was coming home today, although he enjoyed time to himself, he missed his wife. Sunday in Green River was a quiet affair, church was the beginning of the day followed by Sunday lunch. Jim did not force religion on Jake, he let him decide for himself. Just like the younger generation religion was not the most important subject in their lives, as the generations go on, values are lost along the way. The last generation has been brainwashed on modern technology, mobile phones and the internet are a prime example. The weather was still mild for this time of the year and the avid gardeners were out in force, tending to their lawns and flower beds. Jim estimated that they should be home by lunchtime so timing was essential to make sure that lunch would be ready when they arrived.

He was making a pot roast with all the trimmings, a family favourite for the Rogers, Jim prided himself on his roast. A family recipe taught to him by his mother, he paused for a moment to give Jake a call.

'Hi Jake, how are you doing for time?' Corrine picked up the phone because Jake was driving. 'Hey Dad! It's Corrine, Jake's driving, we should be home in an hour, Mum is behind us so we are nor far.'

'That's great, I can't wait to see you guys, lunch will be ready when you get here so don't pick up any take out OK!'

'No problem, we are very hungry, see you soon.' Corrine switched off the phone and looked at Jake, 'Lunch will be ready when we get home,' said Corrine, 'I bet he's cooking pot roast! That's his special dish, man, I'm more hungry just thinking about it. Pass me some potato chips, they will hold my hunger.' Corrine turned around towards the back seat and leant over to get the potato chips from the bag for Jake. Before she turned around to face the front, she waved at Debbie who was following behind. Debbie waved back and smiled. They were being followed on the highway by grey clouds but they would soon fizzle out as they approach the warm westerly winds blowing up from Yellowstone.

It was 1pm as they arrived home first Jake pulled onto the drive of their house and then Debbie. The cars came to a stop and Debbie was glad, she hadn't driven that far for a long time, so she was glad to be on her feet. Jim saw them outside and went to the front door and opened it.

'You are a sight for sore eyes, lunch is ready.' Jim came out to Debbie and she put her bag down and they hugged.

He gave her a kiss on the lips and he was happy, 'Awe, look at that, I hope we are like that when we get to that age.'

Jake looked at his parents and said, 'Get a room, you guys.' They all had a laugh and walked into the house. 'I think I'm going to get washed up before lunch' said Debbie, she took her bag upstairs and went to her room.

'Yeah, that's a good idea, we'll do the same, be down in ten minutes, Dad,' said Jake. They both went upstairs to get ready for lunch. This just left Jim to go to the kitchen and get lunch ready to serve.

A few minutes later they were all downstairs. Jim had already laid the table out and he asked them to sit down, he was going to wait on them. The food was brought to the table. Jake opened the bottle of wine and poured out into the glasses. Everyone was going to have wine today.

'Mmm, that smells great!' said Corrine. 'Yeah, Dad, looks good.'

Jim carved the beef while Debbie passed the vegetables around.

'Pass your plates,' asked Jim, he handed out cut pieces of beef as they passed their plates to him. 'How has the shop been, Dad?'

'Just fine, a little quieter than normal, lets enjoy our lunch and then we can relax and talk about you and the rodeo,' said Jim, they all agreed and got on with eating, they were hungry and soon finished their plates and Jim was only halfway through his. 'Gee, you guys really must have been hungry,' Jake helped himself to some seconds.

Corrine was full and so was Debbie. 'I don't know where you put all that food Jake, slow down a little, you still got pecan pie and cream later,' said Jim, Jake's face lit up as he continued eating with a smile on his face.

After dinner was finished and they had eaten their dessert, Jim helped Debbie and Corrine in the kitchen. 'Isn't this nice, this is what I missed,' said Jim.

'This is a family thing, isn't it darling?' said Debbie.

'Yes dear!' Corrine smiled. 'You two are so good together.' The kitchen was all done and they brought coffee to the table, it was time to give Jim the low down on the rodeo. Debbie started by describing the events leading up to the

268

rodeo, when Corrine and her drove up to Newcastle and their shopping adventure. Jake then took over; he explained that pure adrenalin took over when he faced El Toro! Corrine was less than enthusiastic about that! She was scared for Jake; Debbie was also a little scared but she had faith in her boy. After Jake had gone through his account of the rodeo, Jim was in awe.

'It sounds amazing! I wish that I had gone now,' he looked at Corrine. 'What do you think of Jake now, do you think he was right to do this show?'

Corrine looked at Jake, 'I was scared, I just wanted the rodeo to finish and for Jake to be safe.'

'Well, it's all over now, back to reality,' said Jim. Jake changed his facial expression to that of guilt, he didn't tell them everything, Corrine looked at him, 'What happened Jake, are you alright?' 'The thing is, Bandy said that he might have another show lined up, and this would be the big one! It would be in Texas.'

'But Jake, you said that this would be the last, you just wanted to get this out of your system. That's what you said, right!'

Jim could see that Corrine was uneasy. 'Look, let's all sit down and I will put on a movie, we can just sit and relax for the rest of the evening, how about that?'

He got up and walked to the lounge and headed towards the television, 'That's a good idea, we have had a long trip let's just sit down and relax, tomorrow is another day.'

The following day, Bethany called Jake on the phone. 'Hi Jake, I heard all about the rodeo in Newcastle, and got some pictures. From our sister newspapers, they also wrote a piece on you. It seems you again made the headlines!'

'I can't believe you guys, so is this going to be in the paper?'

'Of course, you are news, Jake and people want to read about you, you know, our circulation has increased by 40% since you were first reported on.'

'I suppose I will have to get used to the fame, thanks for the heads up.'

Chapter Sixty-Nine

The next few weeks went by without any incidents, the rodeo was almost forgotten by all apart from Jake, who was waiting for a phone call. He was dreading the phone call but was silently excited at the same time, how would Corrine take the news and what would she do? Jim was looking at his son, and he could tell that he had something on his mind. He walked over to him. 'A penny for your thoughts, son?'

'Oh, hey Dad, I just got a few things on my mind.'

'Yes, I know, look son, I know that I said that you ought to do the things you want to in life, but you also got to be aware of your circumstance as well.'

'You are married, you have a responsibility to Corrine.'

'But this is work, and I make good money as well.'

'But you have a good job here too son, and all this will be yours one day.'

He shrugged his shoulders. 'Aw, I know Dad, but this is my dream, it's just that when I think about the rodeo, it makes me feel real good inside.'

'I can't tell you what to do Jake, but Corrine is a good girl and you would be a fool to give her up for the rodeo.'

'Who said that I was going to give her up!'

'Think about it son, the rodeos are not local, you will be travelling all over the country, you could be weeks away from home. What kind of life would that be for the two of you,' Jake looked down at the ground. 'What do I do, Dad?'

Jim put his arm on Jake's shoulder. 'I'm sure you will make the right decision son, just think about it carefully before you make that decision, it could change your life,' Jake looked at his dad. 'Thanks for that Dad, as always you are right.'

Nathan came up to Jake. 'Hey Jake, I heard you was a real macho man again, this is becoming a habit for you.' He gave Jake a piece of paper. 'Can I have your autograph please?'

Jake smiled at him and took the piece of paper. 'What can I say, shit happens!'

'No man, but seriously, there is something about you, I don't know what it is, but you attract danger but in a good way, what's next?'

'Well, I'm not really sure, there is another rodeo in Texas that I'm considering.'

'Well, if you need someone to go with you, I'm your man.' Jim was trying to get Nathan's attention to try and not build up Jake's interest for next rodeo, but Nathan saw him too late and looked a little puzzled.

Jake walked off and Jim spoke to Nathan, 'I don't want to let Jake think about the rodeo, he needs to make a decision about his future, and you are not helping.'

'Oh, I…sorry Mr Rogers, I just get carried away sometimes, but he is a badass!' Jim looked at him sternly, 'Sorry, I mean.'

'I know what you meant, haven't you got some work to do?' Nathan looked apologetic and went off to finish his crating.

The shop phone rang and Jim picked it up. 'Good afternoon, Rogers Stoves,' Hey Jim, how you doing, it's Bandy.

Jim's face dropped, this was not good timing, 'Hi, Bandy, listen if this is about the next rodeo, Jake needs time to sort his life out first, can you give him a miss this time?'

'Do you realise what you have there, Jim, he is heading for legendary status, why he already has a following, people know who he is.' Jim looked around to see where Jake was, he was just going out to get some coffee and he waved to his dad as he left the shop. 'Look Bandy, all I'm saying is, give him a chance to get over the last rodeo, I mean it's only been less than a few weeks.'

'I know what you're saying Jim, but he needs exposure, and as a favour to you I was going to put him in the smaller rodeo to gain a little more experience, before the big one in Texas. But we will be OK without him on this one, but I will need him for Texas, there is too much riding on that one.'

'Well thank you for the rest bite, but Jake will have to decide on his own what he wants to do for the future.'

'I understand Jim, and I will respect whatever he decides what he wants to do.'

'Thank you for that, and when is the Texas rodeo?'

'It's in four weeks' time, it should give him some time to decide what he wants to do.'

'Well, we will have to wait and see, thanks for calling, and thank you again for understanding.'

'No problem, but just remember, you can't keep a good man down, it's in his blood.' Jim put the phone down and looked worried, he wasn't going to tell Jake about the phone call, but would wait until Jake settled down a little more. He would try and get him more involved in the running of the shop, give him more roles to take over, this might make the difference.

Chapter Seventy

It was an overcast day in Houston, the largest city in Texas, Bandy and some board members were going to meet at the NRG Stadium, to discuss Jake. The board owned a large share of the stadium and had their head office there, the stadium could hold up to sixty-five thousand people and was rebuilt on the site of the Houston Astrodome. Bandy was in town to meet up with the consortium that ran the rodeo circuit in the United States. He arrived at the William P Hobby Airport; the time was 11am. This was going to be his biggest payday, and fifteen years of building up his company would make him one of the biggest players on the rodeo circuit.

Bandy hailed a taxi from outside the airport, there were a few yellow cabs queuing up and one stopped in front of him. The driver got out quickly and approached Bandy. 'Hello sir, where are we going today?'

'Marriott Courtyard Hotel please,' said Bandy.

Very good sir, the driver took his suitcase and put it in the trunk. Bandy got into the back of the taxi and sat down; they were off towards the centre. He looked out at the scenery and started reflecting on his life. Thinking back to his time as a rodeo clown, very similar to Jake's situation.

Bandy was married then and he was young as well, but he didn't have parents who looked after him, he was a loner and didn't have property, after he got married, he got a job in a bar by the railway tracks and they rented a house in Green River. He didn't tell Jim that he lived in Green River, and Jake was not born then. They were happy for a little while but money was always the governing factor in their lives. The rodeo came to town and Bandy caught the bug! And before long, he was working at the rodeo, he moved with the rodeo to the next town and his wife went with him. But after two shows, she couldn't hack the lifestyle. She would stay at home and get a local job while Bandy would travel with the rodeo. He would send home money every month, and that's how it stayed for the next year. Bandy would come home every other month and things would be fine. But he didn't know that his wife was seeing another man while he was away. He was in a rock band that played in Green River a couple of months ago, they hit it off and saw each other more frequently.

Three years later, Bandy's world came to halt when he met up with a bull in the arena in Texas, that changed his life literally. He was badly injured and after spending a month in hospital, he never recovered from his injuries. His wife came to see him twice in the hospital in Houston and on the last visit, she gave him her wedding ring and never came back. Bandy was alone, and when he finally recovered, he could only get work helping out at the rodeo. He was a big name on the circuit but now he just helped out and his money was a lot less as well, he struggled with the work and took to drinking. He soon lost all respect for himself and turned to the bottle more and more. The rodeo where he first met his wife was going to be his downfall! He lived in trailers on the road while with the rodeo and soon the people who revered him were turning their backs on him.

One August day he decided that he would go back to Green River and try to get back with his wife, he didn't have any money and was forced to ride the freight trains. This was a mode of transport that didn't cost but it could be dangerous to your health. He arrived early in the morning and jumped off the freight train a few hundred yards before the town. The scenery brought back some good memories of his past life. It seemed a lifetime away and how he wished he could turn back time.

His clothes had seen better days and he needed a shower real bad, but this didn't bother him too much, he got some unwelcome looks from passersby as he walked towards his home. He got to his home and saw his wife outside picking up the newspaper that was thrown earlier, as she picked up the paper, she noticed a figure staring at her. She stopped for a moment and looked up at his face.

'Oh my god, Bandy!' He smiled and waved at her, she did not know what to say to him, she looked around to make sure people were not looking. 'What are you doing here?' He tried to speak and then a figure appeared at the front door, it was a man dressed in a dressing gown. Bandy's face dropped, he knew that he had lost his wife, he wished that his life would end right there and then.

She felt bad that he had to find out that way. It was too late to say anything, Bandy turned away and walked back towards the direction of the train station, he got his closure, there was nothing left for him now. All that he knew was the rodeo and resigned his life to living the rest of his life at the rodeo. The evening grew nearer as he waited further along the railway tracks just outside Green

River, when he got near to the station, he looked behind a few times. He was looking to see if his wife had changed her mind and wanted him back, but she was not there and it didn't look like she was coming down.

Eventually the freight train had arrived and it took a little while for the carriages to be emptied of their cargo, and once the new cargo was loaded on it was ready to pull out of the station. The freight train always pulled out very slowly because of the weight it was carrying, this gave the freight train riders a chance to jump on and get a free ride. Years ago, they were known as Hobos, tramps who jumped the freight trains on a regular basis. Today they are known as FTRA (Freight Train Riders of America), sometimes they have been linked to crimes and derailments.

Bandy waited for his moment, he could see that there were no guards and he made his attempt to board the train, there was a sliding door that was hooked on by a latch and there was no padlock on it, this was his target. The train was travelling at ten miles an hour and he ran alongside the train until the door was in reach, he started to jog a little to get momentum and managed to unhook the latch. When the door was in range he jumped up and got hold of the handle and rested his feet on the platform at the base of the door. He forced the handle in an upward motion and the door was open. He pulled himself into the compartment and once inside he pulled the door shut, it was dark inside but there was moonlight shining through the slats in the door.

The train was travelling in the direction that he wanted to go and when he got close to where was going to go, he would jump off and then would get another freight train. There were stopping points along the way where other freight hoppers would congregate and have a fire going and cook dinner and a chance to freshen up. A truck stop, if you like! They would rest there and get some sleep and get ready for the next journey, somewhere along the way, Bandy decided that enough was enough. He would not go down the route of destruction. He would turn his life around and make something of himself. And that is what he did, it took him a few years but he made a name for himself again and decided that after his taxi ride what had to be done with Jake.

It was approaching lunchtime and the roads were very busy. 'It's very hectic this time of day,' said the cab driver, he was Indian, he had arrived in Houston five years ago from Delhi and has made a home in America.

'Are you here on business sir?'

'Yes, I have a meeting this afternoon.'

'Oh, very fine sir.'

'You know, there are a lot of nice eating places, do you want me to drop you at a restaurant?'

'No, it's alright, hopefully they will have lunch laid on.'

'I am going to get off this road and use the Will Clayton Parkway, it's quicker.'

'You are the driver, I am in your hands, what's your name by the way?' 'Oh, my name is Ashok sir, and here is my card,' he passed Bandy one of his cards.

'If you need a cab any time, just ring me directly.' Bandy took the card and put it in his jacket pocket, 'Thanks!'

They had arrived at Bandy's destination and Ashok stopped the taxi outside the Courtyard Marriott Hotel on South Main Street. 'That will be $25.00 sir,' Bandy took out his wallet from his jacket inside pocket and took out some cash, he handed $30.00 to Ashok. 'Keep the change.'

'Oh, thank you sir, don't forget, if you need me, ring.' Bandy took his suitcase out of the cab and walked to the hotel doors, there were three wood arrow shaped desks in reception and he approached the middle one.

He had booked a king room a few days ago, he didn't like using credit cards, but in this day and age, he had no choice, he longed for cash to be back in business. Once he had checked in a porter took his case and showed him the way to his room, it was on the sixth floor. The hotel had a pool which on hot days was a welcoming site, the porter pressed for the lift and it arrived within seconds, they got in and was soon on the sixth floor. He stopped outside 601 and opened the door with a swipe card. Keys were also a thing of the past. The porter entered the room and put his suitcase by the door.

'Here you are sir,' he handed Bandy the key card and Bandy tipped him $10.00. 'Thank you very much, have a pleasant stay.'

He turned to the room after the door was closed and picked up his suitcase and put it on the bed, he paused for a moment and looked out towards the window, it was all the way to the floor. The net curtains draped from ceiling to floor, he had a view of the tree lined courtyard in front of the hotel. There was a sofa and footstool to one side and a desk with attached base cupboard and television above. He noticed a small bar downstairs as he was getting into the lift, he might visit that later. He unpacked a few things and put them neatly away. Bandy had stayed in many hotels on his journey so this was second nature to him, he had time to get freshened up before attending the meeting.

Chapter Seventy-One

Bandy had called Ashok to pick him up from the hotel entrance and take him to the NRG Stadium for his meeting. He walked out of the hotel and towards the taxi, it was part of the Yellow Cab brand and Ashok owned his own cab which he bought after four years.

'Hello again, Mr Bandy, you are looking fresher just now,' Bandy opened the back passenger door and got in, 'Hello yourself young man, to the NRG Stadium please.' He set off towards the direction of the stadium, 'It won't take long, should be fifteen minutes sir.'

Bandy had worked out what he was going to tell the board and this would include the exclusion of Jake Rogers, they were not going to like it, but there was no option. He was not going to ruin Jake's life, even though Jake loved the rodeo, his father was right, Jake and Corrine belonged together. After being dropped off, he paid Ashok and said that he would call him later. The stadium was huge, it had a capacity for 70,000 spectators, it had 196 suites, 100ft screens and was used for NFL Rodeo Basketball, music concerts and other functions.

'Good day sir, how can I help you?' The girl at the reception desk spoke to Bandy, she was dressed in a bright blue dress and had auburn hair and in her early twenties.

'Hi, there, I have a meeting with George Lambert.'

'Oh yes sir, Mr Lambert is expecting you, if you take this badge and take the lift over there, he is on the top floor.' He smiled at her and took the badge which he clipped onto his jacket pocket, and headed off towards the lift which was about fifty feet away. There were a couple of people waiting for the lift when he got there, he waited for the doors to open and walked in.

There was someone pressing the buttons for the various floors, 'Fifth floor please,' said Bandy and the gentleman acknowledged him and pressed the fourth-floor button. Once he was out of the lift, he immediately could see another reception desk with a secretary sitting behind it, he approached her and stopped in front of the desk.

'Hi, I'm here to see George Lambert, he is expecting me,' she looked up at him and smiled, 'Certainly sir, can I take your name please?'

'Goldhawk! Les Goldhawk.'

'I'll let him know that you are here, kindly take a seat,' she pointed to some sofas near her desk. Bandy went over and sat down and waited, the secretary picked up the phone, 'I have a Mr Goldhawk in reception, he has an appointment with you,' she paused for a moment while she was receiving instruction, 'Thank you.'

'Mr Goldhawk, Mr Lambert will be with you shortly, can I get you a drink?'

'No, I'm fine thank you,' replied Bandy, the walls were wood-panelled the same colour as the doors and the carpet on the floor was plush light beige, must be a nightmare to keep clean thought Bandy to himself.

Just then the door opened and a portly gentleman was in the doorway, 'Les! Nice to see you, glad you could make it, come on in,' he ushered Bandy into his office. When Bandy got to the door George held out his hand implementing a handshake, they shook hands and George pulled Bandy into the room gently while shaking his hand. 'Did you have a good flight?'

'It was as usual, pleasant.'

'I hate flying, try not to do it if I can help it.'

'Take a seat by my desk,' he pointed to the two upholstered chairs in front of his desk, the office was large with big windows overlooking the pitch. There was a bar which was well stocked.

'Can I offer you a drink, whisky on the rocks!'

'Bandy looked towards the bar and could see the bottles of whisky, only the best labels were adorned at the bar.'

'Yeah, why not!' George was at the bar and took out a glass and opened the Jack Daniels bottle and poured Bandy a drink with some ice. 'Here you go, Les,' he handed him the drink and had one for himself. He then went behind his desk and sat down in his leather swivel chair. Fantastic show at Newcastle, the board loved it. This chap Jake has got a bright future ahead of him, a lot of plans being drawn up for him, and, thank you for finding him.'

Bandy waited before he responded but thought of Jake before he did speak, 'Now that's what I came here to talk about, you see, Jake, is not the man for the job.'

George put his drink down and his jaw dropped a little. 'What do you mean?'

'Well, after thinking about the boy and what his future would bring, I can't let him go through this, he has a loving wife and a family business to take care of, I can't ask him to give all that up just for the rodeo.'

George got up and walked to the window, 'You see out there, Les, that's where the money is, the crowds! They want to see thrills and spills and they don't care about how happy the person is giving them the excitement. They are not interested in the home life of their hero, they just want to cheer on their hero, and Jake is that man!'

'I thought that as well, he is talented and he is a natural, but he is happily married and I can't let the rodeo ruin his life like it did mine.'

'That was a long time ago, and the industry has changed, there are more safety clauses now.'

'That's not the point, the rodeo will keep them apart and his mother and father's business which is to be handed down to Jake, well he won't have time for. That is if he is injured while doing his duties.'

Bandy got up from his chair and put his drink down on the desk. 'I'm sorry if this puts pressure on the board, but you will have to find someone else.' George was not happy, he paced up and down along the window. 'This is not what we agreed! You have an obligation to me and the board, you have been paid handsomely for your part in all this, you need to find a solution and quick.'

'Leave it with me, I'll see what I can do, I'll be in touch,' and with that comment Bandy left the office and made his way to the lifts. He phoned Ashok to pick him up at the NRG Stadium and take him back to his hotel. He was going to stop off at a place to have some lunch as his meeting was cut short, he made up his mind to go to Green River and speak to the Rogers family and let them know what he had decided. He felt better in himself and had some ideas of who he could get to replace Jake, he had a smile on his face for the first time in a long while.

Chapter Seventy-Two

Back at Green River, it was approaching lunchtime and Jake was at the shop just going to pick up his dad's lunch and get something for himself at the same time. 'Dad, I am going to get lunch. Won't be long.'

'OK Jake,' said Jim as Jake left the shop. Jake was going to the Verizon Coffee House for his coffee and rolls, his father liked their chicken and salad rolls and Jake was partial to the cured ham and salad. Nathan brought his own lunch in. His mother made it for him fresh every morning, she was doing better now and started a new job recently.

Debbie was coming into the showroom as well later to carry out work on the invoices and petty cash receipts Jim didn't like to get involved with that side of the business, he was more hands on. He was at the desk in his office going through some orders when the phone rang, he picked it up and answered it.

'Hello, Rogers Stoves!'

'Hi Jim, it's Bandy.' Jim's expression changed. 'Now don't worry, it's a good call, I have some good news for you and your family, but I will need to tell you in person.'

'Where are you now?' asked Jim. 'Well, I am in Huston just having some lunch.'

'Is this the big meeting that Jake said you were going to?'

'Yes, but like I said, I have some good news for all of you, I will be arriving in Green River this evening on the red eye.'

'OK then, we will see you tonight, I suppose you will be wanting dinner?'

'That's nice of you, Jim, I'll see you later, bye.' He put the phone down, still not certain what Bandy was talking about, Jake had already made up his mind to go to the rodeo and he didn't know what Bandy was going to say. Debbie had just arrived at the shop and opened the door. Nathan was minding the desk at the entrance.

'Hi, Mrs Rogers.'

'Hi, Nathan, how are you?'

'Oh, I'm fine.' He was having his lunch at the desk but he knew that if a customer came in to move his lunch to the kitchen. Debbie went into Jim's office, 'Hi dear, what are you up to?' He looked up at her and smiled, 'Oh, just sorting out these orders, how are you feeling today?'

'I'm good, just in the right frame of mind to go through these invoices and petty cash.' Jake had come in by now with their lunch, he walked into the office and gave his dad his lunch and sat down at the desk to eat his lunch. 'Have you had lunch, Mum?' asked Jake.

'Yes dear, I ate before I left, you carry on, if any customers come in, I will see to them.'

'Oh, Bandy called.'

'What did he say?' asked Jake, 'He said that he had some good news for us.'

'What does that mean?' asked Debbie.

Jim gave a puzzled look on his face, 'Oh and one more thing, he is coming for dinner.'

'Jim! I have to clean the house and get some shopping in, what time did he say that he was coming?'

'In the evening, that's all he said.'

'Marvellous!' She said. 'Well, I had better go and pick up some things for dinner, I will sort the paperwork out tomorrow.' She left the shop and headed for the shops, Debbie had an idea for what she wanted to get for dinner, Jim and Jake finished off their lunch and carried on working, Jake was thinking about what Bandy had to say, and what was the good news! The afternoon went by quickly and the weather was changing, the clouds grew darker, Jim looked out of the shop window.

'Looks like rain!' He said.

Nathan came over to the window. 'Damm! I have to ride home in this.'

'It's OK, Nate, I'll give you a lift in my car,' said Jake and they went back to what they were doing. Jim was finishing up with his paperwork in his office. Jake locked back shutters and was switching off the electric fires in the showroom and Nathan took the trash out and emptied that into the industrial bins outside the shop.

Debbie had finished shopping and was on her way home, she had picked up steaks for dinner tonight. She wanted a simple dish with not too much fuss. The rain started coming down and it was heavy, she parked the car and quickly took the shopping bags and ran into the house. She could not remember when it rained so heavily before, the skies were very dark, she was praying that it wasn't going to another tornado! They saw their fair share of them in the time they lived in Green River. Jim had closed the shop and Jake was giving Nathan a lift home, he put Nathan's bike in the boot of his car, people were running to get out of the rain in the town as Jim drove off towards home. Debbie was aiming to get dinner ready for about eight o'clock, that should give everybody enough time to get ready.

Jim had come by now and quickly entered his house shaking the rain off him as he closed the door behind him, 'Hi honey, Jake is dropping Nathan home because of the rain so he won't be long, do you need any help with anything?'

'No, I'm fine, you get into some dry clothes and pour yourself a drink, dinner will be around eight.'

Jim went upstairs to change into his house clothes and freshen up, Debbie was just preparing the food, she wasn't going to cook the steaks around sevenish. She was making her famous potato salad with gherkins. Her mother taught her how to cook and she still uses the same recipe. Jim had come down and was making a drink for himself.

'Do you want a drink dear?' asked Jim.

'Yes, why not, I'll have a glass of white wine please.' Jake had come home and again shaking off the rain as he entered the house.

'Boy, it's raining cats and dogs out there, I hope it's not going to be another tornado!'

Debbie turned around and looked at Jake, 'That's what I was thinking,' she said. 'It's not looking good out there, but there has been no news on the radio, I'll check the TV to see if there is any news,' said Jim, he turned the television on and sat down on the settee, he flicked several channels to see if there was any information regarding the weather. There was news on one of the weather channels, and they were saying that a tornado was expected but it was to the west of them, they would just experience the aftershock. Which was the edge of the tornado, so it was not that serious. But in America especially in Tornado Alley, they took any kind of warning very seriously, their lives depended on it.

'It's OK, we are in the clear, just heavy rain and winds, nothing too serious.'

'Oh that's a relief,' said Debbie. Corrine came over from her house, Debbie had spoken to her earlier and explained what was happening tonight.

'Hi Mum, Dad, it's nasty out there, I hope there's not going to be a tornado!' They started laughing at her comment. She looked at them puzzled, 'What did I say?' She said.

'It's nothing dear, it was just that we all said the same thing earlier but were fine, it's going to miss by a long way,' said Debbie.

Corrine got the joke and smiled and went over to Jake and gave him a hug. 'How have you been today,' she asked, he hugged her back.

'Just fine, even better that you are here now,' replied Jake who gave her a hug back.

'Apparently Bandy is going to give us some good news tonight,' said Jake.

'Yes, your mother said, I wonder what it's about!' said Corrine. They looked at each other and Jake shrugged his shoulders! 'We will soon find out.'

Chapter Seventy-Three
The Final Chapter

Later that evening Bandy was sitting in his first-class seat on a flight from Houston, the plane, a DC10, as it was on its final descent to Green River Airport. He could see the lights of the town below through the rain, it was easing a little though it was still windy, the pilot made an announcement. 'Folks, I don't want you to worry, but I might have to make more than one attempt on landing, because the extreme winds could push us off course.'

The passengers were talking among themselves and they looked out at the weather outside, the attempted landing was aborted and the plane had to pick up speed and climb up again. The captain had to circle around the airport and try to land the plane again, it's lucky that the fuel tanks were half full so the captain had time on his hands. The passengers were asking questions to the cabin crew who were asking them to keep their seatbelts on and get ready for landing. The cabin crew themselves had to buckle up after making sure the passengers were all safe, the captain tried for a second time. This time he took a chance and guided the plane onto the runway. It was a bumpy landing as the plane as the plane thudded onto the runway and the brakes were slammed down with some force. They were safely down and the passengers clapped and cheered, Bandy was pleased and couldn't wait to get off the plane. When the plane finally came to a stop, the passengers didn't need reminding. They were up and standing in the aisles with their bags, ready to leave the plane.

Bandy was one of the first to walk out of the plane because he was in first class, the cabin crew were wishing them all a pleasant journey and thanking them. Bandy was outside the airport and waited under the shelter for a cab to pull up, he got in and gave the driver the Rogers' home address. 'That will be Jake Rogers' home, he is a hero you know, building himself a rep in this town.' He breathed a sigh of relief as he sat back and relaxed at last, he smiled at the taxi driver's comments. Within twenty minutes, he arrived at the house, he took out his suitcase and paid the driver and then walked towards the house. Jim opened the door, 'Nice to see you, come on in out of the rain,' Bandy shook his hand, and came into the house and put his suitcase by the door.

Jake got up and walked towards Bandy. 'Jake, my boy! It's nice to see you all again, I tell you; after the flight, I wasn't sure that I was going to make it here.'

'Why, what happened?' asked Debbie. Bandy explained what had happened and they were shocked.

'Well, you had better have a drink; what would you like?' asked Jim.

'I'll have a whisky on the rocks please, Jim.'

'Coming right up, go and take a seat and I'll bring it over to you.' Jake walked with Bandy to the settee and Corrine said hello to him. 'You are looking as lovely as ever, Corrine.'

'Thank you' said Corrine. Jim had brought Bandy his drink and he sat down next to him on the settee.

'Dinner will be in half an hour,' said Debbie. 'That's nice, Debbie, thank you for going to all this trouble.'

'Nonsense, you are welcome any time, and you are staying here tonight, and I don't want any arguments,' said Debbie sternly. 'Well, thank you again, you are most generous, and that brings me to why I am here. I had my meeting in Huston and came to a decision. And I have decided that Jake is not going to Texas and take part in the rodeo.'

'But why?' asked Jake. 'It's not a decision I took lightly, Jake, I remembered what happened to me when I was a little older than you and decided that this life is not for you, Jake.'

Jake could not believe it. 'Before you say anything, Jake, the rodeo life is like a bug, and once you are bitten, it's hard to get rid of it. That's not the life for you, my boy!'

'I have thought long and hard about this Jake and believe me it's better that you walk away now with no regrets. You have a great wife in Corrine and a family that loves you, I wish that I had all that, this is the best way forward Jake and this is my decision.' Jim and Debbie were happy and Corrine was even happier, she could now make plans for their future and she had an announcement to make as well.

'I'm glad that you can now plan your future, Jake, and I have an announcement to make,' they all looked at her in anticipation. Corrine held Jake's hand. He was still upset at the news that Bandy gave him. 'We are going to have an arrival next year, in about eight months' time.'

Jake's face changed. He was still thinking about the rodeo but heard what Corrine was saying. 'You mean, we are going to have...'

'Yes, Jake, a baby!' Debbie had a big smile on her face and Jim was also very happy.

'This is wonderful news,' said Bandy.

'Let's drink to that!' said Bandy, they all raised their glasses and toasted the news.

Jake had now come to terms with Bandy's news and was over the moon with Corrine's news, he put his arms around her.

'I love you,' said Jake. 'This is the right way forward, I'm sorry that I was only thinking about myself all this time. We are going to be alright.' They all congratulated Corrine and there was happiness in the Rogers household.

Debbie got up to start dinner. 'Jim, give me a hand.' They both got up and made their way to the kitchen.

The rain had eased off and the winds died down almost at the same time as Corrine gave them the news. Bandy got up and put his drink down. 'You know something, I feel like you guys are going to be just fine for the future, and if you don't mind, I would like to be part of your lives, if you will let me. I've grown attached to you guys and feel like I have a family at last, if you will have me.'

Jim came over to Bandy and hugged him. 'Welcome to our family.'

THE END